THE TALES OF ZREN JANIN

MANUMINA

BOOK 2

M.L. DUNKER

Publishing Services provided by Paper Raven Books LLC
Printed in the United States of America
First Printing, 2022

Hardcover ISBN: 979-8-9850536-2-3
Paperback ISBN: 979-8-9850536-3-0

Dedication: For every child who has been slapped with a label not of their choosing. You are more than this.

"Whala te iti kahurangi ki te tuohu, koe me he maunga teilei."
- Maori wisdom

"Seek the treasure you value most dearly, if you bow your head, let it be to a mountain."

TABLE OF CONTENTS

Kerek City
Huk River
Vingt
Balza
Huk
Cloa
Sary
Isl
Aldi
Manumina
SALT CLIFFS
KEREK
Ribelo

CHAPTER 1

THE ADVENTURE BEGINS

When I had told Miyamoto Suki I would travel with him over the Northern Track to Vikland, I didn't know how long the journey would take, what it would mean for food, shelter, and safety, or even if I would survive the trip.

For his part, he had only asked me because Ngahuru of the West Islands, a softfoot and diplomat whom he admired and trusted, had told him I had saved her life and that of her brother, Koanga, at least twice as they had fled from Kerek City over the Matasi border to Salisport. Miya and I were unknowns to each other. The other Viklanders traveling with us were unknown to me and some were known only by name to Miya. For a journey which everyone said might mean life or death, I wasn't sure that was a good sign for our adventure.

But Ngahuru had already set sail on a ship to the West Islands and traveling with her was not an option. Ngahuru introduced herself as the daughter of a tailor and the sister of the Storyteller

Koanga. But that was merely deflection on her part. As a softfoot, a spy for the West Islands and her King, the more she minimized herself and her talents, the more people overlooked her, and that was just the way she liked it. I thought of her as a Sailor's Curse, a small curved blade with a wooden knob at one end that fit between the fingers and was used to slash across the face. It was the weapon of choice down in Dockside and Lowertown where I grew up. In the service of her King, Ngahuru was just as dangerous.

I had said goodbye to Ngahuru and Koanga before they set sail home to the West Islands. Then I traveled on a ship of my own to Kerek City with Bima Ritwik and Miyamoto Suki. Miya was smooth and polished, a member of the Viklander diplomatic corps. If sailors or others came to talk to him, they spoke in hushed voices of his upcoming thirteenth crossing of the Northern Track. It didn't take me long to figure out most people did two or three crossings across Kerek and hated every moment of it. For Miya to do so many journeys and survive made others think he was brilliant and brave, or foolish and lucky. Miya never said what he thought.

Bima Ritwik was a different sort. He had the sly cleverness I saw in the most successful gang bosses and gamblers in Lowertown. He spoke well and dressed well, and the others on the ship had nodded at him as if they thought he was their better. But I felt uneasy when I was about him. It was the sense that Bima

Ritwik could pry out my secrets without me ever understanding the harm I was doing to another.

Bima and Miya were about the same age. Maybe mid-thirties, maybe more, maybe less. There weren't a lot of birthdays celebrated in Lowertown, and I wasn't good about guessing people's ages. But they were Viklanders through and through. Golden skinned with straight black hair tied back into their braids of honor. They wore dark pants and shirts and polished black boots. The Viklanders I saw in Kerek City, or Salisport, or anywhere really, never tried to fit in with their surroundings. It would be like hiding a hawk in a little brown wren's nest. I had never seen any of them commit an act of violence, not even on their patrols in Lowertown, but they didn't need to. They wore their confidence and their competence in their fighting abilities like a skin or a smile. Especially, the Viklander women.

In Kerek, women needed to live with their father or their brother until they were married. Women did not travel alone, women would never think of carrying a weapon, or wearing anything other than heavy skirts. In Matasi, the country to the south of us, women had a little more freedom. They could work where they wished and could travel alone. Men and women in Matasi dressed in bright colors and both wore wide legged pants to make it easier to work in the fields and orchards. Their curly dark hair was short and to the nape of the neck. Their olive-hued skin was closer to my own cinnamon color than the milk-faced Kerekis.

The Viklander women, on the other hand, were unlike anyone I had known. The ones I had met so far were soldiers, softfoots, and ambassadors. They walked the Kerek and Matasi streets in pairs or groups, crossbows and short bongs slung easily across their backs. They dressed in the same dark pants and shirts as the Viklander men, walked freely wherever they chose, and looked you in the eye when they talked to you. In Kerek City, they were given as wide a berth as the Matasi missionaries with their large cudgels and books of the Lost God. It never paid to be too curious about someone who looked—and acted—so differently.

I stretched and reached out to the little shaft of sunlight touching my bed and my blankets. I had had less than three decons of sleep last night and this morning. Bima and Kern had taken me softfooting over the interior walls of the diplomatic compounds as we breached the Conrosan embasado which had been closed for a generation or more. I smiled to myself. Within those walls, we had found Raumati of the West Islands and escorted her to the Viklander ambassador here in Kerek City. The last West Islander hiding from the Kerek King.

And now I was walking up to Trouble again and reminding her I was out and about by traveling the Northern Track from Kerek City to Vikland with Miyamoto Suki and a handful of Viklanders. I marveled at my foolishness.

Accompanying us would be a bowmaster and healer I had never met called Rell Huena, and a bongmaster named Song Yao with whom I had sparred the day before. Song had been training with multiple partners all morning before I came along, and that was the *only* reason she didn't drop me on the floor as well. There was also Kern the Softfoot, who had already led me astray the previous night, and Chul Swyler, a firemaster, whatever that was, who had been injured and was on his way home to Vikland for healing.

I lazily scratched my head and wondered where I could find a bath, clean clothes, and first meal, not necessarily in that order. I looked over at the other empty beds in the room. The Viklander embasado looked impressive from the public rooms. There was elegance in the ground floor reception areas and hallways with their beautiful tapestries, paintings, and ancient weapons illustrating the Vikland sagas of Warriors and Monsters, visual reminders of the Viklanders cherished virtues of honor, courage, fighting for justice, and defending the defenseless. But the dormitory rooms, where I had been placed with the other soldiers and staff, were large square rooms with six beds in each, a wall of hooks for clothes, and such an empty look it made it easy to see I was the only one still in bed.

The knock at the door interrupted my daydreaming. Without waiting for an answer, an aide pushed open the door.

"Only the Empress has her first meal in bed, and she says she needs a fever to get it. When no one saw you in the dining hall this morning, Bima Ritwik said you may not know enough of our rules and ways to know how to get about. He told me to tell you, he has left with a patrol to purchase tickets on a ship sailing today for the West Islands if there is one, Matasi if there is not. He has asked me to ensure you are ready to go when the Kerek army paychest, soldiers, and horses arrive." She looked at me, still under the bedcovers, and sighed. "He gave me Kereki clothes for your trip, and I was told to stay until you were dressed. Bima warned me you hadn't probably changed your small clothes since you put them on ten years ago."

And that was Bima Ritwik for you. Just when you thought he was doing you a kindness out of the goodness of his heart, he would cut open the gift of fruit and let you see the worm inside. I huffed, threw back the covers, and threw my bare legs over the side.

"Fine. Watch me dress. I suppose that means there is no bath." Ever since my first one, just handfuls of days ago, I had learned I loved baths.

She smiled. "There is. It's down the hall. You can take the clothes from me, walk down to the last door on your left, take your bath, and swear to Bima up and down that I watched you put every stitch on," she paused with a smile, "or you can give up your bath—which you will not get another for nearly a fortnight—just to make him happy. The choice is yours."

"Give me the clothes. I am not crossing the frontier without taking a hot bath while I can." I groused. "After today, I will never see Bima again in my lifetime; his happiness is not my concern."

Now she laughed. "Careful what you threaten, Zren Janin. Bima Ritwik has a way of appearing and disappearing like smoke in the wind." She handed me the clothes. "Thanks for this. I'll go down to the kitchens and see if I can find you some food. I will put a plate on your bed if I am successful."

CHAPTER 2

FELLOW TRAVELERS

After my bath, clean clothes, and the plate of bread, cheese, and fruit, I wandered the hallways looking for someone I knew. There was a lot of hurrying about. I remembered Miya telling me the day before we would be taking letters and packages back to Vikland from the ones who still had another season or more left on their service here in Kerek City. The word had gotten out there was going to be another Northern Track crossing, and three different strangers came up to me to carry letters for them.

I had looked at the first letter given to me and saw the beautiful curved letters of the Vik language. The soldier was still there however and plucked the letter from my fingers and then turned it around.

"Well, I guess I don't have to worry about my secrets if you are trying to read it upside down," he said sarcastically. I shrugged and walked outside. I didn't know how to read any language, not just Vik.

The courtyard was full of people, two wagons—the heavy kind known as settler wagons because they were big enough to carry a family and their worldly goods. There were different horses about, some would be outrider horses, carrying those who would have to be ever watchful for bandits and outlaws which liked to prey on the traveler along the way, large cart horses, and all the bits and pieces that horses needed. I saw Song Yao carry out her travel bag, and three bongs, one long—the jeong bong— and two short, what Miya had called "tahn bongs." She placed them in a cart already filled with long flat wooden crates.

Four soldiers came out carrying what looked like a fluffy feather bed, and I wondered just how fancy we were going to be traveling. When I had traveled with Ngahuru and Koanga down the Coast Road, we had been rough camping with only two waxed and oiled canvases, cooking over a fire, and sleeping in our travelers cloaks. I watched as the Viklanders threw the bed on top of the flat crates and then, tented a canvas over the wagon.

Kern came out and called, "Last chance for letters!" in both Vik and Keresh. She walked among the crowd like the buskers in front of the inns, with an open traveler bag collecting letters and tiny packages. She stopped in front of me, and I dropped my handful in.

"I heard you're riding a wagon, Zren, not as an outrider. You'll have to tell me what you promised Miya so I can get the same special treatment." She laughed, patted me on the cheek, and walked on. I was still tired after only three decons of sleep, but Kern was in the same rough condition. Now she was going to be riding a horse all day? I didn't envy her.

The Kereki soldiers traveling with us to Vikland came before midday. There were four of them, two as young as I was, or nearly so, and the other two much older. All were clean shaven and had short blond or light brown hair. With faces as pale as unbaked bread, and dressed in their sand-colored uniforms and soft leather boots, they looked like dull little house sparrows next to the Viklanders. The two young ones seemed wary—almost skittish—surrounded by so many Viklander soldiers, but they were on embasado grounds and unless Vikland wanted a war, no harm would come to them here.

We were packed and ready, horses selected and both wagons loaded. Once the Kerekis added their wagon to our train, our horses were harnessed and saddled, people mounted, and we were on our way. The crowd of Viklanders who had loaded us down with letters for their families, friends, and lovers back in Vikland stayed outside in the courtyard to see us off.

Three of the Kereki soldiers and Kern were outriders, Miya drove the other wagon filled with Vikland gifts of West Islands steel, and one of the old Kereki soldiers drove their own wagon. Song Yao sat beside me on the wagon bench, reins resting easily in her hands. She would teach me to drive today, she said, and be an outrider tomorrow. Our wagon had the feather bed and Chul Swyler, the firemaster I had met on the ship posing as a Matasi missionary. He had been carried out to the wagon and carefully arranged on the bed under the canvas.

Somehow, no one would tell me exactly what had happened, he had been injured in the fires and riots of two nights ago. I wasn't quite sure if he had disobeyed Joon's command not to leave the embasado during the riots, but if he had, First Soldier Joon had forgiven all, because they were parting as nearly best friends.

Underneath Chul's platform bed were blankets, and the four trunks of West Islands steel which had traveled with us from Salisport. I was told it was pots and pans, fishing anchors, farm implements, and kitchen knives.

When I questioned how we seemed to be taking a lot of risk on the Northern Track for what seemed to be the worldly goods of a peddler's pack, Miya had just smiled at me and said, "I'm just a lowly foot soldier, Zren. That's what we are told."

A waterproofed canvas top covered our wagon to give Chul shade and protection from the rains. The Wet could be starting its first few showers before we reached Juisiti, the city of the Empress within the country of Vikland. I still wasn't sure how long the trip was going to be.

Two spare crossbows were propped against the inside of the buckboard within my easy reach. When I shamefully told Song of my inability to hit the target—even missing the straw bales—in the practice yard, she only replied, "If the bandits are coming over the side of the wagon, Zren, I have confidence you can slow them down enough for me to take care of them with my tahn bong." I liked her already.

The Kereki soldier had insisted on the middle position for his wagon, which is where Miya had wanted him all along. They had a chest with multiple leather bands and buckles, with an iron hasp which they had shoved in the very front of their wagon, and then their traveling bags, food, and other supplies. I didn't see the canvas lean-to tents like I had used all the way through Kerek to Matasi. Maybe the Kerek military had ones which looked different from the ones Koanga and Ngahuru had used.

The last wagon was driven by Miya with Rell Huena on the seat beside him. She was the only Viklander I had not met before this morning. She was shorter than Kern and Miya—about my size. Kern had said she was pretty, and she was, but I would have described her as serious. She had checked the horses on all the wagons, even the Kereki army wagon, while we were climbing up to leave. I heard her talk with the Kereki young ones about their horses, nod, and then clamber up on the wagon next to Miya. Her crossbow was larger than the ones in our wagon and rested upright easily on the wagon floor beside her. I had been told she was also our healer, and there were chests of her medicinals and bandages in both wagons—in case we lost one to bandits. I wasn't getting a good feeling about all of these precautions.

We drove slowly out of Castle Court, down Embasado Street, and out into the heart of the city. There were pushcarts, street vendors, and crowds of walkers who came so close they brushed against our wagons. A few people watched us, probably wondering why Viklanders and the Kereki army were traveling together, but no one looked too curious. It didn't do to ask too many questions in Kerek City. People took offense easily, and everyone assumed the Kerek King was corrupt, foolish, or both. Minding your own business was a good way to ensure your survival.

Once we got out of the crowded city streets and passed the first ring road, Song relaxed a little. It wasn't like we could get lost on the wide dirt road called the Northern Track. According to the map Miya had shown me earlier, Kerek City was shoved up tight against the sea and grew outward in a lopsided circle. There were several ring roads all about the city linking up to the Northern Track, the road to Aldi, and the Coast Road. Miya told me the city was so big, it would take us nearly half the day to leave it. He said the city had sprawled nearly to Vingt, but without any of its charming features coming along. I wasn't sure what he meant, but I didn't ask.

Song was silent for a while watching the track between the broad backs of the horses. I had grown used to traveling with Koanga who loved to tell stories or talk about the West Islands. And then I had traveled on a ship with Miyamoto Suki and Bima Ritwik who had answered any question I asked and listened carefully to anything I wanted to talk about without making me feel foolish or stupid. I was hoping Song was easy to talk to as well, or this was going to be a long day.

"Are you all right with us talking in Keresh? I do not speak Vik," I started hesitantly.

She smiled broadly at me. "I am fluent in Vik, Mata, Wester, and Keresh. As long as you don't ask me to speak Conrosan, I think we will get along just fine."

I scowled. I knew, because Ngahuru had told me, Vikland was surrounded by mountains on three sides and the tiny country of Kerek on the fourth. Therefore, children were taught many languages from the time they could walk, so they could travel outside Vikland's borders and see the world. But it was one thing to have Ngahuru tell me this and another to encounter it continuously among the Viklanders.

I asked her how she had learned to drive a team of horses. She said she had grown up on her family's sheep holdings in Vikland near the Matasi border. She had ridden horses there as well.

"I am a second child, Zren. My older sister was the daughter of my father's first wife. She went to the academies and then to her military service, but always treated me kindly even though there were so many years between us. She was assigned to Matasi and then the West Islands. To a little sister who camped rough during the Dry and watched the sheep on the hills, her life in her letters sounded so wonderful."

Song let the reins lay loosely in her hands. "I learned the bongs at home and practiced my forms on the hills." Song looked at me with a half-smile. "There is a lot of time to practice when you are watching sheep. I asked my sister what I needed to do to be accepted into the diplomatic corps—we call it the 'Diplo,' Zren. For children such as us, with no parents or grandparents who wear a nobleman's name, we would need a valuable skill to be accepted, one Vikland needed. My sister told me to study languages. So I found teachers during the Wet and practiced my conversations with the sheep during the Dry." She glanced at me to see if I was smiling. I was.

"When I reached the academies, I found I was far ahead in languages, astronomy, and the short bongs, and far behind in math and… don't even get me started on the subjects taught in the Academy of Elements! I found I also had advanced well with my jeong bong. Because I did not have traditional teachers, and I used the bongs as weapons against the animals which would prey on the sheep, the bongmasters said I was difficult to fight against. I continued to win matches and to advance."

Song shrugged. "Have you ever been punished for doing well? Because I was nearly unbeatable on the bongs, I spent my military service going from garrison to garrison with another bongmaster to train and test the others. It was *not* the glamorous life my older sister had written about. I never got out of Vikland!" She cut her eyes at me. "But after my military service, I did get in the Diplo. I thought it was because I was fluent in Vik, Mata, and Keresh. When my first assignment was to work in an orchard tracking people smugglers, I wondered if I would ever leave farm work."

"Be careful what you wish for, huh? You ended up in Kerek City." I smiled.

She smiled back at me. "All Viklanders end up in Kerek City at some point in their rotations. It's the closest training we have to war and civil unrest. It trains us to be sharp and always on our guard according to First Soldier Joon, but after a season of it, everyone just wants to go home or somewhere else."

"Where else have you been?" I asked idly.

"My first posting was the West Islands, of course." She looked at me mischievously. "Since Wester was the one language I did not speak when I left the academies—besides Conrosan—it was inevitable the Vikland Diplo would send me to the West Islands first."

I laughed with her.

"I served two years in the West Islands. It is everyone's favorite posting. If you can ever go there, you should." She shrugged. "We also have those who have duty in the Spice Island, and while they say the weather and people are nice, it is not so wealthy, and the dialect of Wester they speak is a little different then what we are taught in the academies. We have two small outposts there beyond the embasado." She paused. "No offense, Zren, but after spending almost three years in Kerek City, I think I am ready to try anywhere else." She gave a deep sigh. "Where have you traveled?"

I thought how casually she said, 'where have you traveled?' Not 'have you traveled?' Or 'If you could travel, where would you like to go?' Did she assume all people must travel as much as the Viklanders, or did she assume because my skin was cinnamon-hued and Ngahuru had told me I was a Conrosan, that of course I could not be from Kerek?

"I have traveled to and through Matasi," I said. "I traveled with Ngahuru the Softfoot, and her brother Koanga, a Storyteller of the West Islands."

She gave me a long look. "I'm surprised our ambassadors let you leave with Miyamoto Suki and did not lock you up with our softfoots until all of your secrets about Ngahuru were told." She turned back to the road. "The West Islands know there is trouble brewing between the three of us—Kerek, Matasi, and Vikland—but they are across the sea and want to remain neutral. They are not our problem." She grinned at me. "Now if you had said you had been in the Kerek King's bedroom and heard all *his* secrets…"

I shook my head and tried to smile. But I was troubled at her words. I thought Bima Ritwik had been so nice to me on the ship because he had unsuccessfully abandoned me in Salisport and was sorry for it. Now I wondered if there had been another reason—he wanted to see if I would tell him any of Ngahuru's secrets. I sighed. I was beginning to think Koanga was right; I wasn't sure I liked Bima Ritwik either.

I pointed my chin at the dusty track ahead. "I can see the appeal of somewhere else, if this is the road home. Somehow, I thought the Northern Track would be nicer, more like the Coast Road, where 'the giants of old built the road,'" I quoted Ngahuru.

She raised an eyebrow at me and said slowly, "I don't know who built the Coast Road, but I am told the Northern Track is nothing more than just wagon after wagon: settlers, military, or people just traveling through from their holdings and smaller settlements to the market towns. The Kerek King is supposed to grant safe passage on this road to everyone, there are treaties signed back in his great grandfather's day. But the current King doesn't care, and that's why the bandits and thieves have taken over. There is no one to stop them.

"In Vikland, some people talk about this road with nostalgia, remembering the terror they felt, but if they emerged unscathed, they almost romanticize it. Others have lost friends, family, or almost everything they own. They will threaten to take the passes unguided over the Silver Mountains during the Wet season before they take this road again."

I was startled. "You were told? You don't remember your last crossing? When did you last travel the Northern Track?"

"I have never been, although Miya showed me maps of what our journey should be like." Song explained, "I came over the Silver Mountains five years ago and have not been home to my family since. I did travel through Matasi, but it was with others who had been many times and I didn't ask enough questions because I was afraid to appear foolish. Then I sailed to the West Islands, where I did learn to ask questions, foolish or otherwise, and then to Kerek City. I do not think my parents expected me to be gone so long, although my little brother has taken over the sheep herding. He probably appreciates me not telling him how to do everything. So I do not know what to expect on the Northern Track."

We passed through Vingt, and I remembered my plans with Primo Resoro so many days and days ago. I had tried to direct Primo Resoro to the Ring Road where two others had been hiding to rob and hold him for ransom from his wealthy father, the Treasurer of Kerek, and a personal friend to one of the Kerek princes. The thieves had only seen my slight build, heard my tongue speak Castle Keresh, and offered me coin to befriend a nobleman's son. They had not considered I had a face too honest for my own survival, and would respond to the kindness of the nobleman's son and tell him everything in hopes he would take me away from Kerek City.

Instead, Primo Resoro had used his cane to beat me and throw me out on the side of the road. As I looked about me, I wondered if he still had wealthy land ownings here. If he bragged about his close call with thieves in Kerek City, or had he stayed on his lands and never ventured further than his local village?

Without warning, Song starting talking about the foods she missed most in Vikland. I loved hearing her descriptions, but it was making me hungry. It seemed like a very long time since we had left Kerek City.

The Huk River came down from the Cold Mountains to the north of us and ran parallel more or less to our track. At one of the river bends, a Kereki soldier, the tall one with the friendly face, trotted up. He noticed Song holding the reins, raised an eyebrow, but said nothing.

Song smirked and said cheerily, "He's teaching me to drive!" Then she took a calculated look back to Rell with her large crossbow at her feet, and back to the soldier, "Well, you certainly didn't expect only the women to do all of the murder and mayhem, did you?"

The Kereki soldier ducked away to hide a smile. "Your leader—"

"That would be Miyamoto Suki," Song agreed.

"He would like to stop for the night soon. He wants to camp by the river and set up before dark. He wants plenty of time to see to the horses because it is their first day."

Song nodded. "We'll stop and he can pass to lead us to the place he chooses." She pulled back on the reins and so did the wagon behind us. Miya and Rell trotted their wagon ahead and a few furloughs later pulled off the track to a fringe of trees at the river.

As we all dismounted, I wondered how camping rough would be with the soldiers and the Viklanders, but Miya stepped in as if the Kereki soldiers were part of his command. Chul was too injured to move, so Rell and Kern rolled up part of one side of the canvas and tied it to the frame so he could see us as we made camp. Miya had me put up one canvas lean-to—it was nearly identical to the one Ngahuru and Koanga had in Kerek and Matasi—and he and Song, speaking softly in Vik, put up the other before she left to gather firewood.

The Kereki soldiers stood by their wagon and watched us. Now I could see them clearly without the crowdedness of the Viklander courtyard. Two of them looked almost as young as I was, another had the hardened look of a bitter man, and the fourth just looked wrong somehow. Even just watching him made the hair on my arms rise. When Miya noticed them standing around doing nothing, he pointed out the trees where they could hang their canvas. I stopped what I was doing to listen in to their conversation.

"Thought we would be staying in the inns along the way. They're just a day's ride apart." It was one of the young ones—the tall one again.

"They are," Miya agreed easily. "But if you pull into an inn with an army wagon and those uniforms, every person there is going to think you're hauling payroll. And one of two things is going to happen: You have to haul in the payroll chest up to your rooms, and everyone will know for sure you have the King's coin. You'll be trapped in your room with no escape when the thieves come for you in the night. Or you can leave the chest in the stables and have to sleep out there to protect it. In either case, you'll have your throat slit before morning for coin that isn't even yours." He let the news settle for a moment. "I told your captain we would be sleeping rough and to supply you with canvas. Did he?"

The other young soldier looked in the wagon, as if he expected the tents to appear. "No."

Miya grinned again. "Well, I will be happy to sell you two of ours and we'll double up." He went to his wagon and threw two tents down at their feet. "Since two of you will have to be on sentry duty at any given time, this should be the right number."

The grizzled soldier snarled at Miya. He pointed to the two youngest soldiers and then the tents. "Get 'em up."

With the loss of the two extra tents, I assumed I would be sharing with Miya. So I was surprised when I came back from getting water to find Kern drop her travel bag and bedroll next to mine.

"Good. You're back, Zren. Help me gather more wood."

We met Song at the edge of the clearing. "Miya wants you to cook tonight, he'll show you where everything is," Kern said to her. "Rell's got the care of the horses." She stopped and watched as Song walked into the campsite. We walked further away from the others and she started picking up downed branches and talking, "Miya, Rell, and I dropped back a little bit today. We told the Kereki outrider it was to get clear of the dust, but we had a chance to assess our friends. The two young ones will be fine. They probably signed up for the army to get out from their father's thumb or to get off the farm and see the world. Miya thinks they will do as they are told, and we only need to be kinder to them than old Bitterboots. I call them Farm Boy 1 and Farm Boy 2. I haven't learned to tell the two apart."

I stared at her in astonishment. There was probably two hands' width of height difference between the two. One had dark brown hair and one had very light brown, almost blond hair. Both looked like they worked outdoors, maybe a farm, maybe something else that required muscles and hard work. But one had a wide open face that looked like the world had always treated him well, the other was shyer and more reserved. Kern looked up, saw my face, and laughed.

"Oh, Zren, if you could see yourself! I was joking with you, truly. I just haven't come up with better names. I had as little sleep as you did last night. Anyway, the two older soldiers are probably being sent out to the outposts as punishment. Bitterboots seems to be the leader of the four, but the other one..." She wrinkled her nose in distaste. "Miya doesn't want any of us ever alone with either of them. If we had our weapons with us, it would be fine, but men like that never look for a fair fight. Miya also said you would have to split the watches with him until we can trust them more. Then he can work them into the rotation. I'm sorry, I know you didn't get much sleep last night. But only Song is truly skilled in hand-to-hand fighting. Rell and I? Our crossbows aren't going to do you much good in the dark of the night."

I grinned at her. "We all have different strengths. I plan on cowering behind the buckboard while you and Rell use your crossbows to pick off bandit after bandit riding towards us at full gallop."

She laughed deeply. She had a smile that made me want to smile back at her, or figure out what else to say to have her laugh again.

"So...How did I lose the dice throw and end up with you in my tent?"

She looked at me, and then laughed again when she saw my smirk. Moving in close enough not to be overheard, she whispered, "Song's and Miya's strengths are the bongs—both long and short. In bong training, we learn to work together to defeat multiple foes. Miya says your strength is close hand-to-hand fighting. You three need to defend us if we are ambushed within the camp." She grinned at me again. "That is, if you have recovered from hiding behind the buckboard."

"What about Rell?"

Kern hesitated before she whispered, "Rell Huena could clear the camp of any bandits *and* the Kereki soldiers before the rest of us could find our weapons. And Chul is not as helpless as we make him to appear. The three of us are your strength for a distant enemy. I should not say more than that."

Our arms loaded with branches, we headed back to camp.

CHAPTER 3

MISTAKEN IDENTITY

The first thing I learned sitting around the fire was Song was not the cook Koanga had been along the road to Matasi. Two bites and I missed his food. I wished I had paid better attention, but at the time, I hadn't realized that was also one of his many talents. Before I had met the West Islanders, I had never been outside Kerek City for more than a night, and I didn't realize cooking over a fire was so difficult. But the Kereki soldiers all ate theirs and asked for more, so apparently rations in the Kereki military were pretty tasteless.

The four Kereki soldiers were sprawled along one side of the fire, and Kern and Chul were in his wagon eating. I was surprised to see the tip of a crossbow within Kern's reach. I wondered if all the Viklanders were nervous about the Kereki soldiers, or if this was just supposed to be an "I am watching you" message of strength.

Rell, Miya, and I were sitting along the other side of the fire in front of our lean-tos. Bitterboots, as Kern had named him, kept watching Song, his eyes following her as she moved about the fire serving us. Miya noticed it also, and his eyes narrowed. He spoke with a bite in his voice.

"So, today, the Viklanders have served as your hosts. We have given you lodging," Miya tipped his head towards the two lean-tos the youngest soldiers had put up. "We have fed you, and we will provide tonight's watch." He sat even straighter and pushed command into his words. "From this moment forward, we expect you will provide a soldier for each watch, gather wood, cook, and clean up the evening meal from your rations. We will prepare first meal and food for the midday break."

"We are already providing three outriders to your one," Bitterboots pointed out.

Miya considered. "True. We can take turns driving the wagons and riding out. I request to exempt Chul," he nodded at the wagon, "and Zren from outriding."

"Why?" asked one of the young soldiers, the brown haired shy one. I wasn't sure which Kern had decided was Farm Boy 1 or Farm Boy 2. I would have to ask her later.

"On this trip, our women are better fighters," Miya shrugged.

Farm Boy sniggered. "In Kerek, we keep our women protected from such things."

"I imagine the number of widows would double overnight if Kereki women had access to more weapons than just pitchforks and pigstickers," Rell responded drily.

The fourth soldier fastened his eyes on Rell, and I studied him unobserved. He looked whole, but my instincts were screaming at me to fight or flee. He was damaged, and my body knew it even if my eyes didn't see it. I tried to puzzle out who I had known in Kerek City with that same dead-eye interest in everything and nothing.

Mouser. My stomach twisted with the realization. Mouser had been a pirate that had floated in with the flotsam in Lowertown. He had coin, no one knew from where, but he would lurch up and down the streets of Lowertown wearing Trouble's face. He would grab the little street runners, the Lost Boys and the Lost Girls, the broken bodied beggars, and cut them for fun, or drag them into an alley. He was a monster hidden in a human body.

It wasn't just the children he preyed on. If anyone interfered or stepped in Mouser's way, they got a knife in the back or the belly for their efforts, depending on where and when, Mouser found you. He didn't fight fair; he didn't fight at all. It was just sneak attacks and lying in wait. I never knew his name. I didn't know that anyone did. Everyone just called him 'Mouser,' and we all knew who we were talking about because of his predatory hunting of the little ones.

I took a deep shuddering breath. I would call this one 'Mouser' as well, I decided to myself, and never turn my back on him. I wondered how many days to the Earles cut-off where the soldiers would turn north and leave us. I wondered how many nights I could go without sleeping.

Kern came back to the fire with Chul's and her empty plates. "He's resting," she said to the group, and sat down beside Rell. The silence stretched uncomfortably.

I suddenly realized how much I had looked forward to Koanga's stories of the West Islands on the long walk down from Aldi to Salisport. I thought how the three of us, Koanga, Ngahuru, and I would have an easy evening around the fire in Kerek or visiting the towns in Matasi. This was different. We needed what Ngahuru called a *titiro mai ki ahau*—a 'look at me'—if only to break the scrutiny of Bitterboots and Mouser from our fragile alliance. I thought about what Ngahuru would do.

I wasn't as good at telling stories as Koanga or Ngahuru, but the others didn't know that. I thought about a story to tell and decided on one of the Conrosan fairy tales Ngahuru had told us when she was still trying to figure out what I knew about myself.

I cleared my throat. "So. How much do any of you know about Conrosa?" I began, "Nothing. Nothing, I am guessing because the journey is all too far for non-sailors like you." I smiled easily at everyone around the circle. In the deepening twilight, the fire picked out the faces, casting shadows and highlighting the interest of the Farm Boys, the amused look from Miya and Kern, and the puzzlement from the others.

"So let me tell you a story about Conrosa. A country next to the land of the fae, who can do wonderful and terrible things. All Conrosans tell their children these stories so they can be ready to do battle or be gracious when they meet those from another land."

Bitterboots snorted then, but I ignored him and continued on with my tale:

"In the days of long ago, the border between Conrosa and the fae was not so well guarded as it is today. Sprites and goblins, monsters without names, and mists without faces would dance in the land of the humans to cause trouble and strife. And why wouldn't they? For Conrosa is a land of forests and meadows, waterfalls, mists, and four seasons. It is the land of plenty and there is time at the end of the day for song and story, laughter and kindness.

Now in these times, there was a hero born. No one in Conrosa knew his parents, his age, or his place of birth. He called himself 'Zren Janin.'"

Song chuffed and Miya poked her to be quiet.

"On this fine morning, Zren Janin was on the road to the Citadel of Wisdom. He was well pleased with the day and himself and why should he not? He wore new boots of fine soft leather, there was food in his leather pocket for midday, and belted about his waist was his magical Sword of Courage. Ah yes, it was a fine day, and Zren Janin knew himself to be a fine man.

The road continued and up ahead, Zren Janin saw a forest of close fitting trees. He knew those woods and knew there was no way to go but through them. As he sauntered into the Woods of Woe, Zren heard a soft voice cry out, "Woe is me! Woe is me! My life is over before it has even begun!" Zren touched his magic sword for courage and then looked about him. At last, he finally noticed a small butterfly resting on a leaf.

Zren Janin crouched down before the butterfly and asked, "What needs to be done?"

"It's so dark in these woods, and the sun cannot shine down to touch my wings and dry them. I shall die here without sunlight, and flowers, and other butterflies."

Zren raised an eyebrow, the butterfly didn't seem to be injured. But he lifted it on his fingertip to his shoulder and there it perched as he walked through the Woods of Woe. When they reached the clearing and the sun fell full upon them and warmed them, the butterfly cried out, "Oh! Oh! This is far better than I possibly imagined!" Zren saw other butterflies in the field and walked towards them. As the butterfly caught sight of them, she cried out, "Oh! Oh! I am no longer alone!" She flicked her sun-warmed wings and flew towards the other butterflies.

Zren waited for a moment watching her, and then he walked on to the road that led to the Citadel of Wisdom.

Not long after, he reached the Meadow of Melancholy. He touched his magic sword for courage, and then he started his way through the tall grasses.

Soon he heard a voice cry out, "I cannot go on! All is lost! Life is too much to bear!" Zren looked about him, above him and below, and found a small kipi, a shy animal with four gangly legs and a gentle spirit.

Zren Janin crouched down to where the kipi was lying, nearly hidden in the tall grass. "What needs to be done?" he asked.

"I don't know!" cried the kipi. "My world is crushing me, and I cannot see what to do in front of me or beside me. I am overwhelmed and cannot go on! All is lost!"

Zren Janin scratched his head. "Well, let me carry you for a while, and you can tell me all about yourself and what you wish your future to be." So he picked up the kipi and nestled it into his arms.

"Oh look!" cried the kipi, "There is blue sky and wide open spaces!" As they walked through the Meadow of Melancholy together, the kipi and Zren talked of their hopes and dreams, and the fears that kept them from reaching them.

At the edge of the meadow, the kipi asked Zren to set it down. "I feel much better, but if you don't mind, I would like to walk with you a little longer," the kipi said shyly.

"Of course," replied Zren, "the way is more pleasant with two." The kipi and Zren carried on together, sometimes talking, sometimes not, until the kipi said it had quite recovered itself and wished Zren a good day.

And so Zren continued on. At last he could see the Citadel of Wisdom in the distance. Only the River of Regret ran between Zren and his destination. He reached the bank of the river and began to remove his Sword of Courage and his fine new boots and his clothes to carry above his head to keep them dry as he waded across.

Then he heard a wavering voice cry out, "I am ruined, I shall never survive this. If only I would have taken another road in life!"

"What's this?" Zren called out. He looked all around him up and down the river's edge. At last, peering about some rocks, he found an old man sitting on the riverbank. He crouched down and looked the old man in the face. "Well, what's to be done?"

"Nothing can be done! I have done nothing in my life but the will of others. I thought I would always have more time to come to the citadel and learn for myself. Now I am too old and too feeble to cross the river and here I will die. If only I could live my life again."

Zren Janin tilted his head to his side. "And how would you live your life differently, if you could?"

"I would love those I cared for, but seek my own path. I would be kind to those I meet along the way, but not linger and get lost in their lives. I would seek truth and justice, and not be swayed by comfort and ease," sighed the old man.

Zren Janin considered the old man's words. "Well, I have never thought it so late one cannot begin again, so climb on my back, and I will carry you across the River of Regret." And with the old man on his back and his bundle of clothes and boots on his head, Zren touched his magical sword for courage, and began wading across the water.

Now the River of Regret is a raging monster that has drowned thousands of those who cannot give themselves permission to move on from their mistakes or allow others to be free from judgment. But Zren Janin's heart was brave and true and wide open to all those he met. He crossed the River of Regret and set the old man gently on the bank. He pulled his clothes and boots and sword from the bundle on his head and dressed himself again.

The old man started down the road to the Citadel of Wisdom. He turned to see if the young man who carried him across the river was coming along to walk with him.

But the road behind him was empty.

The old man smiled to himself. He knew he had just received help and forgiveness from Zren Janin, a changeling fae so fond of humans, he decided to be their champion.

When I finished, the fire's snap and sizzle was the only sound in the darkness. I waited for a moment to let those around the fire listen with their hearts to what their ears had heard. I wondered if they would have the same questions I did, when Ngahuru had first told me the story on the road to Salisport.

"Why is it called a magic sword?" Rell asked. "He didn't kill any monsters with it. In a Vikland saga, there would be a trail of scary beasts with their blood soaking into the mountains."

I nodded quickly. "I asked that same question when I first heard the story. I'll tell you what Ngahuru told me. Zren Janin touched his Sword of Courage each time he carried someone across the Woods of Woe, the Meadow of Melancholy, and the River of Regret. Each one of those can be a formidable monster to those who face them. Don't think of the magic sword as a weapon of bloodshed and violence, but as a weapon which defends and protects others."

"That's what Viklanders believe!" Song replied. "Defend the defenseless and protect those who need our care. I wonder if the Conrosans took the Viklander beliefs and made it into their stories, or the Viklanders heard the Conrosan story and added it to their traditions," she mused aloud.

I heard Koanga's voice in my head, *"Labeled, sorted, boxed, and buried."* I started slowly, "I'm not sure it matters where or who had it first, but rather it is something we all should hold in our hearts."

One of the Farm Boys spoke next—the shy dark haired one. "Do you think," he said quietly, "we could have another?"

"We will," I assured him. "But not tonight. I learned from one of the famous storytellers of the West Islands, only one of the great tales should be told each night so people have time to have their heart learn from what their ears have heard. I'll be happy to tell another one tomorrow." I glanced at Miya, who nodded at me and smiled. My heart warmed at his approval.

I sat there awkwardly for a moment and then, "I have a watch later tonight, so I will turn in now." I stood, stretched, and made my way to the woods first to take care of night business, and then to my bedroll. The others sorted themselves out and I saw Song and Rell take the other lean-to as Miya prepared himself to take first watch.

I lay with my eyes closed, thoughts warring in my head. It wasn't only the bandits and thieves we had to be worried about on the Northern Track. Would the Kereki soldiers attack us the first night while we were still sorting everything out, or would they wait until further down the road? Did they wonder what we were carrying in two heavy settler wagons to Vikland? Did Bitterboots have enough control over Mouser, or would his sickness ride him like the demons the Matasi missionaries were always nattering about?

The next thing I knew Rell was shaking me awake. "Zren, you need to take watch. I'm to sleep here with Kern. Miya is with Song. All is well."

I rubbed my eyes and rolled to my hands and knees. Next to me, Kern was stretched out asleep, her smoke grey cloak over her bedroll.

"I've got an idea. Rell, give me your cloak. You can sleep on mine." I twirled her red cloak around my shoulders, tipped the hood up, and scrambled backwards out of the lean-to. If Mouser woke early and had enough light to see the color of the cloaks, he would think he was seeing Miya and Song in one lean to, Kern and I in the other. He would assume Chul was passed out in the wagon, and that left Rell on night's watch all by her lonesome self. I pulled my Sailor's Curse from my traveling bag and tucked a steel dagger in each boot sheath.

"Wish me good hunting," I whispered to Rell. "No matter what you hear, don't let Kern shoot me with her crossbow." She raised an eyebrow but said nothing.

I skirted the perimeter of the camp and checked on the horses. Earlier, Rell had taught me how to remove the saddles, feed and water the horses, and buckle and set the hobbles. "Not a lot of demand for that knowledge in Kerek City," I had muttered under my breath, as I struggled to get it right.

Rell had laughed. "That's the reason you have me along." She showed me again, and then had me do the rest.

I made a second pass around the camp. This time I stopped in the moonlight in the Kereki soldiers' line of vision and deliberately scuffed my foot in the dirt. I saw one of the soldiers roll over and still. I started another round, this time widening the circle a few steps closer to the river and farther from the fire. I shortened my footsteps, trying to remember Rell's walk. A complete circle, and I was again in the clearing with the moonlight behind my back.

Yes! One of the bedrolls in one of the Kereki lean-tos was empty. I walked the length of a long bong, put my back against a tree, drew one of my daggers from my boot sheath, tucked my Sailor's Curse between my knuckles, and waited.

He came at me from the left, grabbing the front of the red cloak and spinning me around. I jammed my dagger into his belly and jerked upwards. At the same time, with my left hand, I slashed the Sailor's Curse above his eyes and across his throat. He fell forward and I stepped to the side, twisting the knife free as he landed heavily on the ground.

The fight had been noisy enough the camp burst into activity. I heard a command given in Vik, and my name 'Zren,' but it didn't sound like Miya's voice. Immediately, the Viklanders held their weapons at rest. One of the Farm Boys put a stick in the coals and held the flame high.

I gasped in surprise. It wasn't Mouser at my feet. It was Bitterboots, his astonished expression staring sightlessly at me.

I looked at Miya and started babbling, "I'm sorry. He grabbed my cloak and I thought it was bandits! I was so surprised I just fought back! I had no idea it was Bitterboots!"

Mouser crossed his arms and snarled, "Liar." He paused for the insult to sink in. "I believe only you were surprised it was..." he smirked, "...Bitterboots. All of the other words that have fallen from your mouth were lies. That red cloak is not the one you wore on the wagon today." He looked at the body and spat on the ground. "You will find none of us sorry he is gone." He looked at Miya and then at me. "And now we know how well you will defend the King's gold."

Mouser said nothing more and then sighed. He looked up at the sky, the first tinges of dawn barely at the horizon. "We'll take his body to the other side of the river while you're preparing the morning meal. Might as well pack up and get an early start." He grabbed the burning torch from one of the Farm Boys and motioned them to pick up Bitterboots. Dragging the body between them, the two soldiers staggered to the river. The rest of us were silent until we heard the splash of feet struggling through the water.

"I don't know whether to say 'Thank you' or 'What a mess you've gotten us into,'" Kern said. "But I need to teach you how to spin a falsehood. If you ever want to be a softfoot, you are going to need to be much, much better."

"What made you take Rell's cloak?" Miya asked quietly.

"In Lowertown, there used to be a man called Mouser who preyed on children. The way that one…" I waved my hand at the soldiers over the river, "looked at our…"

"Warriors," Miya interjected quickly.

"…warriors made me realize I needed to hunt him before he hunted us," I finished weakly.

"And yet, it is Bitterboots that is dead. Kern is right. Your face won't let you lie. So the one you hunted still lives and knows you don't trust him. Now they think we won't protect the King's gold, and we aren't working together. You have put Trouble on notice." Miya looked at Kern and Rell and snapped, "Your reactions were too slow. Zren's body should be riddled with bolts."

Rell smiled sweetly. "He told me not to let Kern shoot him. I believed he meant me as well."

"We survived," I said heavily. "But I hear what you are not saying. Next time I will talk with you first."

"Thank you." He turned back to camp. "So who needs to learn to cook over a fire? Zren and Song get water. Make sure you go a long way upstream from where they crossed. Song, bring your tahn bong. I don't expect trouble from the soldiers this soon, but you're my best. Be prepared. Kern, you're cooking. Rell, try to wash the blood out of your cloak."

Miya was back in charge.

CHAPTER 4

WE ARE NOT THE ENEMY

The Kereki soldiers had said little at first meal. Miya said we would provide another outrider, if they would allow us the use of Bitterboots' horse. Farm Boy brought it over, and Rell volunteered to ride it, saying she had heard the Kereki saddles were different than Viklander ones and she would like to try one.

Kern questioned the young soldiers if either could shoot a bow—either a West Islands short bow or a Viklander crossbow. Both shook their heads—a little warily—and Kern whispered to me, "Guess it is safe for you to take lead then." Miya heard her and scowled, but told me I would take the same wagon Song and I had driven yesterday. Chul would be sleeping in the back of mine and I would lead us out. Song, Rell, and Miya would be our outriders, and Kern would drive the middle wagon.

Rell's red cloak was still a soggy mess from where she had tried to wash out the blood in the river. It was damp out and chilly for her to be without, but she didn't complain. Before we rode out of the clearing, I heard Chul call to her. When she returned from his wagon, she was wearing Chul's cloak of deep green.

"She's a soldier, Chul," Miya said exasperatedly, "She has had worse days behind her."

"Forgive me for a kindness, then. And she's no longer a soldier, she's in the Diplo—that makes her as soft as you and all the other diplomats," Chul shot back. "I have your bedroll in here to cuddle up in if I decide to take a chill. Let it be, Miya."

We drove through Balza midmorning. The area around the village well was empty of people. We filled our waterskins, and the Viklanders casually filled their flasks of West Islands steel. I saw the Kereki soldiers look covetously at them. I wondered if Miya was deliberately asking for more trouble. Rell showed me how to open and fill a traveling water bag for the horses in case we didn't camp along the river that night.

"How do you know all this?" I asked. "Even the other Viklanders watch you."

"I like horses," she said. "I was around them a lot growing up, and my family taught me to take care of them." She brushed her hand down the nose of Bitterboots' horse. "Someday, I'll live where I can ride every day again." She looked at me and smiled. "Until then, I'll volunteer to care for the horses in order to avoid campfire cooking."

We laughed and took the rest of the horses to the animal trough to water. A few people on the outside streets stopped and furtively watched, but no one spoke to us. I'm sure we looked a strange group of soldiers and nations. I didn't know if all of Kerek would be like this, like Lowertown, where to show curiosity where it wasn't wanted was nothing more than an invitation for a dance with Trouble. But I knew here in Balza, the nine of us were most of all outsiders and best to be avoided.

With the coming Wet, damp breezes were already kicking up, hinting at the rain for the season to come. I had always hated this time of year as the weather was only going to get worse. I knew I had ruined Rell's cloak and should give her mine, but I loved how warm and dry it made me feel. I asked Miya if I needed to buy Rell another cloak while we were in Balza. I wondered how I would pay for it since I had poured all my coins into a Matasi boy's hands back in Salisport.

He looked around at the empty streets. "No. I'm not happy about this. Let's keep moving. If it rains, we'll all be cold and wet." The Kereki soldiers heard him refuse me, but I just shrugged. I saw the shy one duck his head away quickly when he saw me looking at him.

We strung our way east and left the eerily quiet town behind. A few furloughs out, I watched as Miya looked back. He wheeled his horse around and trotted back to me.

"When did we lose Farm Boy?"

"Whoa!" I called to the horses. They stopped, and I turned to look behind me. Kern was driving the middle wagon. Rell, with her crossbow hanging from her pommel, was her outrider on the right, and Song was on the left, a tahn bong crossed diagonally over her back and a jeong bong balanced easily in front of her. Close behind them should have been the payroll wagon and the two Kereki soldiers trailing as outriders to guard our rear. Instead, Mouser was on the wagon far behind us, and the other outrider was nowhere in sight.

"It wouldn't make sense for him to be killing his fellow soldiers," I said slowly.

"Unless his plan isn't to go to the Earles garrison at all. He may be gambling we would be happy just to see him ride off alone," Miya suggested.

"With an entire garrison's payroll from the last two years?" I arched my eyebrow. "Are we happy with that?"

"I'm not sure I'm inclined to let our remaining Farm Boy spill out his life on this dusty road." Miya grinned at me. "I'm a little partial to strays with all kinds of talents."

"If he can cook, I'm all in," I said fervently.

Underneath the canvas in the back of the wagon, Chul snorted in laughter.

"Did we wake you?" Miya called.

"Can't get any sleep with you two chattering like crows out there." There was silence, and then, "I see what the problem is. The remaining outrider is closer to Kern's wagon than his own. Does he think he's in danger? And from whom?"

Kern had finally pulled her wagon up to ours. Song and Rell urged their horses into talking distance to the rest of us and turned to face the last wagon.

We all saw it at the same time. A horse and rider closing fast on the last wagon.

"Rell, Kern. Load your crossbows. Song, grab the extra short bong and give it to Zren. Zren, use it as a club if you must, but don't give up this wagon." Miya barked out his commands. "Crossbows up!"

"Stop. Wait! No, it's Nebs! Don't fire!" The other Kereki soldier rode up fast. "Please! It's just Nebs catching up to us. Don't fire!" he begged.

"Weapons down!" Miya called, and then turned his horse to look at the tall Farm Boy. "How'd he get so far behind? Your wagon too?"

"When we were at the well, Nebs heard this one," he pointed at me, "ask if he could buy a replacement cloak for Rell. When you said no, Nebs told the old man he was going to do it. The old man gave him coin and he was supposed to catch up to us." He looked around at the scrubland. "It's not like you can get lost out here."

The second rider had caught up to the payroll wagon, and we all watched silently as together they pulled up to our group.

"Everything all right?" Miya asked coldly.

Mouser held the reins loosely in both hands. "Yep. The boys here didn't think it too kind of you to push through Balza without a bit of shopping. Since...Bitterboots," there was that smirk again, "isn't around to collect his paypacket, we thought he could at least pay for the cloak he ruined." He nodded at Nebs, who urged his horse forward and presented Rell with a tightly wrapped package in brown paper. Mouser continued, "There is nothing offered or implied in that, girlie. We are not your enemy."

Rell looked at Miya and he nodded. She untied the string and unrolled a travelers cloak in a deep rich red, darker than the one I had ruined. She untied Chul's cloak, laid it across her lap, and swirled the new one about her shoulders.

"I'm sorry, Rell. They didn't have that other red color you had before," Nebs said quietly.

"This one is very beautiful. Thank you," she paused, "… Nebs." Rell smiled at him cautiously.

"I appreciate your thoughtfulness," Miya added stiffly. He reached forward to take Chul's dark green cloak from Rell and placed it in my wagon under the canvas. Without another word to anyone, he wheeled his horse about, "Fall in!"

I snapped the reins and we lurched forward. It didn't take long for the wagons to stretch out a bit, and I was lost in my thoughts when I heard, "Zren?"

"Chul?"

"Did you notice how the Kereki soldiers know the girls' names and not ours?"

"I noticed."

"You were raised in Kerek City. Is that just because of how Kereki men treat their women, or should we be worried?"

"We should be worried."

"Oh." Silence.

"Chul, what did you say when I was fighting with Bitterboots last night?"

"I said, 'Don't move. Zren won.' And it wasn't a fight. I was awake and saw the whole thing from the beginning. Don't ever let me get on your bad side."

"I'll give you plenty of warning." We clopped along in an easy silence. "Chul, you aren't going to die on me, are you? How bad are you hurt?"

He snorted, "Bad enough. The liquid fire splashed on my leg. It's painful, but I'm not going to die from it. I couldn't get it treated in Kerek City because of the fires and the riots down by the docks. There would be too many questions. First Soldier Joon thought it would be good to get me out of Kerek City for a while and back to my labs, and Miya had a plan."

He paused. "Miya always has a plan. So now I get to sleep all day on top of crates of West Islands steel plows and farm implements, and then join each of you for all the watches at night." He paused again, "You should know this, Zren. Miyamoto Suki likes to be underestimated. I bet he is sitting on his horse right now, chuckling that the three remaining Kerekis think they are traveling with a cripple, one skinny boy, a soft diplomat, and a group of women as frightened and submissive as their own."

I was silent for a long moment. "They're not?"

Chul gave a deep belly laugh. "Have you ever seen Rell Huena shoot her crossbow? If Farm Boy wouldn't have ridden up to stop us, she could have taken out all three of those Kereki soldiers, even the one at full gallop, before the rest of us could see their faces." He sobered. "Since we don't know if we can trust our friendly neighbors, we need to keep all our skills hidden, especially while you're out luring old men into a dance with your knife."

"I'll keep that in mind." I nodded to myself.

"You do that. Right now, the Kereki soldiers know you are no longer just a skinny boy too useless to know how to ride a horse. But they don't know about anyone else. Since your watch tonight is only four decons and mine is eight, I better try to get back to sleep. Thanks for my cloak for the way. I don't know what Miya was trying to do back in Balza; it wasn't Rell's fault her cloak was ruined." His voice let me know exactly whose fault he did think it was.

"The town wasn't safe to strangers. I didn't see anything, but I felt it. He did too." I straightened my shoulders and stretched. "Thanks for looking out for me last night. I had told Rell and Kern not to shoot me with their bows, but I still could have taken a solid hit with a bong." I rubbed my shoulder absently. I still remembered how numb it had felt after Song had hit me at the Vikland embasado—and that had only been practice.

"That's what I'm here for. Say Zren? Do you cook?"

"No. Never needed to learn."

"I was afraid of that. Let's hope it is a skill the Kereki soldiers consider useful." I heard Chul turning about under the canvas behind me and sooner than I expected, the quiet stillness of his sleeping.

CHAPTER 5

THE POWER OF NAMES

It turns out cooking is a valued skill in the Kereki army. The tall soldier—I wasn't sure if it was the one Kern called Farm Boy 1 or 2—was in charge of cooking that night when we stopped a few decons short of Huk. Mouser didn't do much beyond putting up his canvas lean-to, but he didn't order the other two around either. They were talkative and cheerful as they gathered wood and water, rummaged through their food packs, and put together stew and cornbread. The one who had bought Rell's cloak I knew now was Nebs. But I didn't know if it was a birth name or a byname. Several times I heard Nebs call out "Rygee," and it took me a while to realize that was the other soldier's name.

We sat around the fire sopping up the juices with our cornbread, praising Rygee every time we stopped him to give us another ladleful.

"You did not learn this skill in the army," I said around mouthfuls.

"No. I learned at home. I enjoyed it more than some of the other chores, and since I had no sisters to help my mama with all the things that needed to be done for a farm our size, my papa allowed me to help with the baking, cooking, and preserving. He had my three older brothers to help him. I still learned by his side to run a farm of my own, so no one minded."

Kern held out her bowl and he walked around the fire to serve her. She flashed him one of her big smiles, and I remembered how she had dazzled me when we had first met. She may be one of Bima's Softfoots, I thought to myself, but she wasn't the softfooting-in-the-dark kind, even though she had helped us in the Conrosan embasado. She was like Koanga, drawing so much attention to herself the rest of us around the fire could have disappeared in the dark, and Rygee wouldn't even notice.

I wondered if Miya had told her to charm Rygee or if she was acting on her own.

"Your papa was a smart man. A man who cooks well? A prize indeed. Yes," she grinned wickedly. "You are a prize indeed."

Startled, Rygee paused for a moment and then stepped back closer to Nebs. He blew out a long slow breath. "Maybe. But if so, my papa didn't see it. At the beginning of this Dry, he decided I needed to be married. My older brothers had all married to the farms next to us, increasing our size with each one."

"Let me guess," said Nebs. "The only farm left touching your borders didn't have any daughters, but only a widow old as dirt and well-tilled bottomland." Everyone erupted in laughter, even Rygee.

"No." Rygee gave a grim smile. "The farm my papa wanted was on the other side of my oldest brother. The daughter was nice enough and not too much older than I am, but I realized if I agreed to my papa's wishes, I would be following someone else's orders for the rest of my life."

"So you joined the army?" Nebs asked incredulously. More laughter.

"No. I refused to marry where he bid me. My papa was angry. He said he had made a mistake, I was too strong-minded for my own good, but it wasn't too late for him to fix it."

Rygee looked off to the river and then turned and watched Miya carefully as he finished his story. "The King posted the decree that he would forgive three years of tithes and taxes to anyone enlisting and serving in one of the remote outposts or border garrisons. My papa packed my bags, my brothers tapped me on the head, tied me to the wagon, and delivered me to the garrison south of Pagta. I woke up in the barracks. I was told my papa told the commander I was sleeping off a celebration. Now here I am."

I looked at Miya who had a perfectly blank face. I watched Rygee who turned away and gave a half smile to Kern and then moved about the fire serving the others. We were silent for a while each thinking our own thoughts.

I had grown up on the streets of Kerek City. But somewhere at some time, someone had cared enough to keep me alive, taught me castle Keresh and not the rough language of the docks. I had no memory of that person, or if it was more than one, but I always believed I had ended up on the streets because they could no longer care for me, not because they could get three years of not paying taxes from a distant king.

I wondered why Rygee had told us his story when we had barely learned his name. I couldn't imagine what that cost him to say so much in front of strangers. Then I remembered how he had looked at Miya as he spilled the story of his father's betrayal. How Miya had said nothing. I felt there had been an entire other conversation than the words that had fallen from Rygee's mouth. I wasn't sure what I missed, although I knew I had missed something.

Mouser shifted his weight, and everyone snapped their eyes to him, breaking the moment.

"Not everyone that starts out for the military garrison shows up there," Mouser muttered.

"I know," Rygee said morosely. "I'll probably be dead before I get there." He shot a quick glance at me.

Mouser shrugged and said nothing more.

Nebs looked at me. "Um, last night you said you would tell us another story?"

"I did." I stretched out by the fire to make myself more comfortable. "Tonight I will tell another tale of Conrosa. This one of the Queen and her daughters." I watched the others move their empty plates aside and settle in. "This one is a tale when the fae decided to cause great mischief in Conrosa and how the Queen and her daughters solved the problem.

"Long ago in the country of Conrosa, there lived a Queen, her consort, and her two daughters. Now you should know, Conrosa borders the land of the fae to the north and to the west. The ocean laps the southern shore, and the Shale Mountains kiss the sunrise before the Conrosans greet the day. It's a tidy land with well-marked borders and no wars. The Queen was wise and her daughters well-cherished.

Now one night, a fluttering of fairies crossed into Conrosa to find merriment and music among the humans. Many of the fae are very long lived and when too much time and too little work abound, well, Trouble is sure to follow.

Over the hills and down in the valleys, the fairies searched for fun. At last they came upon a village wedding. The vows had been spoken, the food had been eaten, and the musicians were tuning their fiddles for the dancing to come.

Delightedly, the fairies enchanted the musicians so they would never tire in their desire to play their best. Then the fairies threw dust over the guests so they would never remember, and enchanted the bride and the groom so they would never forget.

Then they danced.

The moon was high in the sky and still they danced. They danced with the groom until he begged to rest and then they enchanted his feet so he could not stop. They danced wickedly with the parson and the proper ladies and laughed at their wild abandon. They circled the bride and danced while she cried for her enchanted husband and her ruined wedding. Once the first fingers of dawn touched the horizon, they ran down the road laughing as they imagined what everyone would think when they woke in the morning, disheveled in the grass, and believing the worst of what they had done.

Just as the sun was stretching and ready to begin her day, the bride and groom could feel the enchantment loosen. They looked about the wreckage and decided the Queen must be told the fairies had trespassed. For while it was only one day of their long married life together, the groom and the bride knew the fairies would not stop if they did not have a reason.

The bride and the groom came to Wisdom, the city the Queen called home, and told their tale before the court.

Now the Queen was already training her two daughters to act carefully with the trust placed in them by the people of Conrosa. So she gathered them together and asked what could be done to keep the fairies from harming what was not theirs. For while the fairies merely regarded their antics as a night's mischief, to the bride and the groom this was a grave injury that should not happen to others.

The princesses retired to the great library and began to read and study the old legends. At last, they had a plan. They would visit Fairyland with many musicians to perform the song cycles the fairies had never heard before. If they wished, the princesses proposed, the fairies could keep one musician for a year and a day and then return the musician to Conrosa with a wish fulfilled for payment.

And so it came to be. The High King of Fairyland selected a bard for a year and a day. And when the musician returned home, she had a new harp which played so sweetly anyone who heard it offered her food, drink, coin, and shelter to stay and play for them. She could sing for her supper and enjoy a life of ease for the rest of her days.

It wasn't long before the fairies grew bored without their favorite musician. This time, when they fluttered into Conrosa, they scattered from village to village, knocking down the bell towers of all the churches. They tumbled the bells out of the steeples and rang them about the villages. In the morning, like a naughty child who has forgotten their belongings outdoors, the bells were left scattered and broken in the dirt.

People from all the villages which had their bells broken and their night's sleep ruined came to see the Queen and demand she put a stop to the trespassing of the fairies. The Queen and her daughters gathered together to find a solution.

This time the princesses sent an appeal throughout Conrosa for help, for they knew many minds can solve many problems. Within just a few days, a woodsmith showed his face at the castle and begged the Queen and her daughters for an audience. He asked to be sent to Fairyland and work for a year and a day in order to have a boon granted. The Queen smiled and cautioned him against tricksters and to be careful in his words and actions. But the daughters and the Queen granted his request.

Now the Queen had known the woodsmith was not just anyone. She had known of fae who had fled a dance with Trouble in their land and had settled in her own country. She hoped her family and her subjects had treated the strangers so well that if the woodsmith was one of them, he would return to the High King of Fairyland and bring a solution.

She thought the woodsmith in front of her might be the great Zren Janin, said to be a changeling fae so enamored of the humans he *stepped in to be their champion. But while the Queen thought quite a number of things, she could not see the future, and had to trust the woodsmith could accomplish peace between the two Kingdoms.*

The woodsmith left for the land of fairies. For a year and a day, no Trouble danced over the border.

At the end of the agreement, the woodsmith rode up to the castle on a fine brown horse. The saddle was soft leather, the trappings were silver, and the saddlebags were full.

The Queen's Guard circled the horse and brought it into the courtyard where they escorted the woodsmith into the throne room and into the presence of the Queen and her daughters.

"And were you treated well, my woodsmith?"

"Yes," Zren Janin answered. "It was good for me to see Fairyland. I fulfilled the terms of our bargain. For a year and a day I built drums which never faltered in their beat, fiddles which never sang out of tune, and harps of grace and beauty. I thank you for trusting me to meet with the High King on your behalf." He bowed low before her.

"For this honor," he continued, "I have brought you a gift as well. This saddlebag has a horn made by a metalsmith known to me. If you or your daughters shall ever need a courier to travel to Fairyland on your behalf, just blow, and someone—fae or human—

will appear to do your bidding. Let us hang this horn in your castle and protect Conrosa from the mischief of the fairies who stray from their home and hearth."

The Queen considered him and then nodded. "It will be as you say. But what boon did you ask for yourself?"

Zren Janin heaved a great sigh. "You and yours have been welcoming and kind to any who enter your borders. Years ago, my mother's family was banished from their home. Your twice great-grandmother, the Queen upon the throne when all this happened, granted the exiles a safe haven. Now the High King says he can no longer remember why they left his court, and he has forgiven all, if there was anything to forgive. I will leave your presence today to seek my mother's family out and let them know they can return if they wish. It is not that you have been unkind, but only that they miss their home."

The Queen leaned back in her throne. "Daughters, have you heard the words that have fallen from the woodsmith's mouth? And those he has not said?"

The sisters looked at each other, but not a word crossed their lips. Finally, the youngest looked at her mother and replied, "We are in agreement, my sister and I. His gift will be accepted, and his request shall be granted. Hang the horn in the castle. Zren Janin has earned the right to bring his family back to their homeland. As long as his heart is free and he can hear the horn to save us from ill-intent, he shall be able to pass back and forth between the two Kingdoms."

As I told the story of the woodsmith and the bargain struck for a year and a day, I felt the softening of the barriers between us. *All stories do that*, I thought. Listening to Rygee's story and tasting his food made him a man with talents, and hurts, and dreams. Stories remind us there are many ways to look, to listen, and to learn what the world is beating on our brains to teach us.

I suddenly realized Rygee had told his story to tell us the man we saw in front of us was more than a soldier of a King who held Viklanders in contempt. He would not harm us.

I finished the tale as Ngahuru had taught me. *"And that is why even to this day, Conrosa is a land of peace and prosperity with borders open to all who wish to work towards knowledge and kindness."*

I let the silence of the after-story set in and waited for someone to break the quiet.

"Why would you leave Conrosa?" asked Nebs quietly.

"To see the world, of course," I quipped. "Since I left, I have been to Matasi, Kerek, and now I am on my way to Vikland." I squinted at him. "Isn't that why you joined the Kereki army?"

Nebs barked out a harsh laugh.

"You can think about it, Nebs, while you take first watch with me," Miya said easily. "Zren and Rell, you have second watch, and Song and Rygee, you have third watch."

* * * * *

Later that night, Kern whispered to me, "Where did you learn those Conrosan fairy tales?"

"From Ngahuru. She had read them in a book and told them to me to pass the time as we fled Kerek City and down the Coast Road to Matasi."

"Huh." She grunted. "I can't even imagine what that would have been like, to have someone as great as Ngahuru teach me on a journey as long as Kerek City to Salisport." She rolled over so her back was towards me, but I still caught her parting shot. "It seems it wasn't all wasted on you."

CHAPTER 6

DEATH

I could feel the damp breeze as soon as I got up in the morning. Because I had the middle watch with Rell during the night, I felt like I could sleep for a long time to come. But Song and Rygee had the last watch and had already gotten water for the fire to cook first meal. There was no help for it, it was time to get up.

Miya came back from the river with more kindling in his hands. He carefully fed the fire, and as I came back from taking care of morning business, he asked, "Your turn to cook?"

I shook my head. "In Lowertown, I stole my food or went without. I don't know the first thing about the magic of fire and food."

Miya gave a dramatic sigh. "A wagon train of assassins and weapon masters and not a cook in sight." He looked over his shoulder at Rell leaving to tend to the horses. "Rell! Come cook first meal. It's your turn."

Rell turned and gave him a scathing look. "Miyamoto Suki, each morning and each evening I care for the horses. This morning, as I am walking to take care of the horses—yet again— you call me to make first meal like I am some cadet in the first year of my military service." She paused. "I am not."

Miya bristled, and switched to Vik as he spoke sharply to Rell. I watched as she stretched to her full height and responded evenly and without apology. Then without another word, she turned and walked down the path to where we had hobbled the horses for the night. I looked across the fire at Song and Rygee. Song had a small smirk on her face. Of course, she understood Vik. Rygee just looked concerned. Miya stood up and walked out of the clearing to where Rell had disappeared.

"I can cook first meal," Rygee offered. "Can you give me food? Our packs are a little light. We are going to need to stop for supplies soon."

Song got up and pulled over the traveling bag stored in the other lean-to. "We need supplies too, but whatever is in here is available for you to use." She handed it to Rygee. "I'll bring you more kindling and cooking wood for the fire. Zren, come help me."

I had just stood up when Mouser came back into the clearing. He saw Rygee looking through the food bags for ingredients to make a meal. He scowled and looked at Song and then at me.

"This is not what we agreed on. We are not your Kereki housewives meant to fetch and cook for you."

"Don't worry about it, old man," Rygee said easily. "I volunteered." He gave Song a cheeky smile. "Better to cook than to taste someone else's cooking sometimes, eh?"

Song laughed and waved her hand at him. "Works for me. I'll get more wood."

Instead of going with her, I helped Nebs and Kern as they tore down camp and loaded the wagons. Rell and Miya came back to the clearing as the smells of first meal drifted through our spaces. Rell had a small satisfied look on her face, but Miya just looked discouraged. He looked about the clearing and sighed.

Kern laughed at him. "Miya, Miya. While you were off thinking about how hard it is to run a wagon train, your 'assassins and weapons masters' decided to get the real work done. I am starting to see a pattern here, Miya."

He threw up his hands, but smiled at Rygee. "Thank you." He pressed his palms together and said it again, "Thank you."

* * * * *

Usually, I led the wagon train with Chul asleep behind me. It wasn't like I could get lost. The road was nearly straight east.

Small half-tracks wandered off to the south and north leading to settlements and small villages farther away from the main track.

But today, Miya put me and Chul at the end. Song drove the first wagon with Miya as her outrider on the south. He bunched the Kereki soldiers in the middle, which Mouser seemed to prefer, although I couldn't understand why.

Mouser always drove the wagon with the Farm Boys as outriders. Miya rotated who drove the Viklander wagon in the last spot in the wagon train. When I had asked why, he only said that after Balza, he liked two Viklander outriders in the back to keep an eye on us and our surroundings.

The sun was no longer shining its watery light in my eyes when we came over a small rise. With the damp breeze behind us, I saw the bodies before we smelled them. It looked like bundles of clothes strewn about on the track on the south side. There were two badly damaged wagons but no horses. Miya raised his hand up, and we halted. Then he called the outriders forward and they trotted towards him.

"Weapons up!" he called. Song stood up on her wagon seat and pulled her long bong, Kern and Rell lifted their crossbows in opposite directions. Nebs and Rygee pulled long knives and faced north and south. I turned on the wagon seat to look behind us. Mouser sat on his wagon still and watchful.

It didn't feel like a trap to me. But this was my first time on the Northern Track and Miya's thirteenth. I heard Chul rustling around in the back of the wagon.

"Chul," I called softly. "There are bodies on the track ahead of us. Miya thinks it may be an ambush."

"I see it. I'm getting fire power ready. When I say get down, get down."

Miya used his jeong bong like a pike and rolled one of the bundles over. His horse sidestepped, but then stood firm. Miya moved towards another, and I glanced towards Rell and Kern. They balanced easily on their horses, crossbows up and ready to fire. Neither one wavered. I wondered how long they could hold that position.

After turning over the third bundle, Miya called, "Weapons down," and swung himself down from his horse. He walked in a widening circle, and we all dismounted to see what he saw. I walked up to Mouser and together we walked to the first body. It was a Kereki woman dressed in heavy skirts and a shawl over her head. The smell worsened, and I breathed shallowly through my mouth.

"Settlers," Mouser grunted. "I bet you Nebs' paypacket, Miya finds out the other wagons and all the horses have been driven off."

"How many bandits would there have to be to take a wagon train this size?"

"More than you got fingers and toes." He looked around. "More'n we got, anyway." He stared hard at the fringe of trees on the north side of the Huk River. "Those girlies of yours fight as good as you do?" he said suddenly.

"Any of them can beat me in any weapon they choose," I said fervently.

He looked at me then. "You believe you're telling the truth on that." He sounded surprised.

"I am," I answered solemnly.

"What's your name?"

"Zren Janin."

"Like the stories you been telling?" He crossed his arms and looked at me suspiciously.

I thought back to Kern's remark when we first met at the embasado in Kerek City. I gave him a sly grin. "Yes. My name giver thought I could live up to it." I paused. "What's yours?"

He grunted again. "I heard the tall one," he pointed his chin at Kern, "Call the young ones, 'Farm Boy.' And you killed 'Bitterboots.' You had a name for me as well?"

I nodded reluctantly. "We called you, 'Mouser.' Or I did, anyway." I looked off at Song, so he wouldn't see my face.

"Mouser." He blew out a noisy breath. "I can live with that." He uncrossed his arms and started walking towards Miya, not allowing me to make any type of remark. "Might as well find out how bad it is," he called over his shoulder.

Miya took Mouser with him, and they walked the battlefield again. Rell walked up to me leading her horse, she looked numb and shocked. I noticed Song had stepped to the north side of her wagon where she was vomiting, hiding between the tall wheels for cover.

I started talking quickly, "In Lowertown, in Kerek City, you see single bodies like this, Rell. Those who didn't make it home from winning in the gambling halls, the street runners carrying a message the gang bosses didn't like, those caught at the wrong end of a forced barter." I paused to let my words soak in. "Rell, this is a lot of death for all of us."

Rell whispered hoarsely, "I was beginning to think Miya was overreacting. Splitting the night into three watches, riding fully armed." She huffed. "I gave him an earful just this morning about how highhanded he has been."

"I think Miya has survived so many crossings because he does overreact. I like following him."

She gave me an odd look, but before I could question her, Miya rode up. "Rell, take Kern and watch the river. Weapons ready. I don't think they're coming back, but if they do, it could only be from the river. I would rather be overcautious and alive." She nodded at him, mounted her horse, and moved toward Kern.

Miya looked at me. "They're all Kereki settlers. We think there were five wagons, ten or eleven horses. We don't see any tracks of outriders, so they probably didn't have any warning or any weapons more than a few pigstickers and pitchforks. Mouser said the bandits probably loaded up the undamaged wagons and put the uninjured horses on a string. We can see tracks heading north of here. They didn't do anything to hide their trail, so either they are a big enough gang not to care, or fools. In any case..." he paused and grimaced. "They're Kereki settlers and the soldiers' responsibility. The soldiers are sorting through what's left to see if there is anything to identify and notify. They should stop in the next settlement and tell the Justice."

He turned, and Song and I looked to see the two Farm Boys in the wagons going through the remaining belongings and Mouser scavenging the bodies on the ground.

I scoffed, "Looks more like the street runners stripping the bodies in Lowertown to see if there was anything the bandits missed."

"I said we wouldn't interfere," Miya insisted, "They all belong to Kerek, and we are only traveling through."

"Are we in any danger?" Song asked quietly.

"From the bandits here?" Miya clarified. "I would say no. This happened this morning, and they are out somewhere sorting through their treasure. I am sure there was food and coin, so they will be arguing and eating for the rest of the day. That said, if the Kerekis aren't inclined to talk to the Justice, we will go through Huk without stopping, not even for the horses at the village well. I'd like to get far away from here before we stop for the night. We'll run a double watch tonight."

Nebs threw some curiously heavy traveling bags to the ground. They clanked loudly and he looked at us, half challenging, half embarrassed. Miya just smiled back blandly and continued talking, "I need to talk to Chul. He may need to make a miraculous recovery from his 'near-death.' If the raiding gangs are this big, we are going to need every person fully armed and ready. We still haven't seen how green our Farm Boys are, and I don't think Mouser is going to defend anything except himself and that paychest."

We continued to watch silently as the Kereki soldiers threw their scavenging into their wagon and made ready to leave. Kern and Rell, who had been watching the riverbank with crossbows ready, saw them. The bowmasters relaxed, and cantered over to us, waiting.

"We're ready to go," Mouser said.

"You aren't going to bury them?" Kern asked surprised. "Isn't that how Kerekis care for their dead?"

"They're dead. It won't matter to them, girlie, and the sooner we move on, the better."

Kern protested, and Miya called her name sharply. She pressed her lips tightly together but said nothing more.

Everyone saddled up. Silently, we left the massacre and slowly continued east. After a bit, I watched as Miya dropped back to the Kereki wagon. His horse kept pace as the two men talked, and I saw Mouser shake his head. Miya said a few words more and then sharply kneed his horse outward. I didn't need to know what words had been said. I was surprised Miya had even asked if the soldiers were going to stop in Huk and report the death of the settlers. Miya may have known what should have been done, but Miya and Mouser were not the same. I knew the Farm Boys wouldn't challenge Mouser, and I knew Mouser wouldn't draw attention to himself and his scavenging by meeting with the Justice in Huk.

* * * * *

We passed through Huk without stopping. It hadn't felt as unfriendly as Balza to me, but there was the same sense of the streets emptying out as we came through the town. Song was still driving the first wagon with Miya and Rell as her outriders. I noticed how tall and straight they rode in their saddles with their braids pulled forward. Both outriders had short bongs strapped across their back, another in their scabbard, and a crossbow on their lap—when had that happened?

The Kerekis, in contrast, just looked like they could disappear into the dusty surroundings. I was also wearing Kereki clothes as I brought up the rear, but I had Kern as my outrider, and she would wave and smile at anyone who stole a glance at us. I tried to figure out if Miya was trying to make us look like a Kereki wagon train full of supplies with hired Viklander guards, or Viklanders parading through with a captured prize.

I heard Chul give a long sigh of relief as we saw the town fade behind us. But he didn't talk, and I didn't know what to say.

It was maybe a decon later when Miya raised his hand for a halt. The Huk River had angled far to the north, and there was open scrubland on either side of the track. Nothing could hide nearby. He turned back to us and waited until the wagons had bunched up and he could talk without shouting.

"We'll stop for a moment. Water the horses from our supplies, but don't feed them. Song, take Rell's outrider position,

Rell take Zren's wagon. I'll need you on crossbow beside Chul. Chul, your supplies will be in the back. Song, drop back to outrider on the last wagon with me. Kern and Nebs, move up to the front outriders, Nebs on the north side. Zren, you'll take the open wagon and lead us out after our midday."

If any of the Kereki soldiers were surprised to see Chul climb clumsily out of the back of the wagon, take a crossbow, and limp heavily around to the front of it, they hid it well. Rell dismounted and set up the open basket watering skins she had filled that morning for all the horses. Kern rummaged through the food bags and handed out fruit, stonebread, and two handfuls of almonds to everyone. We stood, stretching our legs, eating, and watching the high desert around us. The only sound was Chul moving about the wagon seat trying to get his damaged leg comfortable.

The Kereki soldiers joined us. We stood quietly eating until Mouser spoke, "So, your scrawny boy fights like a Lowertown gang boss, and your Matasi giant rises from his deathbed to live and fight another day. Any more surprises, Viklander?"

Miya smiled with too much teeth. He took a long drink from his flask, and I felt the tension ratchet up. There was no warmth in his voice as he spoke.

"No surprises, but I would like you to consider an offer," Miya said, looking each of the soldiers in the face. "Tomorrow, between the towns of Cloa and Sary, we will reach the crossroads where you would take the road north to the military garrison. 'Earles,' I think it is called. If you choose *not* to take the crossroads, you can continue on with us to Vikland. You will be safe there, free to settle, or soldier with our army, as you choose. Your coin will stay in Kerek. We will deliver your payroll chest to the military garrison at Ishes. Or you can remain in any Kereki settlements or towns to come, and we will say nothing of your whereabouts. We will deliver the payroll chest to Ishes then as well. If the chest is lighter than when you left Kerek City, it is because you took out your two years of wages in advance. But to be clear, I will deliver the paychest and at least part of the payroll to the military garrison at Ishes. I will not have it said we murdered you on the way and took the coin for ourselves."

Mouser said nothing for a moment and then, "You are asking us to abandon our orders to report to the military garrison at Earles? To spend the rest of our lives as deserters?"

Miya looked coldly at Mouser. "This, I believe, was your plan from the beginning. Zren removed your captain, and I am willing to keep your new recruits from harm. They have done nothing to deserve death at your hands or mine. Are we agreed on that?"

"Oh, yes!" said Nebs. "You find me a nice little bolthole, and I will just tuck myself away as quiet as you please. No Earles, no Ishes, no Vikland for me."

Miya raised his hand. "No need to make a decision right now, we still have a distance to go to Cloa." He looked around at the empty landscape. "Keep your eyes open today, we're a long way from help."

Miya took another long drink and stoppered his flask. "Are we ready? Mount up. Let's move out."

Later that afternoon, I saw Miya move up to Kern and talk with her for a while as their horses trotted together. She then pulled up and waited as the wagons rolled on by, falling in with the last wagon. Miya cut across in front of me, riding easily alongside Nebs. Their discussion looked serious and then Miya handed over his tahn bong. They talked for a while more and then Miya headed back to me.

"Can you believe it? The only weapons the Kereki army issued them were short blades and a long dagger made of pounded iron. Pounded iron." He shook his head. "I should have questioned them at the first camp. Hold up, I need to pull out another tahn bong for Rygee back there."

I pulled back on the reins and Miya reached into the wagon bed.

"What about Mouser?" I asked. "To be truthful, I still don't trust him."

"Neither do I," Miya admitted, "but we need him friendly. At least with him driving a wagon, he won't be able to handle too many weapons." Miya hung his crossbow over his pommel, tucked a tahn bong into his open scabbard, and another under his arm.

"Rygee has been asking a lot of questions. He's a sharp boy. I think if we can get Mouser to part with enough coin for him, he will come with us to Vikland." He nodded at me to go, and I clucked the horses forward. Without another word, he wheeled his horse away and headed to the back of the wagon train. Soon I saw Kern pass on my right. She gave me a cheeky smile and a wave and trotted ahead and out.

* * * * *

We finally pulled up to camp for the night. It had been a while since we had seen any type of settlement or even a half track, but it was already later than when we had stopped any night previously. We had to drive the wagons a ways off the track to reach the river, but Miya didn't want to have the wagon train where any passing strangers could see it. I told him how Ngahuru had taught me to wipe our tracks clear with river willow branches. He nodded without saying anything and helped me cut a few. I brushed out our tracks while the others set up camp.

We needed supplies badly. Luckily for us, Song had found watercress along the riverbank and mushrooms on some downed elms and with that, Rygee was able to turn a few gristly vegetables into a stew worth eating. We ate the pot clean.

While Nebs was getting water for the washing up, I went to throw my bedroll underneath the lean-to. Miya saw me and came over.

"We've lost Chul's sleeping all day and keeping watch all night. I want to post double watches tonight. Song and you, Rell and I, Kern and Chul. If the Kereki soldiers post one as well, that's three on each watch."

"You expect an ambush?"

"I think we are at greatest risk between here and Ishes. We are only two thirds of the way through, Zren, and the size of that group of raiders this morning is discouraging. It happened this morning, just this morning. It could have been us."

"But they didn't have Viklander outriders and you to lead them," I grinned.

Miya smiled sadly. "If only that would be a plan for success. Anyway, I wanted to tell you I will tell the story tonight. I want to tell one of the great tales of the West Islands, something to make sure the Farm Boys want to throw in their lot with us." He walked off to the horses to tell Kern the plans for the evening.

I looked for Song to tell her we had first watch, but she wasn't anywhere in sight. I asked Rell, and she looked surprised as she looked around.

"Her jeong bong is gone." She pointed to Song's bedroll. "She's probably practicing her forms somewhere."

I looked around the clearing to try to guess which way Song had gone and realized with a sinking feeling Rygee was the only soldier in sight. Rell snarled when she realized the same thing.

"Tell Miya," I said hurriedly as I pulled my boot knife. "I'm going down that path." I pointed with my knife, and Rygee startled when he saw the steel blade. I brushed past everyone and ran down the worn path to the river.

I heard boots behind me and thanked the stars Rell had been able to find Miya so quickly. I pulled up when I heard the voices ahead of me. Song, and a response from Mouser. Silently, I slipped to the edge of the scrubby bushes and saw Song. She was standing with her feet apart, jeong bong held lightly in both hands at waist height. She looked unafraid, but ready for trouble.

Mouser stood well outside the range of her jeong bong. I had heard the wheedling in his voice, if not the actual words. The air was full of tension and menace. I took a deep breath.

"You don't want to tangle with her, Mouser," I called out as I stepped into the clearing. "Miya calls her his best warrior."

He snarled at me, "So Miya sleeps with a different woman every night and we soldiers are just supposed to be content with that? I just asked her to share. No one had to know until you stuck your nose where it doesn't belong."

"You need your toes to count, you old fool? There are six of them and three of us, you touch her, and we all die."

I nearly fell over. The disgusted voice behind me wasn't Miya, but Rygee. He nodded at me as he passed by, but kept talking to Mouser. "You must have a fevered brain, old man. No one is sleeping with anyone. In fact, I bet you the entire Kereki paychest we are hauling, the only reason they are sleeping in the tents the way they are is because of us. If we wouldn't have needed two of their tents, they wouldn't have needed to double up." He held his empty palms up in the air. "I'm unarmed, old man. You do something stupid and either Zren or Song would drop us both before I could scream for help." He paused. "And who would come running to save us? Nebs?"

Mouser muttered under his breath and turned towards me. At the last moment, I saw the throwing knife slide into his hand. Before I could move, Song swept her jeong bong low, dropped him to the ground, double tapped his wrist and arm and his knife fell away, then she gave him a blow to his head knocking him out. Rygee stared at her open jawed. I swallowed hard. I had seen her fight before and knew how fast she was, but I couldn't imagine what Rygee was thinking.

I heard more steps running behind us and turned to see Miya with a tahn bong, and Rell with her crossbow. Rell stepped up, nocked her bow, and aimed at Mouser's body on the ground.

"Is he dead?"

"Not yet," I answered as I looked up at her. I saw Rygee's face whiten.

"Stop it," Miya snapped. He looked at Song. "What happened?"

Song glanced at Rygee before answering. "I was practicing my forms and Mouser volunteered to be my sparring partner. Zren and Rygee came to watch and ensure no permanent blood was spilt. Isn't that right, boys?" I felt her silent challenge not to contradict her.

Miya kicked at the throwing knife laying on the ground. "Sparring partner? With this?"

"Of course," Song lied easily. "You were there in the courtyard, Miya, when Zren showed me how I would be dead on the Northern Track. Once he showed me my weakness in front of *everyone*," she grinned at me, "I spent the rest of that afternoon practicing until I had a way to beat a knife, a riata, and a Conrosan." She paused and looked at Rygee. "I am a bongmaster responsible for training and testing others. I take my jeong bong seriously."

I saw Miya take a deep breath. He started to say something and then stopped. He took another deep breath. His face was carefully blank, but I sensed how much his thoughts and emotions were warring with each other.

He took one more deep breath and finally he spoke, "Zren and Rell go back to camp and take first watch. Song, walk with me. Rygee, stay here and talk some sense into Mouser. Let him know there are no second chances. It is *only* because of Song's mercy he is even waking up to hear your words of caution. Let him know that."

Rygee nodded quickly.

When Rell and I got back to camp, Kern was sitting in Chul's wagon chatting easily with him, and Nebs was packing from the washing up. The setting sun was casting a soft glow. All three of them looked up when we walked into the clearing.

"Zren and I have first watch. Miya is going to tell tonight's story. We'll make an early night of it," Rell said quickly as she grabbed her red cloak, and we went to check on the horses.

It didn't take long for the fire to die to embers and for the others to come back and settle in. Rygee and Mouser came back, Rygee nearly dragging the limping and battered soldier. Nebs started to ask what happened. Rygee cut him off, just saying Mouser was a fool who couldn't count. Song and Miya came back, she was calm—the excitement of the fight was gone, but Miya just looked tired.

Rell and I took first watch, and Miya said he would tell the story. He talked about the Storytellers of the West Islands, how their stories were based on the constellations because they were a seafaring people who navigated by day and by night. He talked about how in the West Islands and in Vikland, gender played no part in the role a person chose in life, all was done by interest and ability. He said how the Seafarer and the Traveler tales were told with all genders, to reflect all listeners. Then he proceeded to tell one of the funnier Seafarer tales with the Seafarer returning with stranger and stranger gifts for a village never satisfied with the treasures brought back from the seas.

Rell and I could only hear bits and pieces of the story as we intersected in circles just beyond the hobbled horses. I noticed she was wearing her new cloak against the chill.

Curious, I asked, "Any problems with the Kerekis after they gave you that?" I tipped my head towards the dark red cloak.

"No. They smile at us, all of us. Well, the Farm Boys do anyway, but none of them say anything beyond 'Good morning.' You convinced them you will murder them where they stand if they so much as look at us wrong."

I blew out a breath. "It wasn't quite like that."

"They saw Bitterboots watching Song that first night—we all did—and they saw you watching Bitterboots. Next thing anyone knows is Bitterboots is dead in the middle of the night, throat slashed and belly gutted. And now Mouser."

"Song took out Mouser with her jeong bong. All I did was watch. It was Rygee who stepped in to try to stop Trouble."

"They may continue to test us," Rell mused. "But maybe not. I do not think the Kerekis understood what a jeong bong can do in the hands of a skilled warrior. You are the youngest of us and slight of build. *I* believe the Kerekis think, if you and Song can do so much damage, then all of us must be a force to be reckoned with. Miya may be displeased you two showed your strength, but I think you may have done us a kindness. For my part, all I ask is that you never mistake me for your enemy." She smiled at me, but I heard the truth in her words.

I moved past her to make the next pass. Soon the people headed to their bedrolls, and the fire was banked until morning. Nebs joined Rell and me on the night's watch, but he said nothing to either of us, and the rest of the night passed uneventfully.

* * * * *

The next morning when I rolled out of bed, Chul handed me a bowl of oats and berries with a small stick of sugar cane stuck in it. I inhaled deeply and took my first bite.

"Why did we hide you in the wagon if you could make a first meal like this?" I exclaimed around bites.

"We were waiting for you to show us any cooking skills," he laughed.

"Do you remember Song's attempts on the first day? You would beg for her to cook again after tasting my efforts." I called a cheery good morning as the others came to the fire.

Miya came to the clearing hauling water. "We'll stop in Cloa today and pick up supplies. Pack up and be ready to leave within the decon."

Miya put Chul driving the first wagon with Rell and Kern as outriders. "All bowmasters in front," he explained. I took the middle with Song and Miya as my outriders, each of them balancing a jeong bong across their saddle and the shorter tahn bongs in their horses' scabbards. Mouser was forced to the last position with Nebs and Rygee as outriders. As I climbed in my wagon, I asked Miya if he was getting even with Mouser by making him eat our dust all day.

"Of course not," Miya said surprised. "If we run into a raiding party, we need our crossbows in front to take out as many of them as possible before they overrun the wagons. Song and I can fight more than one each with the jeong bongs, but you and the Kereki soldiers are only hand-to-hand fighters. We have to eliminate enough of them so you have a chance."

He arched a brow. "Song has told me the matter is settled. She says she never felt fear yesterday in the clearing with Mouser. She only wondered how successful her extra training would be. You should know she said she was glad to see you and Rygee, but she said she was not afraid. I can do nothing but believe her."

He gave me a long look. "Zren, know this now. I would never give up a tactical advantage based on emotions. Ever." He mounted and wheeled away, then came back to my wagon. "That doesn't mean I wouldn't do everything possible to make sure you survive to see Vikland." He gave me a lopsided grin, one I had never seen before, and said, "You have probably figured it out already, Viklander women do not wait to be rescued." He clucked to his horse and moved out.

Now what was I to do with information like that?

CHAPTER 7

CLOA

A long while later, we were angling through a shallow valley when I saw Rell had stopped her horse. She had her crossbow up and aimed at a low rise to the south of us. I followed her gaze and saw what I thought was a distant outcropping of rocks. Miya called to keep moving, but Kern and Miya both pulled their crossbows and angled their horses next to Rell's. Rell said something briefly to them, and then all three had weapons up until all of our wagons were ahead of them.

I kept stealing looks at the outcropping trying to see what was hiding there. It wasn't until I saw movement that I realized what I *thought* had been an outcropping had been horses and riders watching us the entire time as we passed through the valley. I stared at the hilltop as the riders slowly turned their horses to the west and disappeared behind the rise. I shuddered at how easily my mistake could have cost me my life. Then put a blank look on my face as I heard Rell and her horse trot up to my wagon.

"What did you see?" I asked Rell.

"Six horses, five riders. All dressed as Kereki males. One of them looked small, another had a bundle on the back. I thought they might be a family of traders who decided not to use the Northern Track when they saw us pull our weapons. In any case, even if they were bandits, by seeing our crossbows up, they knew we three could defend the wagons long before they could get close enough to harm us," Rell answered.

"You could see all that?" I blurted out. I kept the rest of my thoughts to myself. I didn't want anyone to know I wouldn't have known they were there. Not for the first time, I wondered just who was protecting who on this journey.

* * * * *

When we reached the edge of Cloa, Miya stopped us to make plans. Nebs reminded us a proper Kereki woman would never appear in a market town without wearing a skirt, or without a man by her side. He kept his eyes on the ground the entire time he told us this, and Chul cut his eyes to me and grinned.

Song, Rell, and Kern all gave an exaggerated sigh, but they grabbed their traveling packs from the back of my wagon, and in front of us tied on a skirt over their Viklander trousers, and draped shawls over their shoulders. They helped each other twist their long Vikland braid into a circle and tie it up in pieces of ribbon and cloth on top of their head. They reached into their traveling packs again and pulled out a cloth shopping bag like Ngahuru had used in Aldi. Chul and Miya had turned their backs while the women were changing their appearance, but the Farm Boys and I stood watching with our mouths hanging open. I wondered what else they carried in their travel bags since they seemed to switch so easily who they wanted to be.

Miya asked Nebs and Rygee to escort Song and Kern to the stores for supplies. They could never pass for Kereki housewives, Kern explained to them, but having the soldiers with them would shorten the bargaining that needed to be done. No one added that the presence of the Kereki soldiers would also lower the prices the Viklanders would have to pay. We all climbed back into the wagons and drove into Cloa. Rell, Chul, and Miya took a wagon to the stables to buy grain and another open basket for the horses.

Mouser and I stayed with the other two wagons in the village green and tried to look non-threatening. There were a few notices tacked to the market cross, but I didn't want to ask Mouser to read them to me. He still had a heavy limp this morning. He held his arm close to his body as if it hurt him just to move it, and the deep bruise across his face had darkened to purplish black from Song's jeong bong.

He hadn't said a word since he and Rygee had come back to the camp last night. This morning, both Rygee and Nebs had taken down his lean-to, brought him his first meal, and helped him up into their wagon. I didn't get the feeling they had done it to help him, so much as to keep him out of our sight and our way.

The other Viklanders acted no differently today as they had last night. But according to Miya, my only task today was to keep Mouser out of the businesses in Cloa where people might ask unwelcome questions. Miya said he didn't need a Justice and a town of outraged citizens defending a poor old Kereki man from battle hardened Viklander warriors looking for a dance with Trouble. I had looked at him a long time without saying anything. He had stopped what he was doing and smiled at me.

"It's all about perception and assumptions, Zren. People see what they want to see and write their own stories of what they think happened."

Today, I looked at Mouser again, and wondered what people saw when they looked at him. I still didn't trust him. I thought perception was a fancy word for understanding Trouble when she travels with you. I thought Mouser would continue to poke and prod at our group until he found a weakness. I thought maybe Song should not have had so much mercy last night.

Song and Nebs came back to the wagon with Song visibly upset.

"What happened?" I straightened from where I was leaning against the wagon.

Song gave an exasperated sigh. "The shopkeeper felt free to give me his opinion on Viklander women, and before I could respond, this one," she poked at Nebs, "jumps in and dresses him down for insulting me. I am perfectly capable of standing up for myself."

"That's not the point!" Nebs ran his hand through his hair. "The shopkeeper expected me to defend you. That's how it works out here. Once he knows you are mine and under my protection, then he can deal with you as a customer. A woman just can't go talking to men she doesn't know or who don't know her."

"This is the most backward country I have ever had the misfortune to travel in," Song retorted hotly.

Miya, Rell, and Chul drove up the wagon just to hear the end of Song's complaint. Miya tsk-tsked.

"Are you insulting our hosts, Song?" He jumped down beside us.

Song narrowed her eyes at Miya. He raised an eyebrow but said nothing. I watched—fascinated—as it appeared an entire conversation took place without a word spoken. Finally, Song blew out her breath and turned to Nebs.

"I am sorry, Nebs. The shopkeeper made me angry, and I directed my anger towards you. I understand the importance of following the cultural rules and norms of another country. I beg your indulgence." She flicked her eyes to Miya and back to Nebs. "…and your forgiveness. It will not happen again." She said nothing more but bit her bottom lip as if she was trying to keep other words from escaping.

Nebs blinked, bewildered. "Ah, sure."

"Where are Kern and Rygee?" Chul asked.

"At the toggery," Song replied. "Rygee wanted to buy new pants and another shirt. He said he didn't want to ride into Vikland for the first time wearing clothes so full of dust they could stand by themselves."

Chul smiled broadly. "Well then, he'll be the best dressed of all of us."

Miya turned to me. "You want to buy anything? We can watch the horses." He must have recognized the expression on my face because he suddenly clapped his hand to his forehead. "I forgot! I wanted more of those things Kerekis wrap around their legs. I wanted to have some riatas in the wagon. Come here," he walked me to the far side of his horse and a small saddle bag. Quietly, at his horse's side, he pulled his purse. "I am so sorry, Zren, I forgot you gave all your coin to Ngahuru and Koanga for their trip home. Please take this and buy what you need. And I do want some fabric for riatas, but it can just be whatever scraps the shopkeeper will sell you."

I started. I thought I had told him I had been found without coin by the side of the road. Had Ngahuru told him something else? And why now? I had been without coin since Salisport. Not that it mattered. Miya had not stopped and let us buy anything along the way, until today. I felt uneasy, like he was playing with everyone.

But I was raised in Lowertown. Uneasy or not, I wasn't going to give up a purse freely given. I took the purse and caught up to Kern and Rygee in the toggery. The Patron had put down his cudgel to help Rygee, but quickly snatched it up when I first walked in the door. I quickly held up my hands and the purse so he could see they were empty of Trouble but carried coin.

All three of us were buying the baggy Kereki pants. Kern held a pair up to herself and said she liked them. She pushed them across the counter at the Patron and said she wanted a price. He gave her a hard look and refused to sell the trousers to her. He turned away and asked Rygee what he needed.

Kern said nothing at first. I could see several emotions playing across her face, and I thought she was deciding how she was going to react to that moment. Suddenly, she put on a light cheerful smile, moved between the counter and Rygee, and carefully said she was buying them for her little brother who happened to be just her size. She could imagine how it must have looked when she had held them up to herself, as if she would ever consider wearing attire meant only for men. It was true, she said, she had been born in Vikland, but she could see the value of women dressing appropriately. I noticed she didn't say what she considered appropriate.

I could see him struggling with his thoughts, but in the end, his need for coin won out, and he took her coins and roughly pushed the trousers across the counter to her.

The billowy country shirts were easier to buy, even though the only colors were grey and brown.

"Not a colorful bunch, are we?" Kern said drily.

"We save it all for our personalities," I joked.

Rygee choked back a laugh and Kern smiled. "You can be clever, Zren. Usually when I least expect it." She paused. "Which is always."

I bought a number of fabric ends that could be used as ankle ties or riatas. The shopkeeper was mystified as to why I wanted them, but agreed to sell me some. His ignorance made it possible to buy two handfuls for what I would have paid for six in Kerek City. This was so much easier than thieving them, I smiled to myself. We walked back out into the cool midday sunshine.

We were all in a good mood as we stood watering the horses and filling our waterskins and flasks. Rygee was explaining a dish he was going to make for us that night with the vegetables and spices he had bought. Nebs recreated the exchange between the shopkeeper and him which had gotten Song so riled up. I showed off the wildly colorful Kereki ties I had bought at the toggery. I explained my great bargaining by saying the Patron had no idea why I wanted them, but he was happy to sell me all his scraps and strips and ends of cloth.

"Stop," Song interrupted. "You told us in Kerek City that Kerekis tie these around their calves and ankles to keep the dust out of their boots and creatures out of their pant legs in the outlands." She looked around. "This. This is the outlands."

I gave her a wide open grin. "I said Kerekis in Kerek City tell *strangers* these are used in the outlands. Those who live in Dockside and Lowertown use them for a lot of things, not all of them useful for a victim to know. Bindings and distractions and riatas." I squinted at her. "I may have missed one or two. What we tell strangers is not always the truth." I smiled. "I guess you aren't a stranger, anymore."

* * * * *

We swung out of Cloa the same way we pulled in. The bowmasters in front guarding Chul in his wagon, I was in the middle with Song and Miya as outriders, and the three Kereki soldiers behind us. Rygee and Nebs were outriders, awkwardly holding the tahn bongs.

Once I saw Mouser fall in behind me, I called to Miya, "You know the Farm Boys are just going to use your bongs as clubs or pitchforks, don't you?"

He sighed. "I know. But when I get to the camp at night, I'm just too tired to teach them anything."

I looked at him then. He still held himself upright in the saddle and his eyes watched everything around us, even as he was talking to me. I wondered what it would feel like to believe it was your responsibility to keep everyone safe. When we had come up on the settlers massacred on the road the day before, he had given me a bong and told me whatever happened not to give up the wagon with Chul and the crates of West Islands steel. I thought about Ambassador Lalsy and First Soldier Joon in Kerek City and how easy and familiar they were with Miya. I knew Ngahuru had met him a year ago at the Ambassador's Harvest Dinner, and wondered if she wasn't the only one who minimized who she was to be underestimated by her enemies.

"What?" I joked, "The great Miyamoto Suki, Prince of Vikland, feels such emotions as 'tired?' Where is the man who danced all night in Matasi, evaded curfew, and thought I needed weapons practice before first meal?"

Miya laughed. "Are you sure you only spent ten days with Ngahuru's little brother?"

I sobered quickly. He hadn't looked surprised or embarrassed when I had jokingly called him the 'Prince of Vikland.' I wondered if that was his title, and Koanga had not been joking with me after all when he had said so back in Salisport.

I sighed and continued, "It feels like a lifetime ago since I said goodbye to Koanga. I wonder if I will ever see him again."

Miya looked at me sharply and then away. "Your future is yours, Zren. You can do anything you want."

"Good. Because I want to be just like you—only taller, smarter, and handsomer." I gave him my cheekiest grin.

Miya gave a startled laugh, his shoulders relaxed, and he turned his horse to ride out farther from the wagon.

Time crept by. I thought about how much better the first day of travel had been when Song had been teaching me to drive and I had someone to talk to. And even when Chul was supposed to be sleeping, he would always ask a question or two when he drifted awake, and I could think about his words. But now? I was the only one on the wagon, and there was no one to listen to me.

I watched resigned as I saw rainclouds start to form ahead of us. There was no help for it, we were going to get drenched. Chul saw them too and stopped the lead wagon so he could check the fastenings on the waxed canvas tops. The rain shower felt like a cold bucket of water dumped hard on our faces, and we all huddled under the hoods of our cloaks. I thought it ironic the canvas tops on the wagons kept everything underneath warm and dry when the crates of pots and pans hardly needed it.

We had barely started when Chul stopped us again. The rain continued pounding on us, and Chul checked the coverings so often on the wagons, we barely moved forward for a handful of furloughs. We hunched shivering under our cloaks and hoods, and I hoped we would reach the Vikland border before the rains came incessantly.

CHAPTER 8

DESERTERS

Miya had been awkwardly hunched over his horse for a while, and I was worried he was ill. Finally, he straightened and turned his horse towards Chul's wagon. Kern rode close to them, and I watched as the three talked together while riding forward. I assumed they were talking about how far we had fallen behind, but then Kern wheeled her horse around and trotted back to me.

"Miya says the next crossroads is the road to Earles. We'll stop there and let the Kerekis decide if they are going to report for duty or not," she said it sarcastically, and I wondered why.

"Is Miya all right? I saw him hunched over," I began.

"He was trying to keep his maps dry. The Kerekis may think it is impossible to get lost out here, but there are half-tracks and roads that lead to small settlements and villages. Places we as Viklanders would not want to go. Miya likes to know what is ahead of him." She shrugged. "Do you think the Kerekis will abandon their duty? Or is there an honorable man among them?"

I considered her words. "I thought Miya wanted them to ride with us. If they report for duty, they take the paychest."

Kern gave me a cheeky grin. "Why, Zren! You think more like a Viklander softfoot every day. Or a Lowertown thief." She turned and looked back at the Kereki wagon. "This is not such an easy decision as it appears. If the Kereki soldiers do not arrive with the paychest, will Vikland be blamed? Can we live with the death of the soldiers, even if it is not by our hand, yet we know what the outcome will be? Song has told you Viklanders are taught to defend the defenseless and stand for justice. This would be easier if Kerek taught their King the same."

I tried to think about what Kern wasn't saying. "If Rygee comes to Vikland with us, will he be in danger?"

Kern gave me a big smile. "You would think by now, I would expect the unexpected where you are concerned." Her face grew sober, and she sighed. "Miyamoto Suki may think Rygee could be a soldier in our army, but truthfully? In Vikland, the Kereki would be mocked for fighting for a country not his own. He could be a softfoot for Bima Ritwik in Kerek City, but he has too honest of a face. He should not go to Earles but should fade away like Nebs and Mouser. But who can tell him this?" She slowly shook her head. "It is not my decision to make." She paused. "It is the waste of a good man, Zren. A good man who can cook well, no less." One side of her mouth quirked up. "We will see who turns north on the road to Earles." She nudged her horse forward and out to tell the wagon behind me.

There was nothing remarkable about the crossroads to Earles. Just another dirt track leading north with a few wooden signs stuck in the soft dirt. The words were no longer legible, and I thought if Miya had not had his maps, we would have gone right past it. Since the rain had stopped, Rell dismounted and reached for the food bag. Together, she and Song handed out bakery bread, cheese, a pickle, dried spiced meat, and water. I wondered who had done the shopping for food in Cloa.

Miya unrolled a map from his saddle bag and showed us all where the Huk River would cross over the Northern Track a decon or possibly two before the village of Sary. Then, beyond the village, was a north and south road called the Huntsman's Trail that ran down to Ahni.

Miya looked at each of the Kereki soldiers. "I need to know what your plans are. Do we divide here or not? Do you wish to report for duty to the garrison at Earles?"

Nebs was the first to speak. "I haven't changed my mind. I'll take my wages and I'll stay behind in Sary."

"Change out of your uniform then and leave it behind." Miya paused. "Rygee?"

"There is nothing here in Kerek for me, and I would like to see Vikland. But if I don't like it, can I come back?" Rygee looked worried.

"Certainly. No one is held against their will in Vikland. We are honored to have you on our journey," Miya said formally. I glanced at Kern, and then noticed all the Viklanders looked relieved. I looked back at Kern, but she didn't meet my eyes.

"Mouser?" Miya hesitated over the name.

The man crossed his arms and stood in front of his wagon. "I am leaving you, but I am taking the paychest with me. You said you didn't want to be accused of murdering us all and stealing the garrison's payroll. But the Kerek King will blame you for all that anyway. He sends the greenest and the worst of his soldiers to the outposts. He doesn't care if they are paid, or if they raid their neighbors to keep the garrison supplied. You think you are going to be rewarded for bringing the payroll to Ishes? Ha! You will be murdered as soon as you are inside the gates.

"I will share a portion with Rygee and Nebs, they have a right to it, but the rest—our supplies and horses and wagon are going with me. Your map shows the Huntsman's Trail, a track running from Sary to Ahni, a settlement on the Old Vikland Road. I'll split with you beyond Sary and head south on that." He turned away and called over his shoulder. "We'll leave our uniforms here, boys. Don't even bring them along. No need to risk running into garrison soldiers on a supply trip in Sary, or a Justice who asks to search our wagons, and hear questions we don't want to answer."

Miya didn't say anything more. We just waited while the soldiers changed out of their uniforms and left them at the side of the road. I wondered what the next traveler would think as they passed by. We mounted up, and although everyone looked north as we crossed over the track to Earles, no one turned their horse or wagon.

The road started a steady climb in elevation. Song rode close to me and explained the border along Vikland was all high desert rolling into a mild green climate with coffee farms and huge gardens and orchards near the mountains. She told me of her father's gardens—how he had plants from all over the known world, and an orangery under glass where he liked to experiment with fruits.

"I think I have tasted fruits that have never been grown anywhere else in the world," she laughed. "And there is a reason for that! Some were so bitter, I thought I was being punished when my father asked me to taste them!"

She asked me what I liked best about Conrosa. Awkwardly, I said I had left so long ago I no longer remembered, and so she asked about Matasi. I told her about meeting Miya in Ribelo and going to the baboy—a pig roast—where Miya was probably the oldest one there. I laughed as I told her about the beautiful music wherever I went, and then learning the next day the music was all hymns and praise songs.

"I didn't know a word I was singing, Song, but I joined in on every one!"

"I heard Matasi is very religious," she commented neutrally.

I nodded agreeably. "It's a way of life for them. At first, I really liked it. It was so freeing to be able to travel without having to be afraid every moment of being ambushed or robbed as we are in Kerek. But one day, we didn't understand we needed to stop traveling early, and we reached a town after everything was closed. We had to spend the night in jail and the fines and fees made us too poor to continue on our own." I considered. "There's not a lot of tolerance for mistakes."

Song was silent for a moment. "What did you like most about it?"

"The people," I answered quickly. I thought about the night at Ebla Potenco's home in Anarkio and the kindness of the guards as they let me slip in to Matasi without traveling papers. "I liked the people, the food, and the music. Did you know they make the churches round so there is no corner for the devil to hide in?"

She looked at me skeptically, then over my shoulder. I turned to follow her gaze. Miya was scowling and pointing his bong at Song. She clucked to her horse and moved out and forward to keep an eye on our surroundings.

I knew we were finally getting close as I watched the Huk River turn south. Stands of trees crowding the banks became more than just smudges in the distance. I let my thoughts drift into any direction they chose to go…Would we camp early to dry out our cloaks before nightfall? Did Mouser have his demons under control or had Song's mercy been for nothing? Would Song have killed him if Rygee and I had not found them in time? Why had everyone relaxed—as if they had been holding their breath—when Rygee said he would not go to Earles? What would Rygee make for end of day meal? I thought about what story I would tell around the campfire that night.

Ahead I saw Chul's wagon had stopped. The outriders had bunched up together around it. I pulled up to them and let my horses crop at the grasses with the others. We waited for a moment for the last wagon to drive up. Rygee and Nebs trotted up, reins loose in their hands.

"We can make an early night of it and camp here on this rise, or we can push on and camp closer to Sary or even on the other side closer to the Huntsman's Trail." Miya pointed at the stone bridge spanning the river. "It looks like a good solid bridge, so we won't have to float the wagons, but it is so narrow, we'll only be able to get one wagon through at a time. It will be outriders first, then the wagons." He stood tall in his stirrups and stretched.

"Or we can actually stay *in* Sary, and have a warm bed, a cold drink, and part in the morning," Mouser challenged. "I'd pay for a bath and a shave and a cold drink that doesn't have to be boiled first."

"I'm two days from Vikland. I'm not going to be stupid now," Miya retorted.

"At least let us camp at the bottom, so we don't have to carry water and firewood up the hill," Kern pointed out.

"This is where we part then," said Mouser. "I'm not spending one more night with all of you, not when Sary is only a decon or so from here." He clucked his horses forward and the wagon lurched down the track to the bridge.

Miya scowled. "We'll camp on the other side of Sary, then. It will be another late night. Hopefully, he'll act as a distraction, and we can pass through without attracting too much notice." He looked at Rygee and Nebs. "You boys get your wages?" When they shook their heads, he sighed. "Go on then, get your coin, your supplies, and your travel bags. You can throw them in Chul's wagon." The two kneed their horses and trotted after Mouser.

Miya ran his hand tiredly down his face. "Let's go. I want to make sure Rygee gets the food sack. I don't fancy any of your cooking for the next few days." The outriders urged their horses forward. Chul and I followed with the wagons down the hill.

CHAPTER 9

BATTLE AT THE BRIDGE

There are some moments I look back on with fondness: meeting Koanga, the storytelling night at Ebla Potenco's home in Anarkio, watching Miya, straight-backed and proud on his horse, Ngahuru smiling at me and saying, "That's not the question I thought you would ask."

And then there are the nightmares. The ones I still dream of—the sights and sounds and smells of blood and dying. The battle at the bridge is one of the worst.

Mouser had driven his wagon down the hill and onto the narrow bridge. The outriders were bunched up behind him: Nebs and Rygee to get their belongings and coin, Miya and the Viklanders to ensure it happened without difficulty. Chul had just driven his wagon between the first stone posts and the solid stone sides of the bridge, and I was bringing up the rear still coming down the hill.

Suddenly, children started boiling up out of the river shrubs and out from under the bridge screaming, grabbing, and feinting with Mouser's horses in the first wagon, slashing with homemade knives. Miya understood what was happening first.

He yelled, "Weapons up! Fire at will!" But the children had blocked the first wagon on the bridge ahead, Chul was trapped between the narrow sides and couldn't back up because I was too close behind him, and the outriders were bunched in the middle and couldn't free themselves to face their attackers.

Mouser urged his horses forward. The only hope to survive the battle was to clear the bridge. It was too narrow for horses to pass Mouser's wagon, but the children tried to reach the outriders by trying to slide by or crawl under or climb over the wagon bed. Mouser used his whip on the children and the horses, but then the horses shied and tangled the traces. He jumped off to pull the horses forward and the children swarmed him. I saw him crumple to his knees under an assault of bloodied knives.

I flashbacked to my childhood and my first murder in Lowertown, and I froze. The sounds of the battle suddenly fell quiet. I could see what was happening in front of me but I felt like I was a child again. Helpless. Trapped in fear. Thinking I would never be safe and cared for again. I was completely unable to move forward to help, or away to save myself. I could only watch in horror.

Song was the closest to the Kereki wagon. She jumped from her horse to the wagon bed with her jeong bong. She swept the children off the wagon, fighting the ones grabbing at the horses and her. She hit the horses' flanks, and they jerked forward knocking her to her knees. She shoved the end of her jeong bong hard into a child, pushing it off the wagon, over the bridge, and into the river below. There was no mercy in her today. She hit the horses again, and they surged forward clearing the bridge. The outriders burst out of the trap and off the bridge. They fought to keep their seats on their frantic mounts wheeling about and stomping. The shouting children continued to weave their way through, slashing at the horses, dashing at their faces, and twisting away just out of reach of the bongs.

I was still frozen on the west side of the bridge. Slowly the sounds of the battle came back. Chul was yelling at me and I finally understood what he needed me to do. I turned my team hard to get them clear of the bridge and the fight. With me out of the way, Chul was able to stand and haul back on the reins. He yelled and pulled to drive the horses back enough he could turn them out of the narrow bridge.

Drawing his wagon parallel to mine, he threw his crossbow at me. "Cover me!" he yelled, as he jumped in the back of my wagon. He scooped up a bunch of quarrels and dropped them on the seat next to me. He stumbled, throwing his weight on his bad leg, and yelped in pain.

I saw Nebs suddenly sprouting an arrow in his throat.

"Bows at north, northeast!" I heard Rell shout, as she immediately started firing her own crossbow into the row of archers that stepped out from the fringe of trees.

Miya was everywhere. He used his jeong bong to beat the children away from Rell and Kern as they shot quarrel after quarrel at the archers.

Rygee fought his way to Song who was still trapped on the first wagon, using her long bong to keep the children from overrunning her. He was using the short bong as a one-handed club and stabbed and slashed with a steel dagger in the other. His horse was bleeding from a multitude of shallow cuts.

Chul shouted at me, "Here's a riata! Throw it at their archers!"

I swung the fabric tails in an easy circle and let it fly. It fell just short of the center of the archers, but exploded into fire and broken pottery when it hit the ground. Two of them fell to their knees.

"What was that?" I grabbed the buckboard to keep my balance.

"My specialty!" Chul grinned. "Here's another!" He handed me a lidded pottery bowl, and I wrapped it quickly in the fabric scraps I had bought in Cloa. I wrapped and slung them as fast as he could make them—launching them at the archers Rell and Kern were methodically picking off, and at the children slashing their bloody broken off daggers at horses and riders.

I heard a high-pitched whistle from the river, and just like that the handful of remaining children fled into the trees. I tracked their movement through the shaking bushes as they fled north along the riverbank. Chul was still holding on to one last riata.

"Give me that," I said.

"No, they're gone," he breathed heavily, and I saw the sheen of sick sweat on him. I took it from him anyway and aimed it where I thought the whistle had come. It hit a branch and exploded in the air. Fire fell like raindrops and I heard a scream—not a child—abruptly cut off. A cool breeze riffled the air. There was no other sound.

I looked around. The battle had only taken a few moments, but it was the sheer horror of the children running through the horses slapping and slashing that sickened me. I watched Rygee as he numbly unharnessed the horses in the first wagon to try to straighten the traces.

Everyone dismounted, reins trailing on the ground. I saw Miya take a deep breath, draw his dagger, and his short bong, and walk over to the closest body. He rolled over the child with his bong and walked on. I knew what he was doing, making sure no one suffered a lingering death, but it wasn't easy, nor was it ever meant to be.

I found Mouser. He was dead, as I expected. I had seen him go down under the frenzy of knives near the far side of the bridge. I pulled him away from the wagon wheel so Rygee could drag the horses forward. Rygee pulled, and he called to Song to release the reins tangled in the wagon brake. She didn't say anything, just sat on the wagon with her jeong bong jammed in between her and the buckboard. He realized it as soon as I did, and we both ran and jumped up from opposite sides at the same time. The movement jostled her body, and she slid lifelessly into Rygee's arms.

"Hey! Help! Hey!" I tried to get everyone's attention. Miya stood up from where he had been kneeling next to Nebs. He saw Song in Rygee's arms and started running. Kern was supporting Rell, who had an arrow sticking out of her arm and slashes bleeding freely down her thighs. They limped over slowly. Rell's leg dragged at an odd angle.

I saw the dagger sticking out of Song's side, jammed upward toward her heart.

"West Islands steel," I muttered.

"I know," Miya said hollowly. "We've had people and shipments that never reached home. Once the bandits get their hands on better weapons, they just get more successful."

"But children? Who would put children into the middle of a battle?" Rell blurted out.

Miya pulled the blade and jammed it angrily into the wagon seat. "Think about it! Even though I called 'fire at will,' you hesitated until the archers stepped out from the riverbank. Not one of you fired first on the children, not one! The children ran freely, forcing our horses to wheel and bolt, keeping us from focusing on the archers. I bet their archers usually just picked off their victims, because after all, who is going to hurt a child?" He dropped his shoulders and said somberly, "If Song and Chul had not kept their heads and reminded us all the enemy is the enemy, we'd all be dead." He looked around. "Where is Chul anyway?"

I remembered the grey face and the greasy sweat on his skin, and said sickly, "He's in the back of my wagon."

Miya walked back across the bridge to our two wagons still on the west side. He leaned in cautiously, gave a big grin, and said something too low to carry across the water. They spoke a little longer and Miya's face looked sad. *He's telling him about Song and Nebs and Mouser,* I thought to myself. Then Miya smacked the side of the wagon and walked back over the bridge.

"He has some burns on his hands from the liquid fire. He didn't take the time to put on his leather gloves first. His leg hurts, too much to hold his weight, he says he thinks that means he's still alive." Miya was quiet for a moment. "He doesn't look good, to be truthful. We've got to get him to a healer." He looked critically at Rell. "You need one too." He stared at Kern. "You hiding a mortal wound I can't see?"

Kern gave him a small smile and shook her head. So did Rygee. Miya looked at me and I flipped open my hands, palms up, so he could see.

"Chul handed me the pottery already made to throw. I didn't know what he was doing to make them. I was busy turning them into riatas. He took all the pain on himself."

Miya looked about the group, thinking. "Zren, you and Rygee take Rell and Chul to Sary. Find a healer for their wounds. Maybe they will be so confused by all of your nations," he smiled, "you will get decent care. Take the extra horses with you." He gave Kern a somber look. "We'll have to recover all the quarrels. Vikland can't be blamed for this. We can't take Song's body back with us to Vikland, it's still two days just to the border, and another three to Juisiti. We'll have to fire her on the field. I'm sorry." Kern nodded and looked away. Miya looked at Rygee. "We'll bring both wagons. You have my word on it."

"I should stay and help," said Rygee slowly. "I can find and pull all the quarrels while you burn Song's body. I understand why you need to make this look like a Kereki fight with only Kereki travelers. Then there will be no reprisals, maybe, against other Viklanders traveling through." He looked away and took a deep breath. "I should stay and help," he repeated.

Miya started to say something, but Rell put her hand on his arm, and he stopped to reconsider. "As you wish."

We tied three extra horses to the back of the wagon, and Rell crawled in the back with Chul. The arrow was deep in the meat of her arm and would have to be cut out. But it was the blood flowing heavily down her thighs and how she dragged her leg that seemed the worst of it.

Her pupils were blown wide open, and Kern bent down to whisper in my ear, "She's in much worse shape than she thinks she is, make sure the healer examines her thoroughly. Hold her down if you have to."

Miya stepped close to me and handed me another bag of coins. "Pay whatever they ask to buy their help… and silence. I need all of you to come home with me. News of this won't reach Sary until people fail to come home tonight. By then, the three of us will have rearranged the battlefield and be on our way to meet you." I nodded.

I pulled myself up to the wagon seat, clucked to the horses and rolled across the bridge. I looked back. Kern was looking away to the south, Miya was already lifting Song off the other wagon, and Rygee just stared after me as if he never expected to see any of us again. I looked at the sun. The battle had been so short, a decon hadn't even passed.

CHAPTER 10

MANUMINA

There were few people in the streets when I trotted the horses into Sary. I stopped the first person I met—a woman standing outside a shop—and asked her for the healer's house. She looked to her husband as he walked up and said gruffly, "I don't think I know you."

"You don't need to know me, you just need to know where the healer lives." I kept my temper—just barely.

"Where are you hurt?" he continued.

I snapped the reins and drove up to the butcher shop. I wrapped my reins about the brake, and turned to step down. When I turned again facing the shop, the first one I saw was

...a Conrosan.

I stood there foolishly with my mouth open trying to understand what—no, *who*—was in front of me. All my life I had never met another person who looked like me. No one with the same brown curly hair, the cinnamon-hued skin, and brown eyes the color of Vikland coffee. Ngahuru had told me I was from Conrosa, a land so far to the north of Kerek, they did not have the seasons Wet and Dry. Yet, at some time ships had sailed from there. I was proof of that. And here, at the edge of nowhere, I find a man about Miya's age or a little older who looks more like me than my reflection in a puddle of muddy water.

He said something then, and I shook my head. "I only speak Keresh."

"Why are you here?" He responded. "Who are you?"

"I'm looking for a healer. I have two hurt." I gestured at the wagon. He walked over then and peered carefully over the edge at Rell and Chul.

He regarded me for a moment, and then whispered, "Ambushed by the river?" When I nodded, he stepped back decisively. "You won't be treated here in Sary. Come with me. We have healers at the settlement. It's not far, southeast of here on a different track. It's about the same distance as the river to here, or a little farther." He spoke Keresh with a rolling accent.

I hesitated.

"Come. I won't hurt you. My name is Piffik Qanaq. I live at Manumina."

It sounded like humming to me. *Man u MEE nah.* I shook my head at him. "No. It's not that. But we have others coming after they care for our dead. If I leave with you, they won't know where to find me."

"Ah. One moment." He stepped into the toggery next door and called out a boy and a girl my age or just a little younger. He spoke rapidly to them in the first language he had tried on me, and the girl shot me a curious glance now and again.

Piffik turned back to me. "If we could use one of your horses, my sister, Aajan, will ride ahead and let the healers at the settlement know you are coming. My brother, Zadah, will travel with you and show you the way, and I will stay behind and wait for your friends." He gestured to the wagon. "Your friends? Are they also from Matasi? Or are they Conrosan? Viklander?"

"One is Kereki—that is Rygee, and two Viklanders, a very tall woman, and a man, the shortest of the three. Tell them you are a friend of Zren Janin and they will know you know me."

"Zren Janin? Our folk hero, Zren Janin?" His lips quirked up in a smile.

"Yes." I sighed. "My name giver seems to have had quite a sense of humor." While we had been talking, the siblings had untied Neb's horse from the back of the wagon. The boy boosted his sister up into the saddle, she wheeled about, and galloped out of town.

"She likes to ride fast, that one. Our plow horses don't give her much pleasure. Go now. I'll go meet your friends at the bridge and help them, and then bring you all together."

I hopped back on the wagon seat, and the boy pulled up alongside me on a different horse. We cantered east out of town, and he had me turn south at the first crossroads. I wondered if this was the road to Ahni—the Huntsman's Trail—Mouser had talked about. I tried to pick out landmarks in case this was a trap and I needed to work my way back, but it was just trees, small hills, and the empty track ahead of me.

Then we came around a low rise and the settlement rose from the valley around it. The boy pointed to it and called, "Manumina." It was a stockade with walls as tall as the tallest ship in Kerek City harbor. It was curiously built with all the houses up against the outside stockade walls, built so closely they had common walls and stacked as high as the stockade itself. In front of the houses, were gardens, then livestock pens, and then fields no wider than each house. It was like taking all the Kereki ties and laying them side by side and calling it a village. Before we had even trotted up to the gates of the fort, the gates had swung open. Inside I could see a small village green, and numerous buildings. The boy—Zadah, I remembered—pointed where to go. There were a number of men already there to lift out Rell and Chul and carry them into a sturdy two story wooden building. Neither Chul nor Rell were still conscious.

Everyone gave me a curious look, a few of them said 'hello' or something like it in that same language Piffik had first spoken to me. I nodded in response, and I followed them into a large room with multiple beds. Once they laid the wounded on the beds, the Conrosans silently faded away.

There were two healers; they looked like mother and daughter. They roused Rell and Chul enough to get them to drink a cup of something and then waved a smoky spill of paper under their nose. The older one cut away Chul's pants and when she started to lift them away, he clenched his teeth, gasped, and fainted again. Once she knew he could no longer feel it, she gave a quick rip and took away most of the scabbing and the fibers that had attached themselves to the wounds since we had started traveling. I stared in shock. How he had even remained conscious through the past days was beyond me. I thought of him taking watches, limping, and jumping from wagon to wagon today on a leg so riddled with burns, I would have curled up whimpering and refused to move had it been mine.

The woman sucked in a breath and looked up at me. "Aajan says you do not speak Conrosan?" Her Keresh sounded uncertain, as if she didn't use it much.

I shook my head. "Keresh only."

She shrugged, "Keresh," and then looked at Chul, "This didn't happen today."

"No," I cleared my throat and answered, "Many days ago in Kerek City. He was caught in some riots. Warehouses were burned at the docks." I turned over his hands, already red and blistering. "This happened today."

I thought about how I had looped the cloth and tossed riata after riata, never looking at how Chul had been making them. He had just poured things into the pottery and lidded them as smoke had started spilling out. Miya said he hadn't taken the time to put on his special leather gloves. While it was true Song had gotten us out of the trap of the bridge, without Chul, we all would have been dead. Miya had not been exaggerating.

"Ah, here is our little troublemaker," the younger healer crowed. "Such a tiny little blade."

I looked over to the younger healer. Rell had been cut out of her clothes as well, but in contrast to Chul she had a wide strip of cloth covering her from her neck to mid-thigh.

"And another one." The healer held up a second bloody arrowhead and dropped it alongside other metal into the basin.

She washed the wound in the leg, put pressure on it, and began wrapping it in bandages.

"How many?" asked the first healer.

"Two broken off knife tips and two arrowheads." The healer looked at me. "Your friend was a..." she said a word I didn't know and I shook my head. "A Kereki metal collector," she repeated in Keresh and then sighed. "Someone must do something about the bandits at the bridge, but we believe there are those in Sary who are a part of it." She paused. "We do not use the Northern Track to travel west of Sary."

For a while, there was no sound except the snip of scissors, the gentle splash of rags in a basin of water, and the soft steady breathing of Rell and Chul. I felt woozy and rubbed my hands hard over my face.

"Are you faint?" asked the older woman. "We give our patients something to keep them calm and quiet." She pointed to the empty cups Rell and Chul drank earlier and the twist of paper still wafting smoke into the air. "If you are not used to it, you can become drowsy or ill. You can lie down over there if you wish."

I said nothing but crossed the room to the bed she had pointed to.

* * * * *

I woke up to voices outside the room. I recognized Miya's voice, but he wasn't speaking Keresh or Vik. I looked around and saw the two women were sitting in chairs by their patients. The younger one gave me a questioning look, said something to me, and then gave a shake of her head and switched to Keresh.

"There are more of you?" She pointed at the closed door. "Conrosans?"

I sat up and rubbed my eyes. My head felt fuzzy and my tongue thick.

"There are three more of us. But not Conrosans. Two Viklanders—one of the Viklanders speaks Conrosan. There is also a Kereki, but he is a friend to us. He is almost as young as I am. He cooks," I added stupidly.

"Ah, he cooks. If he cooks well, he will be very welcome among the daughters of Manumina." The younger one made a comment in Conrosan, and the older woman tsk-tsked but turned her head away to hide a smile.

There was a soft rap at the door and the younger one moved swiftly to open it. She blocked the opening with her body and spoke rapidly to the voices outside and then turned to me.

"Your friends would like to see you. We cannot let them in because they have just come from the battlefield and have not…" She struggled for a Keresh word, "…cleansed. They say they are unhurt. Would you go with them?" She repeated, "I cannot let them in."

I stepped into the hall, and Kern gave me a fierce hug. "Thank you for finding this place!"

I gave her a half-smile. "They found me in front of the butcher shop in Sary. I don't know who was more surprised."

The older man with them smiled. "Piffik Qanaq said he had just been thinking of his sister's latest unworthy suitor when he stepped out of the butcher shop and there you were! The answer to his prayers!" Miya and Rygee burst into startled laughter, and even Kern's so very sad face flashed a hint of a smile. All three of them looked tired with red-rimmed eyes and smelled of fire and death.

I turned to the Conrosan. "Piffik saved us. But I was raised in Kerek City, in Lowertown, which is worse. I know nothing of Conrosa, but that it is the color of my skin. I am afraid Piffik is going have to continue praying for a new suitor for his sister." I gave a small Viklander bow. "My name is Zren Janin. My friend Ngahuru, who knows some of the Conrosan fairy tales, named me. I continue to learn what a sense of humor she had when she did so."

"Zren Janin, it is a pleasure for me to be of service to you and your friends. My name is Salik Oqina, and I sit on the Council of Wisdom here at Manumina settlement. I speak Conrosan, Keresh, and I am learning Vik, but I am not so well spoken as your friend Miyamoto Suki is in my tongue. For the sake of you and Rygee, we will speak Keresh. But for now, we have rooms, baths, and food for you. After you have rested, we will meet tomorrow morning to discuss what to do. For tonight, you must pray for your friends that are healing, grieve the loss of those who have departed, and gather strength for your journey ahead." He spoke Keresh formally, very formally, as if he had learned it as an adult, and not casually as a child.

He led us outside where it was full dark. When did that happen? As we walked across the village green, he pointed out the stables where the horses were being cared for. "We have healers for your horses as well." The locked barn where our wagons were being stored, "The locks are for your peace of mind. No one here would break hospitality laws to pilfer traveling clothes." The round church, "We do not worship the Lost God, but this was an abandoned Matasi stockade when our grandparents' generation found it, and so it serves as our Council meeting room." Finally, we reached a house. "This is our guest house. We have prepared a room for each of you," Salik pushed open the door, "but your meals will be in the common area." I could smell cooking and hear voices in the back of the house.

"There is no rush. Take as long as you need to wash away the stink of the day. You will be served individually or as a group when you are ready. The travel packs from the wagons are in the hallway. I am sorry. We brought in all the packs, including those who are no longer with you, but we did not want to presume." Salik gestured up the steps. "I shall have a word with those who are preparing your meal and then I shall leave you. You will only be disturbed this night if your friends in the healers' care call for you."

Miya bowed deeply and said something in Conrosan. Kern and Rygee bowed but said nothing. I imitated Kern's short bow and then Salik Oqina walked away.

"This is like our Matasi guesthouse in Anarkio. Do you remember, Miya? You came for first meal the next morning," I spoke as I led the way upstairs. "It had running water—every place in Matasi had running water. To a boy from Lowertown, I felt I was in a palace." We picked through the traveling bags in the hallway, chose our belongings, and slipped off to our rooms.

I had already shucked my clothes and was ready to step into the steaming tub when I heard a knock and Rygee's voice at my door. I threw my baggy shirt over my head and opened the door to greet him.

"Zren, our farm didn't have running water. Can you show me how this all works? I thought I could figure it out, but..." he spread his hands out palms down.

His room was similar to mine, and I showed him how to turn on the tank for the hot water and then how to mix them for the soaking tub. I found the hard felt stopper and pushed it in so he could see how the sink and tub could hold water without having to use buckets to fill it. While we were waiting for the tub to fill, I told him how the rest worked, and I showed him the chain to pull. "Look, no chamber pot to toss out!"

He watched me carefully. "Do you think Vikland is like this? Because if it is not, I'm never leaving here." I laughed as I clapped him on the back and darted back to my room.

It took a while, but at last I pulled the plug and watched too many days' worth of grime, blood, and sweat swirl down the drain. Dressed in the new clothes I bought in Cloa—*Was it really only that morning?*—I walked barefoot downstairs.

Only Miya was there ahead of me, drinking of all things, a tiny cup of Vikland coffee. His hair was wet and rebraided. He wore different clothes, but his eyes were red-rimmed, and he looked exhausted.

A woman came out from the back of the house carrying a platter of food, set it down in front of him, and asked me a question. Miya answered her.

"Ha! A Conrosan who doesn't speak the mother tongue and a Viklander that does! Today will never end its wonders." She disappeared into the back of the house and almost immediately Aajan came out carrying another platter. She set it in front of me and lingered.

"Thank you for riding so fast today." I smiled at her and waved a hand at Miya. "You have helped us immeasurably."

She blushed. "Your horse is very fast. If I care for it while you are here and healing, may I ride it again?"

I looked to Miya. "This is Piffik's sister. She rode ahead so the healers would be ready when Piffik's brother and I arrived with the wagon." I dropped my voice so only he would hear, "She rode Nebs' horse."

"What is your name?" Miya asked gently.

"Aajan Qanaq."

"Aajan Qanaq, my name is Miyamoto Suki. My friends call me Miya." He paused. "I hope you consider me a friend." She blushed again. "It was not only that you rode fast to help us, but you and your family reached out to a stranger in a strange land. That is a kindness I cannot repay today. But please, let me gift you the horse you rode today as a measure of the esteem in which I hold you and your family. Is that acceptable to you?"

"Oh yes," she breathed. Her eyes danced with happiness, and she rolled her hands in her apron. "Oh yes, yes!" She turned and nearly ran into the kitchen.

Miya smiled at me. "I thought if *you* gifted her the horse, Piffik might not let you go so easily." He laughed silently at his joke. "We have the extra horses, Zren. It's good to be generous here."

I didn't think I would be able to eat, but the food was so good, my platter was half gone by the time Rygee and Kern came down to join us. Kern was also wearing the new Kereki clothes I saw her buy in Cloa. Her damp hair was unbound and swung in a thick black curtain to her waist. I stared as Miya frowned at her.

"What?" she frowned back. "I wasn't going to sit up in my room all night and wait for it to dry in order to braid it again." She looked at me, "You forget who I am?" she snapped.

"No. Just forgot how beautiful you are. Glad you remind me now and again," I said nonchalantly and cut my eyes at Miya. Rygee sniggered. A Conrosan man carried out two more platters of food and set them down in front of Rygee and Kern. Rygee just tucked his head over his plate and started eating.

"How are Rell and Chul?" Kern asked around mouthfuls. "Everyone I ask says they are sleeping, and it will take a long time to heal."

"Chul's burns are bad," I agreed. "I don't know how he was able to bear the pain. They gave them both something to drink and smell, and the healers said it would make them sleep and forget for a while." I leaned back in my chair. "The younger woman took care of Rell. You were right, Kern. There was more than what we saw. The healer cut two arrowheads and two broken off knife blades out of Rell. She also said the many knife slashes on Rell's legs are not good because the knives were not clean. Neither will be able to travel for a while." I paused. "We're safe here. I think."

Miya nodded. "I believe that as well. The land of Conrosa that I studied in my books is a land of pacifists. I think that is also true here. The entire settlement has treated us with kindness, and not everyone we met today could hold back ill-intent if we were intended harm. We'll rest here tonight, attend their Council of Wisdom meeting tomorrow, see how Chul and Rell are recovering, and then make plans. For now, let's sleep if we can. I know it's late, but I'll ask the healers if I can see Chul and

Rell now that I am not covered in filth." He sighed. "It will be good not to have to set a watch."

Aajan came out to clear the platters, and Miya asked if she could take him to see his friends resting at the healers. She nodded and left to take the empty platters into the kitchen. I stood and stretched, as did the others, and we waited for Aajan to return.

Another woman came out, an older version of Aajan, thicker in the waist and with her grey hair braided in a crown. She had on the same color apron as Aajan.

She spoke Keresh as she addressed me, "You are the one who gifted my Aajan a horse? You are very generous to a pretty young girl. Maybe I should be the one who takes you in the dark across the settlement to the healers. I am not so at ease with your friendship, Miya, fellow Conrosan or not!"

The other three choked back their laughter. I actually thought Kern had tears in her eyes. Aajan's mother looked fiercely at me as I stood there speechless.

Miya saved me. "Forgive me, mother of Piffik and of Aajan. I am Miyamoto Suki of Vikland, a friend to your house for the kindness done to me and mine." He switched to Conrosan then and it sounded like a rather long apology, but at last the fierceness left her face.

Miya turned to us and explained in Keresh, "She'll take me to Chul and Rell. Go on to your beds. The sooner we put this day behind us the better. I'll see you in the morning."

Rygee, Kern, and I made our way upstairs. Kern whispered as she opened the door to her room, "You better lock your door, Zren, or you are going to find yourself wedded and bedded before sunrise."

I didn't bother to reply.

CHAPTER 11

SURVIVORS

I had seen death and dead bodies before in Lowertown. I have been close to death myself. I have two distinct memories of being beaten in an alley, for no other reason than I was not as fast as those who chased me. Both times, I only lived to see the next sunrise through the intervention of a stranger who heard my cries for help and had a cudgel and courage to save a child's life.

I had bloodied others and myself to defend what was mine growing up. There was never enough food for those of us abandoned on the streets. Sometimes it was easier to take the food from another child than steal from the street carts and the ever vigilant owners. There were Lost Girls and Boys—pretty little things dressed up in fancy clothes by their minders and protectors to go out and beg coin and assistance from the shoppers and strangers. Assistance was often a small coin or a sweet rather than actual help, but charity from the wealthy usually wore a thin face. If I was quick enough, I could steal the child's food before their minder reached them. It meant I would have to hide for a day until the minder forgot about me, but it worked well enough when there was nothing else to eat.

I knew I wasn't a hunter, or much of a fighter, but I had defended Koanga and Ngahuru on the Coast Road. I had set a trap and murdered Bitterboots. I had never felt a moment of remorse for any of it. I thought of it as choosing my life over those who would take it from me.

And still I had nightmares. I dreamed of Song sliding lifelessly into Rygee's arms. Looking up at Rell's shout and seeing all those archers lined up against the trees against our two crossbows. Nebs catching an arrow in his throat. Miya beating the children away with his jeong bong to give Rell and Kern space to steady their horses and fire. Rygee using Miya's short bong as a club knocking the children down like wild animals. The sharp intake of breath when the healer saw the extent of Chul's burns. I would jerk awake, panting out the fear and the memory, and chant myself to a troubled sleep, "I am safe. I am safe. I am safe."

I woke once during the night without a nightmare hurtling me there. It was a sound, a muffled cry. I jumped to my feet, grabbed my shirt, and padded to the door. Hearing low voices, I eased open my door and peered into the dark hallway. I waited in the silence and was just ready to convince myself I had imagined it, when the door to Kern's room opened soundlessly. At first nothing, and then Miya, barelegged and dressed in only a long shirt, slipped out. Halfway to his room, he saw me. Quirked an eyebrow.

"Nightmares," he whispered. "Are you...?" I nodded and closed my door.

A storm blew up and through. I listened to rains pounding outside the window. *The Wet is here*, I thought. Our journey will be miserable from here on to Vikland. Then I thought about Song teaching me to drive a wagon the first day on the track, her stories as we passed the time and got to know each other. I remembered her calmness and confidence in her skills when I found her in the clearing with Mouser, and her vicious speed as she disarmed him. I smiled when I remembered how she laughed and told me about her father's orangery—a thing I had never heard of nor could imagine. I thought of how easily she and the others had changed to Kereki clothes before we entered Cloa—so confident in their bodies. Then I remembered the battle again and cried myself to sleep.

The next morning at first meal, everyone had dark circles under their eyes. Kern and Miya were drinking the tiny cups of Vikland coffee, their empty plates in front of them. The man serving us offered me coffee as well. I shook my head, and when he brought one to Rygee, I faked a startled look. He tasted it, grimaced, and sipped again.

"They consider that a delicacy in Vikland," I told him. "That's why Miya is desperate for you to travel with us. If coffee tastes like that, you can imagine what the food tastes like." I gave a little shudder and elicited a small sad grin from the others at the table. I dug into the plate of vegetables and eggs in front of me.

I was shoveling it in so quickly, I forgot to chew before I swallowed and started to cough. I saw Miya wrinkle his nose in distaste and quickly smooth out his features.

I reached for the cup of water. More to slow myself down, I asked Miya, "How are Rell and Chul? Did you see them this morning, or only last night?"

"Still sleeping this morning. The healers woke them long enough last night for me to tell them we are all here and safe for now. I promised I would not leave them behind without means, or without talking to them. They are to sleep and heal and rest. I spoke to the healers as well. The older one is Bett, and she was trained at the academies in Juisiti, so she knows Viklander healing as well as her own, she said. She asked if the others knew another language other than Vik. She says it has been many years since she has used it and does not think she will remember it." He looked at Kern. "It may be true, but we should still watch what we say in front of her."

He went on, "The younger one is her niece and has been training with her since she was a child. Her name is Siba Namikk.

She has not gone to the academies, but she is learning everything Bett can teach her. The drink and incense they are using makes the injured sleep very deeply so they can heal. Both are worried about infection, and they want Chul and Rell to stay with them through the entire season of the Wet."

Rygee stopped eating and looked up. "Are we staying that long?"

"Not all of us. I have to find out if there is a safer way to Vikland. One without going through Sary, or the rest of the Northern Track."

"There is." Salik Oqina stood in the doorway. "There is a road from this settlement to the military garrison at Ishes which is less than a decon from the Vikland border crossing. It's more of a half-track really," he grimaced, "but we use the road when we are not so comfortable trading nearby. Piffik left at first light and is in Sary now, hoping to learn what he can of yesterday's ambush. Truly, there have been many who would like to capture that band of murderers and bring them to account for their crimes. We at Manumina think there are those in Sary involved because they always seem to have advance warning. The Justice and the others who search for them never find anything more than cold fires. We at Manumina no longer travel on the Northern Track."

"The children." Kern gripped her cup a little tighter.

Salik Oqina looked uncomfortable. "That is a mystery to us as well. We are not missing children, nor do we know of lost children in Sary."

"They're the survivors of the wagon trains," Rygee said suddenly. "Remember how scared they were? They weren't scared of us; they were scared of the archers if they didn't slow us down enough." He shoved his empty plate forward in disgust.

The room was silent, and I heard a noise as people entered into the house. Salik Oqina cleared his throat. "There are three people I wanted you to meet before I took you to the meeting with the Council of Wisdom." He stepped out of way and two women and a man walked in the room. All were Viklanders.

Kern slammed her coffee cup down on the table and ran around me to hug a short-haired woman nearly as tall as she was. Miya looked shocked, and then his grin was wide and effortless.

"First Soldier Joon told me he feared you had been killed on the Northern Track when you did not arrive in Kerek City. I am glad, beyond glad, he was wrong."

"We very nearly were." The tall woman turned and looked at Miya. "If a wagonload of Conrosans hadn't been going to market that day, we all would have been corpses."

Miya's grin disappeared. "You three are the only survivors?"

"Yes." The man looked sorrowful. "I'm sorry, Miya. I know Ateo was a good friend of yours."

"A good friend and a good soldier. I will miss her, and grieve for her again, now that I know her fate. May her name live on." Miya took a deep breath and smiled at the survivors. "Rani, Malik, and Ceri, I am so very, very glad to see you. Whatever else happens this day, I will count myself among the loved to see you again." He stood. "Let me introduce you to those who saved my life yesterday. Rygee, a soldier and a farmer, who helped us honor our dead on the battlefield. Song Yao, a bongmaster, was fired in the field."

"May her name live on," the Viklanders murmured solemnly.

"We also have Rell Huena and Chul Swyler traveling with us, but they are resting in the infirmary," Miya explained.

"You had bowmasters Rell and Kern? And a bongmaster? Is the nest of bandits eliminated then?" Rani asked. I watched him as he took in the room. He flicked his eyes at me but said nothing.

Miya shook his head. "I don't know. There were eight archers of theirs left dead on the field. We found another one floating in the river. There were a handful of children who received their freedom at the cost of their lives."

Ceri nodded, her arm still around Kern's waist. "That's about the size of the group that attacked us. We didn't have your archers to fight back so we could only flee. But Miya, I thought you were still in the West Islands getting serenaded by storytellers."

"This was true. I will have been in the West Islands, Matasi, Kerek, and now home to Vikland before the Wet begins." At the others' shocked faces, he responded with a shrug, "I go where the Empress commands."

"Ah, so you are going west to east and we are going east to west," Rani mused. "I had hoped you would be our protection." The others laughed with him.

"You are too few now, and the rains have begun," Miya insisted. "You should come back with us, and then go over the Silver Mountains once the Wet is over. I am going to tell the Empress the Northern Track is too dangerous. We saw massacred settlers—a large train—as well as our own battle."

Rani slowly nodded in agreement. "You outrank me, so I'll take your suggestions as orders. According to your news, First Soldier Joon is no longer expecting us. I could spend the Wet by a warm fireplace at home instead of on patrol in Kerek City."

Salik Oqina cleared his throat. "I am sorry, we must leave for the Council house now. I don't want to keep the others waiting."

Everyone filed out of the house. The three Viklanders headed for the stockade's side door and Kern, Rygee, Miya, and I followed Salik Oqina. I gave Miya a long look as if to ask why he hadn't introduced me. I knew Rani had noticed it as well, but I had the sense Rani saw more than most. He reminded me of Bima Ritwik, and I wondered if he was a softfoot.

But Miya was thinking of the meeting ahead, and never met my eyes.

* * * * *

The meeting lasted for a decon. There were twelve on the Council, a mix of genders, ages, and one Matasian, bent over, and crippled with age.

Piffik Qanaq gave his news first. Miya sat in the middle of us so he could translate as Piffik spoke. Once Piffik realized what Miya was doing, he asked the Council if he could speak Keresh so the strangers would know what was said about them. He said he wanted them to feel safe since they were so few in number in the stronghold of another. The Council consented and Piffik began again, this time in Keresh.

He had been to Sary at first light to tell the Justice of the battle at the bridge. The Justice had already heard of it the night before when people reported family members missing. The Justice had taken others and gone out to the battlefield. He thought he had seen Piffik's wagon far down the Huntsman's Trail heading home, but there had been other wagons also and from that distance, the Justice could not be sure.

I felt Miya stiffen beside me as we all realized how close they had come to encountering those coming out from Sary. The Justice had walked the battlefield with others. They had buried the children where they lay when no one claimed them as those of their own or others known to them. The townspeople had found the bodies of Mouser and Nebs, and no other source of weapons than poorly made bows and arrows, pounded iron knives, and a few copper daggers. Some of the wounded and surviving children had come out from the trees when the Justice arrived. They asked for food. The children had said they were beaten if they did not stop the horses and any travelers on the bridge. They said all of their tormentors had been killed by those with long black braids and a green monster that spat fire. They showed the Justice where they had been forced to live and hide.

In the end, there were homes found for the surviving children for the night, and the Justice called it a battle for territory between two rival Kereki bands of outlaws.

"There were no Viklander or Conrosan children in the survivors. I asked," Piffik said. He turned to Miya. "Zadah remembers your Matasian was wrapped in a dark green cloak when brought to the infirmary. Siba says he was covered in burns. It is my understanding the children were not believed about the green monster that spat fire, but I think it best, he doesn't wear the cloak in Sary."

A woman stood and spoke next. "I wish to thank you for the efforts you made to remove all of your Viklander traces from the battlefield. You will be returning to Vikland on the half-track from here to Ishes soon, but we need to live here, and your efforts to make it seem a Kereki dispute among themselves will help protect us." She made a wry face. "There is a common thought that all non-Kerekis look alike."

She paused. "There are some in Sary," she began slowly, "who are not pleased the military garrisons at Earles and Ishes were sold to Vikland last year, and that soldiers, and traders, and settlers have moved in with them to provision them. But we Conrosans have found them to be good neighbors with regular patrols and buyers of our goods. Again, I thank you."

I rocked back in my chair. Earles and Ishes belonged to Vikland? We should have known this before we left Kerek City! If the Kereki soldiers who had traveled with us from Kerek City had reported for duty, Nebs and Rygee would have been captured and killed the moment they walked into the garrison. Why would the King have sent them to a garrison he did not control? What had they done to deserve such a death? Then another thought struck me and a cold finger of doubt touched my neck.

I glanced at my fellow travelers. Rygee looked stunned. Kern shot me a quick glance and dropped her eyes to her lap. Miya looked defiantly straight ahead at the Council. He knew. I realized immediately, all the Viklanders knew. The Kerek King hadn't sold the garrisons to Vikland. He didn't even know he had lost the outposts and the garrisons were no longer his to supply with soldiers and wages. He was too far away in Kerek City to understand Vikland had somehow winkled them out from under his royal nose. Yet Miya had never once told the Kerekis their lives would be forfeit if they reported for duty.

I thought back to the moment we all had stood at the crossroads and Miya had asked one last time to have Rygee travel with them. That was why they all looked so relieved when the Kereki soldiers did not turn north to the road to Earles. Kern had tried to talk to me about it, and I had been too thick-headed to understand.

My thoughts were chaotic, and I missed the rest of the conversations and decision making. Only as people began standing, did I come back to the discussion.

"What happened? What is happening?" I panicked.

"Later, when we are all together with the others." Miya pressed his lips in a thin line. He started walking to the healers' house and I followed him so closely I was nearly tripping over his heels.

"You knew! You knew before we ever left Kerek City, the outposts had been taken over by Vikland troops. We were escorting a Kereki army paychest for a place that didn't exist and soldiers who would never see a paypacket," I sputtered.

He stopped and looked hard at me. "No, Zren. I promised the Kerek King, in front of witnesses, the paychest would be delivered to either the Earles or Ishes garrison. I told the Kereki soldiers if they chose to fade away into the countryside, I would deliver the paychest to the Ishes garrison. I keep my promises. The paychest may be lighter than when we left Kerek City, but I keep my promises."

"You were going to let Rygee, who has cooked for us, stood watch with us, and Nebs who took an arrow and died defending us, walk up to the Earles garrison, report for duty, and be murdered!"

"Zren!" He looked around to make sure we were alone on the green. "This is my thirteenth crossing in the last nine years over the Northern Track. I have survived bandits, corrupt Justices, thieves, and pickpockets on this Track *every single time*. I have lost someone I have known nearly *every single time*. I am tired of the Kerek King ignoring robbery and murder that happens every day in his country while he amuses himself in Kerek City. I am tired of Viklanders as victims for anyone who sees a different skin color and considers us prey." He took a deep breath and struggled to get his emotions under control.

"I did not ask to guard the Kereki paychest. And if I remember correctly, it was you who hunted Bitterboots—thank you for that by the way. I knew Mouser would desert the first opportunity he was given, and you heard me—I *know* you heard me—say the Farm Boys would not die by my hand. But I also didn't think it was necessary to reveal Vikland's plans along the way where the soldiers could have passed along the message to anyone they encountered to get the news back to the Kerek King." Miya crossed his arms, and I saw how tightly his fists were clenched.

"You must understand. Kerek *needs* to have an uprising. The fool on the throne must be replaced with someone who will deal reasonably with Vikland, Matasi, and any other country. I am only doing what needs to be done. I will *continue* to do what needs to be done. I protect my own, Zren, just as you have done. You protected Ngahuru and Koanga in Kerek and Matasi. You have protected us on the Northern Track. You and I, we are not so different. We stand up for justice. We defend those who cannot defend themselves. We protect our own. My own just happens to be Vikland." He turned abruptly and walked into the healers' house.

I stood there, furious. I wanted Miya to be like Ngahuru. I wanted to believe he was kind, and truthful, and brave. I wanted him to be worth abandoning Koanga and following him across the Northern Track. I wanted to believe that he would take me to Vikland and make me a prince like him. I wanted to believe I risked my life for one worthy of my life. I wanted.

I wanted not to be just another fool who loved the wrong person at the wrong time.

I stood there shattered as I felt the first drops of the daily rain fall around me. I thought about standing out there until all my shame and misery washed away, but instead, I wiped my tears on the sleeve of my shirt and turned and walked into the healers' house.

CHAPTER 12

A CHANGE OF PLANS

Siba Namikk, the younger healer, was alone with Miya in the room with Chul and Rell.

Miya stopped talking when I came in. The silence grew uncomfortable until Siba told me gently, "You see the tent over Chul's leg? The weight of the blanket bothers his burns on his leg, yet the room is cold and damp at night during the Wet season. Chul told me how you made such a thing for him to sleep under on the wagon train. You are very clever, Zren Janin."

I looked at her, and I knew she could see I had been crying, but I didn't care. I looked at Chul asleep and breathing deeply. His hands were wrapped in bandages so large they looked like the food platters the Conrosans had used to serve us.

"Is he going to be all right?"

"He'll live. How much will he use his leg and hands?" She shrugged sadly. "My aunt would know better."

"Ah, I thought she was your mother," I offered shyly.

She smiled at me. "I would not tell her that. She is not that old, and she thinks I am too stubborn." She looked at Rell and I followed her gaze. "This one is the problem. It is good she was on horseback. There were so many knife cuts on her legs, and even though most of them were shallow, the knives were dirty. We have cleaned all the wounds, and reopened the deep ones to clean again, but she is fighting very hard to live. I am not sure what my aunt will want to do next."

"Did you take care of the Viklanders that were found just two fortnights ago? The ones that are here now?" Miya asked.

"Yes." Siba gave him a measured look. "Rani had his tunic slashed from shoulder to hip." She drew her hand across her body. "But he was carrying maps and thick papers next to his body, and they saved his life. Ceri, the tall one, had been grabbed by her braid and pulled off her horse. She was able to escape when she cleaved her braid from her head and turned her hatchet on her attacker. Malik, the quiet one, you cannot see her wound, but it was deep. She took a knife here, just below her ribs. She heals, but she will never be strong again."

Siba paused. "And to the question you did not ask me, my friend Piffik gathered the six who did not survive and brought them to Manumina. Ceri said you do not bury your dead, you burn them on a pyre, so he took them over the border to your garrison beyond Ishes so the proper rites could be observed. He did this at great risk to himself—both from the Kerekis who would have murdered him if they found him with Viklanders dead or alive—and from your own garrison within your own lands if your soldiers learned he was carrying your dead without listening to how it happened."

"I continue to owe him my gratitude," Miya said formally. "And also to you, for telling me what I need to know as well as what I ask to know." He paused. "Can the three who were here travel to Vikland? Are they well enough for that?"

Siba raised an eyebrow. "Today? Yes. I would say all of you could leave except for these two. Is that your plan?"

"If the others will agree to it. But I wanted to see these two and ask them. When will they wake?"

"In two decons, we will wake them to feed them and take care of them, then make them sleep some more. It is good for them, to sleep so deeply while they heal." She looked at me again. "Thank you, Zren, for bringing your friends to us. You are brave and true."

I stilled, wondering what she had seen in my face, to say such odd words. She spoke her Keresh as formally as Salik Oqina, but it was the meaning of the words that made me feel as if everything would be good enough and I had done the right thing at the right time.

I looked again at Chul with the blankets tented over his legs and his hands awkwardly by his side on the big bed where they had placed him. His color was not as grey as it had been on the battlefield. In his deep sleep, I could see the laugh lines by his eyes and mouth. I wondered what he had thought when he knew to save us he would sacrifice himself. But I had never noticed a moment of hesitation. He had poured his liquid fire into pottery after pottery, burning his hands, splashing his legs, handing them to me to make the riatas to toss until we were no longer hunted.

I glanced at Rell. How could she have stayed steady on her horse firing quarrel after quarrel at a distant target while all about her knives were cutting her and children were frightening her horse trying to unseat her? What kind of land was Vikland to create these warriors? What had I agreed to when I asked to be taken to Vikland as my reward for accompanying Miya across the Northern Track?

I glanced at Siba, and she smiled at me. She was a Conrosan like I was, but I knew nothing of what that meant, except she had been kind. And she had said I was brave and true.

But Miya was impatient to meet with the others, and so I followed him out without saying anything to her in return.

* * * * *

The other Viklanders and Rygee were already gathered in the guesthouse common room when we arrived. Miya gave a brief summary on Chul and Rell, letting everyone know the healers wanted them to stay through the Wet. He repeated Salik Oqina's offer that we could find sanctuary with the Conrosans. They would find us housing, labor to be useful, and a place at their tables. We would be accepted as theirs, and if we chose to leave or stay, it would be with their blessing.

Miya outlined his new plan. He would take anyone who wanted to go to Vikland. He would leave the extra horses, one wagon, and enough coin to pay for Chul's and Rell's care. He would like one able-bodied person to stay behind with them, so Manumina would not feel the burden of the injured Viklanders. But, he had shrugged, he knew how much everyone wanted to go home. He assured Rygee he would have a home in Vikland as they had discussed before Earles, but if he wanted to stay at Manumina, he would receive the year's pay he would have earned as a Kereki soldier—not just his, but Bitterboots', Mouser's, and Nebs' as well. He didn't say if the coin would follow him to Vikland.

In front of the others, Miya told me our agreement was still true. I would be housed, fed, and educated in Vikland in exchange for getting him across the Northern Track. I could enter the trades or become a soldier, and if he received a posting to Conrosa, I would be taken along with him in order to find my family.

"But I will tell you the truth, Zren Janin, although I have asked for this posting for many years, I may never receive it. If you stay in Manumina, you are already among your countrymen and your mother tongue. Whether you go to Vikland or stay here at Manumina, you will receive enough coin so you are not dependent on the kindness of others. You can also stay now and return with Chul or Rell when they return to Vikland, or travel with us now, but return if the academies and you do not fit well together."

He paused, and took in a deep breath. "I will say it again, Zren, your future is yours. You can do anything you want."

Who does this? I thought to myself. How can he sit there and just discuss everyone's future as if it is just one more item on his list of things that must be done before he can return home? Hot anger pricked me at the thought I could be left all over again without anyone else feeling the pain of it. I pushed my chair back, stood up, and walked outside. I saw one of the Viklanders watch me, the quiet one—Malik, and I heard Miya's voice falter for a moment, and then carry on talking about supplies and wagon drivers.

I stood on the front porch and looked out at the village green. I let my tears fall as I thought of my daydream on the ship from Salisport to Kerek City when I had thought I could go to Vikland and become a prince like Miyamoto Suki. I thought I would find Koanga in the West Islands and show him how educated and fancy I had become, like those merchants I saw in Kerek City with their fine clothes and manners. Now Miya was talking about soldiering and trades. Had I not been listening? Had my daydreaming stopped up my ears to what the Viklanders had been saying? How did I keep confusing kindness for other feelings?

I looked around me at Manumina. It was a very small village on the inside, and it was clear they had to trade with their neighbors to have everything they needed. The houses and gardens and animals on the outside of the walls were not falling apart, so they were able to care for themselves. The people didn't shy away from us like the settlements we had encountered on the Northern Track. People had been kind, had fed us nearly in the middle of the night, and had given us a clean, safe place to sleep.

Miya said he wanted one able-bodied person to stay here with Rell and Chul. I was the only one besides Rygee who was not a Viklander, and who did not have anyone waiting for me in Vikland. Could I live here? Could I learn about Conrosa, learn to speak the language, find my place in the world? Would this make me a person like Rell and Chul who had saved others? Or would

I be walking away from everything Miya had promised me in Kerek City—education at the academies, traveling in the known world, the chance to see Koanga again, to talk with Ngahuru? I looked around the settlement. What could I do here?

The door shut quietly behind me. I turned and was surprised to see it was Rygee. He put his hands on the railing and looked out over the green. Neither of us said a word for a long time. I tipped my head back to stop the angry tears from flowing down my cheeks. I wondered if he thought I had been in the rain and that was why my face was wet or if he would know I had been weeping. I sighed. *He would know*, I decided.

"You should know I am staying here," he said finally. "So you don't need to feel obligated to wait here for Rell and Chul to get better."

"Is that what you want?" I could barely choke out the words.

He shrugged. "I don't want to be a soldier. Not for Vikland, not for Kerek. Joining the army was never my choice, you know that, Zren. Here, I can have enough coin to live, maybe work in the bakery." He laughed abruptly. "Take a bath with running water every day for the rest of my life!" He looked around. "They aren't rich here, but everyone seems to be kind," he muttered under his breath, "so far." He sighed and turned to me.

"Zren, I heard Kern call me 'Farm Boy.' I know she meant it to mock me, and I know the Viklanders look down on me for deserting even though now I understand it would have meant my death. I am a farmer and a good one. I am a baker and a good one. To go to Vikland and be pushed into something I am not because of a culture which is not mine? Then I am following orders for the rest of my life, and I might as well be back at home listening to my papa and my older brothers." He fell silent for a moment.

"I'm not like you, Zren. I was afraid *every day* of this trek. I was afraid of ambushes and bandits, of Bitterboots and Mouser, dying of a knife wound in my back, and dying of shame. When I saw Song beat Mouser to the ground, she wasn't even breathing hard. Miya was right, it was her mercy that let him live. She could have killed him as easily as you killed Bitterboots."

He gave me a sorrowful look. "I thought any one of you could have killed the three of us as easily as you kill a scorpion. I thought as long as I was the best cook you had on the track, you would keep me alive. Do you understand what I am saying? I was afraid *every day*.

"You and Miya, you're different, you take care of things—of people. You straighten your shoulders and you live with your decisions." He blew out a breath. "Anyway, I thought I should tell you I am staying so you can do what you want to do, and not what you think should be done." Rygee waited for a moment, took another deep breath, and then stepped off the porch and walked towards the bakery.

CHAPTER 13

LEFT BEHIND

I opened my eyes and realized it was still very early morning. I heard the voices and the sounds of a house stirring itself. Ceri and Kern had been inseparable the day before and now I heard their soft voices together in the room next to me, making their plans to return to Juisiti. I didn't hear Miya's voice, but below me in the common room, I could hear Piffik speaking Keresh with his rolled 'r' sounds to Rygee, congratulating him on his new work at the bakery and talking about life at Manumina.

I rolled out of bed as the smell of food drifted up. I knew Miya wanted to get an early start. Using the shortcut Salik Oqina had told them about, Miya would be in Vikland by nightfall and in Juisiti, his home, on the third day. There would be no more night watches on Miya's thirteenth crossing.

I had decided to stay.

Miya had accepted my new plans with a somber face. "I thought when Piffik brought us here the night before last, I would lose you to Manumina. I never knew this place existed, Zren. All those years studying the culture and language of Conrosa, hoping I could be posted there as a diplomat someday. And this was here! Just a day's ride from Vikland!" He smiled. "We shall see each other again and share stories and our lives."

His eyes had grown bright with unshed tears. "I am entrusting Chul and Rell to you. We live, you and I, because of them. If either of them does not recover, do not bury them or fire them in the field. Bring their bodies to Ishes, they will be properly mourned in Vikland as befitting them. If only I would have known we were so close with this half-track, I would never have given Song Yao a soldier's passing. She was a bongmaster and deserved to be praised in the city of Juisiti."

He cleared his throat and continued, "I will come to you tonight and give you coin for you and Chul and Rell to live on during the Wet. Vikland needs this settlement to be kind to us. Do you understand what I am saying, Zren? Salik Oqina says they are pacifists and will not choose sides in a war between Kerek and Vikland, but they trade with us, and care for our wounded; I do not believe they are indifferent to our plight. Be generous to them, so they look kindly on us and our plans."

He had left me then to speak with Rell and Chul and let them know he was leaving them in the Conrosans' care. He would tell them Rygee and I would remain behind, and I would have coin for them to ensure all their needs were met. Then he had left with Piffik and Salik for another meeting. I did not see him again until he had come to my room, but I didn't want to think about that now. Pushing it from my mind, I sighed and threw on my clothes from last night and went downstairs to find food and the others.

The common room was full of people, food, and travel packs. Miya, Rani, Malik, Ceri, and Kern had already finished eating and were drinking their tiny cups of coffee. Piffik, Rygee, Siba, and Aajan had just received their platters of food. When I walked in and sat down, Aajan's mother came bustling out with another platter for me. She smiled, set it down, placed her hand on my shoulder, patted me gently, and then walked out without a word. I looked at Miya.

"You straightened it all out then? I'm not in trouble with Aajan's mother anymore? Because it's going to be a truly long Wet if I have to hide every time I see her."

Aajan muttered darkly at her brother, Piffik, and then smiled brightly at me. "You are welcome here, Zren Janin. You are welcome as my friend and as my brother's friend. You are welcome as one who knows the mercy of caring for his fellow travelers and as a friend of Miyamoto Suki who has gifted me a horse for my speed." She looked down her nose at Piffik, "My mother and my brother do not always recognize kindness for what it is."

She smiled at me impishly. "But you and I, *we* know." She settled herself back in her chair with all the self-importance of a child that has successfully won the prize. We all laughed but it was not cruel. It was the laughter of people who know they are safe, they are headed home to family and warm fires and nights without watches. I ate quickly because I wanted to go outside with the others to see them off.

The wagons had never been unloaded except for our travel bags. Miya had already been out this morning and had chosen the healthiest Viklander horses to hitch to the two wagons which would be going. Four horses and the Kereki army wagon were left behind for Rygee or Chul and Rell to return to Vikland once they were healed enough to travel. Nebs' horse had been gifted to Aajan. I looked at Song's horse—also left behind—and wondered if I would ever be able to ride it.

Ceri and Kern drove the wagon with the West Islands steel and Chul's firemaster supplies. Both of them joked that after five days of me driving the wagon, the seat had magically moved forward, like a Conrosan fairy tale, and now there was no room for their long legs.

I smiled as I realized I had not seen Kern ever this happy. She had hidden her broken heart over Ceri's non-arrival in Kerek City, and I hadn't known her well enough to understand she had been grieving. Now that Ceri had been returned to her, I saw how Kern could fill the space so no one had eyes for anyone but her. I had never seen such a thing before. I thought to myself how Ngahuru would love to have her as a *titiro mai ki ahau* within the embasado. Her happiness rained on us like the fairy dust I imagined in the Conrosan folk tales, and I could not turn away from her. I was sorry to see her go.

I could see now Rani was older than Miya. As we were milling about preparing to say good-bye, I watched him as he carefully looked over the wagons, looked at me, and the Conrosans. I remembered Siba Namikk said he had been wearing maps and papers next to his body and they had saved his life. I wondered what that would mean for First Soldier Joon and Ambassador Lalsy if they didn't know what happened to this patrol until the end of the Wet. I wondered again if he was a softfoot. He was sitting next to Malik as she drove the other wagon with the Viklanders' travel packs, supplies, and the Kereki army paychest. I understood now, from the moment the Kerek King had told him the payroll would travel with us, Miya had planned that it would never reach the Kereki army.

Miya's first, and possibly only love, was Vikland. His promises to me were nothing more than ensuring he would return to Juisiti. But I wondered if he understood what promises from such a man of privilege sounded like to a boy from Lowertown.

The paychest was now very light. Last night, Miya had come to my room carrying three heavy travel bags of coin, one each for Chul, Rell, and me.

"It's about two years pay for a Kereki soldier. It should cover anything you need for you and the others until you are able to earn for yourselves. I have given Rygee the same, and he has also received a year of pay from Bitterboots', Mouser's, and Nebs' paypackets. I will take the rest to the garrison at Ishes as I promised." He smiled. "I keep my promises, Zren. I promised the Farm Boys would not die at my hand. I promised you an education and a way to find your family. I promised I would deliver the paychest."

"It's easy to be generous when it is not your coin," I had responded bitterly. "You bought Rygee's silence and his forgiveness, and you hope to ease your conscience with me by leaving me with the Conrosans and filling my hands with coin." I let the frustration out I had been nursing for the past days. Even as the words fell from my mouth, my head was saying I would regret the words later. My heart didn't care. I talked, and I cried, and I talked some more. I said things I didn't even realize I felt, until I saw the pain I inflicted on Miya. But I didn't stop talking.

He said nothing. He didn't move from the chair across from my bed, just sat there with his head bowed and his hands open, palms up on his thighs. Both Ngahuru and Bima Ritwik had told me Miyamoto Suki liked to see himself as a hero. His life of privilege made it easier to be kind and generous without understanding any of the feelings and implications of his gifts to others. He didn't realize his casual rope of promises was a chain of hope and desire for me. I could not share my pain because he could not grasp why I felt that pain. He could not see me, but he stayed to listen. When I was finished, he left without a word.

I could not change him in one night.

I sighed deeply. But that was last night. This morning, Miya was on horseback, on the finest of the undamaged horses. The two days of rest without watches and travel without fear of an ambush had restored him. He sat straight-backed in the saddle, and he was as handsome as the warriors I had seen in the Viklander tapestries and paintings in the embasado all those days and days ago. His long black braid swung down his back, his dark blue cloak was freshly brushed and spread out and over the horse's rump. He would be the lone outrider today as they rode into Vikland: Miyamoto Suki's thirteenth crossing of the Northern Track.

As if he knew I was watching him, he looked over at me and gave me a lopsided smile. We had said everything I wanted to say last night. We parted as less than friends, but more than fellow travelers.

Two young boys stood at the stockade gates. Miya urged his horse forward and to the right of the lead wagon. He raised his left hand and the gates swung open. He dropped his hand and the procession moved forward, wheels rattling, wagons lurching, voices raised in a chorus of goodbyes. Five Viklanders headed home.

PART II

MANUMINA

CHAPTER 14

THE HOUSE OF NATIONS

After the Viklanders left, Rygee and I were moved from the guesthouse to a furnished house outside the stockade walls. The house bore the scents of empty mustiness on the upper levels and old food and old people on the first. Aajan and her mother came over with cleaning supplies and wood and iron buckets to help Rygee and I "freshen it for living in" as Aajan's mother said.

Rygee had asked her, "If we were moving in, did we force someone else to move out?"

She had pinched her lips tightly together and said, "No, and more than that you don't need to know." Both Rygee and I knew enough not to ask more questions. Still, I noticed he asked for the bedroom at the very top of the house, and let me take the room on the third story. We piled both Chul's and Rell's belongings in the second floor bedroom. It was a problem we could deal with once they were well enough to come home, we decided.

I liked the house. I had never lived in one before and could not believe all this space would be just for the four of us. It was built like all the others on the outside of the stockade. Piffik told me only the stockade itself and the round church had been built when his grandmother's generation found this in the outlands of Kerek. But the Conrosans knew how to work together, he said, and so they built their houses just as they would have been built in Conrosa. Up instead of out, with common walls with the neighbors. The houses were two rooms deep, but just one room wide with a staircase that ran against the left wall—always the left wall—and landings on each floor. The second, third, and fourth floor had large bedrooms with windows facing out towards the gardens, the livestock and fields, and then a smaller windowless washroom against the stockade wall.

Almost all the houses were four stories, as was ours, but some had tiny garrets as a fifth floor.

"Parents sleep on the second floor, girls on the third floor, boys on the fourth floor, and if there is a fifth floor? Too many children," sniffed Aajan's mother. The ground floor had a common room with a couple of soft chairs and a small table between them with room for a lantern. There were benches and a larger table for eating. The kitchen without windows was in the back of the house.

The Conrosans called us the "house of nations." Even though at first, the house held just Rygee and me, we knew Rell and Chul would be with us as soon as they were able.

Rygee worked at the bakery. He started the very day Miya and the others left for Vikland. Each morning he left for work before I was even awake, and came home after midday smelling like sweet cooked fruit, fresh bread, and yeast.

For the first few days I slept. I couldn't remember a time in my life when I did not need to get up at someone else's command or to escape Trouble for another day. I would lie in bed, daydream, and watch the sun move across my blanket. If I could have found a way to have food appear, I doubt I would have left my room.

After a handful of days of doing nothing but eating and sleeping, I woke up one morning to find the healer Siba Namikk standing in my bedroom doorway looking me over.

"Are you ill?" She asked in a concerned voice.

I shook my head. "No."

She tapped her finger on her chin. "Are you afraid?"

I wondered why she had asked that, but I shook my head again. "No."

"Do you lack a purpose?"

I didn't know what that meant, and I said so.

"You are a Conrosan, no?"

"My skin is the cinnamon color of a Conrosan, but I didn't know that until just a season ago. I do not know what it means to be Conrosan. At least not like you are."

She smiled broadly. "Would you like to learn? Would you like to know who you are?"

She turned and went out of the room then and soon I could smell food cooking in the house. I dressed and went down the stairs, curious as to what she was doing. On the table in the front room, there was a place setting for one. I sat down and waited.

She came out and put a plate in front of me. It was a folded pocket of stonebread with roasted vegetables spilling out. I reached for it eagerly and she caught me by my wrist.

"Did you wash your hands? If you eat food with your hands, they must be cleaner than the food."

I looked at her surprised. "You give me food but will not let me eat it?"

She repeated, "Wash your hands in the kitchen so I can see you. Your hands must be cleaner than the food."

I pushed myself away from the table and went back into the kitchen. She watched me wash and gave me a drying linen. "This is for your hands." She pointed to another one which looked—to me—identical. "That is for drying the dishes after they have been washed. Do not confuse the two."

I looked at the piece of toweling in my hand and the one still on the counter. I couldn't see a difference. I shrugged as I put the one down and walked into the dining room. Siba followed without saying a word.

The food was good. It was different spices than what Koanga had used on the Coast Road and Rygee had used on the Northern Track, but it was good. I finished quickly and started to lick my fingers to get the last of the juices. Siba caught me by the wrist again.

"Wash your hands. Your hands must be cleaner than what we are going to do next."

I stared at her. "They were going to be clean, and I have already washed my hands today. You saw me."

"Wash your hands," she repeated stubbornly. I sighed. I didn't know what this all had to do with being a Conrosan, but I was afraid to ask.

By the time Rygee came home from working in the bakery, I had learned to make a bed, wash out my dirty clothes in the tub, hang them to dry on a line under the porch roof, and then wash out the dark rings in the tub. At midday, Siba had made a meal for the two of us, and then set me to washing the pottery that had piled up in the kitchen from Rygee's cooking. She made me wash many of the dishes more than once, saying I needed to see they were clean, not just dunk them in the water. She left before end of day meal to care for Rell and Chul in the infirmary, and I went outside and sat on the porch swing, looked at my still drying clothes, and tried to count how many times she had made me wash my hands.

The next day, she came even earlier.

We took the clean clothes that had been drying overnight and she had me hang my clothes on hooks in my room, make my bed, use something she called a broom to sweep the floor and a catcher to take the sweepings and toss them out the door. Then she made a soup for midday and went back into the kitchen to get spoons for us. I picked up the bowl and started slurping down the noodles and broth. It was still very warm, but I didn't want to stop, it tasted so good.

"Zren!"

She startled me, and I spilled some of the broth and vegetables on the table. I quickly bent down to lick it up. Siba pushed her hand between me and the table and I accidentally licked her hand instead. We both said, "Eeeew," at the same time.

Siba took a deep breath.

"Zren," she said softly. "I have a spoon for you." She placed a wooden spoon carefully on the table and went back to sit at her place. She picked up her spoon and began to eat without looking at me.

I scowled. I knew what a spoon was. I had used a metal one made of West Islands steel on the Coast Road as I traveled with Ngahuru and Koanga. But I had spent many more years in Lowertown using my fingers to pinch food from the pushcarts and swallow it before I was caught by the food sellers. On the Northern Track, I had licked my plates clean and nobody had ever made a comment about it. I wasn't sure why Siba was so upset, but if it meant she would keep cooking for me and let me eat as much as I wanted, well then, I could use a spoon to make her happy. I picked up the spoon and began to eat again. It worked. She gave me a second bowlful as soon as I asked if there was more.

After the washing up, we sat outside on the porch swing and watched the afternoon rains come in.

Siba asked me to tell her what my life had been like before I met the Viklanders. I didn't want to talk about Kerek City, so

I told her of traveling the Coast Road from Aldi to the Matasian city of Salisport. I tried to sing one of the Mata choruses for her, but I couldn't remember it well enough. She smiled and told me she had never traveled farther than Sary, less than a half day away. She asked me if I knew I had been named for a Conrosan folk hero. I told her how Ngahuru had told me stories of Zren Janin, and her brother Koanga had told me Constellation tales of the West Islands. He was the Storyteller to the King, I said proudly.

"Ah, I have never heard a single story from the West Islands, Zren. Do you think you could remember one well enough to repeat it for me?"

I cast about trying to remember one. "The King of the West Islands likes the Seafarer ones, Siba. They tend to be funny, and the Seafarer can be any gender because anyone can love the seas and travel them. But I can't think of one right now, so I will tell you one of the Traveler." I leaned back in the porch swing and began.

"A long time ago, and not so far away, the West Islanders were at peace. The Smith had come and gone, and now looked with fondness on his people from the constellations in the sky. But the West Islanders were not forgotten. Mother Earth would send her daughters: Grains, Gems, Fruits, Flowers, Medicines, and Metals, out with her bountiful gifts.

One day, a new person came and stood by the well in the center of the village. Slight of frame and built close to the ground as all West Islanders are, the person wore a woven cloak of bright green. The hood was drawn up and the voice that called out was neither high nor low.

"Greetings! I have no coin, but I seek food and lodging and in exchange I have news and song and a gift from Mother Earth."

Now in those days, the oldest woman in the village that could walk from the village well to her home and hearth was the one to guide the people. Grandmother came out to meet the traveler.

"Well, what is your news? What is your gift? Then we shall see what food and shelter we have to offer."

The traveler chuckled. "News has value only in the first telling. After that, it becomes merely gossip to be bandied about over weeding and gathering."

Grandmother smiled. "True. At least let us see you, so we know no one shall come to harm."

"A pretty boy or a plain faced maid can hide trouble in their hearts, you must accept me as I appear and let not your generosity be based on beauty."

"How shall we call you?"

"You may call me 'They' or 'Them' or the 'Traveler,' for we go from place to place seeking our fortune, returning to family, or singing our songs in a new hearth."

Grandmother considered. "Well, I won't let anyone in the village suffer by your hand, so come along to my home where you shall have food and shelter for one night and no harm shall come to you."

The Traveler sat at Grandmother's table and told all the news from up and down the roads they traveled. After the meal, Grandmother called the village together, and songs and stories were shared until the stars pinwheeled across the sky. The next morning, the Traveler continued on their journey. The Traveler is neither young nor old, male nor female, but comes bearing peace and reminds us always to be kind to strangers in a strange land."

I looked at Siba. "They call them 'roaming regles,' Siba. Anyone may exchange song or substance for food and shelter in the West Islands. No one may cause hurt to host or guest."

Siba smiled at me. "You have a gift for telling stories. To remember a story so well after hearing it only once? To tell it to me so well I cannot wait to hear what is next? That is a talent not everyone can claim, Zren Janin. You should write them down so others could learn them when you are no longer here."

I bristled at her words. I was ashamed I could not read or write, and so I hid it by mocking her. "I didn't take time with letters and papers. There wasn't much demand for it where I grew up."

Siba abruptly stopped rocking the swing. She started to say something and then stopped. She looked out over the harvested garden, the empty livestock pen in front of the house, and sat silently. I could see she was thinking very hard, so many emotions ran over her face. But I didn't know her well enough to guess what she was going to say.

Finally, she spoke, "Zren, it is very hard for me to remember all the Keresh words I need to use to talk to you. I think there are others here in Manumina who know hardly any Keresh at all, but they would like to know such a well-traveled man as you are. If you could be so generous, it would be very kind of you to learn our language. If you could learn to read and write Conrosan, you could help Piffik with his woodworking deliveries, you could shop for those who do not feel safe leaving Manumina without getting mischarged, and you would gain a second language to help you in your travels if you leave here." She turned back to me. "You have so many talents, Zren, I hate to ask one more burden of you. But I would be willing to teach you your letters, so you do not need to go to school with the little ones."

I looked at her suspiciously, but she just started rocking the swing again. Once the rains had stopped for a while, she took her leave saying it was time to check on Rell and Chul. She asked to be remembered to Rygee, and thanked me for all the work I accomplished that day.

CHAPTER 15

A MANABOUT FINDS HIS WAY

Rygee made friends easily. That same wide open stance and friendly face of someone who had been treated well by the world came back to him. On the Northern Track I had thought him barely older than I was, and timid. But it was because he was afraid of all of us and did not want to be a soldier. Here at Manumina, he was acknowledged and praised by the others as one who knew about baking and farming and how things worked in greater Kerek. He did not speak any other language but Keresh, but he tried to learn the Conrosan words he needed to read the recipes, speak with the customers, and the greetings to ease his way. He seemed to grow older and wiser before my eyes.

In the evenings as we ate our end of day meals, Rygee would describe the Conrosans he worked with, and what he did each day. He said the other bakers were kind and very curious about other things he had learned to bake. As the loaves of bread would cool on the tables before the others would come to pick them up for their end of day meal, he made samples of fingersweets for them. After midday, the bakers would sit down with the tiny cups of Vikland coffee and a plate of his treats. The ovens were quiet then and Rygee would bake bigger and bigger batches of his fingersweets and treats. The other bakers thought all of Manumina would like his delicacies. They offered their ingredients to make them and then helped him trade and barter them alongside the daily loaves. Rygee said since we hadn't been here in the Dry, we had no harvest to eat of our own. So the bakers helped him to trade and barter for vegetables, fruits, grains, and spices, and whatever else we needed to eat.

He invited Piffik and Aajan to the evening meal one night, and then Siba and her aunt Bett on another, to thank them for their care, he said. Then Vigdis, the boy who cared for and had mended our horses at the stables, and Zadah, Piffik's brother who asked us countless questions on life outside of Manumina.

Zadah told us he dreamed of sailing the seas and traveling to Conrosa. He was disappointed I could not remember if I had been born there or how long the sailing took. He asked how long it took to reach the sea from Manumina and how he should go about getting hired by a ship captain.

I told him if he did leave to sail the sea, to cross the Silver Mountains from Vikland to Matasi and sail out from Salisport or another city. It had to be better than taking the Northern Track. And Kerek City? Once he walked into Lowertown and

Dockside, everyone would mark him for an easy victim. To try to gain a ship from Kerek City would mean his death. Matasi was definitely a better route to take, even if he didn't speak a word of Mata. Zadah looked concerned, but said nothing more. Rygee told him to talk to Chul and gave me a disdainful look.

I started to take a greater interest in Manumina and the people who lived there. It was a tiny village on the interior of the stockade with various tradespeople and their apprentices. There were only four houses on the inside—the rooms above the infirmary where Siba Namikk and her aunt Bett lived, the guest house where we had all stayed after the Battle at the Bridge, a small set of rooms above the stable where the horse master and Vigdis lived, and a narrow house with outdoor steps next to the gates. Siba said it had been the arsenal when the first Conrosans arrived, but now the children used it for the school. Because children were apprenticed so young, there was a day school and an evening school so everyone who wanted to learn could learn. No one in Manumina could be a journeyman, on the Council of Wisdom, or run a trade without knowing their letters and how to do sums to conduct business, she said.

Piffik's family ran the woodworks. Their house was on the south side of the stockade, but other than that, Siba said, it was just like the one I lived in. Siba thought I would like to get to know Piffik Qanaq better. I had told her how he thought I would be a suitor for Aajan and she had laughed.

"No, Zren. Now that Piffik has seen you for who you are, he would never wish you for Aajan's husband. She has a sharp mind and a sharper tongue, and the best thing would be for her to go to the academies at Vikland. She is meant for a far bigger world than Manumina. Piffik was only startled to see a Conrosan in Sary that was unknown to him. We have heard there are Conrosans in Vikland teaching at the Academy of Geography and the Academy of Elements and he thought you might be one of them. If you spend time with Piffik now, he will not make you spend time with his sister, Aajan.

"I would like you to know Piffik for another reason, Zren. Piffik's father died of a wasting disease when Piffik was younger than you are now. He was apprenticed to his father, of course, and at the time was a journeyman in the woodworks. But because of his father's death, he left school and took over his father's business. Even though he never finished, he has never stopped learning. He still lives at home with his mother, his sister, and his brother, and listens to their lessons in the evenings. He is a traveler to all the nearby towns and villages, and he is known for his fine furniture."

Siba gave me a serious look. "You should know, Zren, Piffik Qanaq is my oldest friend. He is a man who can teach you to be a Conrosan in your heart and in your head." She smiled. "You are getting so much faster with your chores, and I could teach you your letters in the evening at the infirmary. Perhaps you would like to begin to earn your own way as Rygee is doing?"

And just like that I became a *manabout,* which was nothing more than a fancy Conrosan name for a spare pair of hands for anything that needed doing. Piffik would come in the morning and take me along to meet the one who had bought my time for the day. Piffik and my daily master would talk about what needed to be done, and someone would teach me what to do and how to do it. Sometimes it was another manabout, sometimes Piffik, and sometimes, even the person who said they needed my help. I learned about repairing fences, tending livestock, mending wagons, grinding grains, and making and maintaining the metal farm implements. I was never paid in coin, but Piffik negotiated my worth as he taught me to barter for food, clothes, tools, and whatever else he thought I needed.

When no one had bought my time for the day, I would go along with Piffik and build furniture in his family's woodworking shop. Well, actually, I stood alongside the ten-year-old apprentices and prepared and sanded the wood for the more skilled journeymen and carpenters. While the apprentices received nothing but their meals for their unskilled labor, Piffik's mother was generous in her cooking. She had first meal pasties or runsas, midday, and usually something to go home with all of us.

Since Rygee finished his work day before I did, "because I start four decons before you do," he would say, he would wander about Manumina looking for me after he was done working. Sometimes he would talk with the farmer, or the chandler, or the horsemaster who had bought my time, and ask questions about why they did things a certain way, sometimes he said he just liked to watch me work. But then he would disappear. When I came home later ready for food and a bath, I would find he already had end of day meal prepared and ready for us.

He was always happy when I worked at the woodworks. Piffik's mother would usually send enough food home for the both of us and without any cooking or washing up to do, we would sit and eat outside on the wide swing and watch the rains come down while we were dry under the covered porch. We would talk about our day and Manumina, but mostly Rygee would talk about his home in the south of Kerek.

"I have heard from others, Zren, you have also traveled through Kerek—although down the Coast Road which is far west of my home. But you know the warmth of the sun and the rains are more generous in the south and in Matasi then they are here.

"During the Dry, we would get up while the sun was still tucked in her bed to work in the fields, and then when it was so hot we thought we would crisp up like kindling in a fire, we would stop for a few decons and rest and sleep in dark houses. We would wake while it was still warm outside, eat our evening meal, and then go out and work until it was too dark to see." Rygee shrugged. "Here, I am told we do the same amount of work, but it is in such a short time, I find I have a lot of time on my hands. I am not used to being so idle, Zren."

I snorted. "You need to spend time with Siba Namikk. She believes there are not enough decons in the day to teach me everything I need to know about living in a house and being a Conrosan. She said it will take the entire village of Manumina to drag me to the other side of childhood."

Rygee laughed a long time. "I remember her from when we had her over to thank her and her aunt for their care of us. I have noticed her since then as well. She said she is teaching you your letters and how to read and write Conrosan. I think I should learn it as well. Perhaps it would be all right if she came to our house to teach us both. Would that be acceptable to you?"

I nodded. "Just make sure you wash your hands." I looked at him earnestly. "She checks to see my hands are clean before we can even open a book or touch the paper we will write on."

Rygee just smiled.

As the Wet continued, fewer farmers needed my time. Piffik said it always happened during the rainy season and not to get discouraged. The Wet was a time to rest and reassess, he said. People were not meant to work every day from sun up to sun down. He explained the Conrosans practiced a Rest Day. A day when there was no school for the apprentices and other children, they could visit friends, read books, or write letters, and not feel guilty because work was piling up. Of course, the animals still needed to be taken care of and people needed to eat, but it was a day to do what people liked and wanted to do and not what they had to do.

"What do you like to do?" I asked idly. He and I were the only ones in his workshop. I had gone looking for him after first meal when no one had bought my time, only to learn no one would that day. It was a Rest Day. Piffik had only happened to be in the woodshop to look at the apprentices' work without them hovering over him, afraid he would find too much fault and make them do it again.

"I like to learn something new. I know the world is much bigger than Manumina and I wish to learn about it. Chul and Rell are well enough to have visitors now, Zren. I find my feet like to walk to the infirmary even when it is not Rest Day so I can learn from those who have seen and heard and done more than I have."

He smiled at me. "You were given a great gift to travel with them. But do you know, Zren, I do not know how a Conrosan who does not speak Vik—or so Rell Huena tells me—came to be traveling with Viklanders. Is this a story you would like to share with me?"

I hesitated. I had told the Ambassador and the Secondo and Miya everything because I was afraid they would not let me travel with Miya otherwise, and I knew I could not be left behind in Matasi without knowing the language or without coin to pay my way. I had also done it to protect Ngahuru and Koanga who had saved my life by stopping on the road to Aldi. But to tell Piffik Qanaq, a man who had never lived outside of Manumina? What would he think?

Piffik sensed my hesitation. "You do not need to tell me, Zren. You own yourself. But could you tell me this? Do you still have family where you are from? Are there other Conrosans in Kerek which Manumina doesn't know about?"

I shook my head. "You have talked with Chul? Did he tell you he was bought and sold by the Orphan Master of Kerek City?"

Piffik nodded his head. "Is this what happened to you as well?"

I lifted my shoulders and let them drop. "I don't know. I know I learned Keresh—castle Keresh—and not the language of the streets and docks. So someone had the care of me long enough to teach me to speak well. But Piffik, I should have been old enough to remember this person and I do not. I know I was on my own before I learned to read or write, but that is not a skill that is valued in Kerek City. I know I stole my food or went without. I ran faster than Trouble and if I did not, I was beaten for it. I slept in alleys and doorways with piles of other children so we could not be preyed upon during the nights. I know the best that could ever have happened to me was to be beaten and thrown out of a rich man's carriage so Koanga, a Storyteller of the West Islands, and his sister could find me. They tended my wounds, fed me, sheltered me, and took me along with them to Matasi."

I blew out a breath. "In Ribelo, Matasi, we met Miyamoto Suki. I do not know who he is in Vikland, but I know other Viklanders who met us and talked with him treat him with great respect. Koanga called him a 'Prince of Vikland,' but Bima Ritwik said there is only an Empress in Vikland and no princes at all. Ngahuru said I should not travel with her to the West Islands, but I should go with Miya and have him give me a future." I smiled at Piffik.

"But then we found Manumina—or you found us. Miya thought I should stay here with my people and learn who I was and not travel to Vikland with him, although he had promised to take me and he always keeps his promises, he said. But I was hurt and angry and thought if I stayed here, he would miss me too much and be sorry he had not taken me with him." I gave Piffik a wry grin. "You see how well that worked out."

Piffik interrupted. "We are very glad you stayed, Zren Janin. See how everyone has tried to help you learn who you are? All of Manumina is very glad you stayed. No matter the reason, please take comfort in this."

I gave him a watery smile. I hadn't realized how much I still felt the sting of Miya's rejection. I didn't trust my words and so I said nothing. Piffik looked away and then asked if I knew different woods from different parts of the known world had their own unique smell. I shook my head, and then we spent the rainy afternoon going through the wood pieces in his woodshop and smelled every one. He even showed me some special wood—ones the apprentices and journeymen never got to touch—and we smelled those and tried to imagine what the world was like where those trees had been harvested.

CHAPTER 16

RYGEE BRICK

Once I knew Siba Namikk had told me the truth—Conrosans did want to know more about me and about the rest of Kerek—I asked everyone to talk to me only in Conrosan, so I would learn the words quickly. When Siba was not caring for Rell and Chul, she would come over to my house to teach me my letters. She had borrowed a book with letters and words a child could read. We would work together over the book while Rygee would make end of day meal for the three of us and then we would talk about our day. Rygee joked the Conrosan words he was learning in the bakery were all about food so he thought he and I would get along just fine.

When we didn't know a word, we would use Keresh and Siba would give us the Conrosan words and make us spell them and say them again and again. Sometime Rygee would tease her by using a word that would make her blush pink.

Siba was eager to learn more about life outside of Manumina, and she would have Rygee or me tell a story of what our life had been like in Kerek. Sometimes she was so caught up in the story we could switch from Conrosan to Keresh words without her noticing until the end—or until one of us gave it away by grinning. I thought about how small her life had been and why the Manumina settlers were so isolated. I asked her and she gave me a sad look before answering.

"It is not the choice of the people of Manumina, Zren. When our grandparents came here, they built their houses on the outside of the stockade because they were confident they would meet their neighbors and like them. We built our waterworks, our gardens, our orchards, our fields. We went to the nearby towns expecting to trade and to work together. I do not know what happened, it was all before my parents' time. But we were not welcomed with friendship. Our goods and tradespeople were tolerated and accepted because everyone is so far from the ports here; there is little that can make its way from Kerek City or even the ports of Matasi. But it was not always as bad as it is today. The mothers and grandmothers here remember freely riding horses on the plains east of us all the way to the Vikland border."

She sighed. "Our youth would leave for the academies in Vikland or work in the cities. We know they find a new home, letters do reach us here. But now the Conrosan women do not stray far from the shelter of Manumina just as any Kereki woman does not stray far from the shelter of her husband or father."

She paused a long moment before continuing, "I think the problem is the Kerek King. He has allowed laws to be broken, and so all of us stay inside our walls or only travel in groups to Ahni and Ishes and Sary."

"Piffik…" I began.

Siba smiled. "Piffik is a law unto himself. He traveled with his father when he was yet a boy and is known to everyone. He greets those he knows and treats others well where he can, because he says it is easier to harm a stranger than someone who has done you a kindness in the past. He does not carry any weapon to defend himself against bandits, yet he always comes home.

"We used to say, before you arrived, that our Conrosan folk hero, Zren Janin, rode on the wagon seat beside him with his magical Sword of Courage to protect him." She looked to me and grinned. "And here you are, where every child in the settlement can see you!" She laughed gently. "You should know, Zren Janin, all of the children have been much better behaved since you have become known to Manumina."

Rygee laughed a long time, and smiled at Siba, "Don't worry. His secrets are safe with me."

* * * * *

Another time, I asked Rygee why I never saw his clothes pegged to the line on our front porch to dry.

"I take them to the laundry, Zren. There is a laundry here where you can pay someone to wash your clothes and mend them if they need it. You must mark your clothes, all are boiled together in the hot water, but I like to know they are so clean when I must work in the bakeries."

I was quiet for a while. "Why would Siba make me wash my own if I could give them to someone else to do?" I asked him.

"That's a question you should ask Siba," he replied easily. "But I think it is because she is trying to teach you the skills you need to know to live in a house with others. If you disagree with her, you can talk to her about it." He grinned at me. "Or maybe she is worried your clothes might fall apart if they are beaten in the big cauldrons."

I looked down in surprise at the clothes I had on. I was wearing the clothes the tailor had remade for me at the Vikland embasado in Salisport. They had worked well for me on the Northern Track and here at Manumina as I worked in the woodshop, with the livestock, and in the granary, and chandler shop. My grey shirt was clean, but it showed the past stains and tears of the work I had done.

"You don't like my shirt?" I exclaimed.

"I think you should spend some of your coin you got from Miya and buy some new ones." He smiled gently. "You could take those to the infirmary and give them to Siba for bandages. But wait until I can go with you. I want to see the expression on her face."

I shrugged. I still had my clothes I had bought in Cloa. I was still richer than I ever had been in Lowertown.

* * * * *

I came home from work one day to see Rygee out in the fields in front of our house. It was only lightly raining, but I could see holes in the gardens, mending on the fences, and long handled tools leaning against the marker separating our fields from the neighbors. I was too tired to go out and join him. I had been fighting with Salik Oqina's goats all afternoon. I sat on the porch swing and just watched him walking, bending down and picking up clumps of dirt, and letting them sift through his hand. He looked across at other fields, fallow after the harvest at the end of the Dry, and then at his feet.

Finally, he walked back towards me and stopped at the fences which would have surrounded the pens for the livestock—if we had any. He used both hands to push and pull the fence all around, and then picked up the tools and walked to the house.

He startled when he saw me on the swing. "Home already? Or is it later than I think? I am sorry, Zren, I haven't made evening meal. You didn't happen to work at Piffik's, did you?"

I shook my head. "I was at Salik Oqina's. We were making buckling goats into wethers and you do *not* want to know what that means." I sighed. "I think I am too tired to move. I'll just eat and sleep right here."

Rygee smiled. "I grew up on a farm, remember? You'll want to take your bath first. I'll make end of day while you are cleaning up and then you can go to bed."

I grabbed his outstretched hand and let him pull me up. "What were you doing out there?"

"A woman came into the bakery today and asked if we were going to farm our portion next Dry. They have boys old enough to work their own land, but they still live at home and have no fields beyond the family allotment. She said they would like to plant and harvest our land and give us part of the crops. I wondered if you and I should try to farm it, or if we are better off letting others use the fields, the gardens, and the livestock pens and barter for their goods. What do you think?"

He laughed. "Sorry, Zren, I can tell by your face I am asking on the wrong day. And we need to take Rell and Chul into consideration as well. They won't live in the infirmary forever."

I followed him inside and walked heavily up the stairs. I didn't know the first thing about what Rygee was asking, and I would be happy if he would just make the decision for me. I wondered if I would ever know enough to live on my own. It seemed everywhere I turned someone was still helping me. I wondered what my life would have been like if I had stayed in Kerek City.

Bah! I'd be dead by now. I turned on the taps for the water. I stripped out of my filthy clothes and kicked them aside. I eased my sore and aching body into the warm water and sighed. *I would never be as smart as everyone else*, I decided. But I wondered who I would be when Siba and Piffik and Rygee and the entire settlement of Manumina finished dragging me to the other side of childhood.

* * * * *

It wasn't enough that Rygee's fingersweets and treats at the bakery were so popular he was able to barter and sell them alongside the daily loaves of bread the bakers made for everyone. He wrote down his recipes in Keresh, then again in Conrosan, and before he gave them away, he gave them to Siba to read to be sure they were written right.

One night she came over with a covered plate and sly grin on her face. It was later than usual and Rygee and I had already eaten and done the washing up. She put the plate on the table and took the cloth off. The treats smelled so good, somewhere between a kolache and what Rygee called a fetti—a round ring with a hole in the middle. I reached for one quickly.

I thought it would melt in my mouth. I had barely swallowed the first one before I reached for another.

"What are these?" I mumbled through bites.

"Samiss," she said. "I thought I would make them so Rygee did not think he was the only one who knew how to bake something beyond the daily bread." Rygee gave her such a big grin it looked like his eyes smiled at her too. But he didn't say anything.

That night during our lessons, Siba told us the worst of the danger of infection was past, and Rell and Chul should have more people come to see them at the infirmary than just Piffik. She said Salik Oqina and his son Mikale had been to visit after Bett had said it was safe for Chul and Rell. Salik had asked Chul questions about Matasi. He had wanted to learn more about how and why this settlement had been built and abandoned. Who were the people that came here? Was it only a military garrison or had there been families as well? Chul explained he had been orphaned, sold, redeemed, and raised in Vikland. He had no more idea of the origins of the settlement than Salik did.

Siba told me I would have to take a bath and wear clean clothes before I came, but she thought it would be good for Rell and Chul to see how well I was doing and learn about Manumina, to have them hear stories from someone else besides her aunt.

"I do not talk so much, Zren, and my aunt even less. I think Chul and Rell would like to hear something besides the never-ending rains of the Wet."

* * * * *

Piffik had left on a delivery of furniture, Siba was taking care of an infant with a fever and wasn't going to come over and teach us, and the rains were too heavy to go out. Rygee and I rocked on the porch swing and talked about nothing and everything.

Rygee told me he had contracted with the family who had asked to use our lands for a portion of the harvest, telling me, "Now that I do more at the bakery, Zren, I don't have time, and you don't know how. Neither of us know what grows better here than anywhere else. We are better to have our land tended to by someone with a large family then to try to do it ourselves."

I nodded. "I am glad to hear it, Rygee. Sometimes I do not think I could learn one more thing in a day." I smiled at him. "Maybe they could bring our part of the harvest as the food already cooked, and you and I could just sit here on the swing and eat when we come home and not have to do the washing up."

He laughed.

He told me where he grew up, farther south in Kerek, during the Dry he would wrap the sheeting from his bed about the porch posts to keep out the bugs and then sleep on the porch in a hanging bed to try to catch the night breezes blowing through the sheeting.

"Sometimes, it was so warm, I felt like I didn't sleep at all." He and his brothers would ride horses out from the main house to check on the far fences and animals and sleep in little squares of houses that had openings on all four sides to catch the breezes.

"Do you miss it?" I asked.

"Every day, Zren, every day." He looked at me. "Even the Dry with all of the work and the heat. Of course, I liked the Wet better, there was less work on the farms, and it was cooler. My brothers stayed at their houses more with their wives and children, so it was just my papa, mama, and me in the main house. During the Wet, we would read, or plan for the planting in the Dry. There was always something to do and talk about." He paused. "Yeah, I miss it."

In Lowertown, the Wet season had been a miserable time of daily rains, flooded hiding places, and clothes that hung damp and musty on my shivering body day after day after day. I didn't miss Lowertown, Kerek City, or even traveling at all. Each day since I had been found along the road to Aldi had been better than where I had grown up. I hadn't realized it wasn't true for Rygee. It probably wasn't true for Rell or Chul either. But I didn't tell Rygee. I only said I could understand how a warm shelter, dry clothes, and hot food could make such a difference in a life. I told him I thought I would like the Dry season in Manumina as well.

CHAPTER 17

THE ACADEMY AT THE INFIRMARY

So now, every few days, after my end of day bath, I dressed in clean clothes and showed my face at the infirmary to visit with Rell and Chul. Siba would not let me in until after she had inspected my hands to see if I was clean enough. I would laugh at her as she poked at me and sniffed my clothes, but she always appeared very serious.

"You can smell like clean sawdust, Zren, but if you smell like the fields or animals, I will not let you in," she admonished. "You must scrub that well."

While I would visit, she would usually leave somewhere so Chul and I could be alone to talk.

One time, I was telling Chul what I had learned that day, and what Rygee had made for end of day meal, and what I thought I might do the next day, when Piffik came into the infirmary with a long roll of papers tucked under his arms.

He saw me, nodded, and said, "Later then," just as Chul waved him in.

"Come in, come in. I have been looking forward to this evening," Chul said. "We will keep young Zren here as well and speak in Keresh so he can learn where he stands in his new world."

I didn't know what he meant, but Chul asked me to bring a small table over to his bed and then go into the infirmary kitchen and bring a handful of empty pottery. Once I had done so, Piffik unrolled his first paper. Chul had me place the pottery carefully on the corners to hold it down.

It was a hand-drawn map. There was a neatly lettered word inside a circle at the far right side. All around it were lines and drawings of buildings and marks and words. There was a wavy line west of the circle, a thick line from west to east and more triangles, squares, and circles than I could count.

Chul laughed at the expression on my face. "Ah Piffik, you have a new apprentice I see. I don't know if I have ever seen an adventurer so hungry to learn as our Zren."

Piffik smiled at me. "Can you read any of this yet? It is in Conrosan, so if you can, you are better off than our learned friend here." He waved his hand at Chul.

I stared hard at the map and sounded out the letters to myself. *Man u MEE nah.* "Is this Manumina?" I pointed to the word near the large circle.

"It is." Piffik tapped the curvy line. "…and this is the Huk River which flows from the Cold Mountains by Kerek City north of the Northern Track until it crosses here down through Kerek to the foothills of the Silver Mountains." He tapped the triangles and the squares as he spoke. "If you know that, can you deduce where the town of Sary is?"

I looked at the river on the map and saw where it crossed the thick line marking the Northern Track. That had been the Battle at the Bridge, I realized. I marveled that there was a piece of paper in the world which marked where Song Yao had died and was burned on a funeral pyre. I looked closer at the map to see if it felt more special than any other place.

It didn't.

Sadly, I knew Song would only be in my heart from that moment forward. I leaned back and took in the whole map. I remembered Piffik had said Manumina was the same distance from Sary as the bridge had been. I put my thumb on the bridge, looked at the circle that said Manumina and then placed my forefinger on the next marking of buildings northwest of there.

"Here?"

"Yes." Piffik smiled.

"You have been to Sary, Zren." Chul said, "Let us see if you can find a place you have never been. Can you find Ishes? This is where Piffik led the Viklanders through a half-track to get home sooner." I looked at the map to the right of Manumina and saw a square with a flag. I tentatively put my finger down.

"This is also correct. Now if you know—on *this* map—a square with a flag is a garrison or a military fort, can you find others?"

I looked at the map, it was like a puzzle. I quickly pointed to several and then found the garrison north of Cloa.

"This is Earles, isn't it?" I looked up at Chul. "Where the Kereki soldiers were to report," I said. "But Vikland tricked it away from the Kerek King somehow."

Piffik said quietly, "I heard in Cloa, the soldiers at Earles had not been paid for nearly two years. Desertion was high and the settlements nearby were disgusted with the raiding and thievery of the soldiers to feed themselves. Viklander regiments came through with wagons of foodstuff and coin and went to the village first. The Viklanders made the bandits the common enemy and told the village it was now Vikland's responsibility to rid the Northern Track of bandits and cutthroats who preyed on the settlers and Viklanders passing through. No more Kereki soldiers' and settlers' lives would be sacrificed to murderers who disregarded the King's laws. The Viklanders told the settlement they had bought and paid for the fort and gave them food. They asked the townspeople to meet with the Kereki soldiers and tell them the Viklanders had the coin from the Kereki King to pay the wages of the few remaining soldiers if they would take their things and leave peaceably. If they did not return to Kerek City, the soldiers were told, the King would not reassign them to another fort. They were free to live as they pleased and return to their homes. Why would the Kereki soldiers not believe this? The Kerek King had not cared enough to pay them in two years." Piffik paused and then continued, "It is my understanding no soldiers returned to Kerek City. I don't know what the Viklanders were expecting, but Earles was abandoned, and the regiments moved in without a single crossbow fired."

Chul nodded. "I knew of this. It was a gamble. Our softfoots believed the fort was at less than quarter strength, but no one knew what to expect, if the remaining soldiers would fight or not. The commander was a diplomat who said to succeed they would need to secure the village first and then approach the garrison. He was right. If the garrison had been fully staffed with Kereki soldiers, it would have been a massacre. The regiments to take the fort were all volunteers." He paused. "Let me take another look at this map." The two men started talking about half-tracks and Piffik's routes to the various settlements.

Piffik showed Chul where his half-tracks cut across settler lands—which owners had given him permission to cross and which were abandoned. He had circled holdings where he could ask for help or water or a place of safety against the dark. He described hills and places he could camp rough overnight, and areas where he hurried through because there could be Trouble hiding.

He talked about the Justices in each town. Which ones were kind, which ones were corrupt. Where there were those in the shops who bought Manumina's goods and asked after those who made them. He said there were also those who were so busy trying to mischarge him, they didn't have time to talk. It was fascinating to me to see how a map could say all that from one person to another.

* * * * *

After I had heard Piffik's story of how Earles had become a Vikland garrison in the eastern heart of Kerek, I asked Rygee how he had been assigned to go there. Had he volunteered?

Rygee snorted. "Of course not. The first thing I learned in the army is not to volunteer for anything."

We were doing the washing up. Siba would be over later for our lessons. After she had learned I could not count past ten, and she caught me counting on my fingers for those small numbers, she had decided I also needed to know my sums.

I hadn't known numbers were the same in every language. I was shocked the first time she told me I was learning that a handful of days, goats, and pottery always equaled the same number in Mata, Vik, Wester, and Keresh, as well as Conrosan.

"And coin?" I had asked, incredulously.

"Well, no, coins and the value of things are different depending on where you travel," she had replied. I couldn't figure out how the number of things and the value of things could be different and that a small-sized coin could have more value than a larger-sized one, but I knew Siba had never lied to me. I remembered how Ngahuru had changed our coins from Kereki dias to Matasian cals when we had entered Ribelo. So I had shrugged my shoulders and learned what was put in front of me. And now I wanted to learn how Rygee had ended up on the road to Earles.

"I had been in the army long enough to know it was easier than farm work. There were those who were friendly and those who were not. Those who pulled their weight and those who shirked every time they could get away with it. My commander had been in the military a little while, but he had come from a soldiering family and was better than others I had heard of.

"Our garrison was small. We only had to protect the Harvest Road and there weren't enough travelers passing through to make the bandits wealthy. The commander of the fort had gotten the orders to send a handful of men to Kerek City to serve at the King's castle. He thought he was doing us a kindness to have us travel about and see more of Kerek."

Rygee gave me a wry grin. "I had just arrived at the castle two days before. Everyone in the barracks had been telling us new soldiers how wicked Kerek City was and where the best places were to gamble and drink and where to stay away. Our new commander had laughed as he told us the news that Viklanders came to the castle and asked for an escort over the Northern Track. He told us only the worst of the soldiers were assigned to the farthest garrisons. Then he looked at me and said since I had come from a far garrison in the south, obviously I was a problem he didn't want to deal with. I was to report to the castle the next day and travel out with you."

"You didn't know Nebs?" I asked surprised. "I thought you were friends."

Rygee shook his head. "Never saw him before we loaded the wagon to travel to your embasado. Nebs said, *his* friends had told him, he must have angered the Lost God somehow to get attached to the Viklander wagon train. That if the bandits didn't get him, the Viklanders would. He said his commander told him he wasn't a betting man, but if he was, he would bet the entire Kereki paychest, Nebs wouldn't live to make it back to Kerek City." Rygee fell silent, and we both thought about how the commander's words had fallen true.

"After we met all of you, Nebs and I talked it over and decided Miya was a better man to follow than the man you called Bitterboots. If we ever had to choose, we agreed we would align with the Viklanders rather than Bitterboots and Mouser. We hoped you would spare our lives because you needed us to protect your women as well as our paychest." He looked at me and laughed. "How could we have been so mistaken?"

I laughed with him. "It was what you knew. It was how you were taught to think. It was how I was taught to think. It wasn't right or true, but it was what we were taught to believe."

Rygee nodded in agreement. "You had killed Bitterboots, Rell had seen and silently challenged the bandits on the hill—I never noticed them until the movement of their horses gave them away, and Song had injured Mouser. The Viklanders did not need our protection." He blew out a hard breath.

"Miya had told each of us we could slip away and not report to the garrison. I couldn't figure out why. Were you going to kill us one by one as we slipped away? We were already outnumbered two to one. It didn't make sense. After Nebs said he was willing to be left behind and fade away, Kern had taken me aside and suggested I do the same. She said I was too good of a man to waste my life at Earles. I thought she meant the garrison was full of troublemakers like my commander in Kerek City had thought.

"Nebs and I talked again. He reminded me you had killed Bitterboots because he had grabbed you first. Song had nearly killed Mouser because he had threatened her and then you with the throwing knife. None of you had ever treated us badly until we acted badly first. So Nebs thought you knew something about Earles we didn't. We deserted. It wasn't until I got here to Manumina, I learned Earles had already fallen to the Viklanders."

I was silent. From the moment Rygee had told his father he wouldn't marry where he was told, his life had not been his to control. Suddenly, I understood why he had started working at the bakery so quickly. Why he insisted we keep our house clean and I do the washing up and sweeping every day while he did the buying and bartering and cooking for both of us. Why he wanted our fields, and pens, and gardens to be used and not idle. Why he walked about after his work at the bakery and talked with and learned from others at Manumina. Once he arrived at Manumina, his life was his to control again. And yet, he still missed his home.

There was a knock at the door and Siba let herself in. She was carrying another book and more paper.

"Have you washed your hands, Zren?" she called out. "I have borrowed this book from a teacher at the day school. I promised her I would not let you touch it until you washed your hands." She smiled as she came into the kitchen and saw us finishing the washing up.

Rygee apologized, "We were talking and are not quite ready. We will be with you shortly."

Siba nodded. "I understand. Would you like me to wait in the other room for you so you can finish your conversation?"

I shook my head. "No, we are done. I just figured out Rygee is a good man. And Kern the Softfoot told me, a good man should never be wasted."

Siba laughed. "Truer words were never spoken, Zren. I have thought so since I met him."

* * * * *

Piffik had learned to read and write Vik from books, but he wanted to learn to speak it so he could communicate and not just trade with those at the garrison at Ishes. He and Chul would have long conversations in Vik with Keresh words mixed in. They would talk about building things and inventions I had never heard of, places I had never been, and ideas, and governments, and books they had read.

I didn't stay long on those nights, or I would go talk to Rell.

I had stood watch with Rell Huena on the Northern Track, but I had never talked to her about anything except horses. I could say with complete truth, I had known and liked Song Yao the best. But Rell was a good listener and talked without making me feel stupid for not knowing things. When I mentioned something I had learned about Vikland or about Song, Rell commented how traveling together broke down barriers. She said I knew stories about Song Yao she had never learned in the years spent together during their military service and in the Diplo.

"You're easy to talk to," Rell commented once. "I don't know how, you fill up every bit of space in a conversation, but I enjoy your company. You remind me of my brothers." She laughed. "Those words should never be in the same conversation." She laughed again. "Do you have brothers, Zren?"

I shook my head but didn't explain.

"I have so many, I can't even remember all their names." She looked at me slyly, and then burst into laughter at my expression. "Ah, Zren. You make the best faces. So tell me what you are doing between the time the healers let you see me?"

I told her I was learning to be a manabout. When nobody had any work for me, I would go along to Piffik's woodshop and work in there. I talked about how the others all started out making coffins and then furniture and then they could sell their work outside of Manumina for coin they could keep for themselves. That they were called journeymen, but there were women and girls in there too. I said I thought Manumina was like Vikland where anyone could be anything they wanted to be.

Rell smiled. "I think you overestimate Vikland, Zren. But you have never been there, so I can understand. All Viklanders must serve three years in the military after the academies. There we get to travel and see more of our country and other countries. I think our elders hope we see and learn what we want to do for the rest of our lives. To bring back new ideas and new foods and new ways so Vikland continues to grow and stretch. Sometimes we do and sometimes it takes a few tries." She nodded. "But you are right, Zren. No one would be told they could not do something just because of how they looked or who they were."

CHAPTER 18

THE TAX COLLECTORS

I was walking across the village green to see Vigdis at the stables when I saw the door to the round church open. The Council of Wisdom slowly walked out, and I saw Zadah and the chandler come out as well. I was curious, so I stood there until Zadah passed by. I followed him. He saw me and turned.

"I thought you and the chandler were in Ahni selling candles and soap and buying supplies," I began.

"We were." He grinned. "We delivered our goods, bought our supplies, and left there after midday." He added something in Conrosan.

Uncertain, I translated it back to him, "We met ourselves on the track?"

He laughed. "It was a saying of my father. It means we were so quick about our business that we made time go backward and met ourselves coming into the town." He added gravely, "We were in a hurry to return. We needed to tell Manumina the Tax Collector will be coming sometime in the next two days."

"What does that mean?" I squinted up at him.

"It means the Kerek King sends some of his army and a pompous fool or two to come to Manumina and poke about our belongings, our animals, and our young men, and decide what belongs to the King and what we are allowed to keep for ourselves."

"Truly?" I was astonished. "But why?"

"Because he can, Zren. So Manumina needs to be ready for him." He paused and looked at me. "You know we are pacifists?"

"Sort of," I hedged. "Well, actually, I don't know what that means."

"It means we do not fight. We resolve Trouble peaceably. Unfortunately, the Kerek King seems to be deaf to our words that we are Conrosans and not Kerekis and therefore not subject to his military conscription. We pay taxes, more than our fair share, I might add. But we will not fight." He paused and looked me up and down, "How old are you, Zren?"

I shrugged my shoulders. "What age do you want me to be? I think I had a birthday here, but I am not sure why I think so. I think I may be eighteen, but you could convince me otherwise."

Zadah looked surprised. "You seem younger. Hmmm. It may be Salik Oqina may need you to play a part to save us. It would be good to have another man in addition to his son, Mikale, stand on the green. Could you do that, Zren? Could you stand between the Kerek King and Manumina to protect us?"

I thought of Rell and Chul in the infirmary. I remembered Song and Nebs at the Battle at the Bridge. I swallowed hard.

"Will I die?"

Zadah startled. "Of course not! We only need to have a small number of children and young men about—but not ones the army will take. You know Mikale, do you not?"

I nodded. I had worked with Mikale and Salik Oqina when it was time to change the buckling goats to wethers. Mikale was a hard worker and had shown me what to do.

Zadah saw me nod. "You see? You know Mikale is smart and strong and can do many things. But people outside of Manumina only see his withered arm and assume he can do nothing but eat and sleep. He has a brave heart to stand nearly alone on the village green while the rest of us hide in Vikland. It would be good for him to have another, also one with a brave heart, to stand with him when the Tax Collector comes. You should see Salik. Talk to my brother when he returns from his delivery at Cloa. They will tell you the role they need you to play for Manumina." He turned and walked to the stables.

Over the next few decons, the strangest things happened before my eyes. The school teachers released the children from their classes. People took the wagons and plow horses from the stables and loaded them with food and goods. Young men came into the stockade wearing cloaks and carrying travel packs and met with Salik Oqina and others from the Council of Wisdom on the green. They would talk together and then some would take goats and drive them east. Others loaded chickens and rabbits on hand carts, covered them with waterproof canvas, and pulled them east. Conrosan girls—Aajan among them— came out of their houses wearing Kereki male clothes and cloaks, carrying travel packs, and battered brooms to sweep out their tracks behind them. I had just started forward to ask Aajan what was happening when Rygee came through the stockade gates.

"Zren!" he called, "I've been looking all over for you!" He walked up quickly to me. "We need you in the infirmary. You have to help us hide Rell. She's not well enough to travel with the others over the border to Vikland."

"Is that where everyone is going?"

"Yes. Siba says there is a small holding about two decons over the border. It has been abandoned since her parents' time, but there is a cottage and sandpoint well. Vikland does not have guards everywhere and the border is unprotected there, so people at Manumina can cross unnoticed and use the cottage to get away for a while. There are fences and sheds there which the Conrosans use to hold their animals. I guess this happens every year, so the Council has a plan everyone follows."

I tried to keep up with his long legs as we hurried to the infirmary.

"What about us?" I asked as we stepped inside.

Siba answered my question with rapid fire answers. "Chul will have to be a patient here. We can't move him. It is good he looks like a Matasian, and so the Kereki army won't care. We will have to hide Rell upstairs in my room, she is a Viklander and can't be found here. We have a place for her. I hope she does not have a problem with small spaces."

She looked at me. "Rygee is a deserter from the army and can't be found here either. He will travel with the others over the border. The only ones to be left here are the old, a few families, children and men who cannot be conscripted, and a handful of animals. We must look poor and beneath the King's notice. Do you understand that, Zren?"

"What about you?" I asked.

"Only my aunt will be here. I must flee with the other young women to Vikland." She grabbed one corner of Rell's blankets, pointed me to the other one, and Rygee lifted both corners by Rell's feet by himself.

"Up!" Siba called out and Rell rocked in the blanket as we carried her up the stairs and into Siba's bedroom.

There was a large wooden chest extending nearly the length of the one wall. The lid was open and there were wooden trays of botanicals and clothes stacked on the bed and on the floor nearby.

Rell gasped. "I have to hide in there? For days? Are you sure?"

"Everything will be left open Rell. It will be like a bed with sides. Only when Salik Oqina strikes the gong will my aunt have to place the trays in and lock the lid."

"Lock the lid?" Rell repeated. "Put me down on the floor."

We did.

Siba looked sadly at Rell. "I am sorry. I am beyond sorry. Sometimes the Tax Collector walks into the stockade, looks about, and calls out a random number which we must pay for our taxes. Sometimes, they walk through every house, open every cupboard that is not locked, and count every pot and pottery. Because it is different every time, we cannot know what we will face. My mother's generation says they used to take young men and women, and we would never hear from them again. Since then, we do not give them the chance. Maybe things have changed. But we are not willing to gamble anyone's life to find out." Siba looked out the window and back at Rell. "We have to hurry, Rell. The last group waits on the green for me and Rygee. I cannot delay much longer."

Rell took a long shuddering breath and gave a sharp bob of her head. We lifted the corners and gently placed her inside. "Zren, come back and see me after everyone is gone." She almost whispered the last part, "please?"

I nodded. "As soon as I know what is happening, I will come back and see you. I promise." I looked her in the face so she would know I was telling her the truth.

"I have never been so grateful you have a face that cannot lie." She closed her eyes.

I turned and ran down the stairs to catch up with the others.

That night I slept on the floor in Siba's room. Twice Rell woke up gasping and calling out my name. I would sit up, place my back against the chest and talk to her or tell her stories until I heard her fall asleep again. I wondered what would happen to her once we had to close the lid, and I had to go downstairs and stand on the green.

* * * * *

Zadah and the chandler had given us less than a day's notice and yet by the next morning, Manumina looked like I had never seen it before. Instead of people hurrying to their work around the settlement, there were a few people sitting on their front porches, just idling away the day. There was one teacher with white hair who I had seen run up and down the stairs on the inside of the stockade two handfuls of time yesterday. Today, he pretended he could barely shuffle across the green.

There were a handful of goats, a scratching of chickens, barely enough rabbits for a stew pot. Two bakers had stayed behind but only one of the big bakery ovens had been lit that morning.

The Tax Collectors came just before midday. Salik Oqina's son, Mikale, had been the lookout on the south side of the stockade. He had come running in and said he could see the King's standard in the distance. Salik had struck a large gong in the round church, and I had hurried to the infirmary to help Bett with Rell. Bett showed me how to stack the trays carefully on the ridges around the inside to give Rell plenty of room and breathing space, layer the clothes on top, close the lid, and lock it. Rell had kept her eyes closed the whole time, but I could smell the fear on her.

"There are three keys, Zren," Bett said quietly, "I am hiding one in the kitchen infirmary in the largest mortar. I am giving one to you, and I am wearing one. Even if neither you nor I survive, Siba will know where to look to unlock her when she returns."

She looked at my horrified expression. "Your friend is safe, truly."

We went downstairs and Bett said a few words to Chul. She asked if he wanted to be awake and alert, or did he want the incense to cause him to sleep deeply. Chul had given her a pointed look and said he should be awake. He didn't want to be mistaken for dead and carried away.

Soberly, Bett and I took our cloaks against the rains. She said the Tax Collectors would keep us standing there for a long time. We filed out on to the green with some of the others just as a procession of horses, wagons, and a fine carriage all trotted in the open gates.

There were two Tax Collectors who climbed out of the carriage. Both were richly dressed. I had expected them to be both

Kereki men about the age of Salik Oqina—I don't know why, I just did. But one was a Spice Islander with a gold ring in his ear and gold rings on his hands. The Kereki soldiers surrounding the carriage and guarding the wagons of tribute and taxes reminded me of Nebs and Rygee. They looked young and unequipped for the bandits who would be waiting for them along the tracks and trails. Some of them were not even wearing uniforms. I wondered how much of the King's wealth taken from these settlements ever reached Kerek City.

Salik Oqina nodded at the men. "Welcome to Manumina, a Conrosan settlement in Kerek," he began formally. "I am Salik Oqina of the Council of Wisdom, our..."

"Yes, yes, yes." The Spice Islander waved his hands, and I noted how the rings caught the light and flashed in the watery sunshine. "Let's get this over with before the next bout of showers. I want to be in Sary in time for end of day meal. Do you have any wine to make this less tedious?"

"No, we don't, but if you are thirsty I can have someone draw you a cold drink from our well." He gestured to the pump on the green behind him. The Spice Islander sighed.

The other Tax Collector unrolled the papers in his hand. "Salik Oqina, how many people on your Council of Wisdom?"

"Three," Salik Oqina said confidently. I knew there were twelve, and kept my eyes locked on the ground. I wasn't even the one lying and I could feel my body growing anxious.

"Three," the Tax Collector repeated. "Do you have an armory?"

"No."

"An ironworker? A farrier? A healer? A horsemaster? A blacksmith?" The Tax Collector sighed, "Is there anyone who has a shred of intelligence or ambition in this place?"

"No to all," Salik replied, "We are all just living from hoe to fork."

I couldn't help myself. I shot Salik a look of surprise, and the Spice Islander saw it. He walked over to me, reached out, and pulled me forward.

"Who are you?"

I stopped breathing. Salik and Bett said my part was only to be a youth too young for the conscription but able-bodied enough. I was to stand with the other adults in the middle of the village green and be looked at—but not noticed. There were only six of us left behind in the entire settlement to represent the next generation of Conrosans—Mikale Oqina and me, the chandler's daughter, and the one everyone called Ivan who didn't speak but screamed if you touched him. There were two younger ones as well—about the age of Lost Girls in Kerek City. No one had told me what I was supposed to say or do if anyone spoke to me.

"My nephew," Bett sighed loudly. "Nice enough boy, can be taught common chores. Sometimes has trouble following directions. Even simple directions," she gave me a pointed look.

"Fine." The Spice Islander dropped my arm, and I shuddered out a long breath. The other one peered closer at me. "How old is he?"

"Fourteen," Salik Oqina said quickly, before I could even open my mouth.

"Fatten him up a bit, and in two, three years, he'll have learned enough to clean the army stables." The Tax Collector patted me on the shoulder. "How'd you like that, young man? See the world, buy your own drink, eh? Nice job for a fellow like you."

I stared at him. What did he think I was?

The Spice Islander looked about. "Houses built on the outside. Stables on the inside. What were you thinking?" He paused. "We'll check the stables, the arsenal." He pointed to the school building. "The round church, and three houses on each side." He pointed to the soldiers. "Two of you in each house, bring out anyone you find, food and coin lying about. Leave the livestock, I don't want to hear the noise or smell the stench all the way to Sary." He looked at Salik Oqina again. "Are you sure you don't have any wine about?"

Salik Oqina slowly shook his head.

Once the soldiers trotted out of the stockade, both Tax Collectors climbed back into the carriage to wait.

We stayed on the village green. I wasn't sure why, and I thought to ask Bett, but then I remembered I was supposed to be only smart enough to clean stables, so I kept my mouth shut. Thankfully, it wasn't raining—yet.

The time passed. I wondered what Rell was thinking in her enclosed space. I wondered how the ones in Vikland would know when it was safe to come back. I wondered what Chul was thinking and if he had dragged himself up to a window and was watching us. I wondered if he could make liquid fire out of Siba's potions and make the soldiers leave. I wondered if bandits followed the Tax Collectors from place to place. I wondered what might happen if Tax Collectors didn't show up when they were supposed to. I wondered where Piffik was. If he was going to come back today from his deliveries or if he would know the Tax Collectors were here and be able to avoid them.

Slowly, the soldiers came back. Some of them were pushing elderly Conrosans ahead of them. Others had their hands full of food, pottery, and bedding. It all seemed so random to me.

The Tax Collectors climbed out of the carriage again. The one unrolled the paper, and the soldiers began their reports. South side done, east side clear, north side inspected, west side checked. They went back to the wagons and poked through the belongings taken from the houses.

The Tax Collector looked up. "110 dias."

Salik Oqina paled. "We won't have that much coin until next harvest and only if we sell everything and save nothing for ourselves."

"If you had a boy to soldier for us, we could forgive that amount," the Spice Islander said.

I snapped my head up. Is this what happened to Rygee? He said his father had been forgiven three years. Was the Kerek King so desperate for soldiers?

The Spice Islander narrowed his eyes at me. "That's twice now, boy. I think you understand a lot more then you let on." He turned to the other. "Mark the tax, and take the boy. He's too small to fight but the army can use him for other things." He turned back and grinned at me. "You're a lucky boy. You're going to Kerek City to soldier for the King. Run along to the stable and saddle your horse."

I felt lightheaded and sick and afraid all at once. I was safe here at Manumina and now someone else wanted to take that away from me. Siba had said the Tax Collectors used to take people and they would never come back. Zadah had told me I would not die, but what did he know? He was hiding over the Vikland border. I wanted to refuse—*could I refuse?*—but I couldn't make my tongue work, my mouth was too dry with fear. My heart pounded painfully. I was sure everyone could hear it.

"We're waiting, boy. Don't make me order these soldiers to…"

"I don't know how to ride a horse." My words all ran together.

"Oh, for all the steel in…"

"He's too young." Salik Oqina took a step forward to stand between me and the Tax Collectors. "He's too young to soldier, he's too young to be out on his own."

"No. It will be all right," I said in Conrosan. I turned and shoved the key to unlock Rell out of her prison into Bett's hand. "I am Zren Janin." I quickly touched my pocket where I still carried my Sailor's Curse. "I have my Sword of Courage." I felt my eyes fill with tears, and I couldn't say anything more over the lump in my throat, so I quickly walked to the back of the closest wagon and climbed in among the bags and bedding.

CHAPTER 19

ESCAPE

It was full dark when we reached Sary. I had been alone in the wagon with my thoughts, and none of them had been cheerful. Once we reached the stables at Sary and I helped the others care for their horses, I learned many of those traveling with me were also new conscripts. They told me what they knew. The plan had been for the Tax Collectors to take the less dangerous Old Vikland Road first, then the Huntsman's Trail north, and finally west on the Northern Track when they had the most men along to fight bandits and cutthroats. Even the conscripts would fight, they said, for it meant their lives as well.

I tried to remember Piffik's map from the evening in the infirmary when he and Chul had shown me where I stood in the world. If I ran away, would it be enough? I knew I was fast, but I would need to have a destination to run to. I didn't know anyone along the Northern Track. Although Piffik had said that night which Justices were kind and which were corrupt, I wasn't sure which one I needed. One who was corrupt and could be bribed not to turn me back over to the Tax Collectors? Or one who was kind who would shelter me? If I ran, would the Tax Collectors just go back to Manumina and this time catch the others who had hidden in Vikland?

The Spice Islander came out to the stables then and had a small wooden tray of meat pies.

"One apiece," he said, as I reached for two. "The King isn't feeding you until we reach Earles, and I am not a rich man... yet."

Earles. I kept my head down so the Spice Islander wouldn't see my face. I wondered if I could remember the turn off to Earles. I wondered how I could make the garrison know not to shoot their crossbows at me as the wagons lumbered into sight. I remembered what Kern had said about "the waste of a good man" and wondered how many of these conscripts were just men who had no interest in soldiering, but no escape for it. I wondered how Vikland was able to keep its takeover of the Earles garrison such a secret. Was no one allowed to leave once they got there? I swallowed hard. Would I have to worry about the Viklanders too?

We were told to bed down in the loft above the stables. "Only the Tax Collectors sleep in the inn," the Spice Islander said. There were four actual soldiers who were supposed to take watches and guard the wagons. "Not that anyone would be so foolish as to leave," the Spice Islander continued, "We know who you are and we will just go back to your village, farm, or settlement."

That night, I had dreams of a handful of different ways I could die at Earles. I wondered if there was a story of Zren Janin like this and what I could do to survive the next day. I wondered why the Zren Janin in the fairy tales got an entire Legion of Heroes and a Sword of Courage to help him, and I only had a Sailor's Curse and an imperfectly remembered map of small trails and half-tracks.

We were kicked awake at first light.

I helped with the horses again, and then waited while the carriage and wagons were hitched. I still didn't have a plan, but I had information I didn't have yesterday and decons before we would reach the turn-off to the military garrison. If we didn't go to Earles, the next village would be Cloa. I know Piffik traveled there often and used a half-track across fields and pastures, avoiding the Northern Track all together. If I could find it, I could sleep rough and make my way back to Manumina. Either way, the day was better than yesterday when I thought I was going to be dragged all the way to Kerek City.

There was no food for first meal.

The wagons lurched down the road. Those who had them huddled under their travelers cloaks, those who did not shivered against the never-ending drizzle. As we crossed the bridge where Song Yao had lost her life, I let myself weep. My tears mingled in with the rain.

It felt like decons later. I was sure we had missed the road north, and I had been so lost in my misery I hadn't been paying attention. Suddenly the wagons stopped, and I lifted my head to take in my surroundings. It was the crossroads. I could see the same weathered sign now laying in the ditch, and moldy lumps of sand-colored cloth—I realized they were the uniforms Mouser, Nebs, and Rygee had tossed out of their wagon at the beginning of the Wet and left behind. I stretched and took another look all around. The wagon drivers were talking into the window of the carriage. No one would expect me to run *to* the garrison, I reasoned. I could warn them of who was coming and they could do something—I wasn't quite sure what.

The arrow thunked into the wagon wood beside me.

I didn't think. I just fled. Behind me, I heard the yells and screams of bandits and the answering cries of the four soldiers as they bravely tried to mount a defense. None of the conscripts had a weapon, and they were on plow horses, not battle horses.

I slipped into the shrubs and tried to catch my breath. My heart was pounding so hard I could hardly focus on anything else.

I could see three horses surrounding the carriage. The carriage driver was dead, slumped over the seat, and three cutthroats hidden deep in their cloaks were pounding and pulling on the carriage doors. The two men inside must have been able to brace the doors, but they were outnumbered. It would only be a moment before they would be pulled out and murdered. The conscripts on their horses bolted in every direction, but there was a hooded archer on a fine brown horse who sent arrows whizzing after them.

I needed to move. Somehow, I had escaped notice, or was deemed too little to bother with. But that wouldn't last. Carefully and slowly, I watched the tops of the shrubs as I took a step to the north. I remembered how at the Battle at the Bridge I had been able to track the children by the bushes moving as they ran away. I couldn't risk the same here.

It felt like it took me decons. To crawl forward a few steps, use a broken branch with leaves to wipe out my tracks, slow my breathing until I could hear everything around me, and then repeat the entire process. I was sure the bandits were celebrating their good fortune somewhere warm and dry, but it meant my life if I was wrong, and I was disinclined to gamble so casually.

My legs cramped. Tears and sweat and rain washed into and out of my eyes. Still, I crept forward. At last, I heard the distant sounds of living. People walking, horses, the smell of fire and of food. My stomach suddenly growled.

I risked a look. The gates of the Earles stockade were closed of course, but I was only a few furloughs away. I still didn't have a plan for not getting killed with a bolt as soon as I got within range. I was sure any bowmaster could shoot farther than I could shout as I begged for help. I was on my hands and knees watching the fort when I heard a soft footfall. I spun around and was promptly knocked to the ground by a jeong bong. I lay perfectly still with my hands open and away from my body. I felt my heart racing again, and I was sure she could smell the fear sweat on me. It had stopped raining at least.

The soldier stood over me just out of reach of my hands, legs, anything. Meanwhile, she held the jeong bong easily, and I knew she had intentionally tried not to kill me.

"Who are you?" she asked in Keresh.

I talked quickly, "I am Zren Janin of Manumina. A friend to you and yours. I seek sanctuary. I am a friend of First Soldier Joon, Miyamoto Suki, Bima Ritwik..." I glanced at her jeong bong. "I had the privilege to know Song Yao—a great bongmaster of Vikland. It would be a shame to lose my life now at your hand after she saved it... twice."

Her eyes narrowed. "Friend of First Soldier Joon? I hardly think so."

"Well, maybe not friends," I conceded, "but I met him at the embasado in Kerek City. Could you please just take me to your garrison? I could tell the entire story so much better if I had food and a warm fire to sit by."

She snorted, stepped back, and motioned me to get up. I carefully held my open palms out and away so she wouldn't mistake any moves I made for threats. I wanted to brush the mud and leaves from my soggy clothes but I didn't dare. We walked slowly towards the fort.

At the gates, she called out in Vik. She spoke for a while without anything happening so I assumed I was being announced with my entire life story. I wished they had a Secondo who would order a soft bed and a hot bath for me, but at this point I was ready to settle just for food and a dry corner. At last, a small side door opened, and three Viklander soldiers stepped out, all with crossbows up and pointed at me. An older man stepped out behind them.

He asked me a question in Vik, and when I didn't respond, asked again in Keresh, "Who are you?"

"I seek sanctuary. Miyamoto Suki told me this place belonged to Vikland. I am Zren Janin of Manumina. A friend to you and yours. Please, I seek sanctuary."

"Why were you on this road?" He didn't seem sympathetic to my troubles.

"I was taken yesterday by the Tax Collectors in payment for Manumina's debt. We spent the night in Sary. Our wagon train was traveling west and found by bandits at the crossroads. I fled north because I knew you were here and could help me get home to Manumina." I added in a small voice, "I traveled with Song Yao and Rell Huena and Chul Swyler and Kern the Softfoot on Miyamoto Suki's thirteenth crossing. It is how I knew to find my way here."

The soldier took a deep breath, and I found myself holding my breath as well. I knew the next words out of his mouth could determine whether I lived or died, and I had no further say in the matter.

"Blindfold him."

I let out my breath in a long shuddering sigh. I braced myself but kept my empty hands out as a Kereki tie was roughly wrapped about my head and tied. The voices continued talking—now in Vik—but they didn't sound angry. I thought I might have heard, "Kern," but I wasn't sure.

I was taken through the door, and the noises of the fort suddenly got louder. I could smell heat as we passed close to an outdoor fire and then into a dry building. I relaxed. I heard a heavy wooden door scrape open, I was pushed through, and then the door banged shut. I quickly reached for the blindfold and when no one said anything, I pulled it off.

It was a room so small I could reach from wooden wall to wooden wall. There was an empty chamber pot in the corner and a wooden bucket of water in the other one. There was a cut log no longer than my thigh but wide enough to sit on. I was out of the drizzle, with people who spoke at least some Keresh, and no longer on my way to Kerek City. It may have been a Viklander jail, but I smiled at my surroundings.

A few decons later and I was no longer smiling.

Outside I could hear the sounds of wagons coming, voices shouting, horses, and people in a small space. I thought I might have been forgotten and tried to remind myself this was still better than Kerek City. I was out of the drizzle, and no one was hurting me.

Suddenly a door opened, and a dim light threw the soldier in dark shadows. I raised my arm to protect myself and braced myself for a blow.

"Zren Janin," she said, "I shouldn't be surprised to see you here. If you taught me anything on the Northern Track, it was always to expect the unexpected where you are concerned."

I dropped my arm. "Kern?" I straightened. "Kern, is that you?"

She stepped out of the shadows, and I could see it truly was her. She was dressed as a Kereki woman and her long braid was twisted up and under a funny scarf on her head, but it was definitely her.

"Thank the stars! It is you!" I paused. "Kern, I am so hungry. Could I have food, please?"

Kern laughed, even though I couldn't figure out what I had said that was so funny.

"Well, now I know you are definitely the Zren Janin I know. Anyone else would be worried whether they would live to see another day." She paused. "I'll bring you some food, and then we will need to ask you some questions." She turned back to me as she started to walk out the door. "You are safe here, Zren. We only had to put you in here because of something else, not because of you or where you came from. Do you understand? You are not a prisoner."

I nodded and closed my eyes to wait for the food.

＊ ＊ ＊ ＊ ＊

There was a soldier who brought a vegetable stew, bread, and fresh water to drink in a West Islands steel flask. He asked me if I had traveled from Conrosa or had been born at Manumina. I said I thought I had been born in Kerek City, but I had been to Matasi and had sailed on a ship. He didn't seem impressed and left me alone with my food.

Kern and another soldier came a little while later. She had changed back into the dark Viklander clothes, and he was dressed the same. They led me out of my cell, down a very short hall to a larger room in the same building. There were two windows, but both had been covered with grey Kereki shirts. Light came in the room, but I couldn't see out. Kern gestured to a table with four chairs, and the three of us sat down.

Kern pushed a small plate of rough pottery with two kolaches on it to me.

"I'd offer you coffee, Zren, but I know how you insulted Ambassador Lalsy by refusing to drink with her."

I looked at her startled. *I had insulted an ambassador?* Kern laughed and turned to the soldier. "I would like to introduce you to Zren Janin. He traveled with Viklanders on the last official crossing of the Northern Track. He protected us, he fought for us, and he found us a place of sanctuary at the Conrosan settlement of Manumina. They have healed and harbored our soldiers before. It is as he says, he is a friend to us." She paused. "Zren speaks no language but Keresh."

I said nothing. I didn't expect either one of them to suddenly burst into Conrosan, but I didn't know what I would gain by giving the information away either. The soldier said something in Vik, and Kern gave a huge sigh.

"I am sorry, Zren, I shall need to translate. I appear to be working with yet another soldier who couldn't pass his languages at the Academy." She grinned at me. "I promise to make your bravery so impressive he will regret ever volunteering for this."

She said something in Vik, and I watched his face. He didn't look at her, only at me. Kern on the other hand, had the same bemused look I had remembered when she had introduced herself to me in the embasado in Kerek City.

"So. Tell us from the beginning. How did you end up here in Earles?" she began.

I took a deep breath. "The Tax Collectors took me to be a Kereki soldier to pay the debt for Manumina. Remember when we were on the crossing? And Rygee—you remember Rygee?— told us how his father had sold him for three years of freedom of taxes and tithes? I think it was like that. Only the Tax Collector took me without permission."

"How much was the tax?"

"110 dias," I responded.

Her eyebrows shot up. "I shall have to treat you much better, Zren. I didn't know you were so valuable to the King." She laughed and I smiled back at her. She really had a smile that just made you want to make her smile again.

She turned to the soldier beside her and spoke quickly in Vik. He quirked an eyebrow as well, and I straightened in my chair. I thought I needed to look like I was worth 110 dias.

"So I heard you spent the night in Sary?" She looked back at me. "Is this true? Tell me what happened next."

I explained how there were only four soldiers, all the rest of the men were those like me who had been taken to pay the King's tithes and taxes. The two Tax Collectors slept in the inn, one of them was a Spice Islander—he was nicer and had given us all a meat pie, but we were to sleep in the stables with the wagons. We had left at first light and had stopped at the road to Earles.

"I remembered it, Kern, because the sign was still there but tipped, and I think I saw the Kereki uniforms in the mud."

She nodded and I went on. "I was trying to decide if I should run for Earles. What would I need to say so your soldiers wouldn't shoot me with their crossbows? I didn't know what the Tax Collectors would do, would they chase me? Let me go and just go back to Kerek City? Or would they return to Manumina and take someone else."

I took a deep breath. "Then there were bandits. I ran and hid in the shrubs, and then I knew they would look for me if they saw me, so I crawled and crouched my way here. I thought I would beg for sanctuary, and then I would worry about how to get to Manumina later. Or perhaps someone would have a plan and I could follow them." I tried to sound hopeful and helpful at the same time.

Kern didn't say anything, just watched me as she spoke Vik to the other soldier. I noticed how both of them watched me.

"What?" I asked.

The other soldier spoke, and Kern translated, "How many bandits were there?"

I looked at him incredulously. "There were arrows shot at me and you want to know if I took the time to count how many bandits there were?"

Kern laughed and didn't stop for a long time. "Ah, Zren, you make the best faces."

I scowled at her. "That's what Rell says. But that's because she is making up things about her little brothers and thinks I will not know any better."

Kern sobered. "How is Rell? And Chul? Are they still at Manumina?"

I nodded. "They are still living in the infirmary. Chul cannot use his hands. Rell's wounds have healed, but she fought infections for a very long time. Both are still too weak to travel to Vikland."

She nodded sadly. "Take care of them, Zren, we need them both."

"How will I get back to Manumina?" I cocked my head. "Can you make that happen?"

She smiled. "*I* can't, but we are still working on this. It looks like you will be a guest of ours tonight. We hope to give you a better bed than your welcoming cell. This building is small but with only three rooms it serves us well. For now, we will have to lock you in here. I am sorry. Again, it is not you."

Both Viklanders stood. "Is there anything we can bring you?" Kern asked. "You are not a prisoner here. Our accommodations for you are less than the embasado, but we don't entertain here often."

I hesitated. "Could I have dry clothes…and more food?"

"Of course, I will have someone bring some as soon as we can find some that may fit." She gave me one of her dazzling smiles. "It is good to see you again, Zren Janin. I had hoped Manumina would treat you well."

CHAPTER 20

IN THE TENDER CARE OF VIKLANDERS

We passed the other open cell, and I was locked in the same room as before. The chamber pot had been emptied, the log had been replaced with a real chair, and a small table had been added. Soon someone came with dry clothes—I was surprised to see they were the Kereki style baggy pants and a clean sand-colored shirt with a fresh dark brown tunic. There were even boot linings and small clothes and a dry pair of leather boots. The soldier took mine away and said he would try to wash out the mud and at least dry the boots before tomorrow. I hoped that meant I would return to Manumina soon.

I smiled to myself and thought how I would tell this story to Siba Namikk and the others. Then I sobered, wondering if all the Conrosans were back from their quick flight to Vikland, who had unlocked Rell from the chest in Siba's room, if Piffik had made it back without harm, and what they were thinking about me—if they were thinking about me. I sighed.

I wondered about Kern's visit earlier. I knew Kern had been sent to ask the questions because she was known to me, just as I knew the soldier with her understood every Keresh word that fell from my lips. Kern hadn't bothered to translate the entire last part of our conversation, and he hadn't been concerned enough to ask her about it.

I wondered if they would hunt the bandits. I knew the settlements around Earles had been told that was the garrison's purpose when the Viklander soldiers first came. I wondered why the bandits had chosen to strike so close to the fort. I wondered if they had been following us on the southern rises, like the traders had when Rell had spotted them on our crossing at the end of the Dry. I wondered why we had stopped at the crossroads at all. If we were meant to go to Earles, why not just turn and travel north? Why had the wagon drivers all been away from their wagons talking with the Tax Collectors in the carriage when the bandits struck? I thought I would entertain myself by puzzling it out.

When that didn't work, I told myself Conrosan fairy tales so I wouldn't forget them before I had time to write them all down in my books of pressed papers.

I heard hammering outside my wooden door. It sounded like it came from the building I was in, although on the other side. Soon, another soldier came to get me.

"We have a better room for you." I followed her down the short hall to the same room where Kern and the soldier had talked to me earlier.

The Kereki shirts were still covering the windows, but now it didn't matter. Wooden shutters had been nailed over the outside to block out everything. There was a small lantern lit on the table where we had sat earlier, and now there was food there as well. A rope bed had been hastily assembled in the corner away from the windows. No pillow but a thick blanket.

"You can sleep after you eat. No one will come into this room until tomorrow morning. Use the chamber pot in your old cell, there is none in here and I am not bringing it to you." She turned and walked out of the room leaving the door open. She walked out of the building, and I heard the sound of a wooden board sliding across to bar the door.

My first panicky thought was I was trapped inside. Then I reasoned it out. I had food, a bed, dry clothes, and an entire military garrison to keep watch for bandits. If I believed Kern, and there was no reason I should not, then I was as safe as if I were at home at Manumina. I was safe and warm and dry. I sat down and ate my end of day meal, and then tucked myself into bed. After the fear and uncertainty of the last two days, I slept without dreams or nightmares.

CHAPTER 21

A BARGAIN IS MADE

First meal was oats and honey. It was hot and fresh which was the only forgivable thing about it. With the windows barricaded shut, there was no daylight streaming in the room. I felt as if I was getting up in the middle of the night. The soldier who brought my own clothes which I had worn yesterday—now clean but still damp—was as out of sorts as I was. Any question I asked was rebuffed with a curt, "Later."

This time Kern was accompanied by the man who had met me outside the fort and demanded I be blindfolded. I was sure I had him to thank for the wooden shutters. I thought of what I needed to do to convince him to help me get home to Manumina. What would Ngahuru or Miyamoto Suki say or do? I stood from my meal and gave him a small Vikland bow with my hands folded together.

"Thank you for the gift of untroubled sleep. I rested deeply knowing my Viklander friends had provided so well for me with hot food, dry clothes, and a warm bed. Vikland is a true friend to me, Zren Janin of Manumina."

Kern snorted and quickly looked away. The soldier just looked at me suspiciously.

"I am told you do not ride a horse."

I shook my head. "I have never learned such a skill. My Viklander friends, however, have taught me how to drive a wagon, care for horses, and hobble them at night so they do not disappear in the dark."

"We have treated you well yesterday and today," he began and then grimaced, "as well as we could."

I smiled agreeably. This felt promising.

"We would like you to drive a horse and wagon to Manumina for us. Once you are there, either you—or a person who speaks Vik preferably—will drive this same wagon to Ishes, without unloading it, without going through Sary or using the Northern Track. Do not draw any attention to yourself. Do you know your way through the back country well enough for this?"

I nodded my head slowly. He obviously didn't know I hadn't left Manumina since I had arrived there at the beginning of the last Wet. I worried what would happen to me if I was not useful enough to him. But I remembered Piffik's map—a little—and I thought I only had to angle south, southeast until I came to the Huntsman's Trail. From there I should be able to find my way. I hoped.

"What about bandits? Will I have a weapon?"

"The bandits from yesterday will not bother you. They will not bother anyone again. Your wagon will have two Viklanders who need to go to Vikland as quickly as possible. They will be hidden, but well-armed. Obviously, they cannot ride on the Northern Track, and we don't have ways to have so few travel east safely. We ask you to do this for us just as we cared for you and are returning you to your home at Manumina. Is this acceptable to you?"

I looked at Kern. "What about the Tax Collectors? What will happen if I do not show in Kerek City? Do you know?"

Kern looked at the soldier and he nodded. She answered me, "The Tax Collector and his carriage were left on the Northern Track and the Justice of Cloa sent for. The soldiers and conscripts were left where they fell. It will be assumed by those in Kerek City there were no survivors, and Manumina's tax will be considered paid until next year. Remember the massacred settlers we encountered on the way to Huk? We ensured the bandits will not harm anyone again, but the rest of it? It is a Kereki matter." She lifted her shoulders and let them drop.

I slowly nodded my understanding, but I wanted to be clear. "I hear what you are not saying, Kern. In exchange for surviving the massacre of the Tax Collectors and soldiers, I will drive a horse and wagon to Manumina. There I will have another—one who speaks Vik—drive to Ishes. He will be unharmed, yes?" I asked quickly.

"Yes." Kern smiled. "We wish Manumina to be a friend to us. They have offered us sanctuary and we have done the same for you. We are not your enemy, Zren Janin."

"Good," the commander said briskly. "I know the trip will take far into the night or even two days, if it is not safe to drive the half-tracks after dark. The Viklanders are ready to go, food and supplies have been loaded."

"My clothes are still damp." I tried not to whine.

"Take them with you and wear the dry ones you have on. Your cloak is damp—there is no help for it—we don't have another for you. But you are alive and going back to Manumina. Think on that as the drizzle settles on you today."

I grinned at Kern. "Thank you."

She shrugged, but grinned back. "It may be we meet again, Zren Janin. We need to do a kindness for each other when we can."

* * * * *

Kern brought me a travel pack, I shoved in my damp belongings, and then she blindfolded me again. I felt her warm dry hand in mine, and she led me out of the room, the building, and across the fort. The sounds of living quieted as soon as the small door to the outside shut firmly behind us. She took off the blindfold and gestured to the horses and cart in front of me.

"I am trusting you, Zren Janin. Get those soldiers home to Vikland as quickly as possible. Take care of Rell and Chul. Come to Vikland someday and put your feet under my table." She patted my cheek. "Keep that pretty face away from Kereki soldiers!"

And that was how I left her. We were both laughing. A weak sun was just coming up over the edge of the world, and I knew all I had to do was keep it on the side of my face—one side or the other—until I saw Manumina.

At the intersection with the Northern Track, the broken carriage lay on its side. It had been heavily damaged, and I didn't think it could ever be repaired to work again. I looked about for the other wagons, but there was nothing in sight. The bandits had probably taken them with them. But then Kern had said the Viklanders had hunted the bandits and eliminated them... didn't she? So where were the wagons and horses? I turned left and immediately an angry sound came from the back of the wagon.

"No Northern Track."

I stopped and turned around to face one of the Viklanders. He had a crossbow up and loaded and pointed at me.

"I have to… just for a little ways," I explained quickly. "The half-tracks are small and look like wagon wheels passing in the cheatgrass and pastures. I can't just drive anywhere. If the owners find us on their land, they have the right to kill us where we are for trespassing. Trust me. I want to go home too. I am not going to do something stupid."

Not intentionally anyway, I thought to myself. The Viklander put the crossbow down.

"We are watching you."

I scowled. "Well, if you want to be truly helpful, hide that braid of yours, sit up here on the wagon seat with me and help look for the trails."

The two Viklanders talked for a moment, and I looked around. I wondered if any of the other conscripts escaped. I knew I was the only one who headed north, but what about the others? From the little I had seen, everyone had scattered, only the uniformed soldiers had made any attempt to protect the carriage and wagons. *Where were the wagons?*

There was movement in the back and the other Viklander stood up and dropped her braid between her shirt and her neck. She swirled her cloak about her and tipped the hood up, hiding who she was. She stepped over the seat and sat down hard beside me.

Then she turned to me, gave me a quick smile, and said, "Better?"

"Yes," I grumped. I snapped the reins, and we were on our way.

* * * * *

It took us two days to reach Manumina. I didn't care to remember the number of wrong turns I made. Whenever I took a half-track that led to someone's home and fields, I would greet anyone I met loudly in Keresh, so I didn't end up with a quarrel in my back from my distrustful Viklanders. Most people were startled enough to wave back, one even came over to the wagon and gave me directions to where I should have gone. I hastily scrambled down and met him at the front of the horses. The Viklanders had hidden under their cloaks in the back.

By the time I finally recognized the Huntsman's Trail and the breakaway to Manumina just a little ways north, I was so relieved I thought the Viklanders behind me would sense it. And then they would realize I had been lost for nearly half the day.

The gates were closed when we reached Manumina. I talked over my shoulder at the two Viklanders, telling them I would need to get off the wagon, go in the side door, and find someone to help me open the big gates. I told them Conrosans were peaceable. No one would harm them. They jumped out of the wagon and said they would come in with me anyway. They told me to wait until they were fully armed. I waited.

We left the horses and wagon outside the gates and walked inside the small side door.

It looked like Manumina again. There were people walking across the green, children playing. All the sounds of a settlement scurrying to take advantage of a few moments of sunshine before the rains started again. I tried to find one of the Council of Wisdom. I wanted Salik Oqina, but finally decided to take them to the infirmary. I would ask Siba Namikk what to do next.

Siba wasn't there, but Chul and Rell were. There were surprised yelps, and happy greetings in Vik. All four of them tried to talk over each other. Bett came out of the kitchen with a mortar and pestle in her hand to see what the commotion was all about. I told her I had horses and a wagon still standing outside of the gates. She gave me a big smile, told me she was glad to see me again, and then she sent me to Vigdis saying she would sort out the Viklanders.

Vigdis helped me open a gate. He said he would take care of the horses and told me to look for Salik Oqina in Piffik's workshop. I told him not to touch anything in the wagon bed. There were two Viklanders in the infirmary who would hold me responsible.

"They are armed," I said ominously. He smiled at me and said nothing would be touched.

* * * * *

I was glad Salik and Piffik were both in one place. After their initial shock at seeing me return, they sat me down in Piffik's corner where he wrote his orders and made me start the story from the moment I left Manumina.

I told them the Viklanders said the Tax Collectors had died in the battle with the bandits, but Manumina's tax would be considered paid for the year. I said I had met the Softfoot who had been to Manumina in the past, and she said we were not her enemy and they were glad to do us a kindness because of kindness given to them in the past.

Salik Oqina smiled and told me solemnly, "We can never underestimate the good we can do in the world."

I told them what I had promised in exchange for a way home, and Piffik said he would take the Viklanders immediately to Ishes. He would tie a horse behind the wagon, and ride home the same night. He wasn't worried, so I didn't think I needed to be either. I asked if it was all right for me to go to my home and my bed. Both men smiled but agreed.

My adventure was over, and I was glad of it.

CHAPTER 22

ZREN JANIN AND THE VILLAGE GEESE

The chandler had me carefully skim off the dead bees and bits of old honeycomb as we heated the wax. As we worked, I asked her where the wax came from. She said it was from the honeycombs from the ground bees nesting east of the orchards. I didn't know bees, I said. She smiled and told me what they were and how they helped the people of Manumina.

"But you must never disturb their nesting grounds, Zren, we have two people who do nothing but tend the bees and make sure the bees tend our orchards. The beekeepers know how much honey to take and when the honeycombs can be dug out of the ground and shared with me. This is not work anyone can do. The only time you will have to worry about the bees is when it is harvest and everyone is out in the orchards picking the fruit for all of us. They like to sting us then, for they think we are taking away all their food." She laughed at my horrified expression.

We talked as she gathered the other ingredients for making the soft soap everyone in the settlement would use to wash their dishes, their clothes, and themselves. She explained what she had: ashes from fireplaces, the blossoms and powdered leaves from the healers, a little goat milk, a little olive oil all the way from south Kerek or Matasi. I carefully stirred them in the mixture until it looked like a thick soup. I asked her how she had learned to make soap. She said she had been an apprentice when she was younger than I was and took it over when it was her time.

"Do you have an apprentice now?" I asked idly.

"No. There was one who started with me, but she went to the academies at Vikland." She looked sad. "Once they leave Manumina, none come back to the settlement."

I looked up at her. "Are you going to get another one? An apprentice, I mean?"

"Of course. Someday. We know Rygee has found his home in the bakery, and they are glad to have him. We do not know if your two friends in the infirmary are planning on staying or not, and what their talents are." She smiled at me. "We do not know if *you* are planning on staying or not, and what your talents are. By having you try so many tasks as a manabout, you can see if there is something you wish to do beyond all other choices."

We spent the rest of the day working comfortably together. She asked me about my travels. I told her of my favorite night in Matasi listening to Koanga tell West Islands Constellation tales at the home of Ebla Potenco in Anarkio. She said there were others who would like to hear my stories of where I had gone and what I had done. I said I did not think my Conrosan was good enough to tell stories. She said I needed to practice. I couldn't succeed if I never tried. So I asked the chandler to give me all of the Conrosan names of the things I touched and I gave her the Keresh name. At the end of the day, we skimmed the blossoms and leaves and the last of the impurities off the top and poured the near boiling soupy mess into the wooden molds to harden into the finished soap that would be sold to the shops in Sary, Ahni, and Cloa.

We added a little more water to the remainder of the soap in the pots to stretch it for the rest of us in the settlement. The chandler said she would put the word out that night and people in Manumina could just bring a small pottery bowl to collect their share when they had time.

Before I left for the day, she asked me to drop off a bowl of soap for Bett and Siba at the infirmary.

* * * * *

I heard the cries as soon as I walked in the infirmary door. Chul was sitting up in his big chair with his leg elevated and a concerned look on his face. I followed his gaze to see Bett holding Rell and rocking her like a child. Rell was crying, bawling like a Lost Girl who had every coin stolen by another before her protector found her.

"What's wrong?" I asked anxiously.

Chul lifted his shoulders and dropped them. "She started when she woke up, or her nightmares woke her up. Bett can't get her out of her head to talk to her and tell her she is safe."

"Come here, Zren," Bett commanded. "Sit by me, and don't stop talking. Tell her about your day, what you are learning, tell her one of your stories. I don't care. Just talk to her and don't stop."

I panicked. Chul saw my face and said gently, "You'll be fine, Zren. Think of the campfires on the Northern Track. Could you tell us another one of those stories? You could tell another story of Zren Janin, I know we haven't heard them all. Or maybe one of the funny ones of the Constellations from the West Islands. It doesn't matter. She just needs to hear your voice and come back to us."

I nodded and sat down on the other side of Rell. I couldn't bear to look at her, so I focused on Chul. I took a deep breath.

"Rell, this story is called Zren Janin and the Goose." I stopped. "No, it's not. I forgot its name. There isn't even a goose in it. Or at least, a real goose…oh never mind. Here's the story," I began.

"In the days of long ago, the border between Conrosa and Fairyland was not so well guarded as it is today. Sprites and goblins, monsters without names, and mists without faces would dance in the land of the humans to cause trouble and strife.

In those times there was a hero born. No one in Conrosa knew his parents, his age, or his place of birth. He called himself Zren Janin.

Now Conrosa is a land of forests and meadows, waterfalls, mists, and four seasons. It is the land of plenty and there is time at the end of the day for song and story and laughter and kindness.

It was just before midday, and Zren Janin was traveling on the road to Wisdom, the city where the Queen and her two daughters resided. It was the Season of Hope in Conrosa, and all about Zren were the signs of a world coming back to itself after the Season of Rest. Families were planting in the fields, children were walking off to school, goatherds and shepherdesses were ambling along behind their flocks moving them from paddocks to pastures.

It was a fine day, and Zren Janin was a fine man and well pleased with the world and himself.

As the day and Zren ambled along, he came upon a crowd surrounding a girl sitting tousled on the ground, her pony cart upset beside her, and a pony nearly a furlough away cropping contentedly on some fresh tender grass.

"Well, what's this?" Zren Janin cried as he shouldered in for a better look. For Zren Janin was such a curious fellow, he was always looking about at this and that to weave a new story.

"She's spoiling her new frock," cried one woman. "For shame, to be so wasteful!"

"She must have abused her poor pony for him to run so far away! How awful!" an old man pronounced sharply as he waved his shepherd's hook in the air.

"Well, I don't know her. Strangers like that must not know any better. I wish they would just stay where they belong," sneered another.

"She's obviously in trouble. A runaway no doubt. Just one more burden for the village," sighed the mayor.

Zren looked about at all the people crowding around. "Has anyone asked her what she needs?"

"Of course not!"

"No."

"Why should we?"

"It's obvious she's just lazy."

"Would she even understand us? To play in the dirt at her age must mean she is simple-minded." The crowd was indignant at Zren's suggestion.

Zren Janin shook his head at their foolishness. He walked forward and crouched down beside the girl. "What needs to be done here?" he asked her gently.

She looked him steady in the face. "My cart needs to be turned upright, my pony caught, and the traces mended enough so I can travel home to the village beyond the next one. I could do all those things myself, but my crutch fell out of my cart a little ways back. When I reached to grab it, I overbalanced the cart and frightened my pony away."

Zren Janin stood. He tipped the pony cart upright. He rocked it forward and backward to be sure the wheels still turned. Then he reached into his pocket for the apple that was to be his lunch and walked slowly towards the pony. All the while the crowd murmured against him—the girl was only taking advantage of his kindness and generosity; he was only encouraging sloth and laziness; she broke the wagon, she should be the one who fixed it.

Zren said nothing. He led the pony back to the cart and soothed it with soft words while he hitched it back to its traces. He checked them for damage and knew the cart and pony would get the girl safely home to the village beyond the next one.

Then he lifted the girl out of the dirt and placed her gently on the tiny cart. He walked to the front by the pony's head, turned it around, led it by the sullen crowd, and down the road.

"Now tell me what your cane is like, and I shall pick it up for you," Zren told the girl.

A few paces on and the girl pointed out her crutch, half in and half out of the ditch. Zren Janin picked it up, checked it carefully to be sure it was not broken, and handed it back to her. He nodded his head towards her hands. She picked up the reins, and once again they turned and trotted past the crowd. Zren Janin kept pace easily beside her.

Once they were quite clear of the crowd of villagers, the girl said, "Thank you! I would have been pleased just to have you walk back and find my crutch for me, but you did so much more! I can care for myself, but when I stumble, I need a little help from those around me."

Zren nodded in agreement. "I could have done only that. There are people in the world who are like geese. They squawk and honk, but do nothing more than set up an alarm. There are neighbors who would pick up your cane and tip their cap as they handed it to you, leaving you to gather yourself and your cart and your pony and travel on your way. And there are friends, who help you gather yourself, ensure all is well, and then travel with you on your journey a little way or a lot."

He raised an eyebrow and mischievously smiled, "I didn't want to be one of the geese!" He stepped back from the cart as she continued trotting down the road.

It took her a moment to rein in her little pony and turn back to look at the young man who helped her.

The road was empty except for her pony and cart.

She smiled to herself as she picked up the reins and continued on her way to her own hearth and home. She knew she had met Zren Janin, a changeling fae so in love with the humans, he stepped in to be their champion.

I stopped, uncertain on what to do next. Rell had stopped crying, but she was still making great shuddering sighs. Bett had loosened her arms. I suddenly realized the healer hadn't been comforting Rell but restraining her while she was lost among her nightmares.

"Is she going to be all right?" I questioned anxiously.

Even though I was looking at the healer, Chul answered. "She will be. But it will take a long time. This sometimes happens to the Viklander soldiers when they must take a life. Some recover quickly, some learn to manage their trauma at a great cost to themselves, and some never accept what has happened and live hidden away from others where they can do no harm to themselves or others."

I snapped my face to him. "Rell?"

He nodded slowly. "She is a healer and a bowmaster. She cannot forgive herself for firing upon children and for not firing quickly enough to save Song Yao. You see the problem? She will relive that battle over and over until she can find a way through to forgive herself for two opposing deeds. It is up to her whether she can fight those monsters and win."

Bett looked at me. "You will need to come back tomorrow. You and Chul were also at the battle, you can talk to her. Anyone else she will not believe because we were not there. We did not see what she saw. We did not do what she was forced to do."

I nodded slowly. I didn't want to come. *But what would happen if I did not?*

"I have to go now. The chandler sent me here to bring you this." I handed the bowl of soft soap to Bett and once I was out of the infirmary, I ran as fast as I could back to my house on the outside of the stockade.

Rygee was already asleep but had left the door unbarred for me. I slipped the wood in place, blew out the night lantern sitting on the table, and ran up to my bedroom. Once I was hiding underneath the covers, I curled into a tight ball. I wondered what Rell's monsters looked like…and if I would recognize them if they came for me.

CHAPTER 23

CONROSAN PLOW HORSES

One morning I woke to blue skies. No one had bought my time that day. I had finished making my bed, hanging up the cleanish clothes I had tossed on the floor the night before, and throwing my dirty clothes in the washtub. I still did not take my clothes to the laundry as Rygee did, but I had cleverly discovered I could wash my clothes at the same time I took my bath at night. I couldn't believe everyone didn't do it my way. Or maybe they did, and Siba was trying to make me work longer by making me wash out my small clothes and boot linings separately. In any case, I certainly wasn't going to tell Siba, she would think I needed more chores.

I headed downstairs to see if Rygee had left any food I could eat before I went to work in Piffik's woodworking shop. He had. I ate all the fetti on the plate while I waited for the water to heat up so I could wash the pottery from the day before.

Rygee and I had come to a new agreement since I refused to learn how to cook. He would make all our meals for us if I would clean the pottery and pots. I agreed as long as I could do washing up any time I pleased—which usually turned out to be the next day or later. He had given a deep sigh, muttered "small steps" under his breath, and then had gone for a long walk outside.

I had just piled a number of plates and cups into the water and flicked a small chunk of soft soap in with them when I heard a knock at the door. I yelled for them to come in. Aajan walked through the common room and found me with my arms up to my elbows in hot water.

"I would like to teach you to ride a horse, Zren Janin," she began without any greeting. "I have heard from Chul Swyler this is a skill you are lacking. Piffik says I may have been gifted a horse for my speed, but I cannot ride the horse outside the stockade without someone with me. What good is a fast horse if it only stands in a stable and becomes ill-tempered because it is not ridden?" She gave me one of her sly smiles. "Zren Janin, the champion of Conrosa, is here in Manumina and he does not ride a horse. Can you believe such a thing?"

I squinted at her. "I am not going to learn to ride on a fast horse that can dump me on the ground and be to the Vikland border before I pull my face out of the dust."

"Of course not, Zren!" She gave me a broad smile and I began to feel uneasy. "I would not think of such a thing! I have found Old Dris, a horse so slow with a back so wide you will think you are riding on your bed. I have heard you are quite fond of your pillow."

I gave her a pointed look, and she just looked back innocently. "The horses are already saddled and tied to your porch. It would not do for my brother, Piffik, to see you abuse the horses by leaving them saddled and tied waiting half the day for you to make up your mind."

I waved a soapy hand at the kitchen. "You will help me with the washing up when we get back?" I asked.

She gave me a grin. "Of course."

We did not ride long that first day, I could not figure out how to sit well. As Aajan helped me with the washing up, she promised me it would get better.

And it did, little by little. There were several of the old plow horses with gaits so smooth and slow, I could plod along and keep her in sight while she rode Nebs'—her—horse at speeds she and the horse enjoyed. We would go out every Rest Day, or whenever my time was my own, even in the miserable rains when no one else would be out and about the settlement.

We rode farther and farther south and east from Manumina. Either Piffik noticed, or someone said something to him, but one day Aajan came with the horses—and with Piffik carrying a Viklander crossbow. I recognized it as Rell's, as it was bigger and heavier than the one I had carried in my wagon on the Northern Track.

"If you are going to take Aajan so far from Manumina, then you must protect her. You should know, Zren Janin, my mother considers her the jewel of the family, and one worthy of extraordinary care."

I raised an eyebrow. "And if I refuse? Or say I cannot shoot Rell's bow?"

"Then Aajan cannot ride outside the stockade gates," Piffik said simply.

I saw Aajan frantically signaling me from behind Piffik's back. I blew out a noisy breath and held out my hand for the crossbow and the other for a handful of bolts. Before we left for our ride, I dutifully hung it from my pommel on the saddle. I thought I should tell Piffik I couldn't shoot the thing. But I knew it had cost him something, a man of non-violence, to ask such a request of me. I knew he had not made an idle threat, Aajan would be forbidden to ride outside the gates if there was no one with her. It was not that she was weak or helpless, it was only to remain in compliance with Kereki custom of a male protector. I also understood the freedom riding gave her and why she loved it so much. She longed to break free of Manumina's walls as much as I loved to feel them wrapped safely around me.

* * * * *

Siba made me go back and visit Rell.

Chul continued to mend as far as he was able. He had a soft chair next to his bed in the infirmary and a bench with a small table. He would move about the three during the day to relieve the pressure on his body. His burned leg did not bend. And even after the bandages came off his hands and wrists, the scar tissue was so thick he could not fold his fingers. Piffik and Siba made mittens for him with little pockets to tuck in a wooden spoon and fork so he could feed himself. But although they tried many different ways, no one could figure out how to make it possible for him to hold a graphite and draw his thoughts and pictures for his inventions. Bett or Siba would visit with him while they worked in their still room or tended to Rell.

Rell would lay on her bed facing the wall. She did not talk to us. She did not acknowledge I was in the room most of the time. Sometimes she would have tear tracks down her face from weeping all day. Some days she did not eat. I could not imagine a sickness of the mind that would not let you eat.

"Talk to her, Zren," Bett would say and then walk upstairs to her rooms to sleep for a bit.

"Tell her stories, Zren," Siba would say and then would reach for her cloak and walk outside to escape the sickroom for a while.

"Keep her with us, Zren," Chul would rumble and then sit quietly in his soft chair while I sat on the edge of Rell's bed and talked.

I told Rell I had asked everyone to talk to me in Conrosan so I would learn the words quickly, but sometimes I took too long to think about the Keresh word in my head.

"I think I hear the Conrosan words for 'Watch out,' 'Stop,' and 'Don't do…' in my sleep already," I groused. Rell didn't laugh.

I told her how much I liked working in Piffik's workshop. That he had a piece of wood he said came from the West Islands and how I would go smell the wood because it had a scent different from any other piece of wood in the shop. I wondered out loud if the scent was the sea and if I would ever sail to the West Islands.

I told her the West Islands Constellation stories—the ones I could remember anyway. I said I could only tell her one story a night because I had been taught by a West Islands Storyteller the heart needed time to learn what the ears had heard.

I explained to her how I had learned to live in a house. Did she know houses needed care just as a cloak does? They need to be cleaned and mended and looked after. I apologized again for ruining her red cloak on the Northern Track when Bitterboots died at my hand. I explained I had found it again when I was using a broom and catcher on our house, in the room which would be hers, and I had gone to Siba to see if she could fix it. The stains had been left too long, she had said. But Siba had told me the cloak was a very pretty color, and if Rell wished, Piffik could make her a small chest to use the undamaged part of the cloak for a lining.

I also had a chest of my very own, I explained to Rell. Piffik had made a chest of wood for me to place under the clothes hooks in my room. The chest was no bigger than my pillow but it held all of my treasures… and my extra clothes.

"I have more than one shirt Rell, truly! I am that rich! Piffik has bartered for me as I learned to work here at Manumina. I have two more shirts than the one I am wearing, three pockets— one leather and two cloth, two tunics, three pairs of pants, and only one of them has a rip in the leg from mending fences. Siba says I have so many boot linings and small clothes I can wear clean ones every day!"

Chul gave his big Chul laugh and I startled. I had forgotten he had been sitting there. I looked back at him and he smiled.

"Your evenings with Rell are helping, I think. She no longer weeps continuously."

I told her Conrosan fairy tales. I said I liked the ones with Zren Janin the best, but there were others as well, some with wise queens and clever daughters, some with magic and wishes. One time, I do not know why, I told her I did not know my name, but people where I grew up just called me 'Red' for the color of my skin. And then I had heaved a great sigh and told her the rest of it. How Ngahuru had told me stories to find out who I was. I had not even known I was a Conrosan, because I had never met another person who looked like me.

I explained I had stood in front of the Conrosan embassy as a child but had no idea the place was important to me. I confessed I had hated Kerek City and the Wet and being hungry and afraid. I admitted I had pretended not to know who I was so Ngahuru and Koanga would take me along with them as they fled to Matasi. I had only hoped to escape from my previous life in Lowertown, but they had done so much more than that. It was Ngahuru who had given me the name of Zren Janin.

"I did not know what a sense of humor she had, Rell. I did not know if she thought I could live up to my name."

I paused a little before I confessed the last part, "I *like* my name Zren Janin. I like that he goes on adventures with his Sword of Courage, and has his friends—the Wit, the Wizard, and the Warrior—in the Legion of Heroes who help him." I took a deep breath. "I like to think *you* are one of the Legion of Heroes, Rell Huena." I didn't say anything more that night, and after a while I just got up and left. I ran back to my house on the outside of the stockade. I was no longer afraid Rell's monsters would get me. Just afraid they would never let her go.

Days and days and *days* went by. Slowly, Rell came back to us. She was thinner, and her skin was almost as pale as a Kereki. Her braid was pulled apart into a thick mat of black hair, and her eyes had an old look that had never been there before. She would listen carefully as we came to visit her and tell her our news of the world outside. She would talk with anyone, hungry to return to a world without her monsters.

Piffik visited the infirmary nearly every day he was at Manumina. When he talked to Rell, he was shyer and asked many questions about the academies. He wanted to know how big was Juisiti, and how Vikland treated those who were not like them. Rell told me once it was Piffik's desire to have Aajan go to the academies in Vikland, but when she had said he should go as well, he had said he was too old and had left abruptly.

"He's smart, Zren. Very smart. You could learn a lot from him," she urged. "I listen to him talk with Chul and it feels like I am at the academies again. They talk about everything under the sun."

I told her all that he had been teaching me—more than just about woodworking. I told her how the Council of Wisdom had asked for one to speak for us when we had arrived. How Piffik and Siba had agreed to take responsibility for the four of us and how the Conrosans called us the House of Nations, even though she and Chul still lived in the infirmary.

Each time I came to visit, she would ask me what I learned that day. Sometimes she would tell me a story of how her brothers had done something just like I had done and how they had solved a difficult problem. Sometimes I remembered those stories when I was working as a manabout and the person who bought my time would be impressed I was so clever.

One evening, I told Rell I could now read and write Conrosan a little, and Siba had given me a book of pressed papers so I could write down the stories I had learned on my travels.

"The pressed pages are not new paper of course, but paper that has been bleached and cleaned of all the writing so only my words are on them," I said proudly.

Rell shifted her weight on the bed. "Are you mocking me, Zren?" She looked closely at me. "No, I can see you are not." She pursed her lips and thought for a moment. "I didn't realize Manumina was quite so poor."

I shrugged. Everyone here was richer than Ngahuru and Koanga and I had been on the Coast Road. Definitely richer than anyone I knew in Lowertown. I wondered just how wealthy Rell was and who was her family if she thought Manumina was poor.

CHAPTER 24

FOURTH NIGHT AND FORTITUDE

Rygee decided cooking for me wasn't enough. He spread the word through the settlement those who were without a hearth of their own were invited to our house for food and stories on the fourth night after Rest Day.

The first time, the house was so full, people held their platters in their hands to eat. There was so much food and laughter, and people were kind and funny and helpful. I told a West Islands Constellations story of the Traveler. Someone else told a tale of Conrosa I had never heard before about Zren Janin and a too friendly bear. None of us knew what a bear looked like, but we had a lot of fun guessing what it would do and say.

Rygee was exhausted when everyone finally left, but his eyes shone with happiness, and I knew he had found his pleasure. Fourth night food and stories quickly became a tradition and our circle of friends continued to grow.

Days passed and we could begin to see an end to the Wet. First, it was just showers after midday, and then we had bursts of sun with our drizzle, and finally days where the rains tapered off altogether. Manumina came alive as everyone prepared their fields and gardens for planting.

The Wet was over before Rell was finally released from the healers' care. Rygee moved Chul's belongings into his room on the fourth floor, and Siba came over one Rest Day to tidy the bedroom before Rell moved in with us. Siba had given the stairs a long look and then let out a sigh.

"There are others at Manumina who are forced to sacrifice their dignity for our unforgiving houses, but if you give her privacy while she crawls up and down, I think she will continue to mend until they are not her enemy." She smiled at us. "Thank you for giving her the lowest bedroom."

Rell had a different thought. When we told her she had the second floor, the lowest bedroom in the house, she had limped back out into the yard, and called us both out there. Pointing to her window, she commented it was the least secure bedroom in the house, which could be reached from the porch roof if someone had ill intent.

Rygee made his eyes go round. "You are the best shot of the three of us, Rell Huena. You are a bowmaster of Vikland, and we are confident you can keep us all safe." She gave him a searching look but said nothing more to either of us. She grabbed the porch wall and pulled herself up the two steps and into the house. She gave us another pointed look as she reached the stairs leading to her bedroom. Rygee said he and I would finish tidying the kitchen while she settled into her new space. We waited a long time while we listened to her drag herself up the stairs and then as she bumped about in the room above us. Only when it was quiet again would Rygee let me go up to bed.

The next morning Rygee had already left for the bakery when I heard Rell step and thump down the stairs. I hurriedly washed and dressed, but by the time I reached the front porch, she was waiting with her crossbow and bolts. She asked me to tuck a small square of cloth into a straw bale and set it up as target in the field outside our house. As I left for my day of work with Vigdis at the stables, I already heard the sound of bolts thudding into the straw. I wondered how many squares of cloth she had.

Over the next few days, Rygee and I pretended not to notice how difficult the stairs were on Rell as she dragged her damaged leg. We made sure we stayed in our rooms, or in the kitchen, when we heard her first foot drop heavily on the stairs. She tried different ways: scooting down, bracing her arms on the walls, crawling feet first, even sliding her back along one side of the wall, and dragging the damaged leg behind her.

But we had said nothing to warn Piffik when he came over for end of day meal one evening. He had watched in horror as she crawled on her hands, dragging her leg down the stairs to join us. As she used a chair set at the base of the stairs to pull herself to her feet, she smiled feebly.

"This is how I check to make sure the boys have done the daily sweeping, Piffik. Did they do it?" She held her arms out, palms up, and then limped heavily to the sink to wash her hands before coming to the table.

The very next day, Siba sent for Rell to come to the healers' house. While she was out, Piffik and Zadah came over with wooden poles and round pieces used for table legs. Zadah carried precious West Islands steel brackets, well-used but still strong. Piffik had me walk up and down the stairs several times as he measured. Zadah would balance the wood beams to try to bear my weight with the differently sized poles. Before end of day, we had built a railing along the stair wall Rell could use to pull herself up and balance on the way down.

"From now on," Piffik announced, "only Rell's feet touch the treads."

Rell was beyond pleased. She used the railing to drag herself up and down to regain her strength. Some nights when she could not sleep, I would drift awake and hear the slow thick thuds as she forced her damaged leg up and down the treads for what seemed like decons.

I continued to visit Chul after the end of day meal. I often found Piffik or Siba sitting with him visiting when I arrived.

Siba still gave me a sniff test, "You can't have taken a bath if you still smell like livestock, Zren," but now she smiled easily when I knocked. She would slip on her cloak, say she would be back in a while, and walk out the door. If I looked back at Chul, he would be holding back silent laughter. I didn't know what was so funny, but he was definitely amused.

Chul was older than Miya, but while Miya was slim and just a hand taller than me, Chul was tall and broad with a strong Matasi jaw, dark, curly hair, and olive skin. He laughed easily, even though he must still have been in near constant discomfort. I spent my time with him telling him stories—mostly of my foibles among the Conrosans as I tried to learn the language and the way of things. He especially laughed at my attempts to learn to care for livestock.

I admitted I liked building things: fences, wagons, and furniture. I think I bragged for three visits as I told him some of the elderly people specifically asked for me when their houses needed mending. After the other manabout and I finished the repairs, I told Chul, we would stop for a slice of bread and butter or maybe even a fingersweet with the people, and I would tell a story of the West Islands or ask them to tell me one of Zren Janin or another Conrosan fairy tale before we left for the day.

And then, Piffik moved me up from working with the ten-year-olds and other apprentices to making the rough coffins and carry chests that Piffik sold to the Kereki settlements and military garrisons. When Piffik had come over to our house and tried to give me the coins from the sale, Rygee had stepped in and said no. Bartering was one thing, he said, but we had been provided for and there were others who had no one to earn coin for them.

Afterward, Rygee explained to me that we were not Vikland dragons who hoarded coin others needed. But I was still unhappy he had not allowed me to be paid and told him so. He looked at me and said we could have this conversation again when my travel bag of coin from Miyamoto Suki was completely empty. Until then, accepting coin others needed more was not going to happen. He said he was pleased I had become a man who shared generously with others. I knew he refused coin, and now seldom accepted barter, but he was not me, and I sulked for days. He didn't budge and I didn't know how to go and ask Piffik for the coins without Rygee learning of it. I wondered if Rygee was more like his father than he wanted to admit.

I confessed once to Chul I thought the settlement was poor, and I used his coin to pay for his care, and Rell, Rygee, and I paid for our food with the coins Miya left us, but I saw most others barter. He suggested we spend more in Manumina rather than traveling to Sary and buying for our needs. We could pay for lessons in something we wished to learn.

"Like cooking, Zren. You truly should learn. I am not going to tell another's secrets, but I don't think Rygee is going to live with you forever." I brushed him off. After working all day mending fences, tending livestock, and now learning to plant the fields and gardens, the last thing I wanted to do was come back and cook my own end of day meal. Rygee cooked well for all of us, why should Rell and I suffer through my own efforts?

During one unexpected late season shower, I dashed across the village green to find him alone in the infirmary. I used the chance to tell him my worries.

"I have heard nothing from Vikland, Chul. They know we are here. Piffik or Zadah travel to the Ishes garrison often enough that if we had been sent a letter from Juisiti, we would have received it. Do you think Kern and Miya have forgotten us?"

"No," he reassured me, "they are only preoccupied. Now that the Earles and Ishes garrisons are ours and Manumina is a friend to Vikland, they are hurrying to gather forces to move into Sary as soon as the rains stop and the roads dry enough for the heavy wagons."

"Vikland will move in just to remove thieves and outlaws from the Northern Track? Taking Earles and Ishes wasn't enough?" I questioned. "Wouldn't that be like another gang boss moving into a different territory in Kerek City?"

Chul laughed and then turned serious. "Zren, Vikland was promised free and safe passage on any road from the Vikland border to Kerek's sea by the current King's father and grandfather. If the Kerek King does not honor this treaty, Vikland will take the Northern Track by force. Whether it is military garrisons within a half-day's walk of each other, armed settlements, or something else, Vikland must create a secure supply route to a port. Not to fight for this now means Vikland will die. Maybe not in our lifetime, but the next. It is important that we do not accept going over the Silver Mountains as our only access to the known world. We must not allow the Kerek King to believe a Viklander's life is worth less than his own."

I considered this and tried to fit in other information I had heard into a puzzle I could comprehend. I thought of First Soldier Joon and the conversations he had with Miya when I was still taking in everything in wide-eyed wonder at the embasado. I thought of Salik Oqina and his stories of Manumina. What else did I remember?

"Matasi is buying farmland from the border to the Old Fort Road in southern Kerek," I said slowly.

"Yes."

"When Ngahuru sent the children home and escaped through Matasi, she was trying to keep her country neutral so the West Islands King and country would not be obligated to support either Vikland or Matasi and the trouble in Kerek," I spoke my thoughts out loud. "Is she truly that important, Chul? Could this be true?"

"I believe that was her plan. She is important to her King, but it was the children she was trying to protect. As long as no one knew where the West Islands King's niece and nephew were, they could not be harmed or used as political hostages. Her cleverness meant the West Islands are able to stay out of the dance with Trouble the Kereki King is stirring up with his neighbors. I heard your night in the Matasi jail devastated your resources, but even so, I believed she had decided to throw in with Vikland." He winced as he moved gingerly on his bed. "That was before the uprising in Kerek City."

A terrible idea unwillingly bloomed in my head. "The riots and fires in Kerek City. You weren't just caught in them because you disobeyed Joon's orders not to leave the embasado."

Chul sighed. "I wondered when you would see this. Every time I heard you describe me as a victim of that night, I realized you truly believed it." He added quietly, "You do not have a face that lets you lie."

"I was staying in a bunk room with five other men. They didn't come back that night and when I asked Miya he said they were out on assignment," I hesitated, uncomfortable with my train of thought. *Could Vikland start a war and call it an uprising?*

"I don't know whose room you stayed in, so I can't say anything to that."

"Vikland started the fires and the riots and let Lowertown be blamed for it." I could barely believe the words that fell from my mouth.

Chul nodded and said calmly, "Kerek needs a new king. A revolt within Kerek would have been best. But Matasi and Vikland are not going to wait for it anymore."

"Miya knows all this?" I asked.

Chul barked out a sharp laugh. "Miya is in the thick of it. I believe there is nothing that can happen to him he cannot turn to his advantage. He will save or sacrifice any of us depending on what he thinks he must do. Miya is a true son of Vikland."

"He was going to let the Kereki soldiers walk into the garrison at Earles with their paychest to be murdered," I said bitterly.

"Was he?" Chul chided. "I distinctly remember him offering a chance to fade away in one of the villages or go to Vikland with him. I think he is truly sad Rygee has stayed here. As a Kereki, he would be a valuable softfoot in Kerek City. I know he was more than pleased you found this settlement of potential allies. We will never know if we would have received the same help if Rygee had been driving the wagon, if you had stayed behind to help Kern and Miya build and burn Song's funeral pyre. And having the Kereki army paychest to spread around and buy goodwill? That was pure Miya." He shifted his weight and grimaced again.

"I should go. I have overtired you." I didn't want to talk anymore about Miya…or the riots.

"Come back soon. I know Siba makes you take a bath, but it's worth it to talk to me, eh?" He grinned, but didn't ask me to stay, so I left.

CHAPTER 25

THE BEGINNING OF MANUMINA

Chul stayed at the infirmary while he learned to walk again. I was drowning in Conrosan words all day every day, and sometimes it just felt nice to speak Keresh without trying to figure out if not knowing a word was going to cause me pain. One day, when I was nursing an especially nasty bruise on my leg because I didn't know the Conrosan words for "jump over the fence" when a sow took offense to me, Chul told me I should have Rell teach me Vik or Wester.

"For her sake as well as yours, Zren. She needs a purpose, another one to thunking quarrels in a target."

"I would be happy to teach her how to be a pig farmer," I muttered under my breath.

He snorted. "The first time she loses her temper we'd be eating pork until we all squealed."

"Will you teach me Mata?"

He raised his brows in surprise. "Planning to be a missionary?"

I scowled back. "There were times on the track when Miya would switch to another language with any one of you to keep the others out of the conversation. The more I know, the more I can't be left behind."

"Ah," he said cryptically. He didn't say anything for a moment, but his eyes looked sad. Then he straightened in his bed. "So tell me, what did you learn from your stories from the last Fourth Night?"

I knew he was changing our conversation. He had made it so obvious, I knew he wouldn't talk about what had happened on the Northern Track. So I shared the story of the Conrosan settlement which Vigdis, one of the stable hands, had shared.

"The beginning of Manumina," I began solemnly. "The Conrosan ship had been blown off course and limped into the harbor of Kerek City in the time of the current king's grandfather. A king," I said dryly, "who was a great improvement over the current wreck that sits on the throne." Chul laughed, and I protested, "That's what Vigdis said. Truly!"

I explained how that king had invited them to build an embasado next to the castle grounds, and there the Conrosans all lived. "Apparently, it was a small ship," I told Chul. He laughed again and I continued, "Alas, the good king died and the Conrosans decided Kerek was not the country they wished it to be. So some took a ship to the West Islands, some followed the Coast Road to Matasi, and the rest decided to move to Vikland." Chul and I wondered who they had talked to in the embasados on Castle Court to decide who would move where. Obviously, the Northern Track had not been the bandit infested trail it was today if the wagons had rolled along unmolested until they reached Manumina. I cleared my throat and got back to the story.

"Now in Conrosa, there are four seasons: the Season of Rest, the Season of Hope, the Season of Life, and the Season of Harvest, each with a time to do certain things. In Kerek, this is not true. Unfortunately, the Conrosans had started their journey just before the beginning of the Wet. By the time they reached the Huk River, it was raging whitewater that flooded its banks. They camped in the rains by the side of the road for days and days waiting for the river to drop and the rains to cease enough for them to cross. At last came 'the little Dry' and there was enough sun that the river began to smooth out and the ruts began to harden. Thinking the rains were over, the Conrosans floated their wagons across and tied lines so people could haul themselves and their goods to the other shore. Thus they dragged themselves into Sary.

"Now Sary was a much smaller town then, and those who lived there had no time nor coin for such bedraggled refugees. The Conrosans were told of an abandoned Matasi stockade, more than a decon southeast on the Sary to Ahni road. The Conrosans found the fort, took shelter, built the houses as they were in their homeland, bought livestock, and stayed." I quoted Vigdis for the rest of it.

"My grandmother was one of the original settlers," Vigdis had said, "She would teach us the language, tell us the stories, and reminisce about her childhood back in Conrosa. But never once in all her years did I hear her want to go back. And so we remain, safe here, left alone for the most part, until the last ten years or so, when the current king was crowned."

Vigdis had sighed before continuing, "We assumed he would grow into his crown. Instead, we find more dead and damaged travelers on our roads, fewer supplies getting through from the port at Kerek City to Sary or Ahni where we can finally buy them. Then a year ago, we hear the Kerek King was so corrupt and desperate for coin he sold the garrisons at Earles and Ishes. The Vikland army paid the soldiers to leave—and they did—because the Kerek King had not sent the paychests for too many seasons. But it wasn't just the garrisons who benefitted from Vikland's generosity."

Vigdis had looked at me then. "Vikland came with soldiers and settlers, with farm implements, seed, and a dozen horses to Manumina. 'A gift!' we were told from the Vikland Empress. And now, if we have trouble, we are to ask them for help. If we find their travelers, we help them home. When Kereki merchants look at us with harm rather than merely distrust, we pay the extra coin and buy what we need from Ishes."

I finished with, "Did you know this, Chul?"

"I didn't even know this place was here until I woke up in the healers' house and drank Siba's funny tasting potions. When I first opened my eyes, I thought you were wearing a dress, and I could not imagine why you would be softfooting wearing Kern's dress." We laughed, and I made a big show of how long her dresses would trail behind me.

Suddenly, I remembered when I saw Miya slide out of Kern's room on the first night here in Manumina. I debated saying anything, but then I decided I would not know unless I asked.

"Chul, were or are, Miya and Kern together, as you know, together?"

Chul's brows shot up. "Saints, no! What would make you think that?"

So I told him. I said I had heard a noise in the guesthouse on the night of the Battle at the Bridge. Since I wasn't sure what kind of a noise, I had gone to the door and had watched as Miya had walked bare-legged out of Kern's room and into his own. I looked at my feet.

"He said she had a nightmare."

"Oh, Zren! Look," Chul hesitated. "I saw how your eyes would follow him about. How eager you were for his approval. But Miyamoto Suki isn't for the likes of you and me. Kern's family isn't noble enough for him. He has his eyes set on one of the Empress's daughters, and he is ambitious and handsome and rich enough to succeed. If Miya told you Kern had a nightmare, I would believe it to be true. Take peace in knowing he cared enough about you to tell you the truth."

He looked out the window. "Kern had a lover, but she didn't survive her crossing from Vikland to the Kerek City embasado. Their group never showed up in Kerek City at the beginning of the Dry and we didn't come across them on the journey out here. We'll probably never know what happened to them. That's why it's so important to replace the Kerek King and get the Northern Track and other roads from the border open again to safe travel."

"Ceri?" I realized suddenly Chul had been sleeping under the healers' potions and had never heard of the others we had found here at Manumina or the story of their rescue and safety.

"Kern talked about her? They have been together since their days in the academies. Almost as long as you have been alive. She was a soldier from the farthest east settlements where they are trained for defense on axes and hatchets instead of the short and long bongs."

"Oh, Chul! You didn't know! Ceri and Rani and Malik were here! They had been found by Conrosans in the early morning, half dead from an ambush by the same bandits who hurt us, and brought back here to recover. They went back to Vikland with Kern and Miya, with your supplies and the West Islands steel, and the almost empty paychest. But Ceri was here! Kern saw her and they traveled together to Vikland. Ceri was here safe!"

Chul sank back in his bedcovers. "I love a happy ending, Zren, I truly do. But this is just one more reason Vikland needs to take back its safe passage."

I recognized what was to come next as Chul slipped back into his thoughts as to why the Kerek King had to suffer, and so I excused myself to think.

CHAPTER 26

THE SEASON OF HOPE

At last the Dry was here for good. Everyone was outdoors in a flurry of fieldwork, farrowing, and foaling. If I hated livestock before, my feelings now ran to loathing. My small size and narrow hands made me the manabout of choice to assist with the births and stick my hand up the mare, or cow, or ewe. My arm would be bruised from the pressure, and I would need two baths to feel clean enough. When I would complain to Chul, he would laugh until tears ran down his face.

"I would offer to help you Zren, but..." and he would hold up his huge, thickly scarred hands and start laughing again.

Piffik would have me help in the woodshop for an afternoon for a break, but then would send me back out to the farmers, saying in Manumina everyone worked together for the good of all. Only Rygee seemed sympathetic.

"I am the youngest son, Zren, so I know exactly how you feel. I was far younger than you the first time my father yelled for me to help with a difficult birth. The calf was turned. My father said to stick my hand up and follow the legs until I could find the calf's face. We didn't know there were twins. I had found the second calf's face when I started pulling." He let out a noisy breath. "It did not end well. I cried when my father explained to me what must have happened. He was not angry with me, but said a farmer has many disappointments and we must learn from them."

He grimaced. "Then my older brothers found me and mocked me for crying and being such a delicate flower." He sighed. "It is not easy to be a farmer. That is why our bodies are made to die if we do not eat. So we learn to do the hard things in order to live another day."

I looked at him. He was taller than Piffik and strong. I had seen him lift the bags of flour at the bakery for the others and they looked like the size of a small child. "But who was going to do it while you were in the army?"

Rygee laughed. "I have been too big for many years. One day my father said my hands and feet had grown to match the size of my head, and they would have to get a hired boy to help with the birthing. I didn't care he was calling me too big for my britches. I only cared that I would never again carry a bruise from my wrist to my shoulder bones." He grinned at me. "You eat everything put in front of you, Zren. I can't help but think you will soon be too big as well, and they will have to look for another manabout."

* * * * *

Piffik and Zadah were very late coming back from a delivery. Their destination had been Pagta, a town on the Old Vikland Road far beyond Ahni. It was a town with wealth and King's agents and Piffik had earned a fine commission there. Their plan, Piffik had said, was to deliver the wardrobe, buy supplies, and be out of the town the same day they entered. He knew he and Zadah would need to sleep rough each way, but the coin was very good, and with late nights and early mornings they would be home in five days.

On the fifth day of their absence, Siba came over for end of day meal and our Conrosan lessons, but she was so distracted, there was little point in reading out loud to her. Rell was in her chair, massaging her damaged leg, and the two were both constantly looking out the window towards the Huntsman's Trail.

I wondered what they would have done if we had been facing east or even north. Climbed to the rooftop? Waited in Manumina's lookout?

As darkness fell, Rygee reassured them both Piffik merely decided to stay in Pagta and see the sights, and he and Zadah would be home the next day. It was not an unreasonable extension of time, he said. It would be foolish for us to lose a night's sleep for worry over a man who knew the half-tracks and hidden trails of Kerek as well as Piffik did. Rygee lit the lantern and offered to walk Siba home so she would not need to cross into the stockade in the dark.

I didn't sleep well that night. I thought of all the kind things Piffik had said and done for me. Now here I was lying in a soft bed while no one in Manumina knew if he and Zadah were hurt or dead or lost in the dark. I hoped they were merely lost and holed up in a quiet place waiting for daylight to see the paths again. I remembered my adventure with the two Viklanders coming back from Earles all those days and days ago and how easy it was to miss a half-track in the twilight. I wondered if they carried extra food. I wondered why Manumina would let two brothers travel together without a weapon against bandits.

CHAPTER 27

AN UNEXPECTED GUEST

It was barely first light and Rygee was shaking me awake.

"Zren, it's Piffik's wagon. Come help me open the gates."

I was awake instantly. Rygee was already dressed and walking to the door. "Hurry, Zren. If he is traveling this early, it means there is trouble."

I threw on my clothes and ran down the stairs to catch up. Rygee and I slipped through the small side door and together we opened the large gates so the horses and wagon could drive straight through. We stood there waiting, the sun barely peaking over the horizon.

"How did you know?" I asked yawning.

"I was walking to the bakery to start the ovens, and I saw movement down the Huntsman's Trail. I know we have no close neighbors in that direction so it had to be someone who had driven all night." Rygee gave me a half smile. "The only one I know so foolish or so brave to do that is Piffik."

We could see only one sitting on the wagon seat and Rygee's smile disappeared. "I'll get Siba up," he said sharply. "Tell whoever it is to drive straight to the infirmary. Leave the gates open and follow quickly. We may need you to help us carry him in." Rygee turned and hurried inside.

Only as the wagon got closer, could I see it was Zadah on the wagon seat.

"Go straight to the infirmary," I shouted as he trotted by. He nodded. I tried to pull the large gate closed before I abandoned it halfway and ran to the infirmary to help.

Piffik was climbing out of the back of the wagon his hand and shirt spattered with blood. He gestured inside the wagon and Rygee, Siba, and Zadah crowded about another man. Zadah and Siba rolled a blanket underneath him and the four of us quickly lifted him up and out of the back of the wagon, through the door, and on to an open bed in the infirmary. I looked to Chul. We had awakened him, and he was groggily watching us. I looked down at the man we had carried in and yelped.

It was the Spice Islander. The Tax Collector who had taken me during the Wet to pay Manumina's tax of 110 dias was lying on the bed with a fresh knife wound in his back. I looked up startled as Piffik, Zadah, Rygee, and Siba all calmly worked on him.

"No," I cried as I started to bat their hands away. "We can't help him. He's the Tax Collector. He was supposed to have died at the crossroads to Earles. If he sees me, he will know I didn't go to Kerek City. I didn't die at the crossroads, and Manumina didn't pay its tax."

"That was a long while ago, Zren. This can't be the same man, this wound is recent. From yesterday, no earlier than that," Siba assured me. She kept pressure on the wound now that Piffik had moved out of the way.

Bett came out of the infirmary kitchen with a steaming bowl of water and a handful of fresh clean rags. She had heard my words.

"I would think Zren would remember. You were all in Vikland that day. Let me see, I was there too." She put the bowl down and moved Zadah aside to get a better look.

"It is him." She blew out a breath. "Well. Yes." She looked about the room. "This is what we must do. This man is in no shape to see outside of this room for days. We are all safe until then. I will tell all of you when you must keep yourself out of sight. Zadah and Piffik, you have done your part. Go home, sleep. We can wait to hear your story until after you have restored yourselves.”

“But you can’t mean to help him!” I looked at her appalled. “He’s the Tax Collector!”

“I do and I will, Zren.” Bett looked at me. “It may be we do a kindness and are rewarded for it. It may not. I cannot decide whether I will help or not because of what I may gain or lose. Now all of you leave. I need to have a clean room in which to work, and Chul wants to go back to sleep.” She made a shooing motion with her hands, and we all scurried out of the infirmary.

Outside on the green, Rygee gave Piffik and Zadah a resigned look. “Zren can take care of your horses. I’m going to work today and bring you end of day meal. We can hear your story then.”

Piffik looked at both of us. “It wouldn’t have changed anything. Even if we knew who he was, Zadah and I would still have stopped to help him.”

* * * * *

The Spice Islander was out of his head with fever for the next few days. He spoke Wester as all Spice Islanders do, and Chul reminded Siba and Bett that our Rell spoke Wester. It would be in all of our best interests, he reasoned carefully, if Rell was there to translate what the Spice Islander said in his fevered dreams.

Then the Council of Wisdom could decide if Manumina was in danger or not, and what steps they wished to take. He also told them Rell had been a healer in Vikland, but she was afraid to ask Siba and Bett if she could help them.

Bett said they could certainly use her talents. And it would be good to know what their patient was saying in his ravings, but it should be Rell's decision—she was risking herself as a Viklander.

I sighed. I knew that meant Rell would be helping to care for the Spice Islander, and I was right.

It was two handfuls of days before Rell came home again. She said the Spice Islander was finally lucid—which she explained to me meant he was back in his head again. She said the man was asking for Zren Janin of Manumina. But at my shocked expression, she promised me she and the other healers had pretended they didn't understand what he meant.

She said it was up to me if I wanted to let him see me. But she would stand behind me with her crossbow and if he meant me or Manumina harm, she would take care of the problem. I looked at her, shocked at her coldness. She laughed.

"Truly, Zren, don't you think I can protect you? Why did you and Rygee make me practice in all weather during the Wet and the Dry if I was not supposed to regain my bowmaster skills?"

When I said I did not think she would miss, just whether or not she would want to take a man's life without a battlefield, she grinned at me. "I think you will not be afraid to meet this man—with or without me standing behind you."

* * * * *

Only Chul, Rell, and I were in the room with the Tax Collector. He was sitting up, although we could see he was sitting stiffly forward to keep his bandages from touching the back of the chair. His long brown hair was brushed and clubbed back, and I realized he was still wearing all of his rings on his fingers and in his ear. He had not been robbed. *A man who had been found with a knife in his back in the outlands of Kerek who had not been robbed. Huh.*

"Hello," I said cautiously. "Rell said you wanted to see me."

"Zren Janin of Manumina." He smiled agreeably. "I am glad we meet again. I have heard you like stories. That you have a gift for remembering a story—even if you have only heard it once— and you have a gift for seeing the meaning behind the tale. I would like to tell you of my adventure and see if you can make meaning out of this. Is this acceptable to you?"

I sat down on the open chair. "I am listening."

"I am Buku Pramana of the Spice Island. I am a *kapene kaipuke*—a captain of a ship which trades only between the Spice Island and Matasi. Last year at the end of the Wet, my ship was caught in a storm at sea. We were driven far off course running ahead of the winds. My sailors were better and stronger than the wild seas and we prevailed. We limped into Kerek City, savaged, but not sunk. We purchased supplies and worked to repair our ship. For almost the entire Dry, we worked to rebuild and restock. Our cargo—our profit—had been lost to the seas, so many of my men had taken work within the city to earn the coin to pay for our repairs so we could all go home." Pramana smiled at me. "This is what the Conrosans do, no? All work together so all can share in the reward."

I nodded slowly.

"When we were ready to leave, my men who worked in the city returned to the ship, and those who had repaired the ship made ready to sail out on the next tide. But before the waters turned, a group of soldiers, the Harbormaster, and the Kerek Port Tax Collector boarded the ship and demanded to be paid in coin for the privilege of living and working in Kerek City. There were fees and charges for anchorage and advice, bills for food and drink which I know had never been delivered to the ship, and all manner of coin I had never heard of or imagined. All needed immediately for us to be able to leave." Buku Pramana raised his shoulders and dropped them.

"We had none of it. We did not know. It is not how the Spice Island runs their ports. Nor the ports of Matasi, and those were the only ports I knew. The soldiers forced us off the ship. The Harbormaster claimed the ship for the Kerek King, and we were all marched to prison. Now I ask you this, Zren Janin, how can a man work to pay to free his ship if he is locked in a cell no larger than a fishing boat?

"We languished. Our cell had daylight, but what did it matter? Our cell was mostly buried below ground and the window was so small and so high overhead, we could only see the feet of those who passed by. Rain, or mud, or slops would all run down the wall and puddle on the floor. Truly, I despaired we would ever step foot on a ship again. No one in Kerek City or the Spice Island knew we were there who would care to bring Spice Islanders home."

Pramana smiled weakly. "And then, as the Matasians would say, 'We had a miracle of the Lost God.' A boy called to us from the barred window high above our heads. He spoke Wester as a Spice Islander would, and asked us if our ship was the *Kororia o te Moana*? 'Yes,' we called to him, 'did he have news of her?' He did, he said, and asked for a man who could make decisions for all of us. He said one man would be redeemed for a price. My men gave my name. The boy left without saying another word. Our spirits were crushed and hopeful at the same time.

"Two days later, I was freed. I was told by my jailors I had been redeemed so I could earn the coin to free the others. I was reminded the Kerek King did not want any to benefit from his generosity in providing food and shelter far from home. I needed to remember, the ship and the crew would remain captive until all the fees were paid. But I was free. What I did with that freedom? The Kereki jailors did not care.

"As I walked out into daylight, I saw the boy who had called to us waiting for me across the way. He was a Spice Islander as I had suspected, but he wore no gold in his ears nor on his fingers. He called me by my name and then took me to a Viklander. A Softfoot. The man said he did not speak Wester, but if I would be so kind to hear his words in Mata, he thought I might like what he had to say. We walked and talked and the boy followed closely behind keeping watch."

Pramana gave me a measured look. "I cannot tell you all we talked about that day, the Softfoot and I, but I will tell you he offered me a plan to free my ship and my men. He asked me to become a Tax Collector for the Kerek King. To write down the routes and the days for him. To note the men who could be bribed and already were and by whom. To see how much coin made it to the King and how much disappeared into pockets along the way. If I could do this for him, over all three of the routes in Kerek, he would free my men or my ship immediately, and then when I returned, he would pay the fees and fines of the other and we could sail for home and Kerek would be none the wiser.

"I ask you, Zren Janin, as one who has lived by his wits and his work, what would you have me do?" Pramana raised his shoulders and dropped them. "I told him to free my men immediately and I would do as he asked."

Pramana looked at Rell Huena. "It is not so hard to become a Tax Collector in Kerek. I would have thought I would be forced to pay for the privilege. But I understand, it is not a position known for a long life. Do you, as a Viklander, know why that might be?" He gave her a knowing smile.

"Let it be said, Zren Janin, there are many people in Kerek with a Viklander heart, if not a Viklander face. In towns and settlements, I would be given names and places to drop my information. In the next town, I would be given coins and directions, and requests of things to confiscate for taxes, and things to leave behind in stables and inns. Once, early on, I left a message saying my fellow Tax Collector was too suspicious. I didn't think I could continue. Two days later, he died in his sleep from an open window and a knife wound.

"After I had traveled all three routes, I returned to Kerek City thinking my task was done. The same boy found me and took me to meet the Softfoot. He said he was more than pleased with my work and my papers. He said he would redeem my ship and I could tell my crew to sail for the Spice Island. But as for me, I would be given one last route to run and then I would be taken to Matasi where I could take another ship and return home. If I refused, I would need to find my own way and my own coin to free my ship. He said Vikland had no disagreement with the Spice Island. But he needed to find his allies where he could.

"I said that was not what we had agreed upon. He had shrugged and started to walk away. I knew I could not win this dispute with honor. So I asked him to let me see my men and my ship sail safely out of the harbor and it would be as he said. I told my men to take the ship home and rejoin their families, and I would follow them before the Dry had ended. They had doubts and suspicions, but I was the captain. Together the Softfoot, the Spice Islander boy, and I watched as the *Kororia o te Moana* sailed out of the harbor and made her way towards home."

Pramana looked at me. "On your journey, my last, I was told to conscript two boys—any boys with enough sense to drive a wagon and find their way home: but one had to be a West Islander from Aldi and one a Conrosan from Manumina. The plan was to have the Viklanders rob the Tax Collectors at the crossroads to Earles. There were only to be three survivors—the three the Viklanders could easily pick out at the other end of a crossbow—the West Islander, the Conrosan, and me. Your purpose was to transport softfoots from Earles to the Vikland border, the West Islander was to take softfoots to the Matasi border. You both would do this in gratitude for your life as you were to be rescued from the cutthroats by Viklanders.

"But it did not go according to plan. Oh, the Viklanders got the Tax Collector's coin, wagons, and horses. But the West Islander had run away at Pagta. You turned out to be cleverer than anyone expected, and ran *to* Earles instead of getting rescued and offered a chance to pay back a debt of gratitude. So the Viklanders had to hide you away while those who had pretended to be bandits returned to the garrison with the goods, the coins, the wagons, and horses. There were those who were concerned if you were clever enough to rescue yourself, then you were clever enough to know it was Viklanders as the bandits, and to note you were the only survivor." He held out his hands, "In addition to me, of course.

"Lucky for you, another Viklander softfoot—Kern—was there and said you had a gift which gave you away every time. You had a face that could not lie. What you felt in your heart and your head was as clear on your face as the sun over the horizon during the Dry. Once they were sure you believed you had been truly set upon by bandits, and you had lived by a miracle and not by intention, they went ahead and had you transport the two Viklanders to Ishes."

Chul laughed his big Chul laugh. "Oh, Zren. No one in this room will tell this story. You can continue to tell of your escape and bravery just as you have been. In fact, I truly like your version better."

Rell just patted my hand. "It took courage to do what you did that day. It doesn't matter the why and the what, if you didn't know who they were."

Pramana nodded. "I am only telling you everything, Zren Janin, not to make your story small, but so you understand people make hard decisions and sometimes those decisions have nothing to do with you. When I was here at Manumina, I knew I had to bring a Conrosan. But the Council of Wisdom is so clever, I was appalled at my choices. The children were too young, the adults were women or not believable as conscripts. I treated you roughly because I needed to be convincing to the other Tax Collector. I told you Earles because I could not risk having you run away. But whatever gods the Conrosans pray to were watching out for you and perhaps for me. You played your part so well, I knew if Trouble found me, I could come to you for help.

"After you had left, I learned there were no plans to return me to Kerek City. Instead, I was now promised they would take me east to Vikland and over the Silver Mountains. I asked if that were true, why not send me with you and the other Viklanders? I was told the trip over the mountains could only be done during the Dry. And since I didn't speak Vik, it made sense to them I would wish to stay with the Viklanders at Earles and help them softfoot through the rest of the Wet." Pramana snorted.

"Zren Janin, I told you I am a *kapene kaipuke* who only sails between Matasi and the Spice Island. The Matasi have so many rules, one cannot be cheated by another without the Fist of God or the Rule of God joining in the conversation. A Spice Islander wouldn't cheat another because we live together on a small island and the treachery would be known from one end to the other. So I was unprepared to understand the Trickster's bargain I had made. The Softfoot knew the fees and charges were continuing to grow while I was acting as a Tax Collector. By having my ship and crew sail away, he had no more expense, but I was still trapped into doing his will. He gained his desire by convincing me my ship and crew were safe from Kerek." Pramana took a deep breath. "I did not know I had more than Kerek who meant me harm.

"Two days before Zadah and Piffik found me, another soldier at Earles, one who had chosen to cut his braid so he could pass more easily in Kerek, or so he told me, said he would take me to Vikland. There I could find a guide to take me over the Silver Mountains and then across Matasi to the coastal cities. He said he disagreed with his commander and said I should have been allowed to leave with you. He said to tell no one we were leaving and to take nothing with me which would alert the others. He gathered two horses and we set a fast pace. The first day, I thought he was merely chasing half-tracks which would take him around the Northern Track. But the second day, he seemed distracted, and I stopped to challenge him thinking he was lost. I sail upon the seas, Zren, I know when I am taken southeast. We argued. I turned to ride away and find my own way due east."

Pramana pinched his lips tightly together. "I do not choose to remember the rest of what happened that day until I heard the wagon wheels of Piffik and Zadah. I called out for help. They stopped and gave me water and put pressure on the wound. I could see they were Conrosans, and I asked if they knew Manumina. They said yes, it was not far. I said if they could help me to Manumina, there was one there named Zren Janin. He had been given sanctuary at Earles where I had been and now I begged for sanctuary and help from him."

Pramana opened his hands and showed me his empty palms. "And now here I am, Zren Janin, seeking help to get home to the Spice Island."

I looked at Rell and Chul. "Could this be true?" I asked.

Chul nodded sadly. "It is. Remember when you brought those two Viklanders back with you? You didn't know what to do with them so you brought them here to the infirmary to ask Siba."

"I knew them from the Diplo, Zren." Rell added. "They were not softfoots—not Bima's softfoots anyway, but they were part of the Earles garrison and needed to get news and documents they had recovered from the Tax Collectors quickly to Juisiti. I cannot confirm all of Pramana's story, but I do not doubt it is true."

"So *Vikland* is acting as bandits and outlaws? It is the very thing they say they cannot accept from Kerek. Those boys with the Tax Collectors, they were just like me. They did not choose to be soldiers. They were sold for their taxes and tithes, just like me. How can you do this? They were just like me." I stood quickly and left the room. No one tried to stop me.

* * * * *

Manumina offered sanctuary and healing to the Spice Islander. Although I stayed away from the infirmary for the rest of the Spice Islander's stay, there were others who did not.

Piffik had once told me he thought the reason his brother did not marry was because he was going to run away to the sea. As we watched Zadah walk to the infirmary again and again and again, Rygee and I both recalled the time Zadah had come to end of day meal and asked every question of me on how to find a ship captain who would take him sailing on the seas.

And now the ship captain had come to Manumina.

But if Zadah was going to run away to the sea, then Chul and Rell were going to make sure he got there. They had both crossed the Silver Mountains and told Pramana and Zadah how to find a good guide to take them over the passes. The travelers were told not to cross too late in the Dry. Deadly mists came down obscuring all footpaths and making the rocks too slippery to walk on. They were told how much things should cost. Rell told them where to go to buy horses and told them to give her letter to the innkeeper *before* they started to bargain. They wouldn't be able to take the horses over the mountains, but there were many in the foothills who would buy them—and then sell them back to Viklanders who were traveling from Matasi to Vikland. When Piffik suggested they could save coin by not buying horses at all, both Rell and Chul protested—no one walked in Vikland on the country roads.

Rell taught both Zadah and Pramana the formal Viklander greetings and instructed them on their use. Chul explained how to travel in Matasi. They told Pramana how good it was he spoke Mata and already understood the rules of the Triune Council at the seaports. They reminded both men to speak Wester or Conrosan first when asking for help in Vikland. While few people would know either, they could then speak Keresh and the Viklanders would treat them as if it was only a common language, and not as Kereki troublemakers.

At first Pramana did not understand why Chul and Rell were making maps for him and writing letters for him to carry for people they knew to help him.

"Vikland…" he protested.

Chul had shaken his head. "Vikland paid for your ship and your crew to leave Kerek. I do not know who your Softfoot in Kerek City was, but when you and your secrets were left on the outlands to die, that was when I knew you were of no further use to Vikland."

No one mentioned they were not doing this for the Spice Islander, but for Zadah, because he was Piffik's brother. The two men would still have to cross all of Matasi and find a ship in one of the port cities sailing to the Spice Island. I remembered my own journey through Matasi, and I thought Pramana would probably have to sell all the gold on his fingers to get home to his family and his ship again.

Piffik came to borrow coin from Rygee. Zadah would need it for food and shelter, the horse to travel across Vikland, and to provide for himself until he learned to be a sailor.

When Piffik suggested the terms for repayment, Rygee had questioned, "Shouldn't it be Zadah talking with me?" Piffik had shrugged and said Zadah was his brother, and it would be difficult to send coin across the seas.

I heard of all these plans and more from Rygee, but I continued to stay away.

The morning Zadah and Pramana left Manumina, I ran up the stairs near the arsenal wall to watch over the stockade gate as Piffik's wagon turned east. As I saw them slowly disappear down the half-track, I wondered who had been the Softfoot who had first promised Pramana a way out of the Kereki prison in Kerek City, and the one who had left him and the secret of his betrayal to die on the outlands. I wondered how Vikland could claim to fight against injustice and to defend the defenseless, when they could take a man from the Spice Island, one who had no argument with Kerek or Vikland, and force him to such choices to protect those in his care.

I wondered what I would be willing to do to find my way home.

CHAPTER 28

CHUL'S BASTONO

Sometimes when walking from field to field or across the inner stockade, I would see Chul using his canes and trying to walk in his stiff-legged gait. He would throw his burned leg forward, balance awkwardly with the canes, and take a step with the other. But his scarred hands couldn't close tightly around the canes, and he wobbled a lot.

One morning, as I was on the way to Piffik's woodshop, I saw Chul lurch across the village green, drop one cane, and just stand there looking at it. I realized he couldn't bend down to pick it up, and he couldn't grip it tightly once he could get it back in his hands. He couldn't move forward, and he couldn't balance there much longer. I hurried over.

"Ah, Zren, as of this moment, you are my favorite person in Manumina! I need you to help me back to Bett's, find Rell, and send her to me immediately. This is such a matter of great importance that whoever has bought your time today shall have to do without." He chuckled. "You can tell them I said so. Not that it would do you much good."

"He won't mind." I hurriedly added, "I was on my way to Piffik."

"That's even better. Let's go immediately to Piffik." Chul smiled, "He's smart enough to know what I need without Rell drawing a picture first."

I spent the rest of the afternoon with the two of them. Chul explained to Piffik he knew his hands couldn't hold a cane, so what could be used instead? His arms—there was nothing wrong with his arms!

"I am imagining, Piffik, wooden legs resting in wooden arms attached to my body. But these legs must fold away when I lift my hand to wash my face, to comb my hair. They need to be strong enough to bear all my weight and more when I lift trays in my working rooms, twist to reach for something, and step up on a landing or a platform."

Piffik nodded as Chul talked. "Yes," he said once. "I see." Finally, both men stood there silently looking at Chul's hands stiff and scored with thick scar tissue from his burns.

Piffik finally looked at me. "We need your help, Zren. Has anyone bought your time today?"

I shook my head. "I was just on my way to see you when Chul needed me."

"Ah, good. Would you go to Vigdis and ask him for a broken harness? It must have a sound buckle, but the leather can be as short as your arm. We will start with that and then once we know what works, we can ask him to cut others to size."

I ran to Vigdis and asked him for all the broken harness he had. I knew Piffik would need more than one, and I didn't want to keep running back and forth. Vigdis looked at me with a hurt expression.

"You say that as if you think I will give you two handfuls! How far behind do you think I am on my repairs?"

I took a deep breath. Now I understood why Piffik would only ask for one. "Of course, I know you probably have none at all, but Piffik is making a special cane for Chul and he wanted to only use a broken harness until he has it perfect." I tried to smooth things over. "You have known Piffik longer than I have. You know I have the right of it."

Vigdis chuffed and walked back into the tack room. He came out with three different lengths. "All of the buckles are strong on these. I was only waiting on new leather to rebind them. See if these will work for the Matasian."

When I dashed back into the woodshop, Piffik was already sawing deep notches on opposite sides of a shallow kneading bowl. It was the long narrow kind the bakers used for rising bread, but this one had not yet been oiled for use. It must have been a new apprentice's work for the rough gouges and uneven shape would make it unusable. Piffik lined it with a thick piece of wool he used for polishing and asked Chul to rest his forearm inside.

Chul nodded thoughtfully. "It's long enough I think, but too wide. My arm could roll and if I am not centered on top of the legs, I could overbalance."

Piffik agreed. "Zren, could you go to my house? Someone should be there. Ask them to give you the narrow wood pieces that have no heartwood. They are on the fireplace." Piffik looked to Chul. "Sometimes the sawmills have wood that is missing from the inside. I get them, because they are already curved and hollow." He smiled, a little shyly. "I find them pretty."

I ran out over the green, cut through the newly planted gardens to the southern wall, and found my way to Piffik's house. Piffik's mother opened the door, and I could see Aajan bent over books and papers on the table in the common room. I explained what I wanted, and Aajan protested.

"Are you sure he said those pieces, Zren?"

I nodded.

Aajan gave her mother an odd look, but she went to the fireplace and lifted down three different sized pieces. She gave them to me and told me to be careful. I noticed each one had a different smell, and I breathed in deeply before cradling them close to my body and running back to the woodshop.

Piffik had not waited for me but had already started going through the round poles and pieces from the lathe to be used for table and chair legs.

Then Piffik sent me to the blacksmith for metal fastenings—pounded iron—and back to Vigdis for leather strips both the size of my palm and as long as my arms.

All afternoon Piffik made oddity after oddity under Chul's instruction, which I would test out, and then Piffik, and only when we knew it wouldn't collapse, Chul would try it. Then they would start all over again. Piffik made suggestions to shorten the cradles and to put grooves underneath for the canes. Chul wanted hinges to have the wood swing out of the way if he lifted his arms, even if it meant they would be less sturdy. At the end of the day, Chul had two contraptions one for each side. Attached to a set of buckles and leather were two walking sticks with curved tops that would rest on the ground whenever Chul stood still and move forward like insect legs when he walked. Those buckles and leathers would wrap around his forearms as they rested in the cradles of wood.

When linked together, they looked like an open cage and could stand by themselves when Chul unbuckled them. Piffik said it was so they wouldn't fall to the floor where Chul could not pick them up. The final pair were too tall for me to test them first, but both Piffik and I walked across the green with Chul as he tried his invention.

"This," he kept saying. "This."

When I asked what they were, Chul called them *bastono*. "It's a Mata word, Zren. You can translate it, but I will tell you it means 'freedom,' yes?" He laughed his big Chul laugh.

I didn't understand what he meant. But I walked in with him to the healers' house where Siba and Bett were cleaning the infirmary. Bett glanced up and then took a long look.

"Well, that's it then," she smiled broadly. "Now that you're on your feet, we need to throw you out of here. If you stay any longer, I'll have to marry you to stop the wagging tongues."

Chul laughed again. It was the deep laugh of a man who had regained his independence.

* * * * *

Rygee and Rell and I had all made a special meal the night Chul came home to us. As he clumsily moved about the house in his new bastono, we deftly moved our chairs and belongings out of the way. He roared at us to leave everything alone, he had to learn to move about more gracefully, and we weren't going to be around forever to hold his hand.

He sat down heavily in a chair. "I am sorry. I am so very sorry. I'm frustrated and angry these are my limitations, and I took it out on you. You, who have worked so hard to make me a place I can come home to, who delayed your own journey to Vikland to wait for me. I am an ungrateful man, and if you feed me right now, Rygee, I won't be able to say another word I will regret later."

After the meal, he lumbered over to the stairs. He wasn't smiling. "I'm assuming you had a good idea here. Tell me your plan, Zren, and let's see what we can figure out together."

I cleared my throat. "I was going to move in with Rygee and you were going to have my room. It's on the third floor."

Rell jumped in. "The railing only goes up to the second floor. You could have my room, Chul, and I can move to Zren's. I'm better on the stairs than when I moved in here. I don't need the railing at all anymore."

Chul looked at Rell. "When you moved in, you could pull yourself up with your hands on the wooden bar Piffik put in for you." He held up his scarred hands palms out. "I can't even curl my hands enough to do that."

In the end, we partitioned off a corner of the first floor sitting room for him. Rygee and Rell assembled the extra rope bed I carried down from Rygee's room, and I pounded in wooden hooks for his clothes on the wall. It was very late when we all went to bed, but we were back together.

Chul made us all smile as he called out, "Ah, it's so good to be back with the three of you and not to have to set a watch."

* * * * *

Chul's spirit was too big for the limitations of his body. Soon he had Rell acting as his hands and helping with his inventions. I hadn't known he had been one of the *creators* of liquid fire. His inventions were so renowned, Rell told me, he had his own rooms and labs at the Academy of Elements in Juisiti. He had even been exempted from his military service, because he was too busy creating invention after invention while he was still a student at the academy.

"I know you don't understand what that means, Zren, but very few do not serve their years in the military. In truth, I do not know of another."

CHAPTER 29

AAJAN QANAQ

Rell threw down the graphite in frustration. "Say it a different way, Chul. I can't picture in my head what you are imagining."

Chul was pacing back and forth on his bastono. The hinges made a curious 'click-slide' sound as they locked into place when he placed his weight, but moved easily as he stepped forward. I was sitting at the table trying to read a book Siba had given me, supposedly another children's book, but I was writing down every Conrosan word I didn't know and the list seemed to be very long for something a child should be able to read easily.

Rygee had left right after the end of day meal for a long walk, he said. He didn't meet anyone's eye as he walked out the door, but both Chul and Rell gave a small smirk. I thought they were making fun of all the dirty pottery and pots he had left behind, but I was already used to doing the washing up the next day, so I just ignored them.

There was a light knock at the door. It was with a sense of relief that I put down the book and went to answer.

It was Piffik and Aajan. I stepped aside to let them into the common room with the others. Piffik greeted everyone and asked how their day and their day's work had gone, but Aajan went straight to her request.

"Zren, I need to go to Sary tomorrow and Piffik says he cannot accompany me because he must make a delivery. Will you come with me? We can ride the two fast horses and be back just after midday with an early enough start. I know you love your pillow—"

"Stop," Rell interrupted. "When did Zren learn to ride a horse? This was not a skill he claimed on the Northern Track." She narrowed her eyes at me.

"I learned here at Manumina," I explained. "Aajan taught me. Piffik would not let her ride the horse Miya gifted her without someone to ride with her. Aajan said horses get irritable when they are not taken out and ridden. She said she could not bear to have a horse as beautiful as that one turn mean-spirited because it could not get out of Manumina and run. She said she asked me, because Zren Janin, the champion of Conrosa, should know how to ride a horse." I gave an embarrassed smile. "It was during the Wet and even her unworthy suitors would not go out."

Chul laughed at the look on Piffik's face.

Rell turned and looked at Piffik. "This doesn't have anything to do with your request to use my crossbow, does it? I thought you were borrowing it to protect yourself on your deliveries."

Piffik just gave her a wry smile. "I needed Zren to protect Aajan."

Rell turned and looked back at me. "Does Piffik know you can't fire a crossbow? Miya said you were strong on hand to hand fighting, but the one time you shot a crossbow in the courtyard of the Vikland embasado you missed the target and even the protective bales of straw surrounding it." She nodded at the shocked look on Piffik's face. "Ah, I see. He didn't know you were as useless as Aajan's unworthy suitors." She looked at Aajan. "And if you knew this, you weren't going to say anything to curb your freedom."

Rell was quiet for a moment and then she shrugged. "I would have done the same." Then she looked at Chul. "Did you know all this was going on?"

Chul nodded. "Actually, you did too. Zren told you all about it when you were in the infirmary. Zren told you the names of the horses he rode, what he liked about them, and where they traveled. He complained about how heavy your crossbow was and remembered the times on the Northern Track when Miya would call 'Weapons up,' and you would hold your bow so steady for what seemed forever. He reminded you that you had taught him to care for the horses on the way, and sometimes you thought horses were smarter than people. You said you preferred caring for the horses over cooking over a campfire. He told you all this and more."

Chul paused. "You were fighting your monsters, Rell Huena. We are glad you are back with us, and even though your monsters took all your efforts, your crossbow kept Aajan Qanaq and Zren Janin safe from harm. You are truly a bowmaster of Vikland who stands for justice and protects and defends the defenseless."

Rell's face scrunched up into an odd look, and I didn't know what to expect. Chul just stood there in his bastono and solemnly and steadily looked at her face.

Finally, she gave a lopsided grin, and said, "Well, then. If Zren can ride a horse, and my crossbow can keep us safe, we should all just go on a pony ride to Sary for a day of buying trinkets."

Piffik blew out a noisy breath. "It isn't that easy, Rell. I can have Zren ride with Aajan while she gets the oils the chandler needs. The chandler cannot go herself because she has already started the soaps, and if she lets the fires out the entire batch is ruined, and our profit for Manumina is lost. Aajan has helped her before and knows how to tell if the Patron of the shop will try to cheat her on selling a lessor oil."

"I helped the chandler," I offered.

Aajan looked critically at me. "The Patron in Sary tries to sell us rancid oils which spoil the soap. Did she have you touch the oils to your tongue so you know which ones are best?"

I scowled. "No."

Aajan didn't say anything more but walked over to the used sheets of paper Rell had scattered about the tables.

"What's this?" she picked up one for a closer look.

Rell sighed. "Chul has inventions coming out of his head and no way to put them on paper." She added drily, "He needs curves and subtle angles and what would a bowmaster of Vikland know about that? I can only draw straight lines." She grinned at Chul. "At least that is what he thinks."

"And these numbers?" Aajan said slowly. "Are they measurements, trajectories? Ah, these are how much pressure is needed."

Chul looked at her skeptically. "You see what I am trying to do?"

"It is similar to a book my teacher gave me." She looked up at him. "I sit in the classes with the oldest students at Manumina, but even so, my teachers give me extra books to keep me out of trouble."

"Take a blank sheet of paper—less blank," Chul clarified.

For the next few moments, we watched mesmerized as Chul described something completely different, but Aajan followed along with his words, only interrupting to say numbers which meant absolutely nothing to me. Chul just kept grinning as he talked until finally he said he was done. We all crowded about the picture.

"Our waterworks!" Piffik said. "That is the drawings of the waterworks piping. It stands underneath the round church our Council of Wisdom uses. But neither of you have ever seen it. How did you know?"

"We have similar waterworks in Vikland, and it is one of the first experiments students at the Academy of Elements must create at a small scale." He looked modest. "I may have taught that class once or twice."

Rell snorted. "Aajan, if you even understood half the words that have fallen from Chul's mouth, I respectfully hand you the graphite." She made a small Vikland bow and made a show of handing another graphite to Aajan.

Chul just looked back and forth from Aajan to Piffik and back to Aajan. "I should have known." He said shaking his head. "I should have known."

Chul wanted Aajan to begin working with him the next day. He said he had so many ideas rattling around in his mind they were giving him headaches. Piffik said Aajan needed to go to Sary for the chandler and then had her schoolwork after that.

It took all of us to come up with a plan, but in the end, I would go to the chandler's and keep the fires hot and her soap soup from ruin, while the chandler and Vigdis would go to Sary. Rell would take care of the horses for Vigdis. Piffik would still make his delivery to Ahni and return in two days. Aajan would work with Chul in that time. If Aajan liked what she was doing, and Chul was still satisfied with her work, Piffik would invite Aajan's teachers to the Qanaq house where Chul could talk to them about what should be done.

Rell leaned back in her chair and looked at me. "See, Zren? All this has happened because you finally learned to ride a horse."

* * * * *

Aajan's skill matched Chul's creativity. She could sketch his words into pictures, measure and transcribe the parts, and write descriptions of the whole. Her clever mind and quick hands could translate his thoughts into drawings; her sharp wit would ease his frustration when what he thought and what he said were not one and the same. She would take their finished drawings and measurements to the blacksmith, the chandler, or to Piffik to build Chul's dreams and inventions, and then, together, she and Chul would present them to the Council to share them with the settlement. Aajan was still known as the girl with the sharp mind and the sharper tongue, but now there was a purpose and a future to her days that had been lacking.

And Chul—Chul Swyler made life better for everyone in Manumina just by waking up in the morning.

CHAPTER 30

PIFFIK

Piffik became my best friend. It was from him I learned the difference between 'friendly' and 'friend.' I learned how kindness and patience with the apprentices meant the difference between one who would learn because they wanted to, instead of because they were scared not to. I learned I could ask him anything about Manumina and he would answer.

Soon I spent all my free time in his shop, and we would talk as he taught me to build Chul's inventions for Manumina and furniture to sell in Kerek. He asked about the world outside of Manumina, and I told him of Matasi. He asked if I missed my adventures, and I told him about Ngahuru and Koanga and fleeing down the Coast Road. I told him I had made a mistake that cost a man his life. I told him sometimes I still had nightmares of Song sliding lifelessly into Rygee's arms. I told him Ngahuru was the first person in my life who made me feel I was not standing alone against the world.

"And you're the second," I told him shyly.

He told me of life in Manumina. He said he still lived in the house he grew up in with his widowed mother, and his sister, Aajan. Now that his brother Zadah had left with the Spice Islander, Piffik had a room to himself for the first time in his life.

He thought when he was younger he might like to travel as I had, but his father had died when he was still in school and there was a woodshop to run. He knew of some who wished to travel so much they had sold their time to Vikland as soldiers for three years, but neither one of us could convince ourselves it was worth the price.

He talked about Aajan. How there was no coin to send her to the Academy of Elements in Vikland for more learning. That at one time, in his parents' generation, all the people would pool their coin to send the best to the academies. But then, those who left because they were the smartest the settlement had to offer, never returned to share their knowledge, but instead, made their way elsewhere. The Council of Wisdom said coin was too precious to spend on so few who would not return.

After every delivery, Piffik would see Rygee and give him coins to repay the loan for Zadah's travel. The first time Rygee protested. He was not a Viklander dragon he said. He had only himself to support and Piffik seemed to be supporting half of

Manumina with his woodworking. But Piffik had explained he had borrowed the coins in good faith that he would be allowed to pay it back. Woodworking was one of the few trades in high demand in Kerek. He had been trained as a journeyman, then a master, and now held the responsibility to teach others. It would not do for such a one to be known for not paying his family debts.

Rygee had given a great sigh then and held out his hand for the coins.

"I am saving it for Aajan and her schooling," he threatened. "Zren and Siba will be my witnesses."

I kept my nose in my book and pretended I didn't hear a word.

CHAPTER 31

A PONY RIDE

It was Rest Day. We had finished washing up after midday, and Rygee was going out for a walk. Chul had just settled in one of the soft chairs with a book Aajan had borrowed from one of her teachers for him. I was sitting at the common table and gathering my papers and graphite to write down the stories I had heard at the last Fourth night. Rell had hardly any limp any more, but moved restlessly between the furniture.

Aajan knocked twice and let herself in. "Zren, I have the horses."

I looked up at her in dismay, "I'm sorry, Aajan. I wanted to write stories down this afternoon. Can we go another time? Or even later today after end of day meal?"

"I'll go," Rell said quickly. "That's exactly what I need—a long pony ride." She gave me a half smile.

Aajan looked pensive. "I saddled a plow horse for Zren. We will need to go back to the stable and use one of the other ones— the Viklander one left behind."

Rell shrugged. "I can help with that. I'm sure the Vik horse needs exercise too."

I shot a look at Chul who was watching Rell. "We aren't in Vikland," he said carefully.

Rell huffed, "Fine, I'll bring my crossbow. Zren, will you run up to my room and get it? Grab a pocketful of quarrels as well."

Chul didn't smile. "It's a matter of numbers. If you are surprised, if you are overwhelmed, if you…"

"I am a bowmaster of Vikland, Chul Swyler. I will not daydream among the flowers. I will not lose my head if Trouble comes dancing. Aajan and I will take the two fastest horses in the stables. Chul," her voice faltered a little, "I will not fail."

Chul's face looked pensive for a moment and then he smiled brightly at her. "Of course you won't. Enjoy your pony ride." He turned back to his book and kept his eyes on the page.

Rell turned back to me. "Not a word to Piffik. And please, can you run up and get my bow and bolts? You're so much faster on the stairs than I would be."

I watched out the window as Rell and Aajan walked the horses back to the stable to get Song's horse, Rell casually carrying her bow in her left hand, her pocket of bolts tied about her waist.

"What should I do?" I asked anxiously.

Chul looked up from his book. "I thought you were going to write down the stories you heard last Fourth night."

"But Aajan and Rell…" I trailed off.

Chul smiled. "Rell needs this. She needs to get back on a horse. She needs to feel she can protect someone who needs protecting. In all the time you and Aajan went riding, did you even see anyone else out there on your rides?"

"No, but it was the Wet. And Aajan said we had to stay between Vikland and Manumina and not cross the Huntsman's Trail—the road to Ahni."

Chul smiled. "I'm sure Aajan will tell Rell the same thing."

I tried to write my stories down, I really did. But all I could think about was the two out there riding horses. I tried to figure out how Chul could stay so calm, but then I realized he hadn't turned the page since the women had left.

A decon passed and then another. The room remained silent as I strained to hear voices, horses, anything to tell me they had returned.

A pair of boots stomped on the front porch. At last! There was a knock on the doorframe and no one entered. Piffik was the only one of our friends who did not knock and then walk in. He waited to have someone open the door and formally invite him.

"It's Piffik," Chul said. "Would you let him in?"

I popped up from my chair and opened the door.

"Is Aajan here?" He explained immediately, "Mother is looking for her. I thought she may have come over to work with Chul."

I stepped back so he could come in. He walked past me and saw Chul sitting in his chair. "Ah, I am sorry. I came here first. I'll check with her school friends." He turned to walk out.

"Piffik," Chul said. "We know where Aajan is, she isn't with her school friends. She is out riding horse with Rell Huena."

Piffik looked at me with a look of hurt and dismay. "How could you?"

"Piffik," Chul said solemnly. "Rell took her crossbow. She and Aajan took the fastest horses. Aajan is safer with Rell

Huena—a bowmaster of Vikland—than anyone else here at Manumina. I believe this to be true."

Piffik took a deep breath. "I have watched Rell shoot her crossbow across the entire village green and never miss the target." He said it like he was trying to convince himself.

I thought of Rell pulling herself up the stairs every day until her legs worked the way she wanted them to, of training with her crossbow to defend our house, of telling us stories of her family until we were comfortable with living with her. How she would tease me that Rygee and I were just like her brothers— only smarter and better looking. I thought of her kindness and laughter and working together with Rygee and me and Chul as we shared a house and became our own family.

"Piffik, I do not know all Viklander women," I said, "but I know when I met the Vikland Ambassador of Kerek City, she told Miyamoto Suki she was sending Rell Huena and she was sending her best." I took a deep breath. "Viklander women do not wait to be rescued."

Chul laughed in agreement. "Viklander women are fierce. Aajan will have good company when she goes to the Academy."

CHAPTER 32

FACES FROM THE PAST

One day Piffik and I were driving a delivery of furniture into Sary when we saw Viklander soldiers everywhere. The soldiers were not carrying weapons, were not even wearing uniforms, but instead the dark trousers and shirts I had seen in the embasados. They were respectful to everyone, careful not to offend, and helpful. But I could tell they were soldiers.

I distrusted them immediately.

Piffik tied up the team and went inside to settle arrangements for our delivery while I stayed outside with the wagon. I had noticed one of the Viklander men watching us from the time we came down the street and now he approached me.

"Are you from Manumina? The Conrosan settlement?" He spoke Conrosan, but so thickly I could barely understand him.

"I also speak Keresh. Is that easier for you?" I looked down at him from my wagon seat.

"Stars, yes. I was just given a Conrosan primer two fortnights ago. It's a pretty enough language, but a lot of extra sounds."

I smiled in agreement. "I think the same of Vik, but then you went and threw a bunch of extra letters in."

He laughed in agreement, and I felt my chest burst with pride. Here was a Viklander who thought I knew languages like one trained from his academies at Juisiti. I turned my head away to hide my grin. Once I thought I had my face under control, I turned back to him.

"Why do you ask if I am from Manumina?"

He told me they had a wagon load of supplies for us. They had missed the half-track from Ishes. He had been told there was another way from Sary but thought it best to ask and be sure. He didn't want to be wandering about the half-tracks and pastures. He had been warned it would not be safe for him as a Viklander.

I tried to remember if I had heard of the Council of Wisdom requesting help from Vikland. News that significant would have spread through Manumina. If it wasn't the Council, who else would have enough coin and connections to demand a wagon be delivered? Rell? Chul? But I lived with them and couldn't imagine such a drastic action without either of them talking it over with Rygee and me. Well, maybe not talking it over with us. But they would at least mention it had been done.

"I cannot take you there without discussing it with our Council of Wisdom. What I *can* do, is tell them of your...*gift,* and they will send someone to meet you here in Sary." The soldier didn't even blink when I called it a gift rather than a delivery, and my distrust went even higher. *Did Chul know what was going on? He hadn't said a word about this.*

I looked around. The Kerek people didn't look alarmed at the soldiers. They didn't look sullen, or angry, or afraid. The shops had a steady stream of Viklanders entering and leaving and I understood the reason why. Viklanders were buying goods with coin. They were bartering metal workings, seeds, wine, and other goods the Sary shopkeepers could not get anywhere else, or at prices they could afford anyway. I watched how kindness and coin would buy goodwill. I listened as the soldiers talked loudly of clearing the Northern Track of bandits and outlaws from Ishes to Earles and maybe to Cloa, so that good honest people could travel in peace to visit families, go to market, and farm in settlements where the land was fertile. Without firing a single crossbow, the Viklanders were working to take away the fear of isolation and danger and replacing it with security.

Piffik came and joined me. He nodded at the soldier, but they didn't exchange words. After driving the wagon around the back, a boy and the owner came to help us unload. The owner was describing the joy of stabling and housing the soldiers.

"We charged them almost double, Piffik, and they didn't argue. Just paid us in advance."

"How long are they staying then?" I knew Piffik was fishing for information, and I ducked my head to my work.

"Just the three days. They are splitting at the Earles track. Some are going to the garrison they bought. They said it needs replenishing because they don't want to be a burden on their neighbors. Another group is going to Cloa for trade."

"Soldiers just out for a ride to market? They don't seem armed, don't they know the dangers?" Piffik shot a quick look at me.

"We told them of the bandits at the bridge between here and Cloa wiped out at the end of the last Dry. The Justice and a search party have gone out there several times since they found all those bodies, but no one new has moved in. The river encampment has remained deserted since then. Whatever troublemakers rode in to take their territory must have reconsidered. We warned the Viklanders, but I don't think there's anything but bones out there."

The Patron shrugged his shoulders. "There's another group near Huk, and possibly one near Earles the Viklanders should be hunting." He stopped and considered. "Although I haven't heard of trouble there since the Tax Collectors were killed. Frankly, if the Viklander soldiers can keep the Northern Track clear enough I don't have to pay double for armed guards on my supplies, I wouldn't mind them sticking around. The Kerek King can't be bothered to stop counting all those taxes he collects from us to see to our concerns."

Piffik joked, "When one suitor is unworthy, another one appears." He gave me a sly smile, and then we all laughed.

Deliveries done, we climbed up on the wagon. Piffik tipped his cap, and I picked up the reins to take us around the village green and out east to the Huntsman's Trail to Ahni and home. I started to tell Piffik about the soldier's request to come to Manumina.

"Zren! Zren Janin!" I heard my name and pulled back on the reins. I turned to look behind us and I saw Bima Ritwik and Solkka Ulani walking fast towards us. Piffik looked at me but didn't say anything.

"Last I saw these two, they were friends." I smiled. "But that was nearly a year ago."

Piffik chuffed, and we waited on the wagon until they reached us. Bima Ritwik put his hand on the buckboard and raised an eyebrow.

"You're not even going to get off the wagon and greet us?"

"Bima, when I first met you in Matasi, you took me out of the embasado, tried to get me lost, and then disappear before our food was paid for. The next time you and I spent time together was a tiny room on a ship back to Kerek City—a city I had just left ten days earlier at great peril to myself. You took me softfooting *after* First Soldier Joon told us specifically *not* to leave the embasado, not once but twice! The last time I saw you, you were explaining to Ambassador Lalsy why I should lie to the King of Kerek and pretend to be a Conrosan diplomat. I probably would have been thrown in a dungeon, if he had one."

I glanced at Piffik whose eyes were round in disbelief. I scowled at the Viklanders. "I see you coming, Bima Ritwik, and I count my coin, check my daggers, and plan my escape, not necessarily in that order."

Piffik choked back a sound, and Solkka broke with a deep laugh. I glanced at him. He gave me a lazy smile, and I just wanted to touch his face. How could one man be so beautiful? I scowled at him too, so he couldn't sense my confused feelings.

Piffik questioned me in Conrosan so they would not understand. "Are we in danger?"

I shook my head at him.

"I thought you said these were your friends?" he said in a low voice. I shrugged.

Bima smiled tentatively. "I think you should know Zren Janin, I sailed from Kerek City to the West Islands to bring Raumati home to her King and country, sailed immediately back to Salisport, Matasi and spent the Wet in Alenti. As soon as the mountain passes were dry enough, I crossed the Silver Mountains. I stopped in Juisiti just long enough for me to meet with Miyamoto Suki and the Empress in order to get attached to this expedition. All this, just so I could see you again and bring you news of Ngahuru, the great Softfoot of the West Islands."

"How is she? And Koanga?" I asked quickly.

"They are well. Truly, Zren, they are well, and it is a tale fit to be told at your table." He smiled. "If we are invited, of course."

"Well, in that case," I launched myself off the wagon seat and gave him a hard embrace. "Is that what you were expecting?"

He laughed and looked down at me. "Yes. Well, perhaps something between the two." He looked me up and down. "It looks like Manumina agrees with you. You no longer look like someone forgot to feed you for a season or two."

"It's true. I'm taller too," I said sincerely. I turned to introduce everyone. "This is Piffik Qanaq. If you have seen Miyamoto Suki, you have heard of the Battle at the Bridge. Piffik found us here in Sary and led us to Manumina to be healed. When Miya and Kern had to leave Chul and Rell behind, I agreed to stay and provide labor and coin for their care." I hesitated. "Piffik is my best friend. He helped us all find a home," I added softly.

Solkka straightened, dropped his lazy smile, and steepled his hands in the formal Vikland greeting. "I am honored to meet you, Piffik Qanaq. I was disappointed when I had traveled from the West Islands to Matasi and over the Silver Mountains to learn the Conrosan, Zren Janin, had not returned with Miyamoto Suki to Juisiti. But I am beyond glad to learn he has gained a home, a friend, and himself, in Manumina." He bowed deeply, and I saw Bima raise an eyebrow. I wondered what I had missed.

I turned to Piffik. "Piffik Qanaq, this is Bima Ritwik. When he could not find the hidden children of the murdered West Islands ambassador, I solved the mystery for him." I gave Solkka a sly look, "And this is Solkka Ulani. He is the reason I am sleeping alone at Manumina." All three gave me startled looks.

"You were going to teach me all those soft words I needed to learn, remember?" I looked at Solkka, and his smiled deepened even further.

"You remembered," he said quietly. I thought I would crisp like cheatgrass in a brushfire, I felt so warm. I dropped my eyes to the ground. What else was there to do?

"We have a wagon of gifts for you," Bima interrupted us. "We have meetings tonight we must attend here in Sary, but tomorrow? Could we come to see you then?"

I looked at Piffik on what to say.

"*Maybe* tomorrow," Piffik suggested. "I need to speak with the Council of Wisdom and earn you a formal invitation. I know Chul Swyler and Rell Huena will be beyond glad to see a face from Vikland to bring them good news," he added. "If the Council grants permission, we will prepare the guest house for you." He looked apologetically at me. "Your house is too small, I think."

"Tomorrow it is," I agreed. "Look for me in the morning. I'll need to arrange not to work tomorrow." I jumped up on the wagon box and reached for the reins. "Until tomorrow!" I shouted, clucked at the horses, and took them at a fast trot out of town.

Piffik said nothing until we were halfway to Manumina.

"I think they were expecting a far different Zren Janin than the one they had the privilege to greet again."

I blew out a noisy breath. "Piffik, I don't know what I felt when I saw them. I was happy and angry and sad. I don't know if it was because it was Bima Ritwik and Solkka Ulani or if it was because they are Viklanders who know Miyamoto Suki. I didn't know what to say. I just wanted to get out of there and think about what it all meant."

Piffik was silent.

I started and stopped a handful of different explanations. I finally gave up and said nothing the rest of the trip.

When we reached the stockade, Piffik spoke, "I have to tell the Council of Wisdom what I saw today and the Viklanders' request to meet us. I can tell the story so that permission will be granted or denied. What do you want to ask me to do?"

I looked up at the sky as if I thought the answer would fall like a shooting star. I took a deep breath.

"Let them come. Once I know what they want, I can decide what I will do. If I refuse to hear them, I will never know how the story will end."

Piffik smiled and I could tell he approved of my answer. "Go and tell the others in your household. I'll take care of the horses and supplies." I jumped off the wagon seat, nodded a quick goodnight, and took the small door out of the stockade to my house.

Aajan and Chul had their heads bent together as she tried to draw what Chul was describing. Rell was in the kitchen helping

Rygee as he was preparing the end of day meal. I heard Siba's voice as well and knew she was over for the evening. This was my home, my family, and for a long moment I just wanted to keep it just like this—safe and enclosed—before I needed to tell them of the Viklanders in Sary.

The six of us sat down to the end of day meal—a rich meat pie with vegetables and gravy. I listened to people tell of their day, events they had coming up, news they had heard while they were out. Rell was describing the uses of borage as a medicinal in Vikland compared to Manumina. I listened silently through the meal to all the different conversations. We were an odd family to be sure, but we had come through it all together.

Afterwards, I volunteered to carry away the dirty platters as Rygee brought out the fingersweets and coffee. When I returned, I cleared my throat.

"The Viklander army has moved into Sary."

Chul's hand stopped in midair as he reached for another fingersweet. Rell leaned back hard in her chair.

Siba spoke first. "What does this mean?"

"It means the Kerek King has fallen and the Vikland army is sweeping to Kerek City to clear the road and set up patrols, or it means Matasi and Vikland are working together to carve up

Kerek, and they think the Kereki army can't stop them," Rell said heavily.

"There's more." I paused. "I saw Bima Ritwik and Solkka Ulani in Sary. Piffik is gaining permission from the Council of Wisdom tonight to bring them out tomorrow."

Chul considered. "Solkka Ulani traveled with Ngahuru to the West Islands from Salisport, and Bima Ritwik with Raumati from Kerek City. Did they confirm the ambassador's children were safe at the West Islanders' court?"

"They said they had. Then they both returned to Matasi, came over the Silver Mountains to Vikland, and now to us," I explained. "Bima said it was a tale fit for our table."

"That's a lot of effort just to visit 'old friends,' don't you think, Chul?" Rell said slowly.

"It is," he agreed. "It is a lot of effort, and yet," he smiled broadly, "don't you think we're worth it?"

We were quiet for a long moment, and then Chul said soberly, "You know they are going to ask, Rell. This isn't a decision you should make lightly. Think of everything you have ever wanted. Don't make it easy on them." Then he asked Aajan to bring the drawings they had been working on, and he spent the better part of the evening explaining his new windmill which would use the power of the wind to bore the hole to the water table and draw up water from the ground for the livestock without hauling water buckets from inside the stockade. As a manabout with no love of animals, I was his most enthusiastic listener. Rell was lost in thought. Rygee and Siba retired to the kitchen where they did the washing up and talked quietly about what this could mean for all of us and Manumina.

CHAPTER 33

GUESTS OF MANUMINA

When I trotted into Sary the next morning on what I still considered Song's horse, I saw a wagon fully loaded but unhitched near the village green. I dismounted nearby, thinking I could catch the eye of the soldiers guarding it and then ask for Bima Ritwik or Solkka Ulani.

Instead, I heard Solkka Ulani call, "Zren!" and I wheeled to see him and the stable boy leading over a pair of heavy plow horses. Solkka was no longer dressed in the dark clothes of Vikland he had worn yesterday, but instead in sand-colored loose trousers and a billowy brown shirt like Kereki farmers would wear. He had two brightly colored Kereki ties about his legs—a vibrant orange on one leg and a deep green on the other.

"I see you finally found a way to tell your right leg from your left. It must make it easier on those forced marches," I said nervously. I wondered why I was being spiteful. He was the most beautiful man I had ever seen, and I was acting like a petulant child.

He gave me a long look. "You've changed since I saw you in Kerek City. I noticed it yesterday. It's more than just a few good meals."

I repeated the words I had told myself over and over again last night before I fell asleep. They could not make me go to Vikland. They could not take what was mine. No matter what Bima and Solkka told me today, Piffik had taught me that I owned myself.

"I have a purpose, a home, and a place to belong," I began nervously. "I'm not scared anymore thinking everyone knows more than I do, and everyone else controls my life. I no longer have to look at every person and try to guess whether they are my friend or my enemy, if they are trying to figure out what I have or what I can do, or if they want it and think they can take it from me."

Solkka cocked an eyebrow and held up his hands, palms out. "Zren, you don't need to be defensive with me. I'm in the Diplo; I'm not a soldier. I'm not going to force you to go with us." He paused a long time and then added, "I mean you no harm. I am your friend." He clarified, "I want you to consider me your friend."

I changed the subject. "You went with Ngahuru and Koanga to the West Islands. What did you find there?"

He dropped his hands and gave me that smile again. "Ngahuru and Koanga were met by her father, the tailor to the King. No one on the island was mourning the missing children. On the third day we were there, Koanga was invited to the King's palace to host a storytelling. Ven Wila and I were invited to attend as well. In a break with tradition, he told two tales instead of one that night. One of the Soldier tales that he said was a favorite of a man he had met in Anarkio, Matasi, and a new Traveler tale. One, he said, in which a trio of travelers trust one another, even though they are beset with many trials and troubles. Through that trust, all reach their destination even though it scatters them across the heavens and only the Seafarer can sail to see them all.

"I thought it was a curious story. I also thought it was curious I never saw Ngahuru again after the first night. She vanished. Both Ven and I stayed in the palace as guests of the King, but we didn't hear any concern over her whereabouts." Solkka gave me a look I couldn't read.

"Then, when Ven and I decide we can learn nothing more and should return to Matasi and our posts; Bima, Raeshon, and Raumati of the West Islands sail into the harbor. That night, that very night, as fast as the news can travel, there are fires and baboys and celebrations all over the islands. The ambassador's children are brought out and introduced as the niece and nephew of the King. And another story is told, not by Koanga, but by the whispers of many voices, how Ngahuru, the great Softfoot of the West Islands, Raumati, a kluba woman who has known and cared for the children since their birth, and others loyal to the West Islands, spirited the children across the ocean. With the help of very great and powerful friends, Zren Janin of Conrosa and Miyamoto Suki of Vikland, everyone from the ambassador's household left alive was brought home." He arched an eyebrow. "You're quite the hero in the West Islands."

I blushed and dropped my eyes to my boots, and then I heard footsteps.

"Thanks, Solkka," Bima said sarcastically. "I had hoped to save that news when I needed to soften Zren's prickly distrust to do me a kindness. Now you put all my coin on the table before the first toss of the dice."

Solkka shrugged easily. "I like to see Zren happy. And if you just remember bits and pieces of all the praise of Zren Janin from your recent journeys, you will have enough stories to 'soften Zren's distrust' to last us the entire Dry." Solkka cut his eyes at me before he finished with a final jab at Bima, "Now I've managed to get the wagon loaded, horses hitched, and Zren collected, while you were whispering soft words to your newest conquest. Perhaps we should go before her father comes home?"

Bima scowled. "How far is Manumina? I certainly don't cherish a day's ride lurching about on a wagon."

I smirked and slipped my reins into Bima's hands. "My dear Bima Ritwik, great Softfoot of Vikland, it would be my honor to have you ride my horse to Manumina. My horse is as brave and true as you are, for she has traveled from Kerek City to Manumina, and lives with the other heroes from Miyamoto Suki's thirteenth crossing of the Northern Track."

Solkka burst out laughing and pulled himself up into the wagon. "There you go, Bima. You can be our outrider, while Zren rides with me and we can teach each other soft words."

* * * * *

I directed Solkka out of Sary to the Huntsman's Trail. Once we had turned south on the track to Ahni and we were safely headed to the settlement, I began peppering him with questions. How was Kern? What did Vikland think when Miya arrived with three missing survivors of the previous journey? Did Solkka know Song Yao's family? Did Rell's family know she was so close to the border? When did Solkka arrive in Vikland? Was Rani a Softfoot like Bima? How did Koanga and Ngahuru look when Solkka left for Matasi?

He didn't answer me, just told me he would only tell the stories once. The Manumina settlement rose distantly ahead of us in the valley, and he marveled at the tall narrow houses side by side marching up the walls of the stockade. I explained how the inside had the shops, wells, and food stores, and how Conrosans held all things in common.

He asked if I liked living in Manumina. What did I do? What was a manabout? Why did I think working with wood was so satisfying? He was telling me a story about his trip over the Silver Mountains to come home into Vikland when he fumbled for a Keresh word. I remembered it in Conrosan at the same time he said it in Mata. He gave a happy laugh, and we continued on in a polyglot of Keresh, Vik, Conrosan, and Mata, substituting freely until we were making more nonsense than sense. For a moment I flashed back to Matasi on the day when I learned to laugh for the joy of living. Ngahuru, Koanga, and I had done the same mashing of languages as Ngahuru had tried to teach us Mata phrases to get by, and Koanga had tried to teach me Wester words. I laughed at the memory, knowing I now lived where I could learn anything I wanted and there were always friends along the way.

Solkka laughed back, his eyes dancing. He pulled back on the reins and stopped the wagon. He glanced at Bima, ahead and to the right. Solkka dropped the reins, caught my face in his hands, and very gently kissed me.

I stilled.

He dropped his hands and pulled back. "I have wanted to kiss you since I saw you again yesterday. When I saw you a year ago in Salisport..." He turned and looked straight ahead. "I am sorry. I have had a year to imagine our first kiss," he picked up the reins, "while you have had a year to forget who I am."

"That's not it, Solkka. I did not forget you." I put my hand on his. "I want, but I don't know what I want. Don't turn away from me, Solkka, please?" I whispered again, "Please?"

He turned his hand over to clasp mine. "I am sorry if I frightened you. We can talk later, or not. We can spend time together, or not. As you said, Zren, you own yourself."

We traveled the rest of the way in silence. I didn't know what to think of Solkka's kiss, so I pushed it away and refused to think of it at all.

The stockade gates were open in welcome, and we pulled the wagon through. I directed him to stop on the village green. Salik Oqina was there to greet them, and Vigdis unhitched and took away the horses to the stables. The presence of the Vikland army in Sary meant this was not going to be a casual visit. The Council of Wisdom was treating this as an official meeting of Conrosan Manumina and emissaries of the Vikland Empress. I had warned Solkka of this as the settlement had come into sight. As for Bima Ritwik, I'm sure the Softfoot could adapt to someone else's plans for a change, instead of only his own.

CHAPTER 34

OLD FRIENDS, OLD TIMES

Rygee was beginning to despair his meal would be ruined when Aajan finally saw the doors of the round church open. She flew out the door and across the green to bring Solkka and Bima back to the guesthouse for midday meal with us.

The common room was crowded, but Chul and Rygee had insisted Aajan, Piffik, and Siba be part of our meal with Solkka and Bima. All three were there, dressed in their Conrosan best.

Rell had taught us all the Vikland greetings and explained how the highest honorific must be used to the person greeted first. She explained this noted the guest was so important everyone knew who they were. Then Chul laughed and said, in Bima's and Solkka's case we could get by with barely nodding our heads. Rell had laughed at that too, but then showed us what to do. She said, if the Viklanders knew the good manners their betters had taught them, they would do the greeting to us in return and tell us how grateful they were we welcomed them.

"I'll give you a direct translation," Rell warned, "so you can decide how kind you wish to be."

I had remembered something like this from Ngahuru when we had been in the embasado in Salisport. She had thanked Miya for his help with a short bow, but he had shaken our hands. In Kerek City, he had asked me to bow when he did to Ambassador Lalsy and First Soldier Joon, but I didn't remember others outside of the training areas. I remembered Ngahuru had said to bow to the most important person first and then wondered if I would know who that was. I wondered if I would ever know how to act in Vikland.

The first greetings were formal and cordial. The Viklanders may have felt they were among friends, but the meeting with the Council of Wisdom earlier conveyed that everyone was taking this visit very seriously.

Piffik had already met both of them the day before, but both were respectful and greeted him first, as if they knew how much influence he had. Rell smirked at me as she watched Solkka and Piffik take each other's measure, but then she stood close to Piffik, put her hand lightly on his arm, and Solkka relaxed.

Bima faltered and then stopped speaking altogether when he saw Chul's bastono in motion. But both of the Viklanders clasped Chul close, taking his heavily scarred hands into their own.

"Miya says he would not be alive without you. His eyes fill every time he has to tell the story of this last crossing. He implored us to make sure you understand how important you are to him, and how much he wishes to see you again," Solkka said softly.

Chul was visibly moved, and before the entire room dissolved into an emotional disaster, Rygee called us all to the table to eat. We were all used to them of course, but both Bima and Solkka watched as Rell put Chul's delicate gloves on his hands. Before the meal, Chul had asked to have a West Islands steel knife and fork in the narrow pockets instead of the usual wooden fork and spoon. He wanted the Viklanders to see how well he could care for himself, he had said.

Over the meal, we asked questions, told stories, and reminded others of how we had changed. Bima told his version of Ngahuru saving the ambassador's children. Stories of the Conrosan settlement brought a flurry of questions, and Bima said he was excited to see it all for himself. Solkka told of the lost travelers, Rani, Ceri, and Malik returning to Juisiti. After their return, the Empress had formally closed the Northern Track to Vikland travel until now.

Kern had returned to Vikland from an assignment in Kerek—Bima had glanced at me—and was leaving the Diplo service to get married to Ceri and be a soldier's wife. Bima was sorry to lose her as a softfoot. Chul and I looked at each other, and he smiled.

"I love happy endings," he sighed.

Rell said little. She answered every question asked of her, talked about her work in the healer's house with Bett and Siba, but dropped her eyes whenever Bima or Solkka talked about a close friend in common. We all talked of Chul's inventions and Aajan's skill in taking his cryptic words and measurements and turning them into drawings and designs Piffik and others could fabricate into reality. Aajan asked a lot of questions about Juisiti and the classes at the Academy of Elements.

Siba cleared the table, and I helped Rygee bring out fingersweets and the tiny cups of Vikland coffee. As the others settled in with their coffee, Bima leaned forward.

"I would like to tell you why we are here."

Chul interrupted, "We know why you are here. You are here to visit old friends and that is what today will be. Zren will give you a tour of the settlement this afternoon. You will have a meal in the guest house this evening with some of the Council of Wisdom and spend the night as guests of Manumina. Tonight, Zren will lock you in your rooms if he must to keep you from counting the goats. Then tomorrow...tomorrow and not one moment before, we will talk of any other reason that would cause you to ride from Vikland and seek us out in our sanctuary."

CHAPTER 35

TELL NO ONE

After midday, I gave the tour Chul and Piffik had planned for me. I was to introduce Bima and Solkka to as many people as possible. The Conrosans would describe their work, their families, and their plans for the future. The goal, Piffik said, was to make the Viklanders see Manumina as people and not a place.

The Conrosans were kind and curious. They asked questions about why Vikland was here in Kerek, about children they had sent to the academies and Juisiti—surely Bima or Solkka would know them. They questioned if it was true all Viklanders were soldiers for a time. Those who had watched Rell practice her crossbow for the past season commented on her endurance and her steadiness. They demonstrated Chul's inventions and explained how they made life easier for everyone.

Bima said little but his eyes traveled everywhere. If we were back in Kerek City, I would have guessed he was a thief measuring how difficult the night's work would be. He commented twice on how poor the settlement appeared.

"They seem to work hard enough, Zren. What seems to be the problem? If they are not lazy or foolish, I cannot see why they do not thrive here."

Solkka offered his own opinion, "Bima, they cannot breathe here. Kerek crowds them all about, there is nowhere for them to dream and build and grow. Imagine what our Viklander women would be like if they were told from the time they were small, they could not be anything or do anything or go anywhere without someone else's permission."

Bima chuffed. "There would be bodies on the ground before that happened."

Solkka shrugged. "Only because they already have that power." He gave me a small smile. "Sometimes, it takes more than one voice for people to understand what they are capable of, to grow larger than the world they grew up in."

I stilled. I felt like Solkka was trying to tell me something. Or maybe, he was just telling me that he had heard me earlier. But I didn't know him well enough to interpret his words.

Bima turned and gave Solkka a long look. "Now is not the time to develop a conscience, Solkka Ulani. You know what we have to do here."

Solkka smiled. "Of course. We need to teach Kereki and Conrosan women to think like Viklanders." He added quietly, "No matter how dangerous that might be to your health, Bima Ritwik." He glanced quickly at me to see if I had heard.

I remembered something Rell had said on the Northern Track to Nebs once when he had said Kereki women were never allowed to handle weapons.

"Rell says, 'The number of widows would double overnight if Kereki women had access to more than pigstickers and pitchforks.'"

Both men barked out a laugh, and we continued on our walk. Once they had seen the narrow gardens and fields, the woodworking shop, and the apprentices and manabouts tending the animals, I took them back to the guesthouse for them to rest and get ready to meet the Council of Wisdom members again at the formal meal that evening.

* * * * *

While the Viklanders and the Council were meeting and eating, I talked with Piffik and Chul about all the things Bima had said. Chul explained why this visit was critical to the Viklanders. As much as we survivors wanted to believe Bima Ritwik and Solkka Ulani were here to see us, we knew the greater purpose was to entice Manumina into an ally. From what Bima and Solkka had casually hinted, the Viklander Empress felt Manumina could not claim neutrality. We had no mountains to hide behind, no stormy seas that would keep the battles away, and no weapons our enemies would fear to face. Therefore, we would need to declare for Kerek or Vikland. In exchange for her protection, Vikland would gain a ready-made garrison fully staffed for her soldiers.

Piffik had bristled then. "Conrosans are pacifists, she thinks we will lay down our generations of beliefs and take up arms just at her desire?"

But we knew the settlement had benefited from Chul's inventions—many inventions—this past Wet. What would happen if our firemaster decided we were the enemy? What inventions had been created in Vikland that we knew nothing about? Vikland had power, discipline, the academies, and training. Kereki settlers along the Northern Track were fighting for their livelihoods, their homes, their families. They may be happy to have a roaming army take out the outlaws and robbers along the road, but as permanent neighbors? Who can imagine desperation when there is nothing else to lose?

And so, now I watched the doors to the guesthouse as some of the Council of Wisdom members filed out. Bima and Solkka came out last. They watched the village green and slowly scanned the interior of the stockade. When they saw me by the village well, they both smiled, and I started forward.

When I reached the first step of the front porch, I asked, "I wonder if you would like to take a moonlight tour of the settlement outside of the stockade? We are safe, no Kereki outlaws stray this far from the main tracks."

They stepped down, one on each side of me. Earlier in the afternoon, when I had led them around the settlement I tried to introduce them to people, to the work they did, to the homes and businesses they had built. We wanted Bima and Solkka to understand the humanness of the settlement, the disruption to people's lives if Vikland moved forward with war with Kerek. I knew Bima and Solkka were too small to make such decisions themselves, but perhaps they had influence with those who made those decisions. Ambassadors listened to them. They knew Miya, and Miya knew the Empress.

Tonight, I wanted them to see the beauty of the place, but also the defenses and the weaknesses. If they could point them out to me with their military strong minds, if they could help me understand what I needed to do to keep me and those around me safe, then I would listen, and I would learn.

The stars were vivid overhead, no cloud cover, just endless points of fire, some bunched up like those in the "bowl of pearls" that Koanga had pointed out so long ago and some strung out in long constellations the West Islanders used to tell time, direction, stories, and their history.

"You've both been to the West Islands," I began. "You've heard the great Constellation stories, or at least heard of the Soldier. He guards the islands from unknown threats—some are from nature, and some are from those who would do the West Islanders harm. The Soldier is brave, he is watchful, he protects those who need his protection." I paused. "You have met the settlers of Manumina, they practice non-violence as they are able." I stopped and looked at them both. "I am Manumina's protection, and I need your help. Show me where our weaknesses are. Tell me how to save the people so we are not starved out in a siege, burned out and massacred, or overrun by Kereki soldiers."

Bima cocked an eyebrow. "I'm a softfoot. I can show you places where I would hide someone to create fear and distrust through single acts of violence and sabotage, but what you are asking takes the mind of someone who can see all the angles to prepare for every eventual outcome. A master of strategy. This," he waved his hand, "is not how I think. Solkka?"

Solkka looked about the valley and then at the stockade. "I have some ideas, but as Bima said, neither one of us is the strategist that someone like Ven Wila is. Still, let's walk and talk and I will tell you what I know."

Bima left us before we reached the end of the first wall. "To talk to Rell Huena," he said. Solkka continued on as if he didn't notice it was just the two of us. When we finished we walked inside the stockade, and he casually put his arm about my shoulder.

"You like living here, don't you?"

"I do. At first I thought it was because we were damaged and afraid, and they were kind, but now it feels like I belong." *I am safe here. Do you understand that, Solkka Ulani?*

"You know Miya would like to see you in Vikland. He says he owes you a life debt."

"He knows where I live. He can come here to tell me," I responded stubbornly. I paused. "Has he made any more trips across the Northern Track?"

"No. As we said earlier, it is closed to us now as too dangerous to travel. The only way a Viklander will be on the Northern Track now is with the army. As for Miya, as soon as the mountain passes were dry enough, he went over the Silver Mountains to negotiate on behalf of the Empress with the Matasi Triune in Alenti."

He hesitated, "Zren, Bima may or may not tell you tomorrow, but Matasi has built armed settlements far into Kerek. They continue to buy up lands and the displaced Kereki farmers are moving north or staying and working their old lands as tenants."

I shrugged. "They were starting to do this when I was in Matasi a year ago. I saw it happen. The new owners were patrolling the Coast Road to keep the travelers safe. What has changed now?" I considered his words, and answered slowly, "Oh. How far north have they gone?"

"As far as the Old Fort Road. They are not just buying one estancia, they are buying *every* estancia. Kerek will have lost almost a quarter of its land if Matasi forced the border north to the edge of their settlements. It is not a big country."

He waited for me to puzzle out the next part. "Where did they get the coin? These new landowners?"

He smiled at me. "That is the right question to ask yourself. The answer is the Matasi government. Bima has placed Raeshon— you remember Raeshon? A Matasian with a Viklander heart. She is now working in the Finance Hall for the Triune in Alenti. A very useful position for a softfoot, though she knows her life is forfeit if she is caught. Matasi and Vikland are not exactly friends but..."

"They are united against Kerek," I offered. "The enemy of my enemy is my friend."

He grinned. "Exactly. The Matasi Triune believes buying the land and helping the landowners defend it is cheaper than a war. It is definitely easier on the hearts and minds of the Matasi people."

"But what happens when the Matasi Triune tells the Kerek King the new border of Matasi is the Old Fort Road?"

"Ah, my friend, if Vikland takes the Northern Track and all the lands north to the Cold Mountains, and Matasi declares a new border to the Old Fort Road, Kerek would be forced to fight a war on two fronts. They have neither the army, the treasury, nor the King to succeed." Solkka gave a satisfied smile.

I swallowed hard. What Solkka described so easily would destroy us at Manumina.

"What are you and Bima doing? You are in the Diplo, not the military. You said it yourself."

He gave me a sly grin. "I came to see you, of course. I have a lot of soft words I want to teach you." He continued on, "Once you found this place last year, Miya thought there might be other towns and settlements where survivor Viklanders might have gone to recover, but not had the numbers or the means to safely return home to Vikland. We are also switching out soldiers at Earles. We are part of the advance: asking about nearby towns to visit, bandits and outlaws that may be operating nearby, patrols we can set up to make the Kerekis feel safer in their own land. Bima is softfooting to see if we can find more lost Viklanders. If we can find them, we can bring them home to great fanfare—the lost have been found—and all that." He quirked a smile at me.

"Is that what happened to Malik, Ceri, and Rani?"

"Actually, Vikland didn't know they were lost. They were traveling east to west. The embasado in Kerek City knew they had not arrived and sent the message with Miya, but then he brought them home. No one has taken the Northern Track since."

Solkka went on to explain how the Empress's strategy was to gather the land north of the Northern Track all the way to the Cold Mountains to build a series of settlements to supply the garrisons. The Empress was a crown with teeth he said, who realized the fool on the Kerek throne and his two useless sons were no longer to be negotiated with. The supply routes from Vikland to the port had been disrupted for nine years. The Viklanders were crying out for a resolution, even if the resolution was war.

We had reached the guesthouse and Solkka invited me to sit with him on the porch swing. I sat down and he put his arm around me again. It felt less... odd than it had before.

"I need to tell you some things, Zren Janin. But I would ask two things of you. One, do not mock me for what I am going to say. Two, tell no one. Do I have your word of honor as a Conrosan, and as a friend of Ngahuru of the West Islands?"

"Is she in trouble?" My stomach clenched.

"No. But I have told no one in Vikland what I have seen, and I must have your word."

"You have it."

Solkka pulled his arm away and turned his body so he was sitting in the swing facing me, one leg casually bent. He told me how he had seen Ngahuru in a formal dress at the Secondo's side in Salisport. While they were talking, she had made a nervous motion as if she were twitching a glove straight on her bare left hand. He noted it because it seemed odd for a softfoot to act as if she wore gloves—like the Empress, or a thief, both of which he knew Ngahuru was not. And then he was called to Miya's group, "…and I saw you." He smiled.

"You looked so fiercely at everyone, but you were nothing but a too-thin boy who had fought and killed to get Ngahuru and Koanga from Kerek City to Salisport. I wondered what Ngahuru had done to earn such loyalty from one she had just met. I had Conrosan teachers at the Academy of Languages, but they were so different from you. I couldn't reconcile what I had been taught in books with the boy in front of me at the embasado. You were a puzzle I wanted to figure out. And then for one moment, you looked at Koanga as he stuffed a pastry in his mouth and your whole being transformed. I thought to myself: what kind of man is this who wears his heart and his mind on his face?"

I snorted. Solkka raised his hand. "You swore on your honor you would not mock me." I thought about his trusting me with his words, and I nodded.

He continued, "I had just finished a year's service in Alenti, so imagine my surprise when I was told I would be accompanying Ngahuru and Koanga to the West Islands to see if I could recognize the children at the palace, and then to travel to Kerek City and let First Soldier Joon know what I had seen and heard. So I asked if you could speak any other languages so we could have a private conversation. I wanted to know if we could meet before I left or when I returned."

He laughed, the smile all the way to his eyes. "You said I could teach you, and I thought to myself here is one I want to get to know better. In that moment, with those words, you became more than a puzzle." He shrugged nonchalantly, but turned his face away from mine, "I thought it was an invitation...Koanga or not."

Then Solkka told me how on the ship to the West Islands he had talked with Koanga and learned he and I had only been fellow travelers. He spent time with Ngahuru and found her to be wise, funny, self-deprecating, and completely unconcerned about the ambassador's children.

"Ven and I would lay awake in our bunks at night and wonder how she had gotten them out of Kerek City when the city was locked down and the entire Kereki army was searching for them."

When at last the ship had arrived in the West Islands, they were met by Ngahuru's father who took them to the palace as an honor guard to eat and rest. And then the next day, Ven and Solkka had lost her. Ngahuru was gone.

The breakthrough came on storytelling night. Solkka had taken a seat in the back so he could watch the crowd. At the doorway to the servant quarters, he saw a white-haired Kereki boy, sand-colored pants tucked in his leather boots, ties about his ankles. At first, he thought it was just another member of a family working in the palace, until he saw the youth twitch a black glove over his left hand. Then he remembered a street runner in Kerek City who often frequented the street where all the embasados were lined up, and where people were always looking for children to deliver messages for a few coins. The street runner wore a glove to keep the paper of the messages clean, or so the rumor went.

Solkka had tried to fight his way through the crowd to the doorway, but by the time he reached it, the youth was gone. "It is Ngahuru, isn't it Zren? She has the ability to change her gender, her age, and her skin, that's why Bima and the others could never find her."

I said nothing.

"Zren, you could not have traveled with her in such close quarters and not known." He sounded exasperated. "By saying nothing, you have convinced me I am right. And this is where I demand you keep your second promise—*tell no one.* If the Matasi, or Viklanders, or—stars above—the Kerekis, know her secret, her life would be worth nothing." He looked fiercely in my face. "Nothing."

"You will keep her secret?" I asked.

"I will." Solkka looked solemn.

"Without a price? Or is that what we are going to discuss next?" I crossed my arms over my chest and looked down at my feet. I had heard of these bargains for bodies in Lowertown.

"Oh, Zren." He sounded so sad. "I would never..." he trailed off. "Without a price. Ngahuru's secret is not harming Vikland, and until she shows up in our palace fluffing the pillows of our Empress, I have nothing to say on the matter to anyone." He looked at me closely. "Zren, I like Ngahuru. I like and respect and admire her. I am not going to do or say anything to harm those I am able to protect. And this I can do, I can protect her secret, and that will protect her life."

He yawned suddenly, and then said briskly, "It's been a long day, and I am headed upstairs. There's no need to lock me in. I'm not going to go out and count your cows, or inventory your weapons, or anything else Chul Swyler has filled your mind with." He stood up and stretched, and I jumped up to keep the porch swing from crashing back against the house. He reached out to steady me. "Look, I learned today you will do whatever it takes to keep those you care about safe. I know that means I am going to go back to Vikland alone. That makes me sad, but now you can imagine what it is like to think of *me* for a year." He pulled me close, kissed me gently on the forehead, and released me. "Goodnight. I'll find you in the morning after the Council of Wisdom gives us their decision."

He walked into the house, and softly shut the door without looking back.

I stood there confused. Confused about what he had told me, confused about my feelings, confused about what I should do next. Then I did what I do best. I stepped off the porch quietly and ran from Trouble all the way to my house.

CHAPTER 36

AND SO IT WAS DECIDED

The Council of Wisdom was not wise. They refused the offer to house a small military garrison of Viklanders with compensation. The council reasoned with Bima that Vikland did have a right by treaty to the Northern Track. But to home Viklanders at Manumina? The settlement's location south of the Track and along the Huntsman's Trail—the Sary to Ahni road—would be in violation of the treaty.

The council refused the offer to move everything they owned into Vikland and find a new life there, abandoning the stockade to the Viklanders and their military.

"We have been refugees before," one of them said, "it is not a life we wish for our children."

The council refused the offer to send their young men and women to Vikland for training to learn to defend themselves and their settlement.

"We have lived here in peace for three generations. The Kerek people know we will heal them if they are injured, feed them when they are hungry, shelter them when they are homeless."

"So you are throwing in with the Kerekis?" Bima questioned sharply.

Salik Oqina looked at him coldly. "The Viklanders know we will heal them, feed them, and shelter them as well. We are a friend to all and enemy to none."

"You are in a valley! Your houses are built on the *outside* of the stockade! They will burn your fields, slaughter your livestock, and starve you out." Solkka was exasperated.

I heard these words with my own ears. The Matasi had built round churches so there was no corner for the devil to hide in. However, a young man, slight of build, sun-dark from manual labor, and strong from a life of running faster than Trouble, could find a perch in the rafters in the shadows.

And so it was decided. The wagon of gifts and supplies was left, not as an enticement or a bribe, Bima said, but as a sincere thanks for the shelter and care given to Viklanders on past crossings. The Conrosans accepted, and stated again, Viklanders would always find a safe haven in Manumina. There were lots of pleasantries, well-wishes, and formal goodbyes, but the message was all the same. Bima Ritwik and Solkka Ulani would be leaving empty-handed.

I waited until everyone had left before climbing down from my perch. When I arrived at home, Solkka and Bima were already there. It was Rest Day, and no one was at work, well except for Aajan and Chul who always seemed to be working on some invention. Bima was telling his version of the meeting, and while I remembered Miya's advice that Bima and Truth did not always sit at the same table, for the most part it was true.

When he finished, Rell looked at me. "You were there. What did Bima fail to tell us?"

"I was." I nodded. "It was as Bima says. The Council of Wisdom believes Manumina can remain neutral if it comes to war."

Chul huffed. "Do Vikland soldiers own the road from Sary to the border?" he asked Bima. He waited until Bima nodded and then, "Will you provide passage back to Juisiti, not just the border?" When Bima nodded again, he paused a long time. "How soon are you leaving?"

"You'll come back with us?" Solkka didn't hide his surprise.

"I'll have to ask Aajan's mother to release her into my care. I formally request Aajan Qanaq be admitted to our academies of learning without cost to her or her family, with a lifestyle and a place to live comparable to the other near royals, as I had when Vikland took me in." He laughed his big Chul laugh. "And there better be a fast horse for her to ride as she wishes." He gave her a wide grin. "I don't want to train in a new assistant who must draw what my head is thinking, and not what my mouth is saying."

"Educating Aajan Qanaq is the price of having a firemaster return to Vikland?" Bima clarified.

"If her mother allows it," Chul acknowledged. Aajan said nothing, but if Conrosans could fly with joy, we would have been looking to the stars for her.

"Done." Bima looked at us sitting around the table. "Anyone else? Rell Huena?"

She looked down at her hands, "They need healers here at Manumina. I'll stay."

Bima looked at her thoughtfully. "There is no shame in what happened at the bridge at Sary." He paused to let the words soak in. "If you change your mind, come home. A fast horse will have you at the border in one day."

She nodded, her eyes bright with unshed tears.

"Rygee, I know that you are Kerek-born, but you also have a debt of thanks from Vikland from the last crossing. Do you wish to stay or go?"

"Siba and I talked about this already." He took a deep breath. "The Conrosans and the Viklanders gave me a life when my father and the Kerek King would have sentenced me to almost certain death in the Kerek army. I will stay in Manumina." He looked at Rell and me before continuing, "It never escaped me for a moment Kern and Miya could have killed me at the bridge when we fired Song's body and set up the battlefield to look like a fight between Kereki outlaws."

He turned back to Solkka and Bima. "Therefore, I will agree to help the Viklander Softfoots. Siba talked to Piffik yesterday when we thought the Council would vote against helping you. He will also be a part of this."

I looked at Solkka. "You are right. I will stay here to protect Manumina, but I will be a part of Rygee's group."

"I will too," added Rell.

Bima's eyebrows almost climbed to his hair. "Do you know what you are offering us?"

"I think I do." I numbered them off my fingers. "Piffik owns his family's woodworking shop that makes deliveries to the garrison at Ishes, as far east as Huk, and all the way down to Ahni. Sometimes those deliveries include coffins and other large chests, large enough to hide people. Siba and Rell are healers with considerable skill which would mean our Kereki neighbors would not need to know about strangers with injuries too severe to ride to Vikland. Rygee is Kereki-born and will not draw attention as he buys and sells, travels, and trades for information among the Justices in all the nearby settlements. Rell, Rygee, and I live together in a home on the outside of the stockade for strangers to find shelter. I know all Viklanders learn as children to speak Keresh along with Vik, but it may be reassuring to those we help to see Rell, a Viklander, among us. Give us friends in the Ishes garrison who won't shoot us on sight, and we can send word, people, and maps, and receive the same within the day." I looked at Solkka and Bima. "That's what we are offering you."

"And if the Council of Wisdom finds out what you are doing?" Bima questioned. "Will you abandon us without warning?"

Rell smiled at Aajan. "Then you are going to have refugee friends sleeping on the floor of your workrooms." She looked at Bima coldly. "We won't abandon you. Viklanders protect those that need protecting as long as we are able."

Solkka was the first one out of his chair. We all stood, and there was a lot of back-slapping and hugging going on. Finally, Chul stepped back and sighed.

"Well, that was the easy part. Now I am off to talk with Aajan's mother."

While he and Aajan were gone, Bima and Solkka left us for the guesthouse to pack up as well. The Council of Wisdom had arranged for Piffik to lead them to Cloa and rejoin the other Viklander soldiers who had left Sary the day before.

Bima left a small purse of Viklander coins on the table. If any of us changed our minds, he said, we were to travel with Chul to Ishes. The coin would pay for food, horses, and inns once we were inside Vikland until we reached Juisiti.

Soon we heard Piffik's boots on the porch. He let himself in the door and greeted us all with a large smile.

"What's so delightful?" Rell asked.

"I just came from my mother's house where Chul and my mother are negotiating Aajan's future. Frankly, Vikland should just send those two to Kerek City. They could argue a truce with the Kerek King before a war begins."

"What does Aajan say?" Rell was curious.

"She wants to go, of course. My mother thinks it will be safer for her to be there, rather than here if there is war and wants her to go. I think this is the opportunity we could never have afforded to provide her, and I want her to go. Chul thinks she would succeed in her own right at the academies and wants her to go. So you think it would be easy, no?" He shrugged his shoulders. "Aajan's worried there won't be horses to ride, Mother is worried she won't be sufficiently provided for, I worry Manumina has not prepared her to live in Juisiti, and Chul— I don't know—does Chul worry about anything?"

Bima and Solkka returned with their travel packs, and we followed them out to the front porch where Piffik had three horses saddled. I recognized Bitterboots' and Song's saddles on the two Viklander horses that would be leaving with Bima and Solkka. It made sense, they were leaving the wagon and the heavy draft horses they had driven down, but it was sad to me to see one more tangible of Song Yao leave my world. I wondered how much longer it would be before I had nothing but a memory of her.

The goodbyes were sober as the men mounted their horses. I stood next to Rell, who was hugging herself tightly. Solkka asked her a question in Vik and she shook her head. He looked pensive and then resigned. Bima looked at Solkka and shook his head. I looked closely at her and noticed her eyes were red-rimmed, and I wondered when she had been crying. I noticed no one used the formal Viklander bows to say thank you or goodbye as Rell had taught us. I wondered what that meant.

"We'll meet again," Bima said to me. "I left you your coin, your daggers, and your escape routes intact." He slid me a half-smile. "I have always liked traveling with you, Zren Janin. I have always liked you. I have always liked how those who disregard you, pay a price for that disdain." He dipped his head just a fraction and nudged his horse to follow Piffik.

Solkka mounted his horse and wheeled around to face me. "In one year, you have learned who you are. You have found your people, learned your language, and become a man with a man's responsibilities. Before we meet again, know this, *Whala te iti kahurangi ki te tuohu, koe me he maunga teilei.* You are my mountain, Zren Janin." He kneed his horse and quickly caught up to Piffik and Bima already trotting down the road.

Rell and I watched them until they were out of sight.

"It feels like the day I watched Kern, and Miya, and the others leave us a year ago." I mused. "I wonder if I will always be the one left behind."

Rell gave me a side eye. "You better learn to speak Wester, Zren." She dusted her hands and turned to go back into the house. "Solkka Ulani is not going to wait for you forever."

I stood looking after her with my mouth hanging open.

CHAPTER 37

CHUL LEAVES US

Chul Swyler was a man who made a decision and didn't waste time once the decision was made. That night as we were all gathered together, he asked Rygee and Siba if they could make a special meal three days from today as a farewell end of day meal. He gave them a bag of coins as large as my palm to pay for the food. Siba looked inside and her eyes grew large.

"How many are we to cook for?"

Chul laughed. "It is to pay for an entire calf. I may never get back to Manumina, and I want to say I know I would be dead now if you had not helped us. It is to acknowledge your mercy, your skill as a healer, and your wisdom. It is the gratitude of a man who has found like souls who can talk about anything under the sun and call it a good conversation. It is the joy of a man who loves a happy ending."

Chul asked me to take down the curtain partitioning off his bed in the front room. He said he no longer needed the privacy.

He was worried his bastono could catch on the cloth and trip him as he packed his belongings.

* * * * *

The day of the special meal, Piffik brought over a wooden chest he had made to carry Chul's clothes and his treasures. It was much larger than mine, with a fancy carving on the lid and stained wood. We all stood around the table and watched as Chul opened it. His eyes grew moist as he saw it had been lined with a portion of Rell's first red cloak. Inside the chest, I had given him a West Islands steel dagger—not the one I had used to kill Bitterboots, I assured him—and a Conrosan fairy tale of Zren Janin, which I had written down on clean white paper. I explained to Chul how Piffik had made a special trip to Sary to buy new paper for me with some of the coin Miya had left and Siba helped me sew the pages together after I was finished because I had been worried about spoiling a page. I knew Chul didn't know how to read Conrosan, but I told him it was the only language I knew how to write. He held up a hand to stop me talking so much.

"For now, Zren. It is the only language you know how to write for now."

I nodded happily in agreement.

Underneath my papers there were four hinges made of West Islands steel, each no bigger than my three fingers pressed hard together. "Perhaps, someday you will have better bastono," Rygee said. "But the hinges are for repairs to the ones made here in Manumina. They represent the bringing together of two parts which work better together."

Siba gave Rygee a bemused look, and then she turned to Chul. "It is to remind you of our secret, which was never a secret to anyone except Zren."

I gave her a startled look, and then turned back to Chul. He shook his head at me, "I warned you to learn how to cook, Zren. I truly did."

* * * * *

Chul's last night at Manumina was like one of Rygee's food and stories nights. People came all evening long bringing more food and their thanks for all of the inventions Chul had given to the Council of Wisdom and the people of Manumina. Piffik's family was there, and Aajan was dressed in her Conrosan best. Her teachers, her classmates, her friends also came to say goodbye. Some were happy for her, some jealous, and some relieved it was not them who would have to learn a new language, new foods, new ways, and still try to keep up in the academies which only took the best students who lived outside of Vikland.

* * * * *

The next morning was much more somber. After first meal, I stepped outside with the others as Piffik drove up with a horse and a small cart. He had modified it with a small cutout opening through the buckboard to fit Chul's damaged leg which still could not bend. He stepped down from the cart just as Aajan came out of the stockade gates riding her horse and leading another. Piffik and Rygee supported Chul as he climbed down the two steps, walked without his bastono to the cart, and then braced him as he pulled in his damaged leg. Rell carried his bastono, and I carried his wooden chest and placed it into the back of the cart beside Aajan's smaller wooden chest and three traveling bags. Piffik mounted the other horse.

Rygee commented the cargo must be valuable indeed to need two outriders. Rell wryly commented they couldn't be outriders if they were all unarmed, and Aajan was only riding because she wanted to ride fast one last time before she reached Vikland.

Chul laughed his big Chul laugh and said it was an honor guard and therefore he must be the secret son of the Empress. Rell smiled and explained to the rest of us, an honor guard was two mounted Viklanders for someone who had the Empress's favor. It was a very rare privilege in Vikland. For Chul to have one as he arrived at the Vikland border? Well, Zren could make stories all day on that.

We all laughed. What could I say? I would talk to anyone who would listen.

"Chul Swyler, do you have my letters to my family?" Rell asked. "My mother will never forgive you if she finds you were no more than a handful of furloughs from the Central Administrative Offices in Juisiti and no letter was posted from there to her."

Chul patted his tunic where he had tied an oversized pocket full of Rell's letters, and another letter I had spent all night writing and given to him just moments ago. He had merely looked to whom it was addressed, looked me in the eye, and said he would deliver it in person. I nodded my thanks. He had hugged me then and said for a man who loved happy endings as much as he did, he couldn't imagine any better ending than the future I had ahead of me.

My throat was too full to speak.

Piffik looked to Chul, and Chul nodded. Aajan moved out to the right, the group turned east to the half-track which ran directly to the Ishes garrison. There Piffik would say goodbye, collect Aajan's horse from her, and turn back to Manumina. The garrison would provide outriders to Juisiti and the palace where Chul Swyler would be welcomed home.

CHAPTER 38

ZREN'S LETTER TO MIYAMOTO SUKI

To Miyamoto Suki, Prince of Vikland, and friend to the Conrosan settlement of Manumina, Kerek:

I write this letter in my own hand and in my mother tongue. You cannot imagine what it means to me to be able to write those words.

I am sad to see Chul Swyler leave us, but as he hands you this letter, I can imagine the look of pleasure and happiness on your face. He has created so many wonderful inventions for us with wind, fire, and water here at Manumina. I think of him as the Smith in the West Islands Constellation tales, bringing a better life to those around him wherever he goes. I know you will look beyond his limp, his cradled canes he calls 'bastono,' and his hands so scarred they cannot bend. Listen to his laughter. I miss him already.

You may have heard from Bima Ritwik, educating Aajan Qanaq is the price to have a firemaster return to Vikland. But you have met Aajan and gifted her a horse for her speed. She is brave and very, very clever. Chul's wisdom in having her educated at the Academy of Elements and continuing to assist him as she begins her own life work is a gift to Vikland—not a price to be paid. But as you said yourself, the Truth and Bima Ritwik do not always sit at the same table.

Rygee continues to do the right thing for the right reason. You would not recognize the confident, open-hearted young man he has become. Or perhaps you would. He has said he knew when he volunteered to stay with you at the bridge before Sary, it would be easy for you and Kern to kill him and steal the Kereki paychest. He knew it could be possible, but he stayed anyway to help you honor Song Yao, and clear the battlefield of Vikland's presence because it was the right thing to do.

And now he has stepped forward again with his offer to help Vikland in the days ahead. There are others here who believe war is inevitable, although it is certainly unwelcome. Rygee's response to Bima and Solkka reminded me of the night on the Northern Track when he told us who he was—a Kereki who did not hate us merely because we looked differently than he did.

Here at Manumina, he has found a life partner in Siba Namikk, the younger healer, whom you met. She is wise and as open-hearted as Rygee. She has taught my head and my heart to work together. She was the first to teach me what I needed to know to live beyond my childhood. She has given me a purpose by teaching me to read and write.

Rell Huena has joined the healers in their work, learning Conrosan medicine and teaching them Vikland's ways. This is hard to write, Miya, and I tell you of the little things, so my heart won't bleed over the big ones. I am not sure Rell will return to the court and the Diplo at Vikland. Her legs healed, although she still limps a little. She has scars from the arrows and knives. But her heart cannot forgive she fired upon children to save our own lives.

Bima told me differently. He believes she feels shame for not firing immediately when you gave the command. That by faltering, even for a moment, she caused the death of Song Yao. Surviving when others did not. Whatever the reason, when her heart is so full she cannot speak, she takes her crossbow and practices for decons. As the quarrels thunk into the target, people come to watch her. She can shoot the length of the stockade and never miss. She is as accurate with her last shot as with her first. She never tires. She is still a bowmaster. She is the defense of Manumina.

I have become a manabout. Whenever anyone needs an extra pair of hands, I am called for. I work where I am needed and I am paid in coin and barter. I have learned about building furniture and fences and caring for orchards and fields. I have been taught all about livestock from breeding to butchering—please, don't ask—and finally, you will be pleased to know, Aajan Qanaq taught me to ride a horse!

I have asked everyone to speak Conrosan to me and only if someone, usually me, is going to be injured, to switch to Keresh and warn me. Rell has taught me the formal greetings in Vik. I never understood how the deeper the bow, the more respected the greeted. I didn't know to not greet someone formally is to think they are beneath you. I missed so much by not understanding what I saw and heard in the Vikland embasados in Salisport and Kerek City. You and Ngahuru were already dancing a complicated set from the very beginning when our paths crossed in Ribelo, Matasi. It is strange to me to think how I witnessed so much without comprehending anything. But I do know this, I thank you for your kindness to her and to me. I realize now your interactions in Ribelo were between Ngahuru and Miyamoto Suki, and what happened to us in Anarkio and Salisport was between the West Islands and Vikland. You are a powerful friend.

It is not enough for me to know how to read and write and speak Conrosan. I have recently been given an incentive to learn Wester. I still plan to visit the West Islands someday. I wish to thank Ngahuru in person for the lessons I learned at her side. She must have thought me hopeless, as well as helpless, as she dragged me from Kerek City to Salisport filling my head and my heart with what I needed to know to live a life beyond survival. I also want to hear more of the Constellation tales from the Storyteller to the King. I truly believe stories tell us who we are.

On Fourth night, Rygee cooks for all of us without a hearth and home of our own. We gather to eat, visit, and tell Conrosan fairy tales, West Islands Constellation stories, and any others we can remember or dream. I wish I would have asked Kern to tell me stories of the great Miyamoto Suki, the famous warrior and poet of a faraway land, and the one I had the honor of traveling with from Kerek City to Manumina. Someday, you can tell me them yourself.

You have made yourself strong enough to do the hard things, Miya. To make treks over the Silver Mountains, journeys across the Northern Track, and sail on the seas between the West Islands, Matasi, and Kerek to bring people out into the world, and supplies and warriors home. You learn languages, and customs, and cultures. You live as a stranger in other courts so Vikland will have a strong voice among her friends and allies. You do honor to your Empress.

I am young and foolish, Miya. When a child grows up on the streets of Kerek City, the child doesn't learn the difference between friendly and friendship, kindness to strangers and affection of lovers. I have slowly sorted out the differences as I live here in Manumina. I am so very embarrassed over my mistakes and misunderstandings in matters of the heart with Koanga, Ngahuru's brother, and with you.

I have forgiven myself and you have never needed my forgiveness. I will continue to live and thrive here at Manumina settlement. Perhaps someday I will appear in Vikland, with or without Rell

Huena. Perhaps someday you will be announced at the court in the West Islands, and find me already there.

Forgive me my harsh words on your last night in Kerek, Miya, my friend. The world is not so kind that we can throw away those who care for us.

Zren Janin

SOME CALL THEM ACKNOWLEDGEMENTS, BUT I PREFER GRATITUDES.

It took the entire village of Manumina to drag Zren Janin to the other side of childhood. It took an entire village of people to hold my hand and calm my heart as we traveled through this second book in the series. And the journey continues.

Thank you to the team at Paper Raven Books. I continue to learn from you all every time I text/email/zoom. Jesus Cordero, you have magic in your fingers to make the books look so awesome. Ashley, you know just the right questions to ask to straighten out those pesky plotlines and contrary characters. Thank you, Karen, for your subtle guidance to keep me moving forward in the same direction as everyone else. Thank you, Morgan, for your NextSteps group. I learn so much from everyone and there are so many people to keep me from falling down rabbit holes! I am so grateful for all of you!

A huge debt of thanks to my beta readers, writing group, and fellow workshoppers. You ask such great questions, catch the tiniest details, and discuss the characters' actions and motivations as if they are your friends, or the snarky person you would cross the hall to avoid. You have lifted minor characters into major ones, demanded to know backstories, and hissed at villainous actions while championing the person behind them. You are the reason the book isn't full of one-dimensional tropes. As the characters continue to unfold in all of their imperfections, I hope you continue to cheer them on. Thank you, thank you.

Angela Lawson, Stephanie Dodge, Gary Dunker, and Florence Dunker – Thank you for holding me accountable! I continue to rely on your good judgment and red ink. Editors, readers, and cultural gurus. I owe you all so much.

Manumina had an entirely different set of people who helped Zren Janin discover himself. I also had so many people inspire me during this book's journey. All I can do is quote Salik Oqina, "*Never underestimate the good you can do in the world.*"

Colleen Oeltjenbruns Dunker – I couldn't decide whether Song Yao or Rell Huena should be modeled after you. Then I realized your bazillion skills and talents could be easily scattered between the two of them and they both would still be Zren's heroes (and mine). You're an awesome sister-in-law, great role model, and can shred the center of any target. I still want to grow up to be you.

Debra Schoenenberger – You handed Siba Namikk her skills and wisdom and turned her into a fan favorite. You continue to be an awesome cheerleader, insightful critic, and faithful reader. I am so lucky!

Katie and Liz – Thank you for the Christmas gift of Bananagrams. You are the reason none of the characters have unpronounceable names that are twenty letters long. (Except for Manumina which is the Latin word for "handwriting" and represents Zren's jump into literacy.) See what my readers would be subjected to without your gift? My readers thank you. I thank you.

Robin Floyd and Susan Schuetrumpf – You were my Manumina when I moved to Georgia. So much has changed since then: our addresses, our jobs, our everything, and yet, here we are.

Greg Dunker – You hold the 'high standards' bar just out of reach, so I have to work to keep up with you, but not so high that I pick up my toys and go home.

As always, David and Bridget (and Sylvia!), Ryan and Briana, Jenny and Zach, Katie and Nelson, Almond, Brandon, Liz, Kaeden, Callie, Peyton, Philip, Lauren, Ryla, Rinoa, Gunther, Lark, Hayden, Max, Nordica, Penelope, Cory, Catherine, and Hallie. You are the readers I write for.

And finally, and most importantly, Steven. You hang the stars and the moon in the sky. New Zealand was only the beginning of the adventure. That pretty much sums it up.

"Sometimes, it takes more than one voice for people to understand what they are capable of, to grow larger than the world they grew up in."

- Solkka Ulani in Manumina

Turn the page for

Manumina Bonus Materials

including a bonus short story: *The Gift of Siba Namikk*

and a preview of Book 3 in *The Tales of Zren Janin: War and Wrens*

READING GUIDE

Need to write a book report?

Try using some of these questions as a launching pad!

1. Zren quickly appreciates and admires the Viklander women and their many talents. Discuss what the Viklander women—Song Yao, Kern the Softfoot, and Rell Huena—represent to you.

2. On the Northern Track, there are two altercations between the Kereki soldiers and the Viklanders with very different outcomes: Zren and Bitterboots, Song Yao and Mouser. Discuss how the differences in Zren's and Song's past upbringing and training impacted their actions.

3. What was your initial reaction to the place called Manumina? How did your impression change throughout the book?

4. From the beginning of the book until the end, Zren only acts independently a few times. Why do you think Zren is so quick to follow the directions of others? How is this different from most main characters in the fantasy adventure genre?

5. The title *A Gift of the Stars* (Book 1 in the Tales of Zren Janin series) referred to Ngahuru. This title, *Manumina,* refers to the place Zren calls home after the Battle at the Bridge. What comparisons can you make between Ngahuru's rescue and acceptance of Red, and Manumina's rescue and acceptance of Zren Janin?

6. The soldier, Rygee Brick, is the only Kereki survivor from Miya's thirteenth crossing of the Northern Track. How do you think this impacts his choice to remain behind at Manumina rather than traveling with the others to Vikland? How does he try to take control back of his life again? What does Zren mean when he says Rygee seemed to grow older and wiser in front of his eyes? How does fear and insecurity make us small?

7. Siba Namikk is one of the first to realize Zren is going to need a lot of help and direction to overcome the intellectual poverty and crippling fear caused by the lack of security (and well, pretty much everything else) Zren experienced in Lowertown. Why do you think she started with teaching him to care for a house?

8. How do Rygee, Rell, Piffik, Siba, and Chul give Zren the sense of family he needs? Why do you think their different methods were more successful than perhaps more traditional ways of teaching/parenting? Which method did you like best? Which would be most effective for you?

9. The Spice Islander ship captain/tax collector tells a very different side of Vikland and the Viklander Softfoots than Zren has known so far. Yet, neither Chul nor Rell deny or downplay the Spice Islander's story. Nor do they dismiss Zren's feelings when he says the other conscripts were just like him. How do you think this will impact Manumina in the future? What could this be foreshadowing?

10. The Viklanders have a very different attitude towards mental health than the Conrosans do. How would Rell's recovery been impacted if she would have been home in Vikland? How does Zren grow in his own understanding of Rell's mental health crisis?

11. How do the stories Zren tells around the campfire (*Zren Janin and the Citadel of Wisdom* and *Zren Janin and the Queen of Conrosa*) and in Rell's recovery (*Zren Janin and the Village Geese*) reflect the setting in which he tells them? What is he teaching his audience?

12. Chul Swyler is a pivotal recurring character in the series who takes a lot of time and effort to teach Zren to think for himself and to understand more of the world around him. He carries on this mentorship when he takes Aajan Qanaq to Vikland to be educated at Vikland's expense. Think of a person in your life who went above and beyond to help you succeed. How did this make an impact on your life?

13. How do you think Zren felt when Chul said goodbye and told him "…for a man who loved happy endings as much as he did, he couldn't imagine any better ending than the future I had ahead of me."

14. Why is Chul's friendship with Piffik Qanaq so important to the both of them? How do you think Chul reconciles his inventions and his role in the Kerek City riots with his love of happy endings? How does Piffik personify his beliefs? How do the two men who have such opposing thoughts keep their friendship?

15. A critical component of the book series is something the author calls "otherness" defined as an unrelenting attitude towards others that says they do not deserve the same treatment or kindness for any reason: lack of wealth, skin color, tenets of belief, gender/sexuality, abilities, lack of opportunities/privilege, or even no

reason at all. Think about conversations and interactions in the book that revealed such casual cruelty such as the Viklanders experiences in Cloa, Piffik's statement that the outsiders would not receive medical treatment in Sary, Miya's minimizing Zren once they arrive at Manumina, the Spice Islander's treatment at the hands of the Viklanders. Why is it so easy for the characters to excuse their own biases?

16. When Zren meets the Viklanders Bima Ritwik and Solkka Ulani in Sary, he acts very differently than they expected. What do you think the Viklanders represent to Zren at the end of the book in comparison to the beginning of the book?

17. When Bima and Solkka leave Manumina, both men realize Zren has made significant personal growth in just one year. In the letter to Miyamoto Suki, we begin to see more of Zren's potential as well. What do *you* think is Zren's most significant moment of self-awareness?

18. Who is your favorite character so far and why?

19. What was your favorite quote?

20. What advice do you think Solkka Ulani was giving to Zren Janin about the future ahead of him when he said, *"Whala te iti kahurangi ki te tuohu, koe me he*

maunga teilei." This translates to "Seek the treasure you value most dearly, if you bow your head, let it be to a mountain." Why do you think he only said it in Wester, a language he knew Zren did not speak?

BONUS STORY

The Gift of Siba Namikk – A Tale Told by Zren Janin, A Traveling Storyteller

Once upon a time, not so far away, there was a healer of Manumina with the name of Siba Namikk.

As a healer, Siba could stir a pot of potions, splint a break, and bandage a wound. These were the healings she had been taught by her aunt Bett, a healer of renown who had attended the Vikland academies in Juisiti.

You know and I know, my friend, in all the best Conrosan fairy tales, our heroes have a bit of magic. Siba Namikk was no exception. Siba had a rare gift: she could see more than what was shown to her, and hear more than the words fallen from someone's lips. This is true, my friends, I witnessed it myself. She could offer solace and healings to mind, heart, and body, not only by acting upon what she had seen and heard, but by what was unseen and unsaid.

Now there are fairy tales where magic wishes are given in threes, and those where bargains are struck for a year and a day, or a great gift is given only to be snatched away through trickery. But Siba Namikk's magic was so much more than that. Her magic was seven times seven and more subtle than a child's lullaby.

One day, when Siba was still a child and just beginning her apprenticeship, a large family of Matasi settlers washed up at Manumina's gates. They had traveled across Matasi and Kerek for an entire Dry with all their worldly goods. But the Wet had already begun when they arrived at Manumina, and they were still so very far from their new home.

The Conrosans knew Manumina had been an abandoned Matasi stockade when their grandparents had found it, so the Council of Wisdom invited the travelers to stay with them until the following Dry. Then the Matasians could continue their travels to build and farm their new lands in northeast Kerek.

It would have been easy during that season of the Wet to keep the Matasians in the guesthouse and empty spaces, to show them where the grain was for their animals, and to allow them to worship in their round church only when the Council of Wisdom wasn't using it. But the Matasi travelers and the Conrosan settlers were all strangers in a strange land. Close quarters made close friendships, and they practiced kindness and shared knowledge with each other.

Because the Matasians had no healer with them, Aunt Bett invited one of the girls to join Siba in her training. Although it would only be for a season, Bett explained to the Matasians, it would be good for Siba to learn more of the world around her, and for the girl to learn a little healing in case their new home was far away from a town or settlement.

So, in addition to Conrosan poultices and potions, Siba learned of Matasi foods, praise songs, and a way of life far different than her own. While the Conrosans held most things in common, practiced non-violence in all ways, and had decisions made by the Council of Wisdom, the Matasians liked owning their lands and possessions, called the Lost God the head of the house, and hunted for their food as easily as they grew it. Siba listened to the parables of the Lost God. She noted how similar they were to the Conrosan fairy and folk tales she had learned from her parents as she was growing from toddler to girl.

But most of all, Siba remembered walking out in the early mornings to gather the plants they would be using in their teachings that day, and seeing all the Matasians sitting on their prayer blankets, facing south. The soles of their feet would be touching together, forearms resting on their thighs, eyes closed in prayer and meditation. She would stand there and watch them, amazed at how even the youngest of them could sit so still and solemn until the morning sun touched them with its rays.

Her aunt had explained to her how Matasi was ruled by a Triune theocracy in which the leaders spoke with the Voice of God, the law upheld the Rule of God, and the military was the Fist of God. That didn't interest Siba nearly as much as everyone sitting silently at daybreak, their straight-backed bodies haloed by the sunrise.

Many years later, Siba met another Matasian who spent an entire season in her care. While he was lying nearly asleep and healing from his burns, unable to move from the bandages over his leg and hands, she shared what lessons and parables she remembered from sitting in a round church with no corners for the devil to hide in.

Chul Swyler told her of traveling on a ship with his parents when he was eight. Pirates had chased and swarmed the ship when they were crossing the wide seas, and while they had been fought off, only a handful of survivors limped into the nearest harbor—Kerek City. He told of the Orphan Master who had met them at the docks, the false promises to find their families in Matasi, the desperation of the other children waiting to be sold on Market Day, and days later, the Viklander diplomat who bought him and the only other Matasi child from their ship.

Siba told him of the Matasi girl who had learned to be a healer with her, and how they would tell each other stories and keep secrets. How she thought the Matasi girl had the best imagination ever to make up all these stories about growing up in Thodport only to be told over and over again, it was all true. Matasi was so different from Manumina, Siba had told Chul, as a child she could only accept what the girl had told her as make believe and fairy tales.

Chul admitted he had been afraid to travel to Vikland with the diplomat's household, thinking no one from his home village would know where to find him. The Viklander had promised to take the children with her to her posting in Alenti and then to Vesaport in Matasi to find their families. But after the betrayal of the Orphan Master, it took many reassurances from the others that Viklanders keep their promises.

Siba told how she would sneak out each morning to watch the Matasi travelers draw their prayer circles, lay down their blankets, and sit so still and quiet in order to hear the voice of God.

Chul told her of the bandits that had struck them while they were traveling on the Northern Track, of the wounded Viklander who had staggered badly as he plucked Chul off the ground and boosted him and Raeshon on an uninjured horse. He had told the boy to ride east, always east, steal horses and food when they needed to, and never stop till they reached Vikland. Chul said he had been too young to understand that man had given his life for him, and he didn't even remember his name.

She told him of the peace she learned from the Matasi and the mercy and kindness she learned living in Manumina where people lived so closely together and shared their stories from generation to generation.

He talked of that desperate flight across Kerek and finding safety at a garrison over the border. He smiled as he told of meeting the Empress and how he was offered a place to grow up in the Vikland court as a reward for surviving, merely surviving. How he was homed in the palace with the other near royals and shared their tutors. How he was encouraged to read and learn and ask questions until soon he had tutors of his own and a seat at the academies. How his size and strength and his ability to learn and create and invent were the very things Viklanders prized most highly.

He said he remembered little of the parables from his earliest years, but he liked to hear Siba tell of them.

But strangers come to Manumina and strangers leave. Chul Swyler left for Vikland taking Aajan Qanaq, their smartest student in a generation, to go with him to the Academy of Elements at Juisiti. He had bargained with the Softfoot to gain Aajan's greatest desire.

Siba thought at first she would be angry since *she* had wanted to go to the Academy of Healing, and *she* had been the one who nursed Chul to walking, and not Aajan. But then she looked at the others who had come with Chul Swyler and realized that dream was not meant for her. She had a different path to follow.

There was the one she first called Rygee the baker, who needed nothing more than time and work to restore himself over the sting of being sold by his father and brothers for the refusal to bend to his father's will. Later she called him husband, but that's a story for another day.

And the Viklander bowmaster, Rell Huena, who suffered from surviving a battle where those she knew did not. A warrior and a healer, her mind had broken when she could not be both at once. Siba knew she could provide comfort and peace, but it would take Rell's own determination and desire to recover herself. No one could fight those monsters but those who had been at the Battle at the Bridge with her.

The last one that had been left behind at Manumina was a Conrosan. Siba had faltered when she considered the last one. He was completely lost to himself and so very broken.

Her friend, Piffik, had been at the Council of Wisdom where Miyamoto Suki had spoken of his gratitude for sanctuary, told of their battle, and his future plans. Viklanders had been ambushed at the bridge before Sary. The Council had sighed, they had lost Conrosans there as well. But Miyamoto needed to return quickly to Vikland with important information for the Empress and her advisors, and only his softfoot and bowmaster, Kern, was well enough to travel. He would leave coin for the care of Rell Huena and Chul Swyler until they were able to return to Vikland. The other two, the Kereki and the Conrosan, "he did not even use their names, Siba!" would be offered a place in the Vikland army, but he wasn't sure they would accept. They were both strong-bodied, if Manumina would offer them a home. He hesitated, "I cannot speak for them, because I did not know either of them before this journey. But Ngahuru, the great Softfoot of the West Islands, said the Conrosan had been found along the road to Aldi, without friends, name, or coin. She named him Zren Janin. Although he is young and slight of build, he defended her life twice, as he defended our lives...twice. He speaks no language but Keresh and knows nothing of Conrosa. He is small, true, but not harmless. Because of your belief in non-violence, you should know men have died at his hand."

Piffik relayed all this to Siba, and told her of his response, "I told the Council I had offered them sanctuary outside of the butcher shop in Sary. Manumina can give them a place to heal, and I can give Zren Janin a purpose to recover himself. I said I would take responsibility for him if Manumina would house him."

Siba looked askance at her friend. "I have seen the boy! Piffik, he is nearly feral! How can you restore him to us if he knows nothing but the wickedness of Kerek City?"

"Through teaching him the value of himself. He is more than the box he climbed out of. Together, Siba Namikk, you and I can teach him safety, food, constancy, and kindness are his whenever he seeks it, for it was the lack of those that broke him."

"I have never met anyone like him before, where would we even begin?" Siba blew out a heavy breath. "It will take all of us here at Manumina." She paused a long time. "We can do this." She smiled weakly at him. "But it won't be easy."

And that's how it began, my friends.

But Zren Janin wasn't the last, oh no! Siba had barely succeeded in dragging Zren to the other side of childhood—with the help of all of Manumina—when a settler's wagon of throwaway children from the streets of Kerek City arrived at the gates.

Siba had walked out early one morning to gather wild plums for the first meal when she saw one of the wrens that had come the day before with Ngahuru. He had no prayer blanket, but he had drawn his circle on the ground. He and his dog sat stiff-backed, eyes closed, facing south.

Siba felt the same sense of calm and peace as the sun rose over the edge of the world and outlined his body in light. Suddenly she knew, this one would be a warrior and a man of so much mercy. He would prevent one murder and commit another to protect those entrusted to his care. He would give almost two years of his life to guide a girl from childhood to a time she could stand on her own, just because a friend had asked him to.

But this wren needed nothing except for Siba Namikk to keep his many, many secrets.

There were other wrens in the settler wagon that needed her.

Nelo who had watched his first friend die at the hands of the monster the children called 'Mouser' in Lowertown. He sold her clothes to buy his first Sailor's Curse and promised her broken body it would not happen to another. He scrambled to find other lost children and save them. But he was a child himself, and there were *so many* children tossed out with the daily wash water and so little coin to buy food for them.

To earn coin, he taught them to be Lost Girls, and pickpockets, and when there had not been food for days, he taught the oldest ones to lure the men like Mouser into a forced barter where he chose the life of the children over theirs. Siba Namikk knew she could listen and forgive, but to redeem a man like that would take Piffik and his ability to build a man out of a boy of sinew and sorrow, and his understanding of putting away a childhood too soon.

The Sinner's District, Dockside, and Lowertown were such harsh masters, even a family was not enough to protect the other wrens who had come with Tiju Tia. Falan who had to stand between her father's greed and the sale of a child's innocence; Callis and Tyra who didn't understand they had a voice to say who they were, what they wanted to be, and how they wished to live. She and Rygee could teach Josef, who had never learned how to be himself at all, and not just what others wanted him to be. She could guide Dica, who thought she was too young and would have let her dreams curdle into a small and bitter life, until Siba showed her she already had the ability and ambition. All she needed was time and teachers.

So many children who needed to learn they didn't need to hide behind a protector, or in the shadows, but could hold a feather light dream in their hands and watch it grow into life. Children who could learn that to stop fighting was not the same as giving up.

Siba Namikk breathed life into their dreams, dusted them off, and introduced them into a life worth living.

This was the gift of Siba Namikk.

Ah, my friends, you noticed it too? Seven times Siba Namikk saved a life by looking for the unseen heart, and the words that had not been said. Rebuilding with trust and truth, a purpose in life, and a promise the future was better than the life left behind.

Of course, my friends, you noted the half-wild boy in the story bears the same name as I do. But I bear the name of the great folk hero, Zren Janin. I imagine many Conrosan parents would like their child to grow up brave and strong and true, and give them such a name to live up to. So whether that Zren is this Zren or not, we need not concern ourselves so much with labels.

Instead let us remember, none of us has so many friends, that we can afford to throw any of them away.

hide in plain sight, and have fingers so light, documents, maps, or coins can disappear into their pockets like dew during the Dry. They wear the faces of every country in the known world. They are between the ages of 12 and 20, and they are ready to overthrow a corrupt King and win a new life for themselves.

But while the Viklanders see the war as fighting for Justice, and the Kerekis believe they are defending their homes, the Wrens and those left behind at Manumina understand the world will consider them traitors. So they begin by sharing their knowledge and sharpening their skills in the Academy of Treason.

The Academy of Treason begins with promises:

- For the Wrens, a life on the frontier, even in the midst of war, is better than the life left behind in Kerek City. If they survive, Ngahuru has promised a life debt for each of them to start a new future.
- For Zren Janin and the others at Manumina, there is hope and help to keep the settlement from falling to bandits or the Kereki army. Zren has finally found a family and a home. He promises to do what he must to keep them.
- For the Viklanders fighting in the war, the Wrens are a face and a helping hand in the unfamiliar countryside. A

promise that Manumina is more than a name on a map.
It is a sanctuary to help them live to fight another day.

And for Ngahuru, who always keeps her promises?

Revenge is a dish best served cold.